TREE OF LIFE

A.M. Leibowitz

Beaten Track
www.beatentrackpublishing.com

Tree of Life

First published 2022 by Beaten Track Publishing
Copyright © 2022 A.M. Leibowitz

Paperback ISBN: 978 1 78645 505 5
eBook ISBN: 978 1 78645 506 2

Cover: A.M. Leibowitz

Beaten Track Publishing,
Burscough, Lancashire.
www.beatentrackpublishing.com

TREE OF LIFE

TREE OF LIFE

Chapter 1

MID-AFTERNOON SUNLIGHT SHINES through the curtain-less windows in the third-floor apartment. The early May breeze ruffles the papers Luke has out on the kitchen table. He stacks them and pushes them under the corner of a scrapbook to keep them from blowing away. Carefully, he takes a letter out of the book and frees it from its envelope to lay it on the table.

Luke stares at the crinkled paper. He's read it enough times to have it memorized. More than a year after Luke left, Greg sent it to him through the college where Luke was taking classes at the time. The words run together, twisting in Luke's brain around his last memories of Greg.

This isn't the letter where I beg your forgiveness and ask you to take me back. It's not the letter where you tell me it's all right and that you'll come home to me. It's the one where I tell you I need help, and I'm getting it. This is the last time you'll hear from me. I hope you have a good life, wherever you go from here.

They haven't seen each other since, and, true to his word, Greg hasn't contacted him again in any other way even though Luke is certain he's out of prison by now. With a heavy sigh, Luke refolds the crumpled page and stuffs it back into the scrapbook where he keeps it. He pushes the book aside and draws his pile of weeks-old mail toward himself. Picking up the top item, he runs his finger along the raised lines of the elegant script. *Misters Antonio "AJ" Mancuso and Adam Foster and their families request the honor of your presence...*

1

Of *course* they'll have a traditional wedding, complete with all the bells and whistles. AJ would be mad at Luke for thinking so, but their ceremony looks to be the perfect picture of polished, upscale gay life. Luke doesn't blame them for wanting to get married, and AJ and Adam are hardly trying to present as the acceptable face of queer America otherwise. Their wedding, though, promises to be the sort of thing one might see splashed on the cover of *Out* magazine in celebration of the anniversary of legalized same-sex marriage. They're both gorgeous, upwardly mobile white men in their prime—the kind of guys men and women alike drool over.

Uninvited, Luke's imagination goes there too as his gaze lands on the enclosed engagement photo. He did his fair share of salivating over AJ, back before they realized they were better off as friends. He was AJ's first, when they were both shy and inexperienced adolescents. Now he wonders what a more mature AJ would be like. Luke knows he and Adam sometimes liked to play. AJ's admitted to inviting an occasional third—or more—party into their bedroom, and they aren't particular about gender. He claims it keeps things interesting. Luke imagines what it would be like to have them together, their hands and mouths all over him.

Disgusted with himself and his train of thought, he banishes the daydream to the wasteland of terrible ideas. It's been too long since he's been with anyone if he can entertain ideas of kissing Adam, whose personality he finds singularly unappealing most days. Or at least he did, when he lived nearby. Perhaps Adam's matured. Luke and his roommate sometimes mess around with each other, but they haven't for a while. He wonders if there's something wrong with him that it takes a picture of his friends to get him thinking about sex again.

He returns his attention to the invitation. There's a space for a plus-one on the RSVP card, but he has no one to bring. Jax, his roommate, received their own invitation. He has no idea if Jax is bringing anyone. They haven't said, but as far as Luke knows, Jax isn't seeing anyone currently.

Before he can make up his mind about which box to check, his phone rings. He looks at the number and lets it go another couple of rings, debating. He finally picks up.

"Hey."

"Luke! How's things out your way?" AJ asks.

"Good, good. Same old." He tries to keep his voice light even though a lump springs up in his throat.

"Glad to hear it. So...you got the invitation, right?"

"Yeah." He swallows to clear the dryness from his mouth. "I did."

"Are you coming?"

He wants to say no. It will be almost unbearable, seeing them all again, having to sit through dinner with every one of his former group talking about how successful they are now. They'll share stories about their tidy lives in their suburban developments, reminding him what a screw-up he is. Then they'll feel sorry for him, working long hours at a greasy burger-and-dogs joint to pay his half of the rent on the shithole apartment they only keep heated because he and Jax sometimes do odd jobs for the landlord when he can't be bothered.

Luke should tell AJ he isn't going, that he has something else or can't take time off or any one of the many excuses at his disposal. Instead, his mouth reacts before his brain, and he hears himself say, "I wouldn't miss it."

"Good!" AJ breathes an audible sigh of relief. "You hadn't sent your reply card back, so I wanted to make sure."

"Yeah...I'm sorry about that. I meant to send it, but you know how things are."

There's a long pause. "I know."

The words hang there, understanding passing between them across the miles. Luke wants to make the most of the moment, to cry out to AJ and tell him everything that's wrong in his life. Except it isn't as simple as a grimy apartment and a bad job and a roommate whose employment isn't always stable. It's the desperate way he misses all of them and the knowledge he's messed up too many times to earn another do-over.

He pulls himself together enough to say, "Should I send the card now? Or should I just tell you on the phone if I want the chicken or the beef?"

AJ chuckles. "You can tell me, but send the card anyway. Easier to keep track. We don't need final count for a couple of weeks." Another silence. "I miss you. I love you, Lukey."

The use of his old nickname almost does Luke in. He brushes at his eyes. "You too, Aje."

They end the call, and Luke sits for what feels like hours, staring at the phone in his hand. Eventually, he tucks the wedding invitation and the engagement photo into his scrapbook, leaving out the reply card. He ticks the box for "chicken," declines the plus-one, and sets it in the bin where they keep outgoing mail until one of them makes it to the postbox. He stands and picks up his keys, deciding a trip to the store for milk and bread will help him get his head in a better place. Somehow, he'll manage. He always does.

＊＊＊＊

By the time Luke returns with the groceries, Jax is home. They don't acknowledge Luke's presence, too busy stretching—or possibly doing yoga—in the middle of the living room. They have on a soundtrack that sounds like it might be audio porn but probably isn't, judging from the occasional instructions to change position. They're not wearing much, only a very small, tight pair of shorts. Luke politely turns his back and puts things away in the cupboards while he waits for Jax to finish. It doesn't exactly bother Luke, but he doesn't understand why Jax never uses their one bedroom for some privacy.

The soft grunt behind him catches Luke's attention, and he waits another sixty seconds before turning around. Jax has already pulled themselves out of a pretzel-like pose and is in process of standing up to cross the room and turn off the audio. They slip on and adjust a pair of soft workout pants, close the tab on the website, and spin around to smile at Luke.

"How was your day?" they ask.

Their words and tone of voice are a mismatch for the situation the two of them are in. Ordinary, as though they and Luke have both come home from office jobs to cook dinner and watch television with the dogs. The phrase hints at nothing about Jax's unconventional employment and ongoing work search or Luke's job he'll leave for in an hour, which he hates and makes him reek of meat grease and onions. Nothing about Luke's perseveration on lost loves. Nor the wedding reply card he didn't take to the mailbox while he was out.

Luke skirts any direct mention of those things. "Just messing around with my scrapbook a little before work. Had to run out for bread."

"Oh, yeah. Sorry for using the last slice." Jax ambles into the kitchen and washes their hands. "You gonna let me look at that book of yours one of these days?"

"Maybe." Jax is the only one who knows about it. Luke certainly isn't going to tell the guys at work and get made fun of for something they think is childish or "girlie." It isn't as though he has a lot of other friends, either. Jax is it, even if they aren't aware of it.

"You'll have more to add after the wedding." Jax directs a pointed look at Luke. "You mail in your card yet?"

"I filled it out."

Jax doesn't miss the way Luke avoids the question. They scrutinize him, and there are things neither of them acknowledge. Prime example: the real reason Luke didn't mail the card while he was out. They both know it, no matter how much Luke tries to hide it. Even AJ doesn't know the whole story. He's also too busy planning the wedding to consider small details like how uncomfortable it will be for Luke to see their mutual friend Connor for the first time in five years. The first time since Luke walked away from the best thing to happen to him after escaping Greg's violence and came back home to find nothing here for him either.

Jax makes no mention of those things. They ask, "Where is it?"

Luke waves at the outgoing mail bin. "I was going to take it, but I forgot."

Jax sighs. "I'll take it on my way out later, since I know you won't, whatever you may say." They step around Luke to pour a glass of water.

A thank-you is probably in order, but Luke changes the subject. "You working tonight?"

"Mm-mm. Had a job for a photographer today, though. Pay wasn't great, but it's something."

Jax is stunningly beautiful, with smooth, bronze skin, expressive hazel eyes, and long, silky black hair. They're tall and lean and look good in almost everything, and they can pull off wearing makeup or not as the mood suits them. The occasional job as a stock photo model is one of Jax's sources of funding; posing for figure-drawing art classes is another one. Some nights, they dance at Thundershock, a local queer club. That's what Jax is best at, the dancing. They were going to go professional, but there was a big blowup with their parents when Jax dared put a toe over the gender line. They lived with their brother for a while before coming back to their hometown.

Before Luke acknowledges Jax's statement about the job, Jax continues. "We, ah, need to talk about something." They look as though the fate of the world hinges on Luke's reaction.

"Okay." Luke slides into a chair.

Jax sits opposite him. They cross and uncross their legs multiple times, finally settling on bouncing their knees. It makes Luke jumpy, and he wants to tell Jax to cut it out. He keeps mum and waits.

"I'm moving out."

The words slam into Luke, knocking out his ability to respond. The last year was the most stable his life has been since he quit school and fled here. His head is spinning with a thousand fears, but he speaks none of them. Instead, he issues a one-word question.

"When?"

"August, but I can go sooner." Jax licks their perfect, plump lips. "Aren't you—I mean, don't you want to know why?"

Luke doesn't, not really. It doesn't matter why. Jax is leaving him on his own to do whatever it is they're planning. Does it make a difference what the reason is? Jax is going to tell him either way, so Luke fakes it for their sake.

"Yeah. It's pretty sudden."

"I got a job. Dancing. With a company, not at a club. I applied to go to school, and I got in. I couldn't accept until I knew I had work." There's another extended silence. "It's in Boston. The Conservatory at Berklee."

Boston. That explains why they need to move out. Luke tries to clear his head. He knows Jax wants to talk about it, wants Luke's permission to be excited. Underneath the restrained exterior and the mask of worry for Luke's well-being, there's a ripple of happiness.

"That's really great," Luke says, trying to put as much enthusiasm into it as he thinks Jax deserves.

"I won't leave you without a plan, okay? We'll make it work."

"Don't worry about me. I'm fine."

Jax looks like maybe they don't agree, but they know better than to push it. Luke already knows what will happen. He'll leave the decision until the last minute, and then Luke will end up begging the landlord to give him just one more month. Long enough to quit his shitty job, pack what little he has and sell off what he can't take, and get the hell out of there. Surely there will be somewhere to go, maybe a place where no one has ever known him. The idea of making a clean start isn't repulsive.

"We can talk about it more later," Jax offers.

"Yeah, sure." Luke is already standing up from the table. "I have to get to work."

Jax stands up too. Luke slips past into the bathroom. He doesn't really need to piss. It's the privacy he craves, a few minutes alone after their conversation. Luke isn't in the mood to talk more right now. He slides down the wall to sit with his back against the door, feeling alone even with his closest friend on the other side of the wall.

Chapter 2

I T'S TWO DAYS before the wedding. Jax is in the bedroom, getting dressed to go out with the others while they're in town. Luke is hiding in the bathroom again.

He stares at his reflection, turning his head side to side and examining his crooked nose. Greg wasn't responsible for that nor for the thin scar on Luke's left cheek. The broken nose was from Sam Whelock at the homeschool co-op when Luke was thirteen. The scar is from the knife one of his older brothers threw at him when he was fifteen, right before they all abandoned him in the middle of nowhere.

Luke draws up his shoulders in an exaggerated sigh. If he goes back out, Jax will try to persuade him to come along to the bachelor party. The wedding, Luke can handle. He can sit in the back and stay only long enough to make AJ happy after the ceremony. The bachelor party is another thing entirely.

It'll be too loud and include far too many drinks and too many questions he's not prepared to answer. Even if they never say it, one question will hang between them for as long as they all live: *Why?* AJ has never asked, not even once. The only thing he did was tell Luke to leave an address, which he did on the promise that AJ wouldn't give it to Connor.

He's kept in touch on and off with AJ, but not any of the others. He was never close with any of them except Connor. He's sure they haven't missed him. Maybe Connor did at first, but if he's smart, he'll have moved on. Luke's not worth wasting that kind of time on. He wasn't then, and he isn't now.

Jax knocks on the door. "C'mon, I gotta get in there and finish up."

Luke opens the door and tries to step around, but Jax blocks his path. "I thought you wanted in."

"Yeah, I do." Jax doesn't step aside. "You can get dressed while I'm in here."

"I'm not going."

"Yes, you are."

"I'm fucking not."

Luke shoves Jax enough to get past and retreats into the living room. There's no point in going in the bedroom. It's not like it's his personal space and Jax can't go in. There's not even a door. That sums up Luke's life, the lack of privacy. He's never had anywhere all his own. Not growing up with thirteen brothers and sisters. Not in the group home. Not the time he tried college. Not with Greg or Connor. Not now, living in the apartment Jax already had when Luke moved in.

He flops down on the ratty sofa and picks up a random travel brochure for a local business. Jax is in it; it's probably a complimentary copy. *Go RV'ing!* the front commands. Luke's only been scanning it for a minute when Jax comes out of the bathroom and stands in front of him. They snatch the brochure away.

"You. Are. Coming. With me. And bring your camera."

Luke scowls and slides down on the sofa. "Did they tell you it was your job to get me there?"

Jax snorts. "No. You know better than that. AJ thinks I should leave it alone and that if you want to come, you will. I think you want to come and won't admit it, so you'll stay home feeling sorry for yourself and wishing you'd gone."

"Fuck off." It's the only response, since Jax is right.

Instead of doing as Luke asks, Jax sits next to him. The press of their leg against Luke's is warm and provides fleeting comfort. Jax leans their head on Luke's shoulder, and Luke exhales as though trying to expel the spirit of his past.

"I understand this is difficult. Think of it this way—you'll have new things to put in that book of yours."

Luke still isn't sure, but he eventually nods. "I'll consider it."

"You have five minutes to get ready."

Jax stands, spins around, and marches back to the bathroom. Luke sits there, staring after them, for another minute. He's down to four, but he can change and make himself presentable in less time than that. He rises just as Jax pokes their head out of the bathroom and delivers a "get moving" glare.

It's more than five minutes by the time Jax is done grooming. They look fantastic, and even in his second-best clothes, Luke feels drab in comparison. Jax's makeup is flawless, a little darker for an evening out. They're wearing a flowing, white blouse and tight, black pants made of some kind of buttery-soft fabric. Luke's dark jeans and plain, long-sleeve T-shirt seem inadequate, and the water he's splashed on his face doesn't make him feel clean enough.

Before he can rush back into the bedroom to find something else to wear, Jax steers him toward the door. "Oh, no, you don't," they say. "I gave you more than enough time, and you look fine."

Jax spends a few minutes messing with the apartment doorknob, which is loose and sometimes doesn't work properly. At last, they get it to lock, and they descend the stairs together. Jax is driving them to Thundershock, where they'll meet up with the others.

The group has booked their private balcony room, which Luke has never visited even though he's been to Thundershock a number of times—and hasn't always left by himself. He's learned not to talk about it with Jax. Not that Jax cares whether Luke goes there or what he does afterward. Which is exactly it: Jax isn't concerned. They told Luke it's not their job to keep tabs. Until then, Luke didn't realize he was looking for someone to do just that. He supposes it's the one way he now has privacy.

Living with Jax gives him the sort of freedom he's unaccustomed to, and he's never fully made peace with it.

The ride to Thundershock is silent except for the metal scraping from Jax's beat-up car. Luke half expects the thing to fall apart any second. It doesn't, and they arrive in one piece. Jax gets out as soon as they turn off the engine, but Luke remains buckled in. He wishes he hadn't come and contemplates slipping away from Jax once they're under the cover of a crowded room.

Jax has apparently developed mind-reading skills because the next thing Luke knows, Jax has the passenger door open and says, "Don't even think about it. You're coming inside *and* to the party."

Luke doesn't protest. He exits the car and takes six deep in-and-out breaths. "Okay. I'm ready."

****

Jax shows the invitation to the VIP room at the door, and they enter the club. As soon as the door closes behind them, Luke is immersed in the techno-blue lighting and the throb of the bass. On an ordinary night out, he might make his way to the neon-and-silver bar. This isn't an ordinary night, though, so he follows Jax up a set of spiral stairs to the balcony room.

It's an open floor plan, so they can still hear the music from the main room. There's an enclosed area behind them. If they went in there, the music would be muffled so they could talk without shouting. Inside is a table, already spread with appetizers. There's a decent-sized group of people on the balcony, leaning against the rail and talking in pairs and threes. Luke is surprised to note that despite this being a "bachelor" party, there are several women here.

One of them spots Luke and Jax and comes over. She kisses Jax's cheek. "Hey, sweetie," she says, like they're old friends. They might be; Luke doesn't recognize her in the dim light.

"Costanza, hey," Jax greets her. *Ah, AJ's sister.*

Luke studies her. She was only ten when he and AJ met. Now she's nearly twenty-three, the same age Luke was when he left his friends without a word, and he barely knows her. Costanza is cute, short and curvy with tan skin and an obscene amount of wildly curly black hair. Her face is similar to AJ's, maybe a touch rounder. When she steps back from Jax, her gaze lands on Luke and her eyes light up.

"You came! AJ will be so glad." She turns her head and calls over her shoulder, "Aje! Look who's here."

The dark-haired man leaning on the rail and talking to a big, burly, blond guy looks up. His expression is the perfect imitation of Costanza's. An instant later, he's flying away from the rail and toward Luke. For a moment, Luke is afraid AJ is going to crash into him. He doesn't; he stops short, breathing a little fast.

"My God," he says. "Lukey. I didn't think you'd come."

"I'm here." It's a ridiculous thing to say, but Luke doesn't have a way to express the traffic jam of thoughts in his head.

They've talked occasionally over the last five years, and Luke's kept up with AJ in other ways when he can. But they haven't seen each other since Luke walked—or, more accurately, ran—away. AJ looks almost the same as Luke remembers. Still tall and broad-shouldered, still perfectly groomed. Luke can't place what's different, but there's something.

Seconds later, it's irrelevant. When AJ holds out his arms, Luke falls into them. He buries his nose in AJ's shoulder, inhaling his scent. He always smells good, if a little too polished and clean. Luke wants to stay there and make everything around him go away. AJ is no longer his, not that he ever was. What happened between them was too many years ago for it to still mean more than two boys figuring out life together. Even so, AJ has always been his safe place, the one friend he could trust.

All too soon, AJ lets go of Luke. He's putting his arm around someone else, and Luke looks to see who it is. *Adam. Of course.* The love of AJ's life and the person he'll make a future with. That's when Luke realizes what it is that's changed. There's a distance between them that has nothing to do with how far away Luke lives. It's the reason why he left, the thing he's sure he'll never be forgiven for.

The kiss Adam gives AJ is meant as a sharp reminder to Luke about his place in AJ's life. He delivers it and then a brief grip of Luke's hand. Every gesture feels like a subtle warning. Adam is taller than Luke, though not as tall as AJ. Even in the weird, dim club lighting, Adam's red hair is blinding. He's grown into himself, filled out a bit. Adam is the reason Greg sent that letter from prison. Adam took a knife to the leg while trying to keep him from killing AJ, Greg's only motive being to get to Luke. Bashing Luke's face in while he was drunk and they were alone in their apartment didn't encourage Greg to seek help. Stabbing a stranger in public in broad daylight was apparently a bridge too far.

Even though Luke knows he has a debt to Adam, he still neither likes nor trusts him entirely. It probably isn't fair, and it's more than half out of envy for what Adam and AJ have and Luke does not. He could have, and he knows it, but he chose to leave instead of facing things head-on. What was it Luke once said to AJ? That he could solve all his problems by having a grown-up conversation with Adam? AJ and Adam both failed the test and learned from their mistakes, and they're getting married in a couple days. Luke should've taken his own advice, seeing how it's worked out so well for someone else.

None of which matters now. Especially not the second Luke's eyes land on the man standing a few feet away, seeming unsure about whether he should approach. AJ notices that Luke's attention is on a point behind him and turns. When he does, it leaves a gap for Connor to step forward.

Luke stares at him for an uncomfortably long time, trying to make sense of the person in front of him. Unlike AJ, he looks different from how Luke remembers. Like Adam, his body has broadened, and he's added muscle. He's grown out his beard too. It's thick and full but neat, and gods, it looks good on him. His brown eyes are gentle when he offers Luke a hesitant smile.

"It's good to see you," he says, and Luke notes his voice has mellowed. Not a change in pitch but in character. Warmer, touched with regret and wariness.

Connor steps closer, and Luke feels the tension of the others around them. Connor is the reason Luke wasn't going to show up tonight. Now here they are, a few feet from each other, Connor holding out a hand in invitation. Luke inches forward too, his chest tight. He wonders fleetingly if he looks as different to the others as they look to him. If Connor sees it.

And then he doesn't have any more time to think about it because he's being swept up in Connor's big arms, solid and strong and wonderful. Luke forgot what it felt like, and now the memories rush in and threaten to crush him under their weight. Long nights talking, holding on to each other while they spilled their hopes and dreams on each other. Falling asleep on AJ's old couch while Connor studied next to him. Connor holding ice on Luke's bruised eye and asking if he was hurting him. Each one a snapshot of the life they'd begun to build before Luke burned the pages of the photo album.

Connor finally releases him. "I can't believe you're here," he says. The words are so quiet Luke thinks they might have been spoken only for his benefit.

"I can't either," he mumbles, which makes Connor's expression go from overcome to startled to laughing in a blink. The sound sends a thrill right through Luke, settling as a warm tingle in his gut.

"I think this is everyone," AJ says. "We can go inside and eat, if you want, or we can hang out here and listen to the music. We've got all night, thanks to these fine folks." He tilts his head at the group of people still lined up against the railing.

They filter into the enclosed room, and Adam shuts the door. They can still make out the thumping bass in the room below, but it's much easier to hear each other now. AJ is still beside Luke.

"Do you know everyone?" he asks.

Luke shrugs. He recognizes AJ's friends Donny—Jax's brother—and Piet. They went to the same Catholic high school as AJ and Connor. The others, he's not sure. AJ's friends or family, probably. More women than Luke anticipated would be there. AJ introduces them, and Luke promptly forgets half the names. He won't see them again after the wedding anyway.

Piet tells everyone to eat up, and they have the equivalent of an open bar. He says there will be entertainment, and Luke assumes this means dancers, from his understanding of the club. Probably of more than one gender, knowing Adam and AJ and given the guests. He wants to relax, but he feels out of place here. A soft hand on his shoulder startles him, and he turns to face the person. It's Lauryn, Jax's sister-in-law.

"It's good to see you again, Luke," she says. He has a feeling there's a hidden message in her words.

"You too," he tells her, even though they both know that he's only delivering an automatic response. Even Lauryn is aware how out of place he is here. Not in the club but with these people, in their lives. He has no home with them now, whether he ever truly did or not.

A moment later, Jax is back at his side. They touch the camera bag Luke has slung across his body. "Make some memories," they say.

"Memories," Luke repeats. "Sure, yeah." He can do this.

He takes out the camera, holding it for a moment to enjoy the weight in his hands. This is the one thing he owns that's worth anything. It's only an entry-level DSLR with a decent zoom lens, but it was on sale when he bought it, and it served its purpose. Besides, what did he need anymore with something higher end? He left that behind him years before.

Carefully, Luke assembles the lens and takes a few experimental shots. When he looks up, he catches AJ watching him. AJ offers a small, secret smile, and it's enough to boost Luke's confidence. He raises the camera, viewing the room and the guests through the screen on the back, and the world begins to make sense again.

※※※※

The party is winding down, and the guests have dwindled to the familiar group from AJ and Adam's graduate school years, when they met. There are only a dozen or so people left. When everyone sits at the table, Luke is shuffled to the end where AJ, Adam, and Connor are sitting. Jax squeezes in next to Luke, for which he's grateful. They're a nice buffer between Luke and the others. Everything about this is uncomfortable.

He's tuned out the conversation, trying to decide what to say if they ask him what he's been up to for the last five years. AJ knows, so surely the others do too. It's different being questioned on it. Luke has nothing to show for all the time he's been apart from them. He told AJ he needed to clear his head, which was true in a sense, but he doesn't think it worked the way it was supposed to. He was meant to erase Connor—and the shame of what Luke did to him—from his mind. Instead, he's now seated a few feet from someone he hurt. Luke is no better than Greg. The difference is, nothing he did would ever land him in jail.

Because he hasn't been paying attention, he misses the reason Connor is now saying, "...take about a month, all said and done."

"What will?" Luke blurts, his admission he's been in the land of daydreams again.

"Connor's going cross-country," Adam says, giving Connor a good-natured punch on the arm.

Connor rubs the spot and laughs. "Sounds like a cliché, doesn't it? I'm driving from Boston to Seattle."

"Why?" Luke frowns. "Just a vacation?"

"Nah. My father died."

"Oh." Luke realizes that sounds rude, so he adds, "I'm sorry."

"It's okay, really. We weren't close."

Jax says, "So did he leave you a bunch of money or something?"

"Not a dime," Connor tells them. "He left me a collection of his writings, and a lot of them refer to something he was looking for. Before he died, he traveled the same route. I guess..." He pauses and taps his lips. Then he curls his hands into fists and places them on the table. His expression is thin-lipped determination. "I wish I'd understood him better when he was alive. After he and my mother split up, she became bitter and angry. He lost his path, but he was documenting something. I want to know what he meant, so I'm tracing his footsteps to the other side of the country."

"I have family out that way."

Luke isn't sure why he says it. Maybe it's the alcohol, making him bold. Or maybe he's latching on to something he has in common with one of them. He hasn't seen his oldest brother in more than twice as long as he's been away from Connor and the others. There are sufficient reasons why he's never visited.

18

"You do?" Connor sounds puzzled, shaded with a bit of disappointment. Of course. Luke never shared much with him about his family.

"Yeah."

AJ reaches out to squeeze Luke's forearm. He knows part of the truth, but none of the others do. They didn't know him well enough back then. Luke used to tell AJ his secrets, often after sneaking away from the group home to see him and touching each other in the dark of AJ's bedroom. He still remembers how it felt.

"You should come with me," Connor says.

When Luke looks around at the others, he realizes he's been set up. He's not so self-centered as to think the whole night was for this purpose, but the conversation was engineered for his benefit. Even Jax looks guilty.

"What about my job? My apartment? I can't just leave them for a month on some whim."

"You hate that job," Jax points out. "And I'm leaving anyway."

Embarrassed now and becoming upset, Luke says, "What am I supposed to do? Quit? Where would I go when I get back? It's not like I have anyone."

There's a stunned silence that follows. It's Adam who breaks it. "You'll stay with us. We'll be home from our honeymoon by then, and we'll get you set up. We want you back with us, Luke."

It shocks Luke to discover he's serious. Adam, who's always been jealous of Luke, wants him there. It doesn't make sense to him, unless AJ did something to convince him it's a good idea.

Luke's face burns. The remaining guests now all have their attention on the conversation at Luke's end of the table. He's not sure what to say. He wants to be angry, especially knowing Jax had a hand in this. His protective but meddling roommate was obviously trying to make sure Luke was taken care of after they left for Boston, but it makes Luke feel like he's being passed around by babysitters. They're all so sure he can't do anything by himself.

"I don't know," he says. It's the only thing he can get out without raging at all of them and ruining the night.

"At least think about it," Connor says. "I'm not leaving for another three weeks. I have to go home, get my shit together, and drive out to pick up the RV for the trip."

An RV. Not quite roughing it but more flexibility than hotel stays for a month. The image resurrects memories Luke had thought long dead and buried. He wonders if there's more to this trip than Connor's letting on. He's not interested right now in figuring it out because he's still stinging from his friends implying he's useless. Some of the hurt is because he doesn't entirely disagree.

"Fine," he says. "I'll think about it."

Connor beams at him. "You can let me know at the wedding."

Two days. That's all the time Luke has to decide whether he wants to upend his entire life and follow Connor on a hare-brained adventure across the country. Does he want a month with someone he can't be certain has forgiven him? A small part of him, which he quickly stifles, knows already what his decision will be.

"I'll think about it," he repeats.

It seems to satisfy everyone, even though Luke's head is still reeling. While he tries to wrap his mind around the previous few minutes, an arm slides around his shoulders, interrupting his thoughts.

"Lukey, how about you break out that camera again, hm?" AJ says. "We should get some group shots."

Luke's hand drifts to where the strap lies across his chest. Glad for the distraction, he agrees and stands to follow AJ.

Chapter 3

L UKE SPREADS THE photos from the bachelor party out on the table. After the wedding, he took the memory card to the photo center so he could print them. The envelopes with the photos from the ceremony and reception are still closed. He sifts through the pictures he's laid out, finding the ones he's in. He let the camera out of his hands only twice at the party—once so Jax could take a picture of him with Adam and AJ and once for the server to take a picture of the whole group.

He lifts the photo of himself with Adam and AJ. Luke is wedged between them, AJ on his left and Adam on his right. Adam's hand rests on his shoulder, leaning in a little and wearing a wide grin. There's no joy in Luke's closed-mouth smile. He can see it in the way his shoulder hunches away from Adam and in the way the upper half of his face remains stubbornly stationary.

Peering closer, he sees something he missed before. AJ's smile is full, but there's something pinched in his forehead. Luke inspects his face and finally finds it. AJ isn't looking at the camera. At first, Luke thought he was distracted by Adam, but that's not it. His gaze is on Luke. He, too, is leaning in, the front of his shoulder pressing against the back of Luke's.

Luke can tell a lot from a photograph. It was how he knew what his brothers were doing and why. He saw it all through the lens of the camera they destroyed when they left him, lost and terrified. It's how he knows now what AJ is thinking even in poor lighting. Luke reads the worry and sympathy in the tight lines around AJ's mouth and eyes.

It's always the same story: Poor Luke. No family. No money. Everyone except Jax—who knows better— imagines him sitting around, waiting for something to come along. Luke runs his index finger over the honey-brown cover of the scrapbook. He traces the tree, a stylized drawing with places to write names. It was inexpensive, something he ordered online because he liked it. He supposes it was meant to be an ancestry album, but he chose not to have it personalized. There isn't anything in his family tree he feels compelled to document anymore.

Maybe they're right, and Luke doesn't have much going for him these days. He's not running a business or going back to school or traveling across the country to find long-lost relatives. He still wishes AJ wouldn't worry so much, even though Luke knows it's in his nature.

AJ and Adam have gone now, farther north to Niagara Falls. The "honeymoon capital of the world." Luke's never been there, despite the promise made to him as a child. Someday, maybe he'll visit for himself and see if it's as grand as he's heard. Or perhaps he'll sit with the illusion of its beauty, content to leave it in postcards lest the real thing fail to measure up.

He still hasn't given Connor his answer even though he promised he would at the wedding. Connor's gone home too, so he can pack. Luke never asked if he stayed in the same college town where he, Adam, and AJ earned their degrees. The same town where Luke tried to make it on his own and failed. Where he left behind his bewildered friends and the employers who treated him as a son and taught him to speak Spanish while he served handmade tortillas in their restaurant. The same town where he left the person he loved.

Luke pushes the scrapbook away. He doesn't have the heart to finish it now. It's foolish anyway, the kind of project a teenage girl might do so she can remember high school decades later when she's old and worn, her life and her identity stripped from her by countless diapers and midnight feedings and fevers and a husband who treats her like one of their children. The kind of book his mother would've made. Or his sister, if things had gone differently.

He crosses his arms on the table and drops his head. Some nights, the loneliness is so deep his bones ache. He wants to cry, but nothing comes. Only the feeling his insides have been hollowed out with a spoon. He wants something, but he doesn't know what. Arms around him, perhaps, but not the kind of thing he can find by way of an anonymous encounter. Not Jax's brand of intimacy either, a quick something to take the edge off before work. Luke wants to rest his head in someone's lap, fingers gently sliding through his hair until he falls asleep.

Once, he had those things. He traded them in for a one-way ticket to an apartment where he can hear the scratch of tiny feet behind the walls and the springs on the next-door neighbor's bed. He gave up his privacy, his steady job, and his only hope for something better in exchange for his freedom.

Now even that will be gone in a matter of weeks. Luke has two choices—to accept Connor's terms and go with him or to search for somewhere else to stay here. He's made a few casual friends; one of them might take him in for a while. He could go crawling back to Adam and AJ in hopes they'll take pity on him instead of judging his failures.

He sits up, needing something to relax his mind and make the decision easier. He doesn't have any weed left. Jax helped him finish off the last of his stash after the wedding. They stayed up until four in the morning, smoking and crying for different reasons and then going down on each other. There was a sadness to it, something more than a parting of ways. Once Jax is gone, Luke knows he's never going to see them again this side of eternity, as his grandmother used to say.

They still have to pack up the apartment, whether Luke goes with Connor or not. Everything Luke owns, shoved back into his worn duffels and backpack. He sighs and stands, stretching. The small bookshelf in the corner catches his eye, and he crosses the room to look. Everything on it belongs to Jax. There are a bunch of books that look like dry criticism of the Bible. Luke snorts; that's about right. Jax, despite their Catholic upbringing, is anti-theist.

One book stands out, though. It's so slim the title isn't on the spine. Luke pulls it out and at first wonders why it's in Jax's collection. At a glance, it looks like typical Bible fiction. When Luke finally gets it, he laughs. Jax was the cover model for this, probably hired by the author and given a free copy.

A Patchwork Splendor, by Es Thornton. Luke flips it over, and his mouth drops open. He's not generally interested in romance novels, but he thinks reimagining the Bible story of Joseph as bisexual erotica doesn't sound too bad. No wonder Jax was all right with this. Luke carries the book to his bed. At least if it's terrible, it'll help him sleep. He slides under the covers and begins to read.

****

"Call him," Jax says for the millionth time.

They make a point at least three times a day of telling Luke to give Connor an answer. It's the first thing they say in the morning, and then they get one in while the two of them are packing up the apartment. Jax saves a final one before bed for good measure.

Luke knows he should. Everything moved too fast after the wedding. Jax accepted Connor's offer of a ride out to Boston, and Luke suspects this was orchestrated to force his hand. Instead, he's made arrangements with the landlord to keep the apartment for a few more weeks until he finds somewhere else.

In the meantime, Luke and Jax are separating their lives into keep, toss, and donate boxes. There isn't much Luke wants to save from the previous few years, and he has almost nothing from before then. It's Jax who's having more of a struggle.

Having given up the fight about calling Connor for the time being, Jax holds up a gray racerback shirt covered in Pride flag hearts. "You want this?"

Luke really likes the shirt, and he almost says yes. It isn't as though it would take up too much space in one of the couple of bags that will hold his entire wardrobe. He hesitates, though. He's never been comfortable wearing anything like that. He isn't like Jax.

"You might as well," Jax says. "You know I'm going to stuff it in your bag later when you're not looking."

"Would you really?"

Jax laughs. "Maybe."

They grasp Luke's hands and fold his fingers around the soft fabric. Then Jax leans in and kisses Luke on the mouth. It's as soft as the shirt at first, then hard and insistent. The two of them haven't done this in a while, and Luke is starved for the kind of touch that consumes him.

Tangled in each other, they roll away from the boxes to fuck, leaving the shirt with the other items for packing. Luke knows it's their last time. He wants to hold on to it, the last trace of the familiar life he's known these few years. His hands slide over Jax's golden flesh, and he struggles to keep his awareness, to burn every detail into his memory. The fit of their bodies fills his senses and drives away all other thoughts.

When they've both found release, Luke feels empty. Hollowed out and blank, like a scrapbook page waiting to be filled. He knows now that Jax won't be the one to do it. He lies there on the living room floor, running a sweaty hand through his blond hair. Jax is half on top of him, gasping, their cheek pressed against Luke's nipple.

They sit up abruptly, grinning. "Call him, hot stuff." They smack Luke's hip and rise from the floor, unfolding like the graceful dancer they are.

Luke props himself on his elbows, watching Jax's firm, round ass as they gather their clothes and head for the bathroom, a sway in their step. Reality cuts through the last of his post-sex high as he sits up. Tears sting his eyes, and he wipes them with the heels of his hands, tensing his muscles to will away any more.

He has a decision to make. For a few minutes, he sits with his arms wrapped around his knees, staring at his phone on the tray table. It wouldn't take long. A simple yes or no, that's all he has to provide.

He won't do it naked. As he stands and grabs his briefs, he hears the water turn on in the bathroom. He yanks on most of his clothes and sits on the couch. Hand shaking, he reaches out for his phone. There are so many things he wants to ask Connor, like why he wants Luke to be the one to come with him. Why not a lover or someone who at least has been a better friend? Why ask someone who lied to him and escaped rather than give him a chance to understand the truth?

He's hitting Connor's number now, praying Jax stays in the shower long enough for him to give Connor his decision. He knows what he should say, which isn't necessarily what he will say.

Connor answers after four rings. "Hello?"

Luke's mouth is dry. He licks his lips. "Hey, it's Luke."

"Luke! Hang on a sec, okay?" There's some background noise Luke can't place, and then Connor is back. "Sorry, just wanted to go where I could hear better."

"Where are you?"

"My mother's house." There's an eye-roll hidden in there; Connor has never gotten along with his mother, for good reason.

"Why's it so noisy?"

"Some kind of home sales party. I didn't ask what. Her latest get-rich-quick scam."

"You're still here in Philly? I thought you were going home-home."

"I did. I'm staying here for a bit to get the last of my crap out of Mom's house before I go."

Doing the same thing Luke and Jax were. "Okay."

"I'm sorry we didn't get more time to talk at the wedding," Connor says quietly. "I wanted to ask how you're doing."

"Surviving," Luke says without thinking.

"Me too."

Luke finds that hard to believe. When he left, Connor had just finished grad school. He was looking for work as a nurse practitioner. Surely he has a good life, something more settled and stable than Luke.

Instead of accusing him of anything, Luke says, "Yeah? What are you doing now?"

"Looking for a new job. I worked in post-op for a while, then for the last two years, I've been in emergency. It's rough."

"Oh." Luke wants to ask about other things, like relationships, but he doesn't. He can't imagine Connor sitting around alone for all that time. But if he were with someone, he wouldn't have asked Luke to come along. Would he?

"Yeah, it's the reason why I'm here at Mom's, getting rid of stuff."

Luke's heart is galloping, and his hands are slick. He takes a few steadying breaths. "Why did you ask me to come with you?"

There's an extended silence, and Luke wishes he could see Connor's face. It was too bold, asking outright. He should've waited.

"The others all thought I shouldn't do this alone."

Of course. And here is Luke, the one among them not securely attached. All of their other friends, now including Adam and AJ, are married. Jax is preparing for their own adventures. Who better than the person who can't gather his life together? Luke knows Jax leaving isn't part of some vast conspiracy among their group, but he can't help being angry all the same.

"Right. And you all thought, 'Hey, Luke has nothing and no one. Maybe he should go.'" His words curl around the edges with bitterness.

"It's not like that!" Connor's protest is too swift.

"Sure, it's not. Because the alternative is that you wanted to spent almost a month and a half with someone who—" Luke cuts himself off.

"Maybe I did."

The soft words bring Luke back down from his anger. "Asking me was your idea?"

"Not entirely. I hadn't found anyone else. Okay, I wasn't really looking, but that's not the point. When Jax said they were leaving and asked for a ride, AJ let it slip you two were living together. I got curious, and...I asked him about you. He said if I really wanted to know, then I should invite you to come with me."

"You don't have someone you'd rather be with?" Luke doesn't ask the real question on his mind; this is close enough.

"Not anymore." There's an edge in his voice, a story lurking under the surface.

"What happened?"

Connor sighs. "We wanted different things."

"Meaning?"

"I wanted someone to come home to at night after a long, horrible shift. He wanted a rotating string of casual hookups while playing house with me."

Luke doesn't mean to, but he laughs, short and sharp, before he suppresses it. "I'm sorry."

Connor chuckles too. "Don't be. I'm happy to be rid of him. Don't get me wrong—I have no problem with casual sex or open relationships or any of it. But it's not for me anymore, and I don't like being strung along by someone faking it because of what he could get out of it."

Luke swallows. He's not sure if the last part was only about Connor's last boyfriend or if it was a dig at Luke as well. He doesn't know what the summer will bring, but he wants to see where it all goes. Connor may or may not have forgiven him, but he wants Luke there.

"I'll go," he says before he can change his mind.

"Y-you will? I guess I expected you to say no, after all this time."

"Just tell me where and when, and I'll be ready."

By the time Luke ends the call, Jax is out of the bathroom. Luke turns toward them, and he can see Jax heard the last part of the conversation.

"Well, hallelujah," they say. "You ready to finish packing up, then?"

"Yeah," Luke says, and suddenly he is.

Then

PACKING, PACKING, AND more packing. Luke's mother threw things into the line of boxes on the bed rapid-fire. She turned around and smiled at him, motioning for him to come farther into the master bedroom.

Obediently, he came closer. She bent to kiss the top of his pale-blond head then straightened up and pushed his bangs out of his eyes. He wriggled his toes inside his grubby socks.

"Isn't it exciting?" Mama asked. "A trip halfway across the country!"

Luke nodded solemnly. Daddy was driving the moving van with James riding along. Luke would ride with Mama, the twins, the girls, and baby Johnny in Peter's RV. Roman, the oldest brother, was driving the RV with the rest of the big boys. They'd never done anything like this. Luke didn't know whether to be scared or excited. A family of sixteen, driving for hours and hours and hours on this big adventure. It was a little overwhelming.

Mama seemed to understand. She paused in her task long enough to sit on the rocking chair in the corner. She pulled Luke into her lap, and he wriggled against the bulge in her belly. He wasn't usually allowed this, not when he would be turning eight before they got back from their trip, and not when he had younger siblings who needed Mama's attention more. Certainly not when there was now barely enough room for him to fit on her legs. It felt nice, having her arms around him.

It was over all too briefly. She nudged him to his feet and then stood. "Help me with the packing, Lukey. Can you go get the diapers from the linen closet?"

On his way there, he heard the low rumble of thunder in the distance. Storms never bothered him much, not with such a big family to keep him safe. Now that he was the big brother, it was his turn to make sure Ruth and Johnny were okay. After he deposited the diapers into Mama's hands, he wandered off in search of Esther. She was eleven and a complete know-it-all, especially now Mama deemed her old enough to babysit.

Esther was in the kitchen, getting lunch for the littles, which probably included Luke. He didn't ask if she needed help, simply rolling up his sleeves and taking over thawing the baby food ice cubes Mama had made. If he were honest, he'd admit he liked taking care of baby Johnny. He was so cute, the way he waggled the teeny fingers on his good hand and made hungry motions with his mouth.

The thawed baby food was for both Johnny and Ruth because even at three, Ruth couldn't eat solid foods. Mama called her a "blessed child." Luke didn't know what was wrong with her, only that Esther and the grown-ups fussed more over her than any of the others. Johnny too, because maybe he wouldn't ever walk, with his feet all scrunched and turned in. But it was Ruth who needed the most care.

Luke peered up through the high windows over the sink. The sky was darkening, and there was another roll of thunder, closer this time. He shivered. Something didn't feel right about it, but he didn't say anything to Esther. She would only laugh at him. Maybe later, after the littles had eaten, Luke would take his camera outside and get some pictures of the storm clouds.

His camera wasn't anything special, just a basic one he'd gotten as a hand-me-down from one of his older brothers. Still, it worked fine, and since it was digital, he could take as many pictures as he liked until the memory card was full. If he was very good and patient, for his birthday, he might be allowed to send away for prints of the ones he liked best. Mama and Daddy were fine with that because Luke wasn't asking for fancy toys or games. And Luke liked it because he could work on his secret scrapbook. Mama knew about it, but Daddy wouldn't be pleased.

Daddy wasn't a mean man or anything like that, but he was strict, and he thought boys and girls were very different. He ran his own contracting company, and so far, all of the grown-up brothers had followed in his footsteps. There were a lot of them. Luke had ten older brothers and one younger, but only the two sisters.

The rule was boys learned to build the outside of the house, and girls learned to tend the inside. No crossover. No change. It didn't matter that Esther was as strong as any boy or that Luke really liked helping Mama in the kitchen. Nobody ever strayed from Daddy's word—it was as good as God's in their family.

The camera, though, was useful. Daddy told Luke he could use it to help out the family by taking pictures of what they were building. Daddy had built a lot of the houses in town, along with the oldest three brothers. Not the one they lived in, an old farmhouse. But they'd outgrown it, and Daddy said they needed to go where there was more land. He and Roman and Peter had already made trips east to build their new home. Luke didn't know what it looked like, but he imagined a castle where he could have his very own room.

They would need it, now Roman and Peter were ready to start courting brides of their own. That's why they had to take this trip now. If they waited, the oldest brothers would be married off and starting their own families. Mama and Daddy wanted everyone settled in first. Now that they had enough money saved up, they could do it.

Luke wandered away from the kitchen and up the stairs to get his camera from the bedroom he shared with the twins. The sound of the thunder followed him, so loud this time that the house shook a little. Still, there was no rain, only a ferocious wind that whipped the tree branches so they slapped against the house, making an eerie, high-pitched scratch when they brushed the windowpanes.

When Luke peeked into the master bedroom, Mama was taping the boxes shut. He left her to it. Packing today, making food tomorrow, and the day after that, they'd be on the road.

Luke crept down the stairs and went to stand on the porch. By now, the air was heavy with the scent of ozone, and the sky was dark as nighttime. A gust of wind made Luke's shirt billow. Lightning struck somewhere close enough that Luke's fine, straight hair stood nearly on end. He shuddered and lifted his camera, taking a picture of the clouds just as he heard the clap of thunder.

And then the rains came.

Chapter 4

LUKE WAKES WITH a start. He's been dreaming again, something about when his family was moving from Washington to South Dakota. A storm. That's all he can remember from the dream, the wind and cracking of tree branches.

With a stretch and a yawn, Luke rearranges himself in the back seat. Jax and Connor are talking quietly. Outside the window, there are only miles and miles of roadway. Luke wonders where they are. None of it is familiar; he's never been this route.

Hours ago, Luke thinks, they drove through New Jersey and part of New York City. He wonders how close they are to Boston. Connor's aunt and uncle, the ones selling him their RV, live in Salisbury. From there, Connor has the entire trip planned down to the detail.

Luke hasn't told Connor—or anyone else—about his family's attempted move all those years ago. It wasn't the same. Fourteen children, and Luke's mother expecting yet another baby. When his brothers abandoned him, he fled to the other side of the country. Back then, New York seemed like the holy city. He never made it there.

"You're awake!" Connor remarks, startling Luke.

"Yeah. Sorry."

Jax turns around and throws Luke a reproachful glance. "Why are you sorry?"

Luke shrugs, but his face is hot. "Where are we?"

"Connecticut," Connor says. "We're getting close to the Massachusetts border. You were asleep for a while." His tone is as apologetic as Luke's was. "Jax, you have an address where I'm taking you?"

"Yeah. Hang on." Jax fishes around in their messenger bag for a slip of paper. "I called my future roommates, so they're expecting us any time after four." There's a tremor in their voice.

"You okay?" Connor asks.

"Mostly. I don't know...guess I'm still wondering what my roommates will think of me."

Luke knows what they mean. Even though Jax is staying with other performing arts students, it doesn't automatically make them open-minded. Jax has said before that dance usually means slotting into a gender and sexuality binary, neither of which applies to Jax. Their roommates supposedly know this, but Jax is still afraid to go where there's so little protection.

"You'll be okay," Connor assures them. "And if you're not, we'll come get you. All you have to do is call."

Jax laughs. "You sound like my brother. He says that every time I start a new job."

"Not often I get to be the older sibling." Luke can see Connor's grin via the rearview mirror.

"I'm sure it's fine. These are other students at the college. I know my job will be good. The company is run by a queer man, and I know for sure at least one of their musicians is a trans guy. I talked to him last week."

"They have musicians? Not just dancers?"

"Yeah!" Jax is enthusiastic now, eager to share details. "They started off with one troupe of Irish dancers, mostly performing in gay bars. But now they've added other choreographers and have parts of the company who do different styles. I usually talk to the Irish fiddler or their vocalist because the main director is deaf, and so are a few other people in the company." They shake their head. "I took this intro class in ASL online, but I don't know how good I am."

"That's pretty cool," Luke says. He hopes it works out for Jax.

"It's way different from what I'm studying, but I think that's good. I can keep some of my other skills sharp. I also set up a website with my portfolio from all those random modeling jobs. I don't have an agent, though, so I don't know how well I'll do on my own."

The three of them are quiet now, and Luke watches the scenery go by. Jax is on the edge of something new and exciting. A scholarship to study dance and already a professional job. Luke still has no idea what he's going to do once he's back from this trip.

"Hey," Connor says. "I gotta piss. Mind if I stop soon?"

"No problem," Jax says.

There's a sign listing gas stations, so Connor gets off at the next exit. Jax offers to fill up the tank, and Connor heads to the mini mart for the bathroom. Luke climbs out of the back seat and stretches. He takes his camera with him and wanders toward the back of the building. There isn't much nearby. This spot is industrial, with the gas station and a couple of fast food places. Beyond it, though, is a county roadway and a lot of trees.

Luke points his camera and takes a few shots. He figures it could be years—or possibly never—before he sees Connecticut again. This isn't necessarily what he expected it to look like. Luke's always assumed there was some kind of clear line, visually, that would make it obvious he was in New England. Mostly it looks like any other highway with a middle-of-nowhere gas station.

Connor emerges with a bunch of stuff from the convenience store: some bottled water, a bag of pretzels, two packs of gum, and some Swedish Fish. He looks sheepish, but he grins at the other two when he arrives at the car. He sets two of the waters in the cup holders up front then tosses Luke the rest of the stuff.

Luke opens the pretzels, and the scent wafts to his nose. He's transported to his childhood, and he freezes with his hand on the bag. His chest is tight, and his stomach clenches as his breath comes in shallow gasps. If he hadn't gone to the convenience store that day; if he'd taken more time—or less—to choose what he wanted; if Sam's older brother hadn't been working; if he'd left his camera home, he never would've seen what his brothers did and recorded it all on film.

"Lukey?" Connor's voice sounds distant and hollow.

"Hey." Jax is in the back now, his hand gently on Luke's where it still clutches the bag of pretzels.

Connor pulls away from the gas pump and into a parking spot. Luke's legs feel numb, and he can't speak. His heart races. At the same time, he wants to pull away, to run as far and as fast as he can even though he can't move. He's shaking now.

Jax takes the pretzels out of his hand. "You're okay. It's not real, Lukey. Just bad memories." They think it's about Greg, like they always do. Luke has never corrected them.

He's aware of what's going on around him. He sees Jax look up and exchange some silent understanding with Connor. He feels Jax's warm skin on his. He can't get his mind off its loop, though. Endlessly replaying the horror and violence of what his brothers had done.

It's not until Connor hands him an open water bottle that he begins to come around. The cool, wet plastic shakes him into full awareness. He reminds himself he's safe, no longer a terrified teenager witnessing a crime.

"I'm sorry," Connor says.

"You couldn't have known," Jax answers. "Hell, I don't always know."

"I'm—I'm okay," Luke manages. He takes slow, deep breaths. "M-maybe I won't eat those." He points to the pretzels.

Jax giggles. "Probably for the best." He snatches up the pretzel bag. "More for me, then."

Connor looks between them, confusion painted on his face. He doesn't comment, though. "Are we ready?"

"Yeah," Luke says.

"I should've asked if you wanted me to drive," Jax offers.

"Nah, it's not that much longer."

"You want me to stay back here?" Jax asks Luke.

"No, I'm fine."

Jax nods and returns to the front. Connor pulls out of the gas station parking lot, and in a couple minutes, they're on the highway again. Luke goes back to staring out the windows. The memory of his brothers and the convenience store has faded, leaving only the vague unrest of questions Luke's never found answers for. His mind wanders to Ruth and Johnny, and the receding anxiety is replaced by sadness.

As the miles go by, Luke alternates between listening to Jax and Connor talking and losing himself in imagining where his youngest siblings are now. Did they stay with Esther? Or did they fall to the same fate as Luke, abandoned to a system that failed them? They pass a billboard with an ad for a clinic, and Luke makes a decision. He'll find Esther when they reach Seattle and find out what happened after he left.

Jax turns around once, and Luke gives what he hopes is a reassuring smile. He won't tell the others what he's planning, but he holds on to that sliver of hope. That's what's on his mind when they finally cross the border into Massachusetts for the final stretch of the drive.

****

Connor inexpertly makes his way through Boston, following the directions given by Jax's future roommates. They'll be living a short way from the college's admissions building with three other students: two upperclassmen and another freshman. At twenty-one, Jax is older than all of them.

At last they arrive, and Luke is surprised to see all three of them come out of the building. After living with Jax for so long, Luke no longer makes assumptions about anyone's gender. There's a curvy bottle-redhead whose hair is a mass of springy curls. They're wearing an aqua tank top and knee-length leggings. A small, slender person with close-cropped dark hair and thick glasses comes out next in a too-baggy white T-shirt and extremely short denim cutoffs. Finally, there's a dark-skinned, muscular person who looks like they came from the studio in a tight, black, sleeveless bodysuit and compression-type shorts. The last one is so attractive Luke has to take a few deep breaths before he can shake their hand.

"Hiya!" the redhead exclaims cheerily. "I'm Aideen, and this is Patrick"—they tap the one with glasses—"and Kobe."

"Are you all dancers too?" Connor asks.

"Oh, no," Aideen says. "Only Kobe. I'm in musical theater, and Patrick's studying composition."

"I thought you were all with the dance company," Luke says.

"You mean where Jax got the job? Kobe is, but we aren't. I don't do any dance except what I need to in a show."

"Jax, you're gonna love it. I'm not dancing right now because of the summer program I'm in, but as soon as it's over in a couple weeks, I'll introduce you to everyone. They're so cool." Kobe leans in. "Most of them are, you know, like us."

Meaning queer, Luke supposes. Jax mentioned it before. It's become clear within minutes that Jax will fit right in.

They look more at home with their new roommates than in the years they've lived with Luke. Happy, excited, ready for this fresh start. Luke and Connor unload Jax's things from the trunk and set them on the sidewalk in front of the apartment building while Jax becomes absorbed in conversation with the other three. Their back is to Luke and Connor, and they're talking animatedly. All four of them laugh at something Luke doesn't catch. He tries not to be jealous.

Jax at last notices the two of them again, and a guilty expression steals across their face briefly. Luke isn't offended at having been forgotten for the moment. He's glad to see Jax is comfortable. One of the others has told them about a student-run nightclub within walking distance, and another is giving pointers on using public transportation. Luke almost laughs; Jax's clunker of a car, now auctioned for parts, was only so useful. They made do more often than not with the bus. It won't be hard for them to acclimate.

Luke and Connor, along with all the roommates, help Jax bring everything inside. They'll be sharing a room with one of the others, dormitory-style. The apartment is much nicer than the one Jax lived in with Luke. He hears Aideen apologize for things being a bit messy in the bedroom. Must be the one Jax is sharing with. Luke confirms it when he sees Kobe slide a possessive arm around Patrick's waist.

At last Jax is settled, the boxes and bins lined up inside their bedroom. Half the life they shared with Luke, about to become part of a new family. Luke swallows around the lump in his throat. Jax's dream is already on its way to becoming reality. When was the last time Luke had something like that?

Connor, Luke, and Jax linger by the apartment door. Jax looks torn between giving quick air kisses and scampering back to their new friends or clinging to Luke for safety. The urge to laugh strikes Luke again; this must be what it's like for an average family dropping their barely adult child off for college. Except Jax isn't his child, and this isn't "goodbye until fall break."

The awkward pause is shattered when Jax grabs Luke and holds on tight. Luke wraps his arms around Jax, and they stand there for a long time, wishing it could last forever. He feels Jax trembling against him and knows they're fighting the same tears Luke is.

When Jax lets go, they put their hands on Luke's cheeks. "Take care of yourself," they say. "Love you, Lukey."

"Love you too." Luke sniffles.

"Here," Jax says, handing Luke a folded piece of paper.

Luke opens it. *"I Believe in You," Michael Bublé*. "Our song," he murmurs, and Jax squeezes his hand.

Jax gives Connor a much briefer hug, and then he and Luke are out the door and heading down the stairs to the car. Luke only allows himself one glance back at the apartment, a glimmer of hope that Jax would've come out again to watch them. It doesn't happen. Luke swallows his disappointment.

It's the two of them now. Connor turns over the engine, and they're on their way again, headed for Salisbury.

Chapter 5

THEY ARRIVE A short while later in Salisbury. It's a quaint, seaside town, exactly what Luke might've pictured from a movie. Connor's relatives own a bed and breakfast, a huge, rambling house with the same sort of almost-fictional feel to it as the town itself.

Connor pulls into the circular driveway and parks. "Enid and Norm are my mom's aunt and uncle. I don't know them all that well because my mother doesn't have much contact with them." He sighs, and his gaze drifts. Luke follows it to the rainbow flag in the post by the entrance.

Luke doesn't know what it's like to grow up with someone like Connor's mother. He's never met her, but from the stories Connor tells, she was open about her hatred for people like them. Luke supposes his parents wouldn't have been happy either, but they never knew. Up until his brothers forced him to leave, he believed his mother loved him. It's for her sake he's stayed away.

He knows families like his are likely as not to despise and fear queer people. He's seen it before, in the likes of the other homeschool co-op families. Mama and Daddy, though, never even talked about it. They never read those parts of the Bible out loud, nor did they discuss them. Once, when Luke was about eleven and too old for children's church, Pastor preached a sermon where he said something harsh. Mama took Luke aside and whispered to him to forget every word.

At the time, it made Luke squirm. He was already taking notice of other boys, but he never breathed a word about it to anyone. Not until the day Sam Whelock kissed him with tongue and then punched him hard enough to fracture his nose.

Connor climbs out of the car, and Luke follows him to the entrance. A kind-faced older woman answers when Connor rings the bell. Beside her, two medium-sized dogs wuffle and sniff. The white one with black and brown patches barks.

"Come on in," the woman says. "You must be Connor. And this is...?"

"My friend Luke," Connor says before Luke can answer for himself.

"Good to meet you. I'm Enid Reilly, but you can just call me Aunt Enid. Everyone else does." She turns and heads farther into the house, calling over her shoulder, "We'll be sorry to let go of Old Tracy, but I'm glad they'll be going to family."

Luke is surprised and amused, both at the pet name for the RV and the fact that Aunt Enid used gender-neutral pronouns. He senses there's a story behind it. Connor traipses after Aunt Enid, and Luke trails behind him. In the bright, sunny kitchen, Aunt Enid offers them a seat. The dogs, now closer to eye level with Luke and Connor, take the opportunity to explore them more fully.

"You two must be exhausted and hungry after all that driving. It's past the usual dinner hours, but I can fix you something real quick."

She begins pulling things out of the giant refrigerator. Luke's never seen one that size, but he supposes they must need it for feeding the tourists who stay there. He looks around, awed by the kitchen.

It's old-fashioned, aside from the modern appliances. Even the wood-burning stove in the corner looks like it belongs in another century. Aunt Enid herself, plump in her floral dress and apron and with her iron-gray hair in a loose bun, seems to have been transplanted from an older time. Luke longs to explore, to take pictures and document their surroundings.

He puts a hand on the bag slung across his chest then lowers it, guilt setting in.

Connor glances at him then leans in. "Ask her if it's okay to take some pictures."

Luke shakes his head, but Aunt Enid turns toward them. "What's that you said?"

"Luke wants to know if it's all right to get out his camera."

"Well, of course!" Aunt Enid beams. "This house is historic, you know. I'm sure Norm could tell you more than I can, as it's been in his family since the eighteenth century. Obviously, it wasn't always a B and B. The family lived here. Now, this was back before they made the town into a resort..."

She rambles on while she heats up some leftovers in the microwave, an odd juxtaposition of town history and current technology. Luke tries to concentrate on what she's saying, but his attention is drifting. Through the lens of his camera, he pictures the people who would've lived here and each new generation adding to the house.

Aunt Enid's history lesson has brought them into the twentieth century at last. She's saying something about how the town used to have a small amusement park which is now nothing more than condos. The way it all faded into history makes Luke sad.

While they're talking, a barrel-chested man with a bushy gray beard comes in with a large basket he sets on the counter. The dogs greet him enthusiastically. He plants a kiss on Aunt Enid's cheek, and she smiles and pats his in return. This must be Connor's Uncle Norm. Like his wife, he seems to be from a long-forgotten era. He has on dirt-covered overalls and a short-sleeved plaid shirt with a tuft of gray chest hair peeking out where the top button is undone. Atop his head is a wide-brimmed farmer style hat, and Luke is almost surprised he doesn't have a pipe or a piece of hay between his teeth.

He washes his soil-covered hands then comes over to the table and extends one. "Uncle Norm," he says, his voice booming and jovial. "Connor, right? Lisbeth's son."

"Yes, sir." Connor stumbles a bit on the words as he shakes Uncle Norm's hand, formal in a way he usually isn't. Luke doesn't miss the way Connor shrinks back a little from the man.

"What's with all this 'sir' nonsense?" Uncle Norm laughs. "I know we haven't officially met before, but you can relax, son. I'm not about to scold you on your manners." He gestures to the dirt staining the knees of his overalls. "I haven't changed or showered yet, and I've been digging up potatoes in the garden." He turns to Luke and offers a hand. "You a friend of Connor's or another guest?"

"Friend of Connor's. Luke Spier." He takes Uncle Norm's hand, which engulfs his own.

"And you boys are here about the RV." Uncle Norm nods without waiting for a response. "Hm. Sorry to lose our old friend, but I'm sure you all will give 'em one last good adventure."

"Last?" Luke can't help asking. He almost claps a hand over his mouth. Uncle Norm may not be the formal type, but Luke's always known better than to speak out of turn to his elders.

"Oh, well, that RV might have a few years left, if kept in good shape. But it's older'n my grandkids, and they're all adults. 'Bout the same age as you two, I'd think. Anyway, you'll make it to your destination just fine. But how long you've got after that is anyone's guess."

Great. They're about to go on a three-thousand-mile trip down Interstate 90, and here Uncle Norm is implying the RV might only barely make it there. Luke knows for sure he doesn't want to risk getting stuck in South Dakota and having his family find him, especially not with Connor there too.

"You sure it's safe?" Connor asks.

"'Course it is," Norm growls. "Wouldn't sell it to you if it weren't."

Aunt Enid sets plates of food in front of Connor and Luke. There are thin slices of a somewhat light-colored pink meat Connor tells him is corned beef. Luke has never had it any other way except on a sandwich and didn't know it could be served like this—braised and topped with a bit of warm sauerkraut. There are fresh green beans and corn and thick, homemade baked beans. Luke can smell the maple and ham in them.

"Everything's fresh," Aunt Enid says. "The 'kraut was finished this morning. Gotta ferment it in ceramic, I say. Comes out better than that nasty store-bought stuff outta the can." She sets a plate of sliced bread and a dish of butter on the table. "Eat up, boys!"

While they eat, Uncle Norm tells them more stories about the town and how they came to be there. He inherited the homestead from his father, but they didn't live there until after their three sons were grown and off to college. Then they moved and turned it into a bed and breakfast with a vast garden full of fresh fruit and vegetables. Their youngest son, along with his family, has come out to help them run the place.

"You'll meet them a bit later. They're off running some errands with their daughter," Aunt Enid says as she slides into a chair.

"Now I've told you some about us, why don't you do the talking?" Uncle Norm suggests. "What's this road trip all about?"

Connor glances at Luke, probably wondering what to say on his behalf. Luke shrugs one shoulder a little, trying to keep it subtle. Connor can tell them whatever he likes.

"I'm off to follow my father's last steps. Dad passed away, and the only thing he left me was a bunch of his writing. He didn't have much money or property when he died." Connor purses his lips. "I always thought he wanted nothing to do with me, but..."

Aunt Enid exchanges a look with Uncle Norm then nods. "I don't like to speak ill of family, but my sister's branch—that's your grandmother—was always a bit too invested in keeping up appearances for my liking."

Connor toys with his fork. "I don't get along with Mom."

That's an understatement if Luke ever heard one. When he met Connor, they were both fifteen, and Connor was angry all the time in a way that worried Luke. He was pushy, aggressive, and self-centered. He changed, thanks in part to his friendship with AJ. Now, though, a little of the old Connor peeks through as he scowls at his plate.

"You don't have to explain it to me," Aunt Enid says. "I'm aware of the way my sister's religious devotion trickled down." She holds up a hand. "I've got nothing against people having their beliefs. It's just that when it gets in the way of loving people, I think they must be doing it all backwards." She sighs. "My sister stopped talking to me because I told her I wasn't going to choose between her and my own son. She didn't understand how I could be all right with him being gay."

Luke raises his gaze to Aunt Enid, and he feels Connor shift beside him. This is obviously news to Connor because he says, "Is that what happened? Sure would explain a lot about Mom."

"Oh, yes. Got to remember, it was thirty years ago. This is our youngest, Justin. I think something in us knew from the time he was little, but we didn't have a name for it until he told us. Your mother would've been only a little older, a teenager herself, raised in that kind of restrictive home."

Another sigh. "We made our share of mistakes too. Things we thought were loving and protecting him, he told us did the opposite."

"I never knew any of that," Connor admits. "Mom never talks about her cousins on this side. It's weird. She ran away with my father, a good Catholic girl marrying a Jewish man because she got pregnant with me. It sounds like something out of a soap opera, the whole 'secret baby' thing. I know my grandparents weren't happy. They were mad she got a divorce too, but it was pretty clear they were happy to be rid of Dad."

Uncle Norm snorts; Aunt Enid clicks her tongue. She says, "Disappointing, but not surprising, I suppose. Anyway, since you're staying another day, tomorrow you'll meet Justin and his husband and their daughter. We usually have family dinners on Sundays, so most of the crew will be here, along with any of our guests who choose to join in."

Luke is somewhere between astounded at Connor's family history and nervous about meeting so many relatives. He didn't know Connor's family was so big. More spread out than Luke's, with his many siblings. But big all the same.

They finish eating, and Aunt Enid sets peach cobbler in front of them. By the time they're done, Luke is certain he'll burst. The sun is finally setting, and he's sleepy.

"Oh, you poor dears," Aunt Enid says. "Let me ask one of the staff to show you your rooms. They're adjoining, with a bathroom in between. I figured you wouldn't mind sharing that." She eyes them up and down. "I suppose I should've asked if you wanted to share a room, too."

"It's fine, Aunt Enid. You've been great. I'm sure the rooms are good." Connor yawns and then laughs. "And even if they're terrible, I'm not sure I could stay awake to be bothered by it."

Aunt Enid chuckles, pulls out her cell phone and sends a text. In a few minutes, a young man appears in the kitchen doorway. Aunt Enid tells him to take Luke and Connor to their rooms, and they follow him up a narrow set of stairs at the far end of the kitchen.

Luke wishes he could focus enough to take in the spacious room and the high four-poster bed, but he can't. The most he can do is fish around in his overnight bag for a toothbrush. Connor looks to be in about the same boat. Luke hurries, not wanting to keep Connor up any longer than he has to.

Back in his room, he lies on the bed and listens to the water running in the bathroom, a quiet, soothing sound. The bed is soft and comfortable, and Luke stretches out. He means to wait up and tell Connor good night, he really does, but the long day and the big meal have made him sleepy. Before he can stop himself, he's pulled under.

Then

THEY WERE SOMEWHERE in Wyoming now. The thunderstorms there were just as bad as the ones back in Washington. Maybe worse, according to his oldest brothers. They'd been on the road for a week, and Luke hadn't seen one until now. He wanted to watch. He stepped outside, but he was only under the RV awning for a few minutes, the rain beating down and the winds whipping up in front of him. A splatter of cold drops hit his face, and he shivered, shrinking back against the front door. He got in one photo of the storm before the door opened and two pairs of hands dragged him inside.

"What were you thinking?" Titus demanded. "You could've been swept up in that wind."

The peal of thunder that punctuated the end of Titus' sentence shook the RV. Luke trembled, afraid now of both the storm and Titus. At fifteen, he already towered over Luke, who was small for his age.

Paul yanked on Luke's arm, dragging him forward. Just two years older than Titus, he tried to be more of an adult than he really was. Luke tried to muffle his cry of surprise and shame. Paul's expression softened, and he gave Luke's arm a gentle squeeze before letting go.

"Stay in here," he commanded, though not unkindly. "Unplug everything."

"Wh-where are you gonna be?"

"Helping Dad. Now, get." He shoved Luke. Not hard, but not kindly.

Luke ducked under Paul's arm and ran for the couch. The storm must be really bad if Daddy needed help. He'd heard from Shallyn Alderwood at their old homeschool group that farther east, they had powerful storms sometimes, with winds that whipped and whirled and took out trees. She said she'd heard about some people whose cars had all been flipped. But surely Luke's family were safe here? Even as he thought it, the RV shivered and shook.

Esther had the babies. Johnny was squirming in her lap, but Ruth was sitting quietly, her favorite blanket clutched in her tiny hands. Luke sat on her other side. He curled his arm around her, wondering where Mama was. She'd been in the bed in the other RV all day, feeling sick. In fact, she'd been like that almost since they'd left Washington. Luke and Esther had done their best to take care of the smaller ones in the meantime.

Esther scooted closer so the three of them were pressed together. One by one, the others made their way into the RV with them, starting with Matthew and Mark, the twins. Luke could still hear the thunder rumbling and the howl of the wind, but only muffled. Matthew and Mark disconnected everything from any power sources. By flashlight, they began quietly playing a board game on the floor.

Mama and Daddy had let them bring some of the boxes into the RV for things to do on the road, books and games and a few toys. Not their schoolbooks, which were packed up and waiting for them to start again when they reached their new home. Most of those were old, recycled from one kid to the next. Mama and Daddy were big on not wasting anything.

These were storybooks. Lots of illustrated Bible tales. Luke liked some of them better than others. They had other books too, about missionaries and people who died because they were sharing the gospel. Luke didn't like most of those. They were either boring or scary. What he did like were the picture encyclopedias. There was one full of glossy photos of horses. Luke could look at that one all day. Another one had famous landmarks. A third one was all the Presidents of the United States.

If Matthew and Mark could play a game while they waited out the storm, Luke could look at a book. He slid off the couch and padded over to one of the boxes. This time, he chose the book of well-known paintings and brought it back over to the couch.

He was mesmerized by the photography. Each one was a work of art itself, and Luke wished he could take pictures like that. The best he could hope for was that his photos of the lightning today would come out well. He traced his finger over the pictures, following the lines of light and shadow that brought out the best in each painting. He didn't believe it was always better to see them in person. Sometimes, it was the photo he wanted to look at. You could tell a lot about the photographer and what they thought was important.

The next clap of thunder was so loud Luke jerked and covered his ears. Esther reached out so her arm was around both him and Ruth. Johnny cried. Ruth screamed. Even Matthew and Mark looked scared. Phil and Tim stopped pacing and stood motionless, staring at the door.

It could only have been a second or two before the explosion. Orange light, far brighter than the lightning, flooded the windows. Luke heard shouting outside. Then a siren's wail sliced the air. The door flung open. Paul was panting, looking panicked. He glanced around at the others and pulled himself together.

"Get out," he said. "RV's on fire. Hit by lightning."

Luke's heart raced. "Where's Mama?"

"She's with Daddy. He took her to the hospital. The baby's coming early."

Without waiting to tell them anything else, Paul picked up Ruth. Esther still had Johnny. They all escaped, Paul running ahead toward the campsite's main building and the others trailing behind.

"We'll be okay," Esther said directly into Luke's ear. "It's safe in the building."

Luke nodded. Back in their old house, they might lose power during a storm. Sometimes everyone still living at home camped out on the furniture in the living room. Those storms hadn't been nearly as bad. There was always a possibility of flooding, but Luke had never been afraid before.

He turned around to look and had to choke back a scream. Both RVs were entirely engulfed in flames now. With his heart pounding wildly, Luke stopped and stared. He tucked his book under his arm and tried to take a photo of the fire.

Esther balanced Johnny on her hip and yanked on Luke's arm "What are you doing?" she hissed. "You could get in real trouble. Come on!"

They made it to the building and sat silently in the lounge, aside from Johnny's light fussing. Luke kept one hand around the book he still held and slipped the other one behind his back under the pretense of adjusting a cushion. With his hand safely hidden, he crossed and uncrossed his fingers three times. If Matthew or Mark caught him at it and reported it to Daddy, he'd be in trouble. Luck, Daddy said, was of the Devil, and superstitions were the Devil's tools. Only real prayer was right and proper.

Luke had learned about luck from Shallyn. She'd had a mini scrapbook where she kept pictures of things she thought were lucky that she'd cut out of magazines. She also had a collection of four-leaf clovers, pressed delicately and kept safe beneath the magnetic pages of the book. Luke was as impressed with the scrapbook as with the contents, and he promised himself he would make his own someday.

Sitting there with the others, tensed and waiting, Luke didn't care whether luck was real or not. If anything could save everyone and make it okay for Mama and Daddy, he was all for it. Luck, prayer, whatever. He would do it all.

Paul left Ruth with them. Esther handed Johnny to Luke and pulled Ruth into her lap. All the big boys were still gone, and Luke had no idea if everyone had made it out safely.

The older boys began arguing over what they were going to do, and Esther tried to step in. Listening to them made the waiting unbearable. Luke tried to get up, but Johnny's weight in his arms prevented him. He set the baby down on the floor and got to his feet. He looked back to the couch. His camera was there, the one other thing he'd managed to bring out of the RV. He picked it up and glanced out the window.

No one would notice. He could sneak out, take pictures, and be back before they finished arguing. Silently, he crept around the others. The door creaked when he cracked it open, and he froze. Esther was still lecturing Mark and Matthew, and none of them turned around. Luke slipped out as fast as he could and shut the door.

The minute he was under the awning, he saw the burning RVs in the distance. Two others had caught fire as well. Even from this far away, Luke was sure he could feel the heat. He snapped a picture, then two. Before anyone caught him, he had half a dozen.

A hand gripped the camera and forced Luke to lower it. Tim towered over him. "Paul told you to stay put." His scowl made Luke shrink away.

"I wanted to see," he mumbled.

"Well, get. You need to stay indoors."

Luke turned and flung himself back inside. The others looked up. Esther opened her mouth to say something, but she saw the camera in Luke's hand and stopped. Matthew took a game off a shelf. Luke came over to the older boys and sat, accepting the red game pieces Mark offered him.

They must've gone through every game in the camp lounge before the door finally opened and Paul entered. His shoulders were hunched, and his face and hands were filthy, but he looked all right otherwise.

Every head turned toward him, even the littlest.

"Fire's out," he said. "Everyone's okay. Got it before it destroyed the whole camp. Good thing the moving van was in the parking lot." Something else was wrong, something Paul wasn't saying.

Then it hit Luke. "What about Mama and the baby?"

Matthew and Mark exchanged an annoyed look. Mark said, "They'll tell us when there's news. Having a baby isn't that fast, you know."

"Mama!" Luke yelled, coming to stand in front of Paul. "What about Mama?"

Paul pursed his lips, seeming to have a debate inside his head. Finally, he knelt down and put his hands on Luke's shoulders. "Mama lost the baby."

Lost...as in, died? Luke had heard the phrase before when Mama looked after Shallyn's mother last year. But she hadn't been nearly as big as Mama, not so close to when the baby was supposed to come.

"Is Mama okay?" Luke's words came out all ripply from his trembling.

"She'll be all right," Paul said. "But we can't go see her yet."

"But...but..."

Luke started to cry. Everything overwhelmed him at once. In a rare gesture, Paul wrapped Luke in his arms. The sound of the others talking about what had happened and what they were going to do faded as he clung to his brother for safety.

Chapter 6

HOT. SO HOT. Luke is burning up. He wakes with a start, his heart hammering. There's a rushing in his ears. He squirms, trying to get away from the source of the heat. If he doesn't, he's going to melt and disintegrate. Kicking out with his feet, he manages to shove off whatever is on top of him, holding in the warmth.

Over his head, rain drums on the roof, and the wind whistles. A shutter rattles. He has to get away before the storm reaches him, and he has to get the others. He runs to the door between the rooms and yanks it open, dashing through the shared bathroom. He pounds on the other door.

It opens, and there's Connor, in only his boxer briefs and socks. He rubs his face. "Luke, what the hell? It's the middle of the night."

"We have to get out! The storm!" Luke doesn't understand why Connor stands there, unmoving. They have to leave. He gasps for air. "Please!"

"Are you okay?" Connor's voice is so calm.

"We have to get somewhere safe," Luke pleads. His head is still sleep-foggy, and he shakes it to try to clear his mind.

"It's just a summer storm."

"No! No. The fire. We have to get out!"

He tries to push past Connor and get to the outer door. If Connor won't listen, he'll find someone who will. Before he gets far, Connor reaches for him.

"Luke." Firm, steadying. "Stop."

But he can't. The fear he woke to is rising again, blossoming into a full-blown panic. All he can think, over and over, is about the crackling sky and the whipping winds and the almighty boom before the gust of hot air. He shakes all over, unable to stop.

"Lukey, shhh," Connor murmurs, pulling him in. "You're okay. It's just the rain."

"So hot..." Luke mumbles into Connor's shoulder. "The fire..."

"What fire? There's no fire. Come on, let's get you back to bed."

"No!"

Connor steers Luke into his room, and they sit on the bed. He puts his hand to Luke's forehead. "You don't have a fever." He presses his fingers to Luke's wrist. "Jesus. Your heart's going so fast."

Gently, he helps Luke lie down. For a moment, Luke tries to pop back up. He still wants to get out. But Connor's hands rubbing his arms feel good, and he takes a deep breath. The room is back in focus, intact. There's no fire or flood, no high winds turning over cars and splitting trees. The rain on the roof is letting up.

"I'm okay," Luke says, more to himself than to Connor.

"Yeah, you are." Connor presses his lips together as if to hold in the words, but he's unsuccessful and they escape. "Is this something to do with Greg?"

Greg? What the hell would this have to do with my ex? The scars Greg left are different. Luke shakes his head. "The storm. The fire."

"What fire?" Connor asks again.

Luke can't explain it now. He's sleepy from the panic and the late hour. He wants to tell Connor what happened, but he can't string a sentence together.

"Tell you in the morning."

He curls onto his side. With a sigh, Connor slips into the bed behind him. There's a brief pause, and Luke imagines Connor hesitating. He wants to tell him it's all right, but he doesn't. Connor puts a hand on Luke's shoulder, but that's all he does. A moment later, the bed moves, and Connor's back is to him.

Connor switches off the lamp, leaving the room in darkness save for the perpetual glow of the porch light. Luke drifts back into sleep, but his dreams are still troubled by thoughts of burning.

*****

The nightmare—and the storm—are forgotten in the morning. When Luke and Connor emerge from the bedroom, they briefly encounter a couple of the other guests. The sound of dishes in the kitchen drifts up the stairs. After a quick greeting, they leave the other guests to their business and head down.

Aunt Enid isn't in the kitchen. Instead, there's a man there, younger than Luke's parents but older than Luke and Connor. Probably not quite old enough to be either of their fathers. He's a little on the plump side, short like Aunt Enid. He looks a lot like her, aside from his full beard. His hair is long, pulled into a low ponytail that hangs halfway down his back. He's wearing a pink T-shirt and gray sweatpants covered in pink stars, a flowered apron is protecting his clothes, and he's swaying his hips to whatever music he's listening to through his earbuds.

On the stove, there's a pan of eggs and a second pan with thick slices of Canadian bacon. The man stirs the eggs and then flips the bacon with a fork. He steps back and peers into the oven, and a delicious smell of baking bread wafts out to mingle with the other breakfast aromas. The man closes the oven door and steps back. When he does, he notices Luke and Connor hovering in the doorway.

"Hey," he says, his full lips breaking into a big smile as he extracts his earbuds. He steps away from the stove long enough to offer each of them a hand. "I'm Justin." His voice has a slight fry, and his sentence rises at the end, almost a hint of a question.

Luke's cheeks burn. Justin is a good twenty years his senior, but Luke finds him very attractive. There's something in him that draws Luke in and holds his attention. Despite Justin's casual attire, Luke still feels underdressed in faded jeans and a worn black music festival shirt. He looks down at himself and wishes he had something nicer. Or even that he'd attended the music festival instead of buying the shirt at a secondhand store because he liked the bands.

Connor elbows him. Luke's taken so long to respond that Justin is already back at the stove, finishing the food. Luke's face goes from a little warm to flaming, and he's sure Justin's noticed. He's still smiling, and his eyes twinkle.

"I'm Luke." The words come out as a strained bark.

"Yes, your friend said." Justin laughs. "Don't worry, I get that reaction a ton. I don't think I'm quite what people expect."

"Not...really." Luke chokes.

"You two want something to eat?" He begins plating the food. Bacon—there's several kinds—eggs, some of the beans from last night. He sets them aside to pull out the tray from the oven. The biscuits look homemade, not the kind Luke is used to from the can. There's a glass dish of butter on the table, along with several little pots of jams and jellies.

Connor digs right in. Luke's more methodical. He carefully butters his biscuit and takes his time choosing a jam. Connor's already putting a bite of eggs and turkey bacon in his mouth, humming happily around his fork. Luke eyes him, amused, and Justin outright laughs.

"Glad you like it," he says. "Learned everything I know from my mom." The twinkle is back in his eyes. "Too bad you're not staying longer. Bet she'd teach you some stuff."

"Not me!" Connor laughs too. "Talk to Luke. He's worked in food service."

"I made tacos," Luke mutters.

"Yeah, but, like, not commercial ones. Way better."

Luke takes a bite of his biscuit to avoid answering. Connor's not wrong. Luke worked for the Guzmans for over a year. He learned how to make tortillas by hand and what they used to season the meat and beans and how to fry the chips and make the salsa. His latest job was heating burgers and dogs on a greasy grill. That doesn't mean he knows much else about cooking. At one time, he'd thought to learn. But school still wasn't for him, and he wasn't able to keep up with his classes.

Justin shrugs. "Anyone can learn."

Some of the other guests have arrived in the kitchen, and Justin offers them breakfast. As soon as the pans are empty, he's already cracking eggs and laying in new slabs of bacon. There's no time for more conversation, for which Luke is grateful.

Connor insists on waiting after they finish to find out from Aunt Enid or Uncle Norm what the plan is for the day. They need to get the RV ready and pack their things inside it, and Connor's promised they'll lend a hand anywhere they're needed here. People may or may not be around for lunch or dinner, depending on whether they added meals to their booking for their stay. Luke hopes Connor hasn't volunteered them to cook.

Slowly, the kitchen empties out, and the other guests retreat upstairs or leave for the day to explore the town. One person pauses to ask about public transit and going into Boston. At last, they're alone with Justin. Without being asked, Connor rises from the table and goes to help Justin with the dishes. He hands Luke a container and the pan of beans to put them away.

"So you're the ones buying Old Tracy, right?"

Connor laughs. "I didn't say anything last night, but where in the world did that name come from?"

"Aideen," Justin says. "My niece."

It's not a common name, and Luke wonders when it jogs his memory. "Aideen? Is she a student at the Conservatory?"

"Yes," Justin says. "How did you know?"

"The only other Aideen I've ever met is my friend's roommate." As much as Luke misses Jax, the connection makes him happy. Jax will be taken care of.

"Small world," Justin remarks. "Well, anyway, she thought the RV needed a name. I think she was about eight at the time. She said it should be gender-neutral, and Tracy stuck."

"Aunt Enid says you have a daughter yourself."

"Step-daughter, yeah. My husband's from his first marriage."

Luke is curious now. "How did you meet?"

"Now that's a story. I was seeing a friend of his right around the time Travis and his ex-wife split. We ended up hanging out a lot. After I broke it off with my boyfriend, Travis asked if I wanted to get coffee."

Luke senses there's more than Justin is saying, but he doesn't pry. There isn't time anyway; Aunt Enid comes in, followed by the dogs. She has a bouquet of fresh flowers that she sets into a vase and adds water.

As she sets it on the table, she says, "You boys sleep all right?"

Connor glances at Luke, but he only says, "Yeah. That bed is really comfortable."

"Glad you liked it. Norm's out in the garden, but he'll be in shortly. He has in mind to help you get the RV road-ready."

"What can we do in the meantime to help out?" Connor asks.

"Care to come out to the garden and help me with the weeding?"

"Sure. Luke?"

Luke shrugs. "I could probably remember how to do green things."

Justin laughs. "Or you can stay in here and help me with the rooms."

"That sounds better." Luke glances at Connor. A slight frown creases his brow, but only briefly before his face relaxes and he nods.

"Awesome. Let me show you where the linens are."

Luke pauses, tracking Connor's progress as he follows Aunt Enid and the dogs outside, and then he hurries to catch up to Justin as he heads up the back stairs. When he glances back, he sees Connor doing the same; Luke ignores the worry lines and faces forward again.

Chapter 7

B Y THE TIME dinner rolls around, Luke is exhausted. He's chased after Justin all day, taking care of the bedrooms and cleaning up after the guests. He's helped make meals despite having said his only skill was with tacos at a takeout place. It's been nice working with all the fresh ingredients, and there weren't too many people at lunch anyway.

The bed and breakfast can sleep up to fifteen. It's full, but the majority of the guests have been out for the entire day. Dinner, on the other hand, is a big event. It's all hands on deck. Justin's husband, Travis, is back from the co-op, where he's traded eggs and fresh produce for meat and milk. He's brought wood too, for the bonfire in the pit later on. Faith, their teenage daughter, is also there.

Justin's grilling outdoors, and Aunt Enid is inside, making all kinds of salads—including at least two involving some kind of beans. Luke wonders if it's normal in Boston to serve beans at every meal or if it's unique to this bed and breakfast. Faith is getting out all the plates and cups and silverware. Travis and Uncle Norm are working on unloading the wood and setting it up to light the fire.

Connor's gone with them, leaving Luke to either help in the kitchen or at the grill. The decision is made for him when Aunt Enid hands him a plate of homemade dinner rolls. He carries it to the yard and sets it on the table under the pavilion. The sky is cloudy, but the rain is holding off, at least for now.

The other guests have started to arrive. It's not late, but because it's overcast, it's darker than it would be otherwise.

Luke comes back into the kitchen to carry more platters to the yard, and he watches the people entering and waving to Aunt Enid on their way up to their rooms with their shopping bags. He has the sense this place caters to a more well-off crowd than he's used to.

In a short time, the food is ready. In pairs and families, the guests come down through the kitchen and out to the yard. Luke follows them. The air is sticky and heavy with anticipation of rain, yet still it doesn't come. The colorful twinkle lights are on now, casting red, yellow, green, blue, and violet light everywhere. Cicadas buzz and trill, and the scents of the salty ocean, the warm earth, and the cooking food mingle.

It takes Luke back to times with his family, before the move, when summers were full of laughter and kids running in the yard and fresh food from the garden. His early childhood wasn't unhappy. He knows most people assume that in a large family, especially one as religious as his was, there's a lack of love or care. That wasn't Luke's experience, not in those days.

He doesn't want to dwell on it now, though. After he sets down the platter, he sneaks off to his room to find his camera. Aunt Enid gave him permission, so he decides to go ahead and make use of it. He brings the camera down to the pavilion.

After snapping a few shots of the tables spread with food, he wanders closer to the water. It's dark on the horizon, with the sun setting in the opposite direction. The waves aren't choppy, but they're stirred up in anticipation. There'll be another rainstorm tonight. Luke seeks the best position to capture the tension on the water.

He lowers his camera and is still looking out over the ocean when there's a tap on his shoulder. He turns to see a young couple, holding hands. Their faces are full of adventure, promise, and love, the same expressions Luke remembers on AJ's and Adam's faces.

"Excuse me," the woman says. She's pretty, with her sweet, round face and her dark hair piled on top of her head.

"Yeah?"

"We were wondering...would you mind taking our picture?"

Luke doesn't answer right away. He was working around the B and B earlier, so it's possible they think he's staff and this is part of his job. It's also poor light for taking elegant posed photographs. He'd only meant to take some pictures of the ocean because he liked the way it looked, not because he thought they would be stunning.

"If it's not too much trouble," the man adds, filling in the awkward silence Luke's lack of response has created.

"Oh. Um...well, I'm not a professional. I was just..." Luke waves toward the water.

"We're on our honeymoon," the woman says with a slight giggle. As if Luke couldn't have guessed that.

"And we've never been here before," the man says. Again, as if Luke wouldn't have been able to figure it out.

"Okay..." Luke sighs. "I don't work here. My friend's family owns this place, and we're stopping here before we set out on vacation." Or whatever the appropriate word is. Luke supposes it's not a vacation if he doesn't have a job anymore to vacate. "Also, it's too dark for your pictures to come out well."

The woman looks disappointed. "I didn't realize."

Luke figures that's true enough. He relents. "Maybe tomorrow? If we try earlier in the day, we could get some really nice ones." When the woman's face lights up, Luke wants to laugh. He also inexplicably wants to see what kinds of pictures he can get of the couple.

"Really?"

"Sure. I don't imagine you have a camera...?"

The man grins. "We do! It was a wedding present, but I have no idea how to use it."

Luke chuckles. "Meet me out here at, let's say, four tomorrow afternoon, and I'll take those pictures. And I'll show you how to use your camera."

The two of them thank Luke, and they all wander back closer to the pavilion. Someone has brought a guitar, and they're singing what sound like Irish drinking songs. There's laughter mingled with the melody. When he's close enough to take a good shot without being noticed, Luke snaps a picture of the assembled guests before joining their inviting circle.

****

There's another thunderstorm overnight, and somehow, Luke has ended up in Connor's bed again. Connor is still asleep when Luke wakes, so he slips out carefully to avoid disturbing him. He dresses quickly and leaves through his own room, descending the stairs into the kitchen. No one is there, so he steps outside.

The sun is out, making the still-wet grass sparkle. The air is misty, and Luke smells the rich, damp earth when he stands facing the ocean on the wraparound porch. Up until this trip, despite the Atlantic being within an afternoon's drive, he's never seen it before. He's glad he remembered his camera when he came outside. Raising it, he snaps a picture of the water from that angle before letting the camera rest against his chest.

The rain brought a cool breeze, and Luke is glad for the flannel shirt he grabbed from his duffel. He closes his eyes, listening to the waves lapping at the sand and the faint screech of the gulls.

A hand on his shoulder rouses him. It's Connor, with a steaming mug in his hand that he holds out to Luke. He's more awake than Luke feels, and he looks good. He's already showered. Luke can smell the combination of soap, hair gel, and deodorant, along with some kind of fragrance. There's a sameness to them, something that reminds Luke of a gift set. He hides a smile behind the cup he's accepted.

They lean against the porch railing, facing the water. "You all right?" Connor asks. He's referring to a second night of Luke waking up, sweating and shaking and crying out about the storm.

"Yeah."

Luke promised himself again last night he would tell Connor about the storms and the fires. Now, in the light of day with his heart rate back to normal, he once again can't bring himself to do it. There's too much to explain about his family that most people don't understand.

Connor picks up on Luke's reluctance and changes the subject. "I'm going to spend some time with Uncle Norm, going over the RV and making sure it's ready for our trip. I've driven one before, so that's no issue. But I want to know about this one specifically. After that, we can move our stuff in so we're ready first thing tomorrow."

"Have you seen it yet?"

"Oh, yeah. It's huge. There are two full-size beds and a twin bunk. There's a ton of room inside. It's like one of those tiny houses on wheels."

Luke grins. "I've always wanted to live in one of those."

"I'd get sick of it after about the first week, I think." Connor laughs. "And yet, here I am, taking a month on the road in something that size. What was I thinking?"

"That you wanted a big adventure?"

"Must be."

"What are you gonna do with your car? Just leave it here until you get back?"

Connor jerks as though the question caught him off-guard. "Hm? Oh. Well, I'm selling it to Justin and Travis's daughter. She needs one for work because she's just gotten her first job."

"Then what are you gonna do when you get back?"

"Buy a new car." Connor shrugs. "I'll sell the RV." He doesn't give any more details.

Their conversation is interrupted by Aunt Enid arriving in the kitchen in a swirl of vibrantly colored, billowing house dress. She pours herself a cup of coffee, adding nothing to it, and comes out onto the porch.

"Morning!" she says cheerily. "I hope you all slept well. That storm was a doozy!"

Luke swallows. "D-do you get those often?"

"Oh." Aunt Enid waves her hand dismissively. "Sometimes, but they're rarely much to speak of. The climate's pretty nice out this way. We get our share of thunderstorms this time of year, on and off until the weather turns. There's the occasional nor'easter in the winter, of course. And once or twice a hurricane's come up the coast, though they lose most of their power by that point. Last night was all bark and no bite, though it's not usual to have a storm two days in a row."

Luke shivers. "We used to get storms like that a lot. Sometimes tornadoes."

"Haven't seen one of those in my lifetime. They don't happen too much around here. Where're you from?"

"Um." Luke hesitates. "South Dakota." It's close enough, though he technically lived less than half his childhood there. "I haven't been there in a long time. It's good you don't get tornadoes here."

Connor's eyeing him, so Luke drops the subject. The storm is over; there's no reason to dwell on it. He finishes the last of his cocoa and takes the cup inside. Connor follows him, and Aunt Enid is right behind him.

"You two want some breakfast?"

"Yeah, that'd be great. Want some help?"

"If you like. We start serving around now, and the other guests will come in as they see fit." She takes food out of the fridge and sets it on the counter, only this time, it's all fresh ingredients instead of reheated leftovers. With her head still in the fridge, she says, "Justin and his family will be by later. Not sure about Henry or Shawn. They sometimes stop by, but they've got responsibilities of their own, and they don't help run the place."

Connor takes the carton of eggs and begins cracking them into a bowl. Luke thinks he should be of some help. Aunt Enid and Uncle Norm are being kind in allowing them to stay there for free while they get ready for their trip. But he'd rather watch Connor, who moves so effortlessly and makes small talk while they work side by side.

He's saying something now about his job, telling a story about something that happened. Luke missed the beginning, and he's not following it now. But Aunt Enid is laughing, and the two of them look content as they make breakfast. Luke looks for something to do and spots the open cupboard with the dishes. He begins setting things out, arranging them on the long counter.

It's not long before the honeymooners from last night arrive in matching rumpled lounge pants, both yawning. The guitar player appears soon after, wide awake and fully dressed—minus the guitar—with their backpack on and a pair of binoculars around their neck, ready for sightseeing. The rest of the guests are not far behind, mostly in singles or pairs, their states of dress and alertness ranging between the two extremes.

"Looks like a good start to the day," Aunt Enid remarks, and Luke only nods, enjoying being caught up in the activity of the moment.

****

Justin arrives by late morning, and for a while, Luke busies himself helping him with inventory of their stock. He likes making the lists and checking off what they need to order. When they finish, Luke joins Aunt Enid and the dogs in the garden. There are weeds to pull and vegetables to pick and flowers to water. It's been years, but it brings back memories of sitting beside his mother, learning how to twist the tomatoes off the vines so as not to bruise them or digging in the dirt for the new potatoes, the soil getting under his nails and clinging to the skin on his palms.

Later, while Connor is in the kitchen helping to chop ingredients for a stew, Luke wanders around the grounds, taking more pictures. The sun is high now, and there are only a few scattered clouds. It's warmed up from the previous day, and Luke has left his flannel shirt in the bedroom. Even so, he's hot, despite the breeze from the ocean.

He follows the same path he took last night down to the water. This time, he toes off his shoes and rolls up the bottoms of his jeans. The sand is gritty and burns the bottoms of his feet as he steps closer to the water's edge. The waves by the shore are blue-gray, capped with white foam. Luke shields his eyes and focuses on the horizon, where the ocean flattens and darkens to navy blue and the sky lightens to almost colorless. It's vast, with nothing in sight except miles and miles of water, still and glossy like a photograph. Luke wonders what worlds lie beneath the calm surface.

His thoughts are once again interrupted by a light tap on his shoulder; this time, he turns to find not Connor but Justin. The heat Luke felt in his presence the first time they met returns. Luke has never thought much about what he likes in a man. His partners have been varied, from the posh and polished AJ to Greg's charmless hypermasculinity. He enjoyed being with Jax, who breaks free from the confines of gender. But there is something calming about Justin, something gentle but with an undercurrent of power. Justin's not afraid of the different parts of himself; he's not ashamed of being a man who embraces his femininity. The combination of his warmth and his strength wraps around Luke like a blanket. He understands it means nothing, but he enjoys being in Justin's presence all the same.

"I called your name, but I guess you didn't hear me over the ocean." Justin smiles, his eyes crinkling at the corners, and it causes a ripple of embarrassment-slash-pleasure in Luke.

He shakes his head. "I'm sorry."

Justin shrugs, a tiny gesture that reassures Luke. Turning toward the water, Justin adds, "I grew up here, so I don't even see it anymore. It's just the ocean, like a tree in your yard is just a tree."

"It's amazing." Luke clears his throat. "I've never seen it before."

"Really?" Justin's expression is puzzled when he turns back to Luke. "I thought Connor said you two lived in Philadelphia, at least for a while. That's not too far from the Jersey shore."

"We did. I still do." At least, to the extent that's where Luke will end up once this trip is over. "But it's not like we ever made that trip."

He doesn't explain about having come to the city with nothing, how being a homeless gay kid didn't give him a lot of opportunity to travel far. Or about the number of times he switched foster homes and the intolerance of strict, religious adults. Or the way he'd followed AJ like a lost puppy instead of taking it upon himself to decide on his own what he wanted to do.

Justin doesn't ask for an explanation; he simply nods as if he understands, even though he knows nothing of Luke's history. "Well," he says, "you're here now." He scrutinizes

Luke for a moment. "And...why are you here? With Connor, I mean. He hasn't said much about what prompted this trip, aside from his father's death and wanting to know more about him. So, how do you fit into that?"

Luke doesn't know how to answer him. His friendship with Connor has been uneasy, aside from the months immediately after Greg. Even then, Connor was on eggshells around him, constantly doing small things to reassure Luke he wasn't expecting anything. A way to prove he was different from Greg.

"He's...we're..." Luke tries, but his mouth sticks between the words.

Justin's fingers on Luke's arm are warm and slightly calloused. "Sounds like you're something different from friends, but not exactly like boyfriends."

Luke blinks. "I don't know. Before this trip, we hadn't seen each other in five years. Then he showed up for our friends' wedding, and all of a sudden, he asked me to come along." He blows out a long breath. He's not sure why he's telling Justin all this, but it feels good to let it out. "I don't understand why he asked me. He keeps saying it's because our friends all thought it would be good for both of us. But I had to quit my job—not that I liked it all that much anyway—and leave my apartment. And...now I'm not sure I should be here or what Connor expects from me."

"Wow." Justin is quiet for a time. He watches the tide, and Luke watches him. At last, he says, "What do you expect from yourself?"

No one has asked Luke that. Not about this trip and not about the rest of his life. When he concentrates, he discovers he has no idea. But instead of that feeling vast and empty and terrifying, it's oddly freeing.

"I think," he begins slowly, "I want to find that out."

Justin doesn't laugh. He nods solemnly, as if Luke has said something profound. Perhaps he has because Justin says, "That sounds like a very good plan."

A warm breeze ruffles Luke's hair, and it carries the sound of laughter. He and Justin both look over. They won't have any more time to talk because the honeymooners from the previous night are headed their way. When they're close enough, the woman waves. Justin looks at Luke and arches his eyebrows.

"I promised them last night that I'd take some pictures and show them how to use their fancy new camera." Luke smiles, realizing he's been looking forward to it despite the couple being presumptuous.

"Well, have fun." Justin leans in. "They took a tour of the town yesterday. I hear they're a little high-maintenance."

"It's okay." Luke grins. "I'm used to it. Connor's a little high-maintenance too."

Justin laughs and rests a hand on Luke's shoulder. "I'll see you at dinner, then."

He departs, and Luke turns toward the newlyweds. Their fingers are entwined, and they look content to be in each other's company. The woman reaches out to take Luke's hand.

"Thank you so much. I know we messed up last night, and I wouldn't have blamed you if you'd bailed on us. We really appreciate that you still showed up."

"No problem. I think we can have a lot of fun with this. Did you bring your camera?"

The man holds up a bag. "Right here."

"Great. Are you ready to get started?"

Chapter 8

IT'S THE EVENING before Luke and Connor set off for the rest of their trip. Another family-style meal, another bonfire. This time, Enid and Norm's older sons, Shawn and Henry, have joined them. Shawn is Aideen's father. His wife has a thick Irish accent. Henry didn't bring his girlfriend.

Luke is a little stiff and sore from using muscles the previous two days that he probably hasn't given much thought to in years. While he was down by the ocean, photographing the honeymooners, he didn't notice. Now, though, everything feels tight. He stretches, working out the cramps. He looks up when a hand rests on his shoulder. It's Justin.

"May I?" he asks, pressing down a little to indicate what he means.

Luke shrugs his free shoulder and winces. "Okay."

Justin's fingers are firm on Luke's neck and upper back, and Luke feels the overuse tension melting away. He closes his eyes, enjoying the warmth of the fire and the deep massage. The air has cooled, though it's still warm from the day's sunshine. The guest with the guitar is playing again, something soft and tender. A love song, maybe, for a person they once knew.

"Better?" Justin asks, letting go of Luke.

"Much, thanks."

Justin returns to his seat and picks up a conversation with the young honeymooners. Luke watches them for a while, thinking about how much fun they'd been during the photo session. He slouches in his chair so his head rests on the back, and he drifts into a state somewhere between sleep and awake, the low hum of voice and guitar weaving around him and lulling him. Connor's presence next to him is comforting.

Over time, the other guests go their separate ways. The fire is burning down to embers, and everything is cleaned up from their meal. Luke stirs and looks up at the few stars peeking out from behind the thick clouds. The night air is cool now, but it's still hot by the fire. Luke is mellow and comfortable, listening to Aunt Enid and Uncle Norm talking with Shawn, Henry, and Justin.

Connor nudges Luke's calf with his foot. "We should get to bed. Early start tomorrow."

Luke nods, but he'd rather not move. Connor sighs and stands then reaches out a hand. Reluctantly, Luke takes it and lets Connor pull him to his feet.

"We're gonna head in," Connor says to no one in particular.

The conversation slows and stops. Aunt Enid hauls herself out of her chair, and the others do the same. She rests an arm around Connor.

"Need anything?" she asks.

"I think we're good." Connor turns to the others. "I don't know if we'll see you tomorrow. We're leaving as soon as we can get on the road."

Shawn and Henry offer polite handshakes to both Connor and Luke. Justin gives Connor a friendly squeeze, but when he gets to Luke, he wraps him tightly. He whispers in his ear, "A song for the road. Put it in your playlist." He pulls a slip of paper out of his pocket and gives it to Luke then pecks his cheek lightly.

"G'night," Connor says, and the two of them retreat into the house and up the stairs.

The only thing left in Luke's room is his small duffel containing toiletries, pajamas, and a change of clothes for the morning. He sets it on the bed and pulls out the pajamas and his toothbrush. He feels in his pocket for the slip of paper

Justin gave him. *"Wake Me Up," Avicii.* Luke folds the paper and tucks it into his duffel. When he looks up, Connor is standing in the doorway.

"What was that all about?"

"What?"

"With Justin."

It's meaningless, just a song. It isn't as though Justin propositioned him or Luke accepted. His interest in Justin isn't any more significant than a passing breeze. Connor's tone suggests much more, and there's a bite to it. Jealousy, fear, anger—Luke isn't sure. He shrinks away. He hasn't seen this side of Connor since high school. It's too much like Greg's constant grilling, and Luke needs distance.

Ignoring Connor's question, he steps into the bathroom and shuts the door. He imagines Connor on the other side, maybe growing angrier because Luke refused to acknowledge such a stupid, petty thing. Fifteen minutes later, Luke hesitates before opening the door. He doesn't want to talk about it.

Connor isn't there, though. The door they share is closed, and there's no sound on the other side. Luke sighs and puts his things away. He's about to climb into the big bed when there's a knock. He answers it to find a sheepish Connor.

"I'm sorry for being a dickhead."

Luke snorts, but he can't help laughing. Connor does indeed look very sorry. "It's—" Luke cuts himself off before he can say "okay." It isn't, and they both know it.

"I shouldn't have said anything."

"Apology accepted."

"Did you want to stay in here?" Connor hitches his thumb back at his room. "I mean...just in case, you know?"

In case Luke has another horrible dream about being trapped in the fire he still hasn't told Connor about. "I don't know."

"Never mind," Connor says. "I was being a dickhead again. I'm sure you can handle sleeping by yourself."

"I've managed it pretty well for some time now, yeah." Aside from sharing a room—and sometimes a bed—with Jax.

Connor cracks a smile. "I mean, successful adulthood and all." He turns sober again. "I thought after the last couple nights...I don't know what I thought. It's probably a bad idea."

Probably, Luke thinks. But he does need a good night's sleep before they leave, and Connor's room is a lot cooler than his own. "Okay."

"Okay, what?"

"Okay, I'll stay in your room."

It doesn't matter if anyone sees them. Several guests saw them emerge together in the morning, and all of Connor's family assumed Luke was his boyfriend already. He can't get rid of it, though, the sense he shouldn't be accepting the offer.

They slip under the covers, and Connor turns out the light. He's quiet for a moment before he says, "About earlier."

Luke huffs. "What?"

"I wasn't trying to say you did anything wrong."

"Kind of felt like it." Luke turns onto his side to face Connor. "I'm not interested in Justin." Or not more than finding him attractive.

"I know."

"Then why did you ask?"

"I wanted to know why you were looking at him that way."

Luke doesn't answer right away. He could think of a thousand things to say, but none of them would be right. He doesn't know what fascinates him about the man. Instead, he stalls for time.

"What way?"

Connor rolls onto his back. "I had this professor," he says. "Freshman year biology. Older, distinguished. He had a brilliant mind, but his teaching was down-to-earth.

He could make anything interesting. I used to hang on his every word. I was young, away from home for the first time, and not under my mother's thumb anymore, but I still wanted to play with fire. I felt like an adult."

"You had an affair with your teacher?"

"You make it sound so tawdry," Connor says. He laughs. "No, I didn't. To this day, I have no idea what his sexual orientation was. He wasn't married, and he never said. What I do know is that he treated my infatuation with kindness." Connor chuckles again. "Didn't really help me get over it— more the opposite. He didn't take advantage of me."

"Jeez. Are you saying your cousin would do that to me?"

"God, no!" Connor bangs his head backward against the pillow. "I'm doing this so shittily. I meant, is that why you got attached?"

"I've known him for less than a day."

"And I'm reading more into it than is there."

"Yes." Luke suspects there's more Connor's not saying, but it feels too nice to have someone worry for him. He can't stay mad, even if it's weird and Connor is acting like Luke isn't mature enough to handle himself. Maybe he isn't, in some ways.

"Okay. I guess it had the same feel to it. Interest in someone safe, someone who can't—"

Connor doesn't have to finish the sentence. Luke knows. Someone who can't hurt him the way Greg did. Only Connor isn't aware Greg wasn't the only one.

"I get it," Luke says. "Look, it wasn't anything."

"Okay."

That's all there is to say about it. They turn over, and in minutes, Luke is drifting off to sleep.

*****

It rains again the morning they leave. Big, thick drops plop onto the sand, and the waves are choppy. The white foam and the gray at the horizon blur into one line. It's not a heavy rain, but it's steady, pattering on the roof of the house and the RV. Luke takes a photo from the porch.

Uncle Norm helps them carry their overnight bags and load them. Connor shuts the door, and they return to the warm kitchen. Aunt Enid baked cinnamon rolls, and she removes two from the pan and plates them. She sets two more aside on a rack to cool.

"For the road," she insists.

She's packed them a lunch too. She gifted them an old-fashioned picnic hamper, and the dry goods are in there. The rest is in the RV's fridge and pantry. Connor planned to stock up when they stopped, but Aunt Enid presented him with the food before he could protest. She packed it earlier in the morning, before either of them was awake.

They stand to eat their cinnamon rolls, already in their jackets and ready to go. Connor wants to be on the road before traffic becomes a problem. Luke thinks it will be anyway, but he doesn't say so. By the time they finish eating, Aunt Enid has the other two rolls wrapped and ready to take.

The rain lets up enough for them not to be soaked as Uncle Norm and Aunt Enid walk them to the RV. Uncle Norm shakes their hands, and Aunt Enid gives them each a tight hug. When she wraps her arms around Luke, he rests his chin on her shoulder. Suddenly, he doesn't want to leave them. He wishes he could stay and help them run their bed and breakfast, maybe learn to make Aunt Enid's cinnamon rolls.

It's silly, he knows. He doesn't belong here any more than he belonged at the foster home or with AJ's family or in Greg's bed or with the Guzmans or in Jax's apartment. But he wishes he could, to stay and belong somewhere.

"Luke," Connor's voice cuts in. "Take a picture?"

"Uh, yeah. Sure."

Luke takes out his camera and points it at Connor, standing between his aunt and uncle. Connor's smile is wide despite the chilly rain. Uncle Norm's eyes twinkle even though his mouth is serious. Aunt Enid leans her head toward Connor, her smile full of warmth and tenderness.

Click.

Luke puts the camera away before the rain can do any damage. He climbs into the passenger seat, and Connor rounds the RV to take his place behind the wheel. He gestures at Luke to roll down the window.

Aunt Enid and Uncle Norm are back on the porch, under the safety of the roof. They wave, and Aunt Enid calls, "Drive safe!"

"Naw," Uncle Norm contradicts. "Drive fast and take chances, boys!" Aunt Enid gives him a little shove, but she giggles.

Connor waves back. "Thanks again for everything!"

The last thing Luke sees as they move off is Aunt Enid blowing a kiss. And then they're on their way, pulling out onto the main road and heading for I-90. They won't stop again until they reach somewhere to fill up the tank at the western edge of New York.

It's just the two of them now, and it feels strange. They had the short stretch between Boston and Salisbury, but it wasn't long. It hits Luke that he and Connor have no one but each other for the next thousands of miles of roadway. Already he's out of things to say. What would they talk about, anyway? Luke's shitty job at the grill? Or his mouse- and roach-infested apartment? The times he picked up a guy who gave him cash because he felt sorry for Luke?

"So...what's up with you and Jax?"

Or that. Luke definitely doesn't want to talk about that. "They're a friend."

"That all?"

Luke sighs noisily. "What would you like me to say? They're a friend I used to occasionally fuck, but now I don't because they've gone to college. Are you happy? Was that the answer you were looking for?"

"Jesus Christ, Luke. It was a question."

"Yeah, one that implied you thought something else was going on. Jax isn't my...whatever the word for a non-binary person you're dating is."

"Sorry I asked," Connor mutters as he turns onto the highway.

"Maybe you should be." Luke folds his arms and stares out the window at the rain, which is now pouring. He shivers, and out of the corner of his eye, he sees Connor turn on the heat.

It's a long time before either of them says anything, but Connor eventually breaks the silence. "You were right. I was...fishing. For answers."

"I know." Luke angles toward him. "Why did you really ask me on this trip? I know why you said, but it doesn't make sense. We haven't seen each other for almost five years, and you act like it was nothing."

Connor opens his mouth and then shuts it again. He blows out a long breath. "I don't know. It felt like the right thing to do at the time. I mean," he backtracks, "it still is. I asked the others what they thought, and they..."

"They what, Connor?"

"They said I should leave well enough alone. AJ said he was going to ask you to come live with them for a while when Jax left. But I insisted, and they let up. Adam actually agreed to help me." Connor snorts. "He's never really liked any of us, has he?"

"Not especially, no. But it's not like we gave him a reason to."

Connor groans. "I know. Hell, AJ should've written me off years ago. I was an ass."

Now Luke smiles. "I remember."

He was, too. Connor was arrogant and self-centered. They barely knew each other at first, but once Luke began spending time with AJ, he saw a lot of Connor. Mostly he remembers Connor trying desperately to get his attention, and he could never figure out why. He thought it had something to do with the fact that by then, Luke and AJ were making fumbled teenage attempts at sex. He's not sure if Connor even knows about that. Did AJ ever tell him?

"AJ knew I needed help." Connor eyes Luke sideways.

Back to this. Luke can relate, though. Everyone thinks Luke needs their unsolicited help. He's perfectly capable of finding what he needs on his own. Even now, with his future entirely uncertain, he'll make it. He'll find another garbage job in another garbage town, and AJ—and Connor—won't have a single thing to do with it.

"AJ likes to stick his nose where it doesn't belong."

Connor surprises Luke by laughing. "Isn't that the truth."

To prevent more conversation, Luke turns on the radio. He knows Connor could easily access whatever's on his playlist, but the radio is faster. He flips stations for a while until he recognizes a song. Listening to Christian radio isn't one of the things he tells his friends about. He's not much of a believer anymore, if he ever was one at all. AJ is—he's always been a good Catholic. But he isn't much interested in this type of music.

It's mainly cheesy, but Luke likes this song. It was popular for about five whole minutes a couple years back. Connor hasn't switched the station or commented, possibly because the song is unrecognizable as religious outside of hardcore fans. The words don't sound like something out of the Bible, and there's no reference to Jesus.

Luke forgets himself for a minute and sings along with the chorus. He only realizes he's doing it when Connor mutters, "Whoa."

"What?"

"You have a nice voice. Also, this song. Is it...?"

"About a blowie, not Jesus? Yeah."

"I kind of like it."

They listen to the rest of the song, and by the time it's over, Luke's let go of their previous conversation. The RV swallows the miles, an endless expanse stretched out ahead of them.

Chapter 9

THEY STOP FOR a break once they're in New York. It isn't raining anymore, and the sun is bravely trying to peek out from behind the clouds. Connor climbs out first and stands by the RV, stretching. Luke is slower, taking it in as he hops down from the passenger seat.

It's a nice place. There are a few people there, despite it still being relatively early on a weekday. An older couple have their dog inside a small fenced-in area. A woman in a long skirt, her head wrapped in a scarf and a cane in her hand, watches two children on the playground.

Luke watches them for a bit too, his back resting against the RV. The little boy, probably no more than five, scrambles around the equipment, which Luke thinks might be designed as a pirate ship. The little girl is making her best effort to keep up with her brother, but she's less steady than he is. The surface doesn't look like anything Luke remembers from when he was young enough for playgrounds, and it makes him curious. He heads for the pirate ship.

When he gets close enough, he stops short. The little girl, now tugging on her mother's skirt, reminds him of his sister Ruth. This girl, too, has Down syndrome; Luke recognizes it immediately. He has to swallow firmly around the lump forming in his throat.

The girl's mother notices him. Embarrassed, he turns away. He doesn't want her to think he was staring at her daughter with ill intent in mind. He reaches down to touch the playground surface, which is what he came for in the first place. It's springy, and as he looks up again at the equipment,

83

he sees all the ways it's been made accessible. Ruth would've loved something like this. Luke blinks away tears as he stands.

"It's neat, isn't it?"

Luke turns toward the woman. She's smiling at him, so he wipes his eyes with his wrist and attempts a return smile. "Yeah. I've never seen anything like it. My sister..." He breathes slowly before he starts crying.

The woman nods. "Makes it easier for both my kids to play together."

"There you are." Connor puts a hand on Luke's shoulder.

"Checking out the playground. Feel this." Luke taps the surface with the toe of his sneaker.

Connor does as instructed. "Whoa."

"Right?"

"So, you have a sister, you said? How old is she?" the woman asks.

"Oh. Uh...she's an adult now, actually."

"Ah, I see. And she's disabled?"

"Down syndrome."

"Same as Katrina." The woman nods to her daughter. "Does she live around here?"

"No." Luke clears his throat. "Seattle." Last he knew, anyway. It's always possible Esther moved again. Luke is glad Ruth's away from their older brothers, but he hasn't seen any of them in more than ten years. He hopes Esther, Ruth, and Johnny are safe. Matt and Mark too, even if they were bossy as hell when they were kids. But the rest, especially Peter and James, he hopes are rotting in jail or dead.

Katrina, who temporarily wandered off while the adults were talking, returns. She has a handful of dandelions, which she presents to her mother. She plucks one out of the center and gives it to Luke. He bends down so he's at eye level with her, and she blinks at him through her thick glasses.

She says something Luke doesn't catch—her speech is less clear than Ruth's was—followed by "sister." Luke didn't realize she was listening while they spoke before.

"Thank you." He sniffs the dandelion, making Katrina giggle. When she runs off again, Luke stands.

"You two have kids?" the woman asks.

Startled that she's taken them for a couple, Luke glances at Connor. "We're not—"

"Nope, no kids," Connor says, and Luke wonders why he doesn't correct the woman.

"Where are you all headed?"

"Across the country," Connor tells her.

She smiles. "Enjoy it now. If you ever have a family, it'll be harder to travel. My wife and I barely make it through a trip across the state." She looks past them to the building, where a lean woman in a baseball tee is emerging with two takeout cups. "Nice meeting you both. Safe travels!" She leans on her cane and makes her way toward the other woman.

Luke and Connor head back to the RV. Connor's set up lunch for them from the picnic basket and fridge. There are the makings of some excellent sandwiches, all with freshly sliced meats instead of packaged ones. Connor doesn't waste any time once the food is out, neither with helping himself nor with asking Luke questions.

"You have a sister?" Way to jump right to the point.

"Two." Luke might as well be honest.

"You never say much about family. I always assumed..." Connor trails off and stuffs a bite of sandwich in his mouth, replacing the foot he'd just had there.

He looks guilty enough Luke doesn't needle him, but he does clear things up, to a point. "You thought I'd been kicked out of my house for being queer." He purposefully doesn't say gay, even though he knows it's what Connor's thinking. It's a bigger subject than his own story.

"Yeah. So were you not, then?"

"It's complicated. I don't think my family even knows. Maybe my brothers suspected, but they never said, and neither did I."

"Wait, you have brothers too? How many?" Connor's an only child, and he's always been more than a little fascinated with bigger families.

"I'm the third youngest. Ten older brothers and one older sister. One younger brother and one younger sister."

Connor whistles. "Is your family part of one of those religious groups, then?"

"Kind of."

"Huh. I guess I assumed you were Catholic, like AJ and my mother. I mean, I know some Catholic families are really big. But that's a lot more than I've ever seen."

Luke doesn't want to talk about it. He knows what kind of family they were—and still are, even with his father gone. He thinks sometimes he's lucky his brothers caught him with his camera when they did. If he stayed...if they all found out about Sam Whelock... It's anyone's guess where he'd be now.

The bite of sandwich in his mouth feels dry, and it's hard to swallow. He thinks about Ruth and about Katrina, the girl on the playground. She's younger than Ruth was when Luke's brothers left him, maybe half her age. Now Ruth is nearly twenty-three. Esther always said she was going to take them to Seattle, but he has no idea whether they made it or if they're still there. She, too, wanted to escape the minute she was old enough.

"I'm sorry," Connor says.

"For what?"

"Asking all those questions. I should've left it."

Yeah, you should. Luke takes a sip of cola. "Well, now you know."

"It's just..."

"What?"

"Nothing." Connor sweeps the trash into a bag and begins putting things away. "Hey, want to go for a walk? There's a path along the canal."

"Sure."

They finish cleaning and step outside again. The day is beginning to warm up, and Luke can tell it's going to be hot. The sun warms the damp ground, making it steam. More people have arrived. The older couple with the dog are gone, as is the woman with the head scarf. The pirate ship playground is full.

"Hang on," Luke says.

He climbs into the front seat and fishes in his bag for his camera, which he brings back out. He slings it across his body, and he and Connor set out for the path. He's never seen the Erie Canal before; it's yet another in a growing list of firsts this trip. Somewhere in the back of his mind, he remembers learning about when it was made and its importance in the trade route, but otherwise, it wasn't of much significance in his education.

They stop at the building, and Connor goes inside. When he comes out, he has a travel brochure, which he hands to Luke. "This has a bunch of stuff about the canal."

Luke opens it and reads a little of the history. He tucks it away, and they walk closer to the water. There's a boat coming their way, but it looks touristy and not commercial. Luke takes a photo anyway. He takes several more after the boat passes, of the canal and the landscape beyond. There are houses across from them, set back from the waterway. Everything is quaint and picturesque.

It's already heating up, so they keep their walk brief. Back at the RV, Luke settles himself. He hopes somewhere along their trip he'll have the chance to print some of the pictures.

"Where are we headed?" he asks as Connor slides into the driver's seat.

"Buffalo. The other end of this canal, pretty much." He glances at the time. "We have a while. I'm meeting up with one of my father's cousins, and they're expecting us around dinner. We won't stay with them like we did with Aunt Enid and Uncle Norm. I've booked us a spot at an RV campground for the night. I have to stop for gas at the next station. There's none here."

"No problem."

With that, they're back on the highway. Luke takes a picture from that angle as they head west toward Buffalo.

****

When Connor pulls over into the Iroquois rest stop to put gas in the RV, Luke ducks into the building under the pretense of fetching them both coffee. Or rather, coffee for Connor and anything else for himself. He's never liked it, and one road trip isn't enough to change his mind.

Before he gets into the long line—apparently everyone else is trying to stay awake too—he pulls out his phone. Pathetic. They aren't even three days into the drive, and already Luke misses Jax so much he's calling them from a New York Thruway rest area.

Jax doesn't answer, which Luke supposes isn't a shock. They're probably busy with their new job or their new friends. It shouldn't sting as much as it does. Jax and Luke were never in a committed relationship, never professed their undying love or made plans for the future or did anything else except occasionally fuck and needle each other about ordinary things in their shared living space. It shouldn't be surprising or painful to know Jax has moved on.

Luke stuffs the phone back into his pocket and waits patiently for an overpriced latte and a hot cocoa that's too thick and burns his tongue on the first sip. By the time he returns to the RV, Connor is leaning against it, texting.

He looks up, and Luke almost laughs at the way his whole body loses its tension with relief when he spots the coffee.

"Here you go. One skim milk raspberry latte, just like you asked." Luke tries not to wrinkle his nose while describing it. He has more success than when he ordered.

"You are an angel." Connor takes the cup and pops the lid to blow on the contents, something Luke should've done with the cocoa.

Gingerly, he takes another sip, ignoring Connor's tiny smirk. The cocoa still isn't very good. "You want me to drive?"

"Nah, not yet. It takes some practice to manage it. I can teach you when we stop at the RV park, though."

"'Kay." Luke's phone buzzes, and he pulls it out. Jax. He's as relieved by this as Connor was about the coffee. "Be right back," he tells Connor, who shrugs and continues to sip his drink.

Luke ducks into the shade of the building to answer Jax. "Hello?"

"Hey, you! I was thinking about you and Connor this morning, and there you were, calling me. What's up? Sorry I missed you a bit ago. I was at the studio with Kobe."

Jealousy bubbles up in Luke's gut, but he reminds himself Jax called him back right away. "Nothing much. Just figured I'd give you an update while we're stopped here at...wherever this is. Somewhere in New York."

Jax laughs, bright and cheery. "You should see if they have postcards. You know, for your scrapbook."

"Maybe."

"Does Connor know about it?"

"It's not like we had a conversation while we were driving, no."

Luke can almost hear the eye roll right along with Jax's exasperated sigh. "Why do you hide it? I think it's so cool. I don't have an eye for that kind of thing at all."

They're right. One time, Luke made Jax a page for some of their professional photos. Jax tried to recreate it for another one, and they gave up halfway through. Luke rescued it and made a few adjustments. He thinks about Jax's question, why he doesn't tell anyone.

"He'll think it's silly, when I could just use Instagram to document my life."

Jax snorts. "You know me. I'd gladly do it all on my phone for the rest of forever. But people still like a real copy they can hold and look at. I mean, take Patrick. He's a composer, and he doesn't only do electronic stuff."

"Wh— Oh. Your other roommate." Another stab of jealousy.

"Yeah. Anyway, I should go. We're gonna make lunch, and then the dance company is performing tonight. I'm going along to watch and so I can meet everyone, even though I'm not dancing with them yet."

"Okay." Luke clears his throat. There's so much he wishes he could say to Jax, but he doesn't know where to begin, and the conversation is nearly over. "Um. Take care of yourself, okay?"

"Hey, that's my line," they joke. "Love you, Lukey."

"Love you too." Words, meaningless when spoken by two people who are one day going to forget about each other.

Luke ends the call and tucks his phone away. He turns to see Connor eyeing him, still leaning against the RV. He must've finished his coffee because the cup is gone.

"Everything okay?" Connor asks when Luke returns to the RV.

"Yeah. That was Jax."

"They settling in okay?"

"Uh-huh. Said they were in the studio with Kobe, and tonight they're going to watch the dancers." Luke feels the bite of every word as he speaks, fresh jabs into the open wound of missing the best friend he's had since AJ.

Connor's face softens. "Why don't you go in and get a couple postcards from the shop?"

Luke stares at him. "What, instead of texting?"

"Everyone likes getting real mail these days." Connor gives Luke a pointed look. "And I know you'll want one anyway as a souvenir."

"Why would I—"

Connor cuts him off. "Don't be mad, okay? I found your book. I don't know why you'd want to hide it, but Lukey, it's fantastic." He holds up a hand to prevent Luke from protesting. "Wait here."

He enters the RV, and Luke hears him opening doors. In a minute, he's back outside with a leather-bound book. He hands it over. Luke takes it and brushes the light brown cover with his fingers. It's buttery soft except for the etching, a beautiful, scrolling tree. The book is similar to the one Luke has only nicer; it looks handmade. He opens it and flips through. The pages are like old-fashioned paper, encased in plastic sheathes.

Inside the first page there are two postcards tucked into the plastic. One is a picture of Boston Harbor at night. The other is a reprint of a vintage Salisbury postcard. It must've come from the bed and breakfast's tiny gift shop. Luke can't help smiling as he touches the postcards through the page protector.

"It's for our trip," Connor explains. "I was going to wait until tonight, but I figure now's as good a time as any." He points to the image on the cover. "It's a Tree of Life. We're not in that big a rush. Go in and pick something out."

"Thank you," Luke finally manages to say, and Connor's face lights up with his charming grin.

Luke hands him the new scrapbook and rushes back into the rest stop to browse the gift shop. He wants to find just the right postcards, one for Jax and one for himself. At last he chooses: One has the outline of New York State, filled in with images of landmarks. The other is an old-fashioned one, another reprint, that says Saratoga Springs. He'll decide later which one to send to Jax. The gift shop also has stamps, so Luke buys a whole sheet of them. He can send Jax postcards from every place they visit.

He returns to the RV, where Connor is already in the driver's seat. Luke tucks the new postcards into the scrapbook. On a whim, he takes out his camera and snaps a picture of Connor, whose smile is shy.

"Enough of that. Ready?"

"Almost. Got any music?"

"Yeah, of course." Connor taps his phone. "Help yourself."

Luke opens the app and finds Connor's playlist. His surprise increases until he's laughing. "Connor, what the fuck?"

"What?" Connor sounds genuinely perplexed, but he could be playing around.

"Why. Why do you have ten goddamn hours of music on here?"

"It's not ten," Connor mutters.

"Close enough and...Jesus." Luke's laughing harder now. "Why these songs?"

"Because I like them, *Janet*," Connor snaps. "Just pick something already."

Luke shrugs and hits shuffle. He can't help the continued random giggles as "Movin' Right Along" plays. He says, "Oh, man. Fozzie's smooth vocals get me right here." He thumps his chest.

"Shut up," Connor replies, but he's grinning as he pulls back out onto the highway.

Chapter 10

IT'S MID-AFTERNOON WHEN they reach the RV park. They set up camp, and Connor shows Luke how to connect everything. It takes some time. Connor says he's done this before, which has Luke curious.

"You've been on a cross-country trip?"

"Hardly." Connor laughs. "No, my parents used to own a camper. When I was little—before all the weird shit happened—we would go up to the Catskills every summer for a couple weeks. Just us and the mountains. Well, and a lot of other families with the same idea."

"Not exactly a wilderness adventure," Luke remarks, bringing out Connor's dimpled grin again. He likes that he's made Connor amused.

"Nope. The place we stayed was more like a resort. I loved it, though. Always made a ton of friends. I stayed in touch with a couple of them for a while, saw them every year until I was about thirteen or so." His smile flattens. "Then my parents split up, so that put an end to our summer vacations."

"That sucks."

Luke knows a bit of Connor's family history, but only from the bits and pieces he shared with their group. Connor's mother isn't nice. Luke met her once, and she acted like she was far too busy to notice or care what her son was doing, as long as it didn't make her look bad. He never met Connor's father before he died.

Connor shrugs. "Yeah. Kind of funny to think I'm sort of going back to all that now."

"We were supposed to see Yellowstone." Luke doesn't know where that came from. He didn't mean to tell Connor anything about it, not yet or maybe ever.

"We were?" Connor frowns.

"No, not us. I mean my family."

"Oh, right. Something happened, and I think you were going to tell me about it?"

They've finished setting up, and Connor has opened the awning on the side, creating a shelter. Laying down a bit of artificial turf to make it more like a porch, he sets out two camping chairs and flops into one inelegantly, simultaneously toeing off his shoes. Luke takes the other chair and settles back into it. He doesn't want to sit, not after their long drive, but the chairs are more comfortable than the RV's cab seats.

The memory Connor is asking about, the one haunting Luke's nightmares, is not the one Luke attaches to his family's move. He thinks about what to tell Connor. Images of the rain and the fire, the smell of ozone and smoke fill his head. Burning, everything burning. Luke clenches his teeth against the fear and turns his mind to the first fire, when the RVs burned.

He doesn't have clear memories of much else immediately after the firefighters came. He remembers Esther tucking him into bed because Mama wasn't there. They all camped out in a motel, while Daddy stayed with Mama at the hospital. What he does recall is the orange light and the booming explosion. If Luke closes his eyes and tunes everything else out, he can still hear it, along with the sounds of Johnny crying and Ruth screaming.

"We were moving," he says at last. "Lightning hit one of our RVs, and it set it on fire. We were in the other one at the time and had to escape fast before it caught too. My mother was expecting another baby, but..." Luke is shivering by the time he finishes explaining what happened. "After all of that, we didn't do any sightseeing."

"Whoa. So did you make it to wherever you were going? Or is...is that how you ended up out our way?" Connor is careful with his words, avoiding asking how Luke ended up homeless.

"No. I was only eight. We rented a couple vans and managed to get there. But we lost everything we'd stored in the RV."

He wishes they hadn't made it. If they'd stayed where they were in Wyoming, or had never left Washington, he wouldn't have met Sam. Everything that unfolded would never have happened.

"Are you cold?" Connor has finally noticed Luke's shaking.

"Kind of, yeah."

"You always did get cold easily. Here, let me get you a blanket."

Connor hauls himself out of the camp chair and retreats inside the RV. A moment later, he's back with a knitted blanket. Luke laughs; it's Connor's college colors.

"Did Lauryn make this?" Jax's sister-in-law had gone through a phase of knitting everything for everyone.

"Yeah." Connor chuckles. "What gave it away?"

"She made one for Jax with Hello Kitty." Luke's face heats up. He'd rather not tell Connor what he and Jax got up to under it.

He wraps himself in Connor's blanket and settles back in the chair. He's not really cold, though it's cooler in the shade. He slouches down so he can lean his head on the camp chair.

"My cousins will be here soon to pick us up," Connor says. "I'm going to go make sure we've hooked everything up properly."

"Okay." Luke nestles under the blanket as Connor disappears inside the RV, and his shivering slowly ceases.

He looks around the RV park, taking it in for the first time. When he thought about campgrounds, he expected something with a bit more wilderness. Trees, maybe a lake. He thinks there is a lake somewhere nearby, but he's not sure, as he can't see it. There are almost no trees in this part of the campground.

"What is it?" Connor asks, startling Luke.

"Hm?"

"You look...confused."

"Oh. I was wondering why there aren't any trees."

"This is the RV site," Connor says, as if that explains everything.

Luke takes another glance around. There are a lot of campers and RVs here, lined up almost in a grid. Not as many, and not as neatly lined up, as in one of those RV superstores, but certainly a lot more than Luke's ever seen in one place otherwise. "Huh."

Connor chuckles. "It's impressive, I guess. The rest of the campground is really nice. We can go explore it, if you like."

"How long do we have?"

"Maybe an hour? I'm not sure. Plenty of time to take a walk. Come on." He tugs at the blanket around Luke's shoulders. "You'll warm up."

Luke stands and stretches then hands the blanket off to Connor. They put the chairs away and head toward the trees. Luke looks back at their RV. It's only their first day in it, but that will be home for the next thirty-eight days. He's not sure what he thinks.

"Wait!" he exclaims. "I forgot my camera."

He dashes back, and in a couple moments has caught up with Connor again. They're both quiet on their walk, and Luke is glad. He wants to spend time taking it in. They reach the trees, and Luke turns back toward the RVs.

He snaps a picture that captures the strange, neat rows and the industrial feel.

There's a path through the trees, and they follow it past the tent campsites. A few people have mini trailers, but they're the kind that doesn't require water or waste hookup. The rest are all a grove of variously dingy-colored tents, some with people outside them, cooking or playing games or reading, and some deserted.

Past the campsites, there's a lodge, and then the entire area opens up to the waterfront and recreation area. Luke cringes; it's touristy, and the noise and crowding are a bit much.

"We can go around," Connor suggests. "There's a hiking trail farther that way." He points.

The rest of their hour is spent in peaceful wandering. Connor does most of the talking, about the last summer he and his father went on a trip. Not camping but to some amusement park.

"My parents had been separated for almost two years and the divorce was finalized that spring. I think he was trying to...I don't know, be the cool dad, I guess," Connor says. "But he never had a lot of money, and he couldn't afford more than the one trip."

"What about your mom?" Luke frowns. He probably shouldn't poke the bear, but he's always wondered why she acted like she did.

Connor snorts. "She tried. That same year, later in the summer." His shoulders stiffen so much Luke feels it when they brush his. "I don't think that summer ended the way she expected. She caught me—" He cuts himself off.

Luke side-eyes him and sees Connor is blushing so red he looks sunburned. "Oh, crap! That sucks. No lock on your door?"

For a moment, Connor stares at him, mouth open. Then he gathers himself and says, "Probably not what you're thinking." He laughs, and Luke's mistake of assuming Mrs. Wasserman caught him jerking off seems to shake him out of his embarrassment, even though it deepens Luke's. "No, she caught me kissing another boy. Some kid I met on our trip to the Jersey Shore."

Luke tries to picture it, Connor around age thirteen, maybe with braces and stray pimples on his nose, fumbling with that first rush of summer love. He wonders if it's anything like what happened between him and Sam Whelock at the homeschool co-op.

"Tell me," he begs.

"About my mother catching us?"

Luke shakes his head. "About the boy."

"Oh, him." Connor's smile is wistful. "He was this tiny little kid, pale skin and a million freckles. His hair was brown, but it turned reddish in the sun, like even it got sunburned." Connor laughs. "That sounds super cheesy. Anyway, we met, and the first thing he announced to me was that he was gay and if I had a problem with that, I could go fuck a duck."

"He didn't!"

"He did." Connor nods, his face purposefully serious before he loses it and breaks out into a grin. "I told him I didn't care. I'm not sure I knew then that I was. My mom sent me to Catholic school starting in sixth grade as part of the separation agreement. It's not like I knew what that even meant."

Luke nods. Connor had already been through two Catholic high schools and was on his third—a mixed-gender one that time—when Luke met him. "Go on."

"Okay, well, this kid, Gavin, dragged me all over the place the whole week we were there. I figured my mother didn't really care because she was too busy with her then-boyfriend to bother with me." Bitterness wraps around the words. "Story of my life. Anyway, I would've followed Gavin to the ends of the earth, I think. I didn't quite get what I was feeling for him, but by our last night, I'd at least figured out I *liked him*, liked him, and I told him so. He kissed me, in the shadow of the beach house. Pretty innocent stuff, but Mom saw because she'd just gotten back herself."

"Shit." It's the only thing Luke can say. He's grateful no one ever saw him with Sam, to his knowledge, though he suspects Sam's mother knew.

"Yeah, well. Nothing to be done about it now. Mom hasn't changed a bit in fifteen years, and I doubt she ever will." Connor glances at his phone. "We'd better get back. Our ride will be here shortly."

They fall silent again and head back toward the RV. Luke stuffs his hands into his pockets and thinks about what Connor told him. It surprises him Connor hadn't sorted out his sexuality sooner. He was always so in-your-face about it, although that may have been due to his mother's demands. Maybe he took a page out of Gavin's book. Luke, despite his family's influence, knew he had "sin" by the time he was ten.

The two of them are only back at the RV for a few minutes before a silver four-seat truck pulls up. A man probably twice their age, lean with salt-and-pepper hair and a neatly trimmed beard, steps out.

"Connor and...Luke, right? I'm Avi," he says holding out his hands. He takes Connor's between his own and presses them, then does the same with Luke. "It is a blessing indeed to meet Saul's son at last. He was a good man, your father."

Connor's eyebrows shoot up, but he's caught himself in time not to say something stupid. Luke will ask him about it later.

"Ready to go?" Avi asks.

"Any time," Connor replies. They climb into the truck, and Avi drives them out of the RV park and back onto the main road.

****

Luke isn't sure what he expected, but the little row of brick townhouses isn't it. Somehow, he thought Avi's family would live in something like Aunt Enid and Uncle Norm's sprawling old bed and breakfast. This looks like a version of the row houses Luke knows from Philadelphia.

Avi parks in the back, and they enter through the basement. As they climb the stairs, Avi talks at them nonstop: what his family is like; what they'll be having for dinner; something about the neighborhood. Luke can hardly keep up, either with his fast pace or his rambling words. He's explaining something about what they do at the townhouses, but it's lost on Luke among all the rest.

The moment Avi opens the inside door, delicious smells waft out to greet them. Luke's mouth waters. Aunt Enid's lunch was fabulous, but it was hours ago, and Luke's hunger stirs. Connor turns and grins at him, and Luke knows he's looking forward to dinner too.

Avi kicks off his shoes, so the others follow suit. He leads them into the kitchen. There's enough room for a small round table, but that must not be where they serve their meals because there's nothing on it except for a vase of yellow flowers. A woman is at the stove, her back to them, her wild, graying brown hair piled on top of her head. She has on a big apron, and she's stirring something and singing softly.

"Ah, Shefele!" Avi says.

The woman sets the spoon down and greets him with a kiss. Then she turns to the others. "Connor?" When he nods, she comes over and wraps him in a big hug and kisses both cheeks. "Hello, bubeleh. And you must be Luke. I'm Sylvia. Welcome to our home."

She envelops him the same way she did Connor, and Luke fights the desire to blurt out that he and Connor are just friends. She lets him go and returns to the stove for another stir of whatever's in the pan.

"It's good to meet you," Connor says. "Dad was your cousin, right?"

"Yes. I'm sorry to hear about his passing. I don't know if it was one of those things where he had a feeling, but I understand he was in touch with a lot of us in the last year or so. Traveling all over the country."

"Yeah, that's what I'm on my way to find out. I'll fill you in at dinner if you want."

"Of course, of course. And we might have some stories for you about Saul."

While they're talking, several more people of varying ages come in. There's a woman and two children, all in shabby clothes; a boy who can't be more than sixteen; and two people who might be college students. Luke wonders where they're all going to fit in such a small townhouse. Sylvia doesn't seem concerned, though. She greets all of them with the same enthusiasm as she did Luke and Connor.

Avi takes a stack of plates and carries it out of the kitchen. Intrigued, Luke steps out to look. There's a dining room right next door, with a little window into the kitchen Luke didn't notice before. Without being asked, Connor picks up the silverware from the counter and passes it through the window into the other room. Sylvia has turned off the burner under the saucepan, and she's pulling something out of the oven. The rest of the crew, even the children, help carry in the food. In a few minutes, there's a feast waiting.

They sit around the big table that nearly fills the small room. Sylvia says a blessing, and then she points out each of the dishes on the table. There's something like chicken fingers, which she calls Buffalo schnitzel chicken planks.

There's a pan of baked zucchini with garlic and grape tomatoes. The salad is cold couscous with pine nuts. Sliced bread is on a wooden cutting board, and Sylvia has promised them a berry tart for dessert.

She introduces Luke and Connor to the other guests. They're not immediate family. Avi is a lawyer, and Sylvia is a social worker. They run a program for housing support. Everyone is there for different reasons, but the townhouses are a temporary dwelling until the residents can move out and be self-sufficient. Sylvia often invites them in for meals.

She says, "We never had children, but we've both always wanted a big family."

Avi smiles at her and takes her hand. "Now we do, and they number more than the stars."

By the time dinner is through, both Luke's belly and his heart are full. He recalls family dinners from his childhood, where the younger ones were expected to be silent and allow the adults to get on with their conversations. Those were usually dull enough Luke had no problem drifting off into his own thoughts.

This is different. Everyone has a story to share from their day, and conversation wraps around each person in turn. It's lulled Luke into feeling content with this peek into Sylvia and Avi's family life. That is, until he hears Avi asking Connor about his father. Luke feels it when Connor's leg stiffens against his.

"I, uh, hadn't seen him for a while before he died," Connor says. An understatement; Luke knows Connor hasn't seen his father since he finished high school, and he wasn't in touch with him all through graduate school. Whether or not they spoke since then, Luke doesn't know.

"He never contacted you?" Avi frowns.

"We spoke briefly, a few weeks before he passed. He said he hoped I would find what I was looking for, and he said to contact you. That was it."

"He was so proud of you," Sylvia says.

Connor looks around at all of the others. His face is pale and drawn. He sets his napkin next to his plate and stands. "I—I'm sorry. May I use your bathroom?"

Avi shows him where it is while Sylvia murmurs, "I hope the food didn't make him sick."

Luke watches Connor disappear around the corner before he says, "Excuse me."

He stands and follows in the direction Avi led Connor. Outside the bathroom door, he presses his ear to it, but he doesn't hear anything. At least he knows Connor's not in there getting sick. Softly, he raps on the door.

"I'm fine," Connor says, sounding anything but. "I'll be out in a couple minutes."

"It's Luke. Can I come in?"

It takes a minute, but Connor unlocks and opens the door. He gestures for Luke to join him. It's doing nothing for the impression Luke wanted to give that they're just friends, but he doesn't care. Connor's upset and needs him.

"Tell me," he says.

"I... I can't. Not now." Connor sinks down onto the closed toilet. "It doesn't even matter anyway. He's dead and can't talk to me anymore."

Luke kneels in front of him. "He can't, but they can." He jerks his head in the direction of the others.

"So, what? I should ask them to tell me all the stories about my father, in hopes somehow I'll understand why he—" Connor cuts himself off.

"Yes," Luke tells him, and he's sure it's the answer, even though he has no idea what Connor's father did or didn't do.

He's sure there's something he's missing, but it doesn't seem important.

Connor looks up at the ceiling and sniffs. "It turns out I didn't even know him, Lukey. And now it's too late."

Luke's not used to being the strong one. He puts his hands on Connor's thighs. "That's why we're here. I thought that's what this trip was about."

"I wanted to follow his path." Connor swipes at his eyes. "I thought—I thought it would help me figure out who I am."

"Maybe it will."

Connor looks down at him. His eyes are bright, red-rimmed. He nods. Luke stands and offers Connor a hand. He doesn't say it, but he wonders if this trip will help him figure out who he is too. He brushes off the thought. This is Connor's world, his people. They have nothing to do with Luke or his family, regardless of what Luke talked about with Justin.

They emerge and return to the dining room. The others are clearing the table, so Connor and Luke join in. Luke accepts a bit of plastic wrap from Avi and folds it around the leftover chicken planks.

"Take them with you," Sylvia offers. "I'll leave them in the fridge until you go."

"Are you sure?"

"Of course." She gets out a shopping bag and puts the chicken in it, along with some of the bread. "Now, how about dessert?" She puts her hand on top of Connor's where he holds the bag's handle. "And I'll tell you a story about the time your father and I sneaked out of our grandparents' house to follow my older sister and her boyfriend to the beach."

Connor chuckles. "All right."

Chapter 11

A VI DROPS THEM off at the campsite hours later, when it's already dark. The clouds from earlier have cleared, leaving an expanse of sparkling stars. Luke gazes up at it, transfixed. He hasn't lived anywhere with this kind of view since he was fifteen. Not that he hasn't ever seen the night sky in all its glory since then, but it hasn't been such an unobstructed view.

He almost misses it when Connor wishes Avi goodnight. He waves, still distracted by the brilliance of their surroundings. Avi drives off, leaving the two of them alone. Someone—either Avi or one of the others—will be back in the morning to return them to the little row of townhouses, when they will see what the family has done with them. For now, though, Luke and Connor are alone.

It's both their first night in the camper and the first they've truly been alone since they set out from Luke's rat-and-roach-infested apartment in Philly. The first time it's been only them since dropping Jax with their new roommates, aside from some time spent in the car. Luke isn't sure what to say to Connor.

Connor bumps his shoulder. "Want me to make a campfire? Or do you want to go right in to bed?"

"I...don't know," Luke says without looking at him. He continues to gaze upward.

Out of the corner of his eye, he sees Connor tilt his head. "It is beautiful out here, isn't it? I know we'll see more like this on the way."

"Where I grew up, this was my view every night." Luke doesn't know why he's telling Connor this. His childhood, all the years spent with his family, are tucked away where no one else can see them.

"Yeah?" Connor replies. "I'm not sure if you've ever said where you lived before." He pauses. "Wait. Didn't you tell my family you're from South Dakota?"

Luke licks his lips. He's not sure he wants to discuss it now. They'll be passing through his home state, and Luke would rather not have to answer questions about why he doesn't want to find his biological family ever again. Except sometimes he does. On the worst nights, he thinks about Ruth and Johnny and Esther, and he wonders what happened to them.

He closes his eyes. "Yes. That's where we moved when I was eight, just outside Mitchell, South Dakota."

"Okay." Connor's voice is soft, as though he's afraid to say much else.

Luke breathes a sigh of relief. Connor isn't going to ask him more, despite knowing their route will take them as close as possible to where Luke lived an eternity ago. He isn't sure if his family or the community built around their church are still there. He called once, back when he lived with Greg, but he hadn't been able to bring himself to speak when Matt answered the phone.

He tried to call Sam once too, a couple months after he was settled in Philly with the family who looked after him. It hadn't ended well. Luke wants to blot out those memories the way the clouds move in again, obscuring the stars.

It's clear Connor won't press for details, so Luke takes out his camera. He wants to capture the sky before it's too overcast. He takes several pictures then slips the camera back into its bag. His new scrapbook remains in the RV's kitchen, waiting for him to have a moment to work on it.

Connor clears his throat. "Maybe we should get some sleep. Avi's sending someone to pick us up in the morning, and later, we'll go up to Niagara Falls."

Now that, Luke's on board with. He's never seen them, even though Philadelphia isn't all that far from here. It's a day's drive, though, and he's never had enough money to spend the night there nor the time to take off work for a vacation. He nods in agreement, and they climb into the RV.

Luke lets Connor go first in the tiny bathroom. He spreads his things out on the bed and stares at his phone. He wants to call Jax again, but they've already talked once today. Instead, he turns over the postcard from the rest stop and begins to write. He cramps his letters so they're tiny and he has more room to describe the first part of their trip. When he's through, he caps the pen and applies a stamp just as Connor emerges from the bathroom.

He sets the postcard braced against his box of brightly colored pens and reminds himself to find a mailbox in the morning. Then he stands and trades places wordlessly with Connor. Quickly, he finishes getting ready for bed and returns to the dinette.

They hadn't discussed sleeping arrangements. There's a pair of beds in the back that can be merged into one larger one, and there's another bed over the cab. Even the seats in the dinette can be rearranged if need be. Luke fidgets, wondering how to ask Connor what he prefers.

Connor is seated at the table, looking over the map, and doesn't notice at first when Luke arrives. He only looks up when Luke sits across from him.

"Hey," he says. He looks around as if taking in the RV's interior for the first time, though Luke knows it isn't. "This reminds me of being a kid and going to the mall with my parents after Christmas."

Connor's growing up must've been radically different from Luke's. He didn't go to malls on a regular day, let alone after a holiday. The first time he set foot in one was with AJ, and it had been more than a little overwhelming.

"What was it like?"

"They sometimes had these big RV and camper events," Connor explains. "Right inside the mall. You could get in them and look around. We had a small trailer-type one, the kind you use for camping. Nothing as fancy as this." He grins. "I'll bet Aunt Enid and Uncle Norm bought theirs at one of those shows. They totally seem the type."

Luke wouldn't know. "And they just let you go in them?"

"Yup. I used to imagine what it would be like. I mean, I didn't think about a road trip. I wanted one for our back yard, so I could pretend I had my very own house. To a kid, these things look freaking huge. Anyway, it was kind of like how you're not supposed to lie on the bedroom displays in the store either. No touching, just looking. And some salesperson stalking you the whole time with brochures."

"The ones we were supposed to take on our trip weren't like this either," Luke says. "A little less like a house on wheels. More like a bus with some beds." He coughs. "Speaking of, um..."

"Right. Sleeping quarters. Well, there's two beds in back, but I don't know if you want to share the room or not. If you don't, one of us can sleep up top over there." He points.

There's something unspoken between them about whether Luke is going to continue to have nightmares. He hopes not, but he can't predict it. And it was nice, having someone in his bed.

"We could both fit back there. It's okay."

"Cool. Well, I'm exhausted, and I want to be up early so we're ready for whatever Avi and Sylvia have planned to show us. I don't know if you caught what they said, but they run a sort of halfway house program. They're gonna tell us more about it tomorrow."

"Okay."

They both head for the bunks. Connor has them set up as twin beds, but there's an extra piece he can put in the middle to join them. Once they're inside, he pulls the curtain shut. It's probably not necessary, seeing as it's only the two of them, but Luke is glad he does.

Luke slides under the covers on his side. The only light is from Connor's phone, which he's put in flashlight mode. Almost the minute Luke's head is on the pillow, he feels the pull of sleep. He watches with half-closed eyes as Connor slips into bed. He shuts off his flashlight, and the darkness feels heavy. Luke blinks.

"Hey."

He turns toward the sound of Connor's voice, and he feels fingers against his arm. He pulls his hand out from under the covers. Connor takes his hand and squeezes briefly then lets go.

"Goodnight," Luke murmurs into the darkness.

*****

In the morning, Luke wakes without recalling any of his dreams. It's already too hot in the back of the RV, and he kicks at the blankets. Connor isn't in the other bed, and Luke sits up, feeling disoriented. He rubs his eyes and combs his hair with his fingers.

Voices drift in from outside the RV, and he isn't sure whose they are. Hastily, Luke yanks on a fresh T-shirt and jeans, wishing he had something cooler to wear. He might have to count his meager savings and splurge on some lightweight pants. He's buttoning up when the door to the RV opens and Connor steps in with two people Luke hasn't met.

"You're up!" Connor says cheerily. "You want some breakfast? Zakhi brought us coffee and bagels."

Luke blinks. "Who?"

"Zakhi, one of the people who works with Avi and Sylvia. He's driving us today."

"Give me a sec."

Luke's not hungry yet, and he doesn't drink coffee. Connor, he suspects, lives on the stuff. Luke doesn't even like the smell. Not when he was responsible for making it every day for his parents and older brothers, and not when he lived with Greg's constant criticism of how he prepared it. He hopes Zakhi and the as-yet unnamed other guest will forgive him.

"...is Rimona," Zakhi was saying, and Luke finally tunes in. "My spouse."

Noting the distinct use of the neutral word, it strikes Luke how similar Rimona looks to Jax. The only significant differences are that Rimona has short, spiky hair and is a bit shorter and slightly curvier than Jax. Their makeup is similar, though, and they have similar features. Even Rimona's smile is disarmingly like Jax's.

"Hi," Luke says, and the word comes out shaky.

"Nice to meet you," Rimona says. "I hear you and Connor want to know more about what we do at the complex." They smile again. "And then Zakhi and I will take you up to the Falls. Have you been before?"

"I have," Connor says. "But not for years and years, and Luke hasn't ever. Right?"

"Nope, never been," Luke confirms.

"Okay, great!" Rimona beams at them. "Ready to go?"

Luke snatches a bagel off the dinette table, leaving the coffee. Connor eyes him then picks it up. Better that it not go to waste. They lock up the RV and follow Zakhi and Rimona out to a four-passenger truck. Rimona climbs into the driver's seat, and Connor, who is just as chatty as they seem to be, takes the front passenger seat. Zakhi catches Luke's eye and offers a tiny smile and a nod at the other two. Luke grins back, and Zakhi's posture relaxes.

He listens to Rimona on the way back to the townhouses. They refer to Avi and Sylvia as feter and tante, uncle and aunt, but it doesn't appear to be literal—more a term of endearment from those associated with their work. The younger pair are equally knowledgeable, having worked with them for several years. Rimona says Avi and Sylvia can fill in how they got their start, but in the meantime, Luke and Connor will have some idea what the Chasah Foundation is.

The townhouses where Avi and Sylvia live are not an ordinary complex. They are a type of halfway house, in a sense, for people who have found themselves without shelter for one reason or another. It sounds similar to the charity that helped Luke after his brothers abandoned him. Except that one mostly helped homeless LGBTQ kids, and Chasah seems more about families.

The townhouses have room for two families each, although not all of the units are always full. Some of the families were at dinner last night. Zakhi and Rimona weren't able to come due to helping one of the families with getting settled in a new home. They talk more about it, and by the time they arrive at the townhouse complex, Luke has a pretty good idea of how they help these families.

Sylvia greets them with more breakfast, and Connor accepts yet another cup of coffee. Luke doesn't think he drank the one he rescued from being dumped, but he's not sure. Connor will be well and truly awake, at least.

They sit down, and in a few minutes, Avi joins them. "Morning," he says. "How did you sleep?"

"Not bad," Connor says. "It's a little weird being away from home this long, but so far, so good."

Sylvia joins them at last. "Zakhi tells me you want to know how we came to be where we are now."

"Sure." Connor looks over at Luke. "Is that okay?"

Luke nods. "You wanted to know more about your family, so let's find out."

"I suppose the first part is really Avi's to tell," Sylvia says.

"I dreamed it," Avi tells them. "I know how odd that sounds, but it's true. Not this, exactly, but about being a father to many children. I was in college to be a teacher, so I thought it was related to that. And then I met Sylvia. So I thought maybe it was literal after all, but one of those things that doesn't mean much other than my sleeping brain picturing the American Dream. You know, the wife, the house, the kids, the yard with a dog. It all sounded nice, if a little ordinary."

Sylvia laughs. "Right. Well, you should know, I was hardly an All-American sweetheart. He's leaving out the part where the reason we met was that we were both part of a student protest group against Apartheid, but we had different opinions on what our activism should look like."

Avi holds up his hands. "Okay, okay. So it wasn't love at first sight." He shrugs. "She won me over, though, and after we graduated, we decided to go on bickering more efficiently by getting married."

"Oh, you." Sylvia mock-glares at him, but she takes his hand. "He told me about the dream he had, of course, and…"

"She laughed," Avi says, nodding seriously. "Right out loud."

"I did." Sylvia blushes. "I did want children, but I wasn't sure about a houseful, even if that dream wasn't literal."

"And then we couldn't have children. So I taught history, and she worked in the financial office for a museum, and we made a good life."

"But we kept coming back to his dream. By then, he'd earned another degree and was working as a school counselor. We decided to become foster parents and began training. Over those years, we took in twenty kids. We learned a lot about how and why families end up separated and children have nowhere to go."

Avi and Sylvia trade off, telling the story of how they turned the complex into a place to keep families together. The townhouses give them shelter, some privacy, and independence. During their stay, Chasah helps find jobs, safe housing, and treatment for those in need. Some of those who have lived in the townhouses joined their team afterward, and others have moved on.

Zakhi was one of those success stories. Avi and Sylvia had taken him in and then worked to reunite him with his mother and help her improve their circumstances. The two of them had stayed on to work with more families after them. He was their first foster child. Although he's since reconnected with his birth family, he's still close with Avi and Sylvia, continuing to refer to them as his feter and tante.

Luke wonders about the teen who was at dinner last night. Is he like Luke was at that age? Someone who has had to leave his home and family? Or was he alone because none of his family could join them?

"Are any of the people you help kids who left home?" Luke won't say *ran away* or *were kicked out*. Neither of those apply to him.

Sylvia nods. "We have some teens who are forced to leave restrictive homes or who choose to leave. It's sometimes harder to help them because their needs are different. We work with other agencies in those cases. The townhouses aren't set up for minors, and there are a host of other legal complications alongside. One of the things we ask families here to do is help one another where we all can, so this is one situation where that works while we sort through the details."

"Is everyone you help Jewish?" Connor asks. It's not something Luke would've considered.

"No," Avi says. "Most, but not all."

Luke isn't sure where the question comes from, but he's driven to ask it. "Does any of this have to do with Connor's dad?" He glances sideways and sees Connor's eyes widen before he checks his shock.

Sylvia folds her hands on top of the table. "Normally, we keep any information about people here strictly confidential. But in this case, I think it's fair. Saul is gone, and you're family."

"Go on," Connor prompts.

She exchanges a significant look with Avi before she continues. "He came to us maybe ten years ago or so."

"Ten..." Connor purses his lips. "Around the time I finished high school."

"I know." She gazes down at her hands as if it's too painful or shameful to look at Connor directly. Eventually, she raises her eyes to meet his. "He'd had some hard times, and he stayed here. He was ashamed, which is probably why he didn't go to your mother or even contact you. We treated him the same way as everyone else. When he was back on his feet, he helped us out for a while. And then..."

"He disappeared," Avi finishes. "We heard from him on occasion, but it was always a long time between calls or holiday greetings."

Luke studies them. There is more they aren't saying, and he isn't sure why. Saul, as they said, is dead. Did they promise not to tarnish his memory? If so, why? Luke was closed off about his own childhood, but now he realizes Connor hasn't said much more than a handful of comments over the years about his father refusing to visit or pay child support.

Connor's figured it out too, but he politely doesn't press them any further. If Luke knows him, he'll get to the bottom of it eventually, whether from this part of the family or another. For now, he seems to shake himself out of it and moves on.

"This is really good work you do here. Can we see more?"

"Certainly," Avi says. "We'll show you one of the units that's currently empty. And then we'll pack you some food to take up to the Falls. How does that sound?"

"Sounds perfect to me."

Chapter 12

L UKE MUST'VE DOZED off because the next thing he knows, he's missed most of the ride up to the Falls. Rimona is pulling into a parking lot when he stirs, and he stretches, almost knocking into Zakhi, who he forgot was the one in the back seat instead of Connor.

They walk from the parking area toward the Falls. There's a viewing lookout where other tourists are walking or picnicking, and when they're close enough, Luke gasps. Like the Atlantic Ocean, he's never seen this body of water before. But unlike the ocean, Niagara Falls never rest. They are massive in a different way, rising up and spilling over in a great cacophony of splashing and roaring.

Zakhi laughs. "C'mon," he says. "Wait until you see them closer up."

They spend the rest of the day enjoying the sights. Luke is overwhelmed by the view from the river, and he hides his panic beneath the plastic raincoat, identical to all the other tourists on the boat. He thinks he's done all right until he feels Connor's hand sneak under the poncho to press against his.

The mighty thunder and spray of the water ignite something long-snuffed in Luke. He remembers the feeling of being inside the raging storm, and he closes his eyes against the drops. Under his feet, the boat sways, buffeted by the current. Why had he thought this would be a good idea?

Next to him, Connor bumps his shoulder. "Isn't this amazing?" he says.

Luke braces himself against another cold spray. He wants to agree, but the whole thing is as shattering and terrifying as it is exhilarating. He squares his shoulders. If he was once able to stand on his front porch, taking a picture of the incoming storm with his hair on end from the electricity, then surely he can brave this one boat ride through the waterfall's mist.

He leans in and puts his mouth by Connor's ear to make sure he's heard. "It's incredible," he says.

When they're far enough away from the splashing, Luke takes out his camera. He snaps a picture of Connor, Zakhi, and Rimona, all laughing as the water runs off their ponchos in thin rivulets.

After the ride, they sit to have lunch. Zakhi clears his throat, and the others glance over at him. He looks sheepish, as though he knows what he has to say might come out wrong. Then he squares his shoulders and looks Connor in the eye.

"We have a favor to ask," he says.

"Oh?" Connor sets down his sandwich. Luke holds his breath.

"Tante Sylvia told us you're heading west via I-90." Zakhi looks at Rimona. "We're moving, starting fresh to continue their work in another city. Can you take us with you to Chicago?"

Connor's eyebrows rise. "I don't know if we can fit everything into the one RV."

Rimona shakes their head. "No need. We're not taking much. The place we're going is furnished, and we've already been out there once. It's just us and a couple of boxes."

It's Luke who answers, surprising everyone. "Why not?"

Connor looks at him, head tilted as if he's searching for an answer. At last he says, "Yeah, why not?"

It's settled, then. In the morning, Connor will bring the RV to the townhouses and pick them up. The conversation moves on, and Luke lets the words flow around him while he continues to stare at the Falls. He's in awe that they were so close up to something with that much power. It's only when

Connor elbows him that he realizes it's time to pick up from lunch and move on.

Later, back in the RV, Luke takes out the new scrapbook. Aside from the postcards Connor donated to the cause, it's empty. Luke hasn't had a chance to have any of his photos printed, and he doesn't have any other souvenirs from the trip. He thinks about what's happened so far. They had a warm welcome from Aunt Enid and Uncle Norm, and Luke misses them. It's been a strange couple of days in New York. Not that he doesn't like Sylvia and Avi or Zakhi and Rimona, but it felt more businesslike. He's not sure what to expect from the rest of the trip.

Connor has attached a map with sticky tack to the wall opposite the cupboards in the kitchenette. He's put push-pins in the cities or towns he expects to visit along their route. The red ones are places they've yet to see, and the white ones are where they've been. He's also put blue ones for gas stops, yellow for tourist spots and highly rated restaurants, and green for the RV campgrounds closest to where they want to go.

Luke shivers when he sees the push-pin near his hometown. He's not sure what he will do when they arrive. It's the last place on the planet he ever wants to see again. Connor is planning to stop in Sioux Falls, not in Mitchell, but they'll pass close by on I-90. It's only a little more than an hour in between. If anything were to cause them to have to detour...

While Luke is thinking about this, Connor emerges from the bathroom. He comes to stand beside the table where Luke is sitting, and he turns to the map. They're both quiet.

"I don't know if I can do this," Connor says.

Surprised, Luke looks away from the South Dakota push-pins to direct his attention at Connor. Up until now, Connor has been full of excitement, talking about how much this trip means to him. Now, he looks unhappy. Luke slides out from behind the table to stand beside Connor. He puts out a hand, changes his mind, and drops it back to his side.

"Why not?" he asks.

"Maybe there are things I don't want to know. What if it's better to leave myself in the dark about my father?"

"What do you mean?"

Connor runs a hand through his thick, brown hair. "I've built this up in my head, imagining my father must've been some kind of great adventurer. He went to see his cousins before he died, and I wanted to follow the same route. But..." The strain is visible on Connor's face when he turns toward Luke. "He never came to see me."

"And you wonder why, if he visited everyone else."

"Yeah."

Luke doesn't think about what he's doing. He folds Connor in his arms and lets Connor rest against him. In that moment, he makes a decision. He's always been the one to let someone else lead him, to go along with whoever he's with. This time, he's taking charge temporarily. He lets go of Connor.

"Hey," he says.

"Hm?" Connor meets Luke's gaze.

"You made a commitment to this." Luke gestures to the map. "You planned it all out and marked the stops. You did whatever you had to at work to take the trip. You can't back out now." *And neither can I*, he thinks, but he keeps that to himself.

"I...but what if..."

"What if you find out something you wish you didn't know?" Luke understands. He's had a lifetime supply of finding out things he wishes he hadn't. Everything would be different if he'd never taken those photos. "Haven't you already learned things that surprised you?"

"And things that pissed me off, yeah." Connor sighs. "I don't just mean what I've found so far. Aunt Enid didn't tell me anything I didn't know. Yeah, maybe it was weird learning that my father was once a funny, charming man or that he was homeless for a while. But it's not like that had a whole lot to do with me."

"Didn't it?"

Connor opens his mouth as if he wants to say something, but no words come out. Maybe he hasn't thought about it like this. Luke doesn't know what Connor's father was like, never having met him. But he's certain there's more to uncover. And if he can convince Connor to be brave enough to finish what he's started, then maybe he can convince himself to follow through on his commitment to Connor.

"I have no idea what's going to happen on this trip," Luke says. "But...we're here together. That has to mean something, right?"

"You'll be here no matter what?" Connor's voice breaks. "Even if we find out something we'll both wish we hadn't?"

Luke nods. "I promise."

Connor puts a hand on Luke's cheek. "It means everything to me that you came."

Not knowing how to respond, Luke only nods. Out of the corner of his eye, he sees the South Dakota push-pin. It seems to swell, standing out from the others for a moment. Luke reminds himself of what he's just said to Connor, and the push-pin returns to its normal size. He'll deal with it when the time comes.

Connor pulls Luke into another hug then lets him go and steps away. Luke watches him head for the sleeping area before he sits back down at the table. He touches the scrapbook one more time before tucking it into the drawer where it's been residing since Connor gave it to him. Soon, he decides, he'll begin filling the pages.

※※※※

The RV park's rental office has a convenience store. Half of it is for camping supplies and firewood. The other half is food and a few random souvenirs. Connor stops by to leave their parking tags, so Luke browses the convenience store in search of postcards.

He picks up one that says "Howdy from Buffalo, NY" with pictures of the city inside the letters and a tacky actual buffalo perched on top of the Fs. He'll send that one to Jax. Then he finds one of Niagara Falls at sunset. He didn't get to see that, but the Falls were impressive enough by daylight. He's never seen anything so powerful.

Once that task is done, he looks around for snacks. There's the usual random selection in any gas station store, so he takes a few things. At the register, he discovers there's a candy counter. A bubbly woman greets him.

"What can I get for you?"

"Um...I don't know." Luke peers into the glass case at the assortment of fudge and hand-dipped chocolates. "What do you like?"

"Are you all from around here?"

Luke shakes his head. "Passing through."

Her eyes light up. "Ooh, I have just the thing." She reaches into the case. "On me. Try it." She slides something in a tiny paper wrapper across the glass.

Luke picks up the treat and bites into it. The chocolate on the outside is dark and rich, and the center is lightly crisp. It tastes of orange and molasses, and it almost melts right away on his tongue. Hastily, Luke pops the other half of the chocolate in his mouth, afraid it'll disintegrate in his fingers before he can enjoy it.

The bubbly woman laughs. "You like it?"

"God, yeah. What is that?"

"Sponge candy. You've never had it before?"

"Nope." Luke looks at the prices. "I'll take the small box of assorted ones, please."

"You got it." She carefully places the candy in the gold foil box and ties it shut with a red string. "It tends to melt, so don't leave it anywhere too hot or you'll have a mess. Enjoy!"

"I will, thanks."

Luke takes the small box out to the RV. At the same time, Connor emerges from the park office. He tosses Luke the keys and climbs into the passenger side.

"I figure now's as good a time as any to learn to drive this baby. You'll be fine. It handles like a truck, for the most part, and we'll be on the highway." He shuts the door.

Luke rounds the RV and takes the driver's seat. Following Connor's instructions, he's got the RV ready to go and oriented toward their destination. Connor points to the little gold box, which Luke has left in the cup holder between the seats.

"What's that?"

"Sponge candy. Go on, have some."

Connor's reaction is the same as Luke's, which makes them both laugh. Connor licks his fingers where a little of the chocolate managed to melt.

"Amazing," Connor says. "Okay, let's go get Zakhi and Rimona, and then we'll be on our way."

Luke is glad for a little time on the quiet streets to get used to driving the RV. It handles well, and with Connor's guidance, he quickly learns the skills he needs to maneuver it.

At the townhouses, Zakhi and Rimona are waiting for them. They meant it when they said only a couple of boxes. They're neatly packed and sealed. The only other things they have are matching suitcases, one for each of them. Connor loads everything into the RV.

While they're packing, Avi and Sylvia emerge from their townhouse. There are tearful goodbyes on both parts, and Luke and Connor step aside to give them space.

A few minutes later, Luke is wrapped in a warm hug from Sylvia. Avi shakes his hand.

"Hold on here for a minute," Sylvia tells Connor. She disappears into the townhouse and then emerges again with a small box. She hands it to Connor. "Your father's," she says. "I believe he wanted you to have it."

"He knew," Connor mumbles. "Or he suspected, anyway. That I would come here, I mean."

Sylvia nods. "I think so, yes."

Maybe this is one of the clues Connor has been looking for. Luke is curious what's inside the box, but Connor doesn't open it there. He gives Sylvia a hug and thanks her for her hospitality. Next thing Luke knows, they're all piling into the RV.

He settles back into the driver's seat, with Zakhi beside him. Connor passes his phone up front before sitting at the table with Rimona. Luke pulls up the playlist and hands the phone to Zakhi to choose their travel music. Imagine Dragons' "I'm on Top of the World" plays, and they all sing along, loudly, until they're laughing too hard to finish the lyrics.

It's early in the day, but it's already hot. The sky is still a dim bluish-purple ahead of them as they head west. This is a good day, Luke thinks, a day he's happy to be free.

Then

MAMA DRAGGED A wagon behind her, filled with jars of jam. She had Johnny strapped to her in a carrier, even though he was almost two now. Ruth sat among the jars, touching them on occasion with her fingers. Luke walked solemnly by Mama's side. He'd offered to pull the wagon for her, but she'd been short with him and said no.

She'd been like that ever since they left Wyoming. They'd had to stay in the motel for three days while Mama recovered and Daddy found them transportation. In the end, they'd rented two big vans. Some people who heard about the fires were nice enough to donate some clothes to replace what they'd lost. It was a good thing they still had all their furniture and most of their belongings in the moving van.

Daddy had made a big deal over Luke because he'd taken pictures. He said that meant they were able to prove it was the storm, and something called "insurance" helped them pay for things. Luke didn't know exactly what that meant, but he did know he liked having Daddy tell him he'd done a good thing.

Some of the big boys rolled their eyes and said they didn't need an eight-year-old's help. They could've done what was needed themselves. But Daddy shushed them and kept on saying he was proud of Luke and how brave he was.

It helped ease the hurt when Mama didn't want to give him hugs or let him sit in her lap anymore.

So now here they were, two months later. Mama had her own car now, and she brought the youngest ones and her jellies. Daddy would be there at the farmer's market too. He was bringing Esther, Mark, and Matt. Luke craned his neck, trying to see them, but there were too many people. Luke thought it was lucky he was still too young for his parents to think he should be away from Mama. It meant he didn't have to look after anyone but the babies, and he didn't have to pretend he would be any good at building or fixing things. Ruth and Johnny weren't either.

Luke did feel sorry for Esther, though. She was stuck because Daddy said with Mama still sort of sick, they had to have someone to help with the household chores. It made Luke cringe to think about her having to do it all alone. He tried to help when he wasn't being dragged around with Daddy and the big boys to take pictures of their work so they could show it off and get more business.

Luke would much rather have stayed with Esther; he liked cooking and taking care of the littles. But he was old enough to have to hide it and start acting like the big boys. Tim, Titus, and Philip did all their schoolwork in the evenings now. They already took on jobs with Daddy. They had to finish high school, but everyone knew they were going to do what all the others did. Luke would too someday, if he could only learn how to be less clumsy.

As Mama pulled the wagon up to the booth, Luke wondered what he would do when he was as old as Tim. He'd have to start learning real quick how to do the kinds of work Daddy did. He pulled jars of strawberry preserves out of the wagon. They were pretty, short and round with a piece of colorful fabric under the lid as decoration. Each jar had a hand-lettered card held on by a string to tell what it was and who made it. Luke wanted to learn how to make those, not how to put shingles on a roof.

Esther came up beside him and wordlessly began helping. She didn't look at Luke, like she was mad at him for something he didn't know he'd done wrong. She grabbed a jar of peach preserves out of Ruth's hands, and Ruth yelled. Instead of comforting her, Esther rolled her eyes and ignored her.

Surprised by how cold she seemed, Luke went to Ruth. "Here," he said, offering her a pair of knitted socks. She pouted for a moment, but then she took it.

At last the stand was set up. Mama pulled Luke and the others behind the table to wait for people to stop by. They'd been doing this for a month now, trying to earn enough money to get back on their feet after the loss of the RVs. Mama dragged Esther, Luke, and the little ones to every possible festival, fair, or show where she could sell her preserves.

Luke could tell some people thought their family was odd. There were so many brothers and sisters, and Mama and Daddy did believe in old-fashioned values, as they called them, so maybe that's what people thought about when they saw them.

All day, he tried to get Esther's attention. He wanted them to go back to how they used to be, sharing the work side by side and bickering a little when the grown-ups' backs were turned. Esther ignored him. Something was wrong, but Luke couldn't puzzle out what it was. Instead, he busied himself resetting the jars every time someone bought one. It passed the time, though part of him wished he could drag it out long enough to figure out what had gone wrong with Esther.

Luke was glad to be here instead of the booth where Daddy had bossy Matt and Mark handing out brochures for their business. If only he could stay here forever, and if only Esther would go back to being her normal self.

Chapter 13

Now

WHEN THEY STOP to fill up the gas tank and switch drivers, Luke pens his latest postcard for Jax. He writes in small, neat print so he can crowd more on, telling Jax how they met Zakhi and Rimona and brought them along. Luke has Avi and Sylvia's address too, but he doesn't think he'll send them a postcard from Buffalo, seeing as they live there. Maybe he'll send one when they get to Chicago and drop Zakhi and Rimona off.

He thinks he should write to Aunt Enid and Uncle Norm or Justin or both. When they make their next location on Connor's agenda, Luke will buy some more postcards for them and another book of stamps. If there's somewhere to develop his pictures, he'll do that too so he can put them in the scrapbook.

Everyone is ready to move again, so Connor takes the driver's seat just as a few stray drops of rain sprinkle down. It doesn't turn into anything more than a light summer shower, and it does nothing to curb the intensifying heat as the day wears on. Luke wishes it would. It's cool inside the RV, but it's so closed in. He longs to open the window, but it's too hot.

They're back in Pennsylvania, though on the opposite side of the state from where they started. Luke doesn't recall a whole lot of geography from his years of homeschooling, but he does at least know the body of water he can see in the distance is Lake Erie. Somewhere else within driving distance, yet he never traveled there.

He puts the window down briefly now, to aim his camera and take a few pictures as the scenery rushes by. He turns to Connor once the window is closed again.

"Next time we stop, can we see if there's somewhere for me to print some of these?" He waves the camera a little.

"Sure. There's got to be a place. I don't think I've ever thought to print any of my photos. Where do you usually go?"

"There was an all-purpose store on the corner near the apartment." He doesn't refer to it as his.

He thinks more about what Avi and Sylvia have done and are still doing. They make a difference for families who want to be together. But what about someone like Luke? He shudders to think of what might've happened if he'd been sent back, or worse yet, his whole family invited there. Grandma Jeanne, the first woman he lived with, never asked questions. She didn't feel an urge to know why a pale, dirty kid with a scar on his face needed a home. Luke is sorry now for all the times he sneaked out, mostly to see AJ.

The RV rattles on, swaying, lulling Luke into a half-wakeful state. It's only mid-morning, but he feels like he could sleep again already. He stretches out his legs, and Connor eyes him.

"You can rest if you like," he says. "I'll keep going until our next stop."

Luke tries to answer, but he can only offer a yawn. He nods and pulls Connor's college blanket over himself. In a moment, he's floating through untroubled dreams.

****

They stop in Erie because Connor spots a store there with candy on one side and fireworks on the other. His reason is that it seems like an interesting combination, but Luke suspects it's because he wants some of the fireworks. Sure enough, he disappears into that side of the store, so Luke waits outside for him. Zakhi and Rimona enter the other side.

The sky is overcast, and it's hot—almost ninety degrees today. Luke's in threadbare jeans and a red-and-white-striped sleeveless shirt so faded it looks pink. Even in lighter clothes, he's still sweltering, almost wishing he'd joined the others inside the store.

He takes a picture of it because he's never seen candy and fireworks in the same place before. This stretch of road is almost nothing but restaurants and businesses. While Luke is standing there, looking down the busy road, a soft, "hey" alerts him to someone else's presence. He turns.

A person who looks like a kid but probably isn't stands right next to him. They have on black skinny jeans, a baggy white shirt, and a backwards baseball cap that hides most of their brown hair. Their arms are well-muscled, and their skin is deeply tanned. They have inquisitive brown eyes and a small, rosebud mouth. Luke has to swallow several times before he can answer. It's been ages since he saw someone who instantly sparked his interest this way.

"Hey," he says.

"You got a couple bucks?"

Oh. Luke holds in his sigh, but he knows before he answers that he'll give this person what they want. He's never been able to say no, not even when he doesn't have any to spare.

"Yeah, hang on." He reaches for his wallet and pulls out what little cash he has in there. He stashed a bit more in the RV, and he has his bank card, not that there's much left in the account—or ever was to begin with.

"Thanks. Hey, you know where the bus station is?"

"I don't live here."

At that, the person's attention perks up. "Yeah? You traveling?"

This is too many nosy questions, but Luke's already said he's not from Erie. "On a trip with a friend." He tilts his head toward the fireworks store. "Waiting for him to get out here."

"You think you could spare a ride to the bus station?"

Luke looks back at the store again. "I don't know. I'd have to ask."

"What, your buddy's in charge?" The person scoffs.

"Kind of? It's his RV." Luke thinks, too late, that he probably shouldn't have said which vehicle was theirs. Though the person might've figured it out eventually, given that there are only two other cars there.

The stranger whistles. "Sweet ride. Well, I'll stay right here with you, since you don't seem like you're gonna give me a real answer."

Luke waits until their back is turned then rolls his eyes. They are nosy and obnoxious, and he's mad that he's still reacting to their appearance. He could do without their personality.

"I'm Jory, by the way." They don't turn around.

"Luke."

"Your buddy, he's one of us, right?"

"Uh..." Luke fights the urge to give this person more details than they need. "One of us?"

"Come on. You know why I picked you and not that guy." They hitch a thumb over their shoulder at the person on the other end of the parking lot, a beefy man in trousers and a collared shirt, talking loudly on his cell phone.

"I dunno. You didn't pick him 'cause he looks like kind of a douche?"

"Yeah, the kind of douche who at best will throw a name at my back when I turn around. Family knows family." They turn toward Luke and eye him up and down.

"Fine. Yes, my friend is 'one of us,' as you put it."

"Then he won't care, and you all can take me to the bus station." They are still holding the money Luke gave them, and they add it to a roll they pull out of their pocket. It looks like mostly ones. "Think I've got enough now."

"Where are you going?" It's Luke's turn to be nosy. He answered Jory's questions, and now it's payback time.

Jory shrugs. "Anywhere but here. I made it all the way to Erie before the last driver left me." They gesture around. "Could've at least taken me somewhere decent, like the goddamn bus station."

Luke observes Jory for a while before answering. "You're lying."

Jory laughs. "And you know this how, by looking in your crystal ball?"

"You're not planning to go to a bus station. You were waiting for someone you thought might take a chance. You'd better be over eighteen, or we're not taking you anywhere except a shelter."

They scoff and turn away again, but they don't have an answer. Luke gets it. He knows what Jory is doing because he did it. He thought he was heading for New York, only he never made it. He was starving and cold and didn't have anything to wear meant for winter weather. At least Jory is traveling in the summer. Smarter than Luke, but then, Jory probably didn't have half a dozen older brothers bent on making them disappear. Or maybe they did; Luke couldn't guess at what had Jory on the run.

Jory turns back to Luke. "Okay, you got me. I need to get farther than the main business drag in Erie. I'm only like three hours from home. And yes, I'm over eighteen. Just because I'm small doesn't mean I'm not a grown-ass adult, and I can show you some ID to prove it. So are you in or not?"

"Depends. We're headed west. That where you want to go?"

"Could be."

Now Luke does sigh, emphasized for Jory's benefit. "Not helpful."

Jory holds up their hands. "I'm not picky. You get me somewhere far from here, and I'll go any direction you like."

Connor exits the store with a bag in his hand, rescuing Luke from having to answer. He stops short when he sees Jory, and his expression is a mix of confusion and concern.

"Hey," he says, approaching more slowly now. "Someone you know, Luke?"

"Not really. We just met. This is Jory."

Jory sticks out their hand, and Connor takes it. "Connor. Good to meet you." He looks between Jory and Luke.

"Luke here says you two might be able to give me a lift."

"I didn't say that!" Luke glares at them, but Jory only grins.

It takes another minute or two of Connor glancing back and forth before he says, "Where exactly are you headed?"

"West," Jory says, and Luke wants to kick them.

"West...right. Well, I'm not sure what you had in mind, so maybe you could give me a bit more detail."

Jory shrugs. "I need a ride to get out of PA. You have this great RV here."

"Yeah, and I also have a wish not to be stabbed in my sleep or have my shit stolen. Plus we have two other passengers who might feel the same. So I'm not taking you anywhere unless you can give me a good reason."

Jory isn't tall, but they draw themselves up to their full height and get right up close to Connor. "I'm gettin' the hell away from the person who did this to me." They pull up their T-shirt to reveal heavy bruising on their midsection. "Now. Are you gonna fucking help me, or are you gonna force me to ask Cell Phone Dickhead over there to take me to the bus station? Because if anyone is in some kinda danger here, it sure as hell isn't you."

Connor backs up and looks to Luke one more time before he says meekly, "Okay. Get in."

Luke takes over the driver's seat while Jory swings up into the passenger seat, leaving Connor to buckle into one of the kitchenette seats. Zakhi and Rimona finally emerge from the candy store, each with a small bag. They climb in and exchange glances with Connor.

"Friend of yours?" Zakhi asks. Rimona is busy introducing themself to Jory.

"No," Connor says. "They need a ride."

"The more the merrier," Zakhi says, and he sounds like he actually means it.

Jory snorts, but they smile.

It's clear Connor has had enough of people for the moment. He pulls out a book, only looking up briefly when Jory tosses their bag back and it lands at his feet. He huffs, but he says nothing.

Jory grins at Luke. "Well, let's blow this place, then."

Luke can't help it. He grins back as he starts the engine.

Then

IT TOOK THREE months almost to the day before Esther cracked. It was after Christmas by the time she said any more to Luke than was necessary. To be fair to her, they hardly had a moment alone. Everyone was busy in the new house. Mama was still selling her jellies all the way up until the farmer's market closed for the season. Now she went to the holiday bazaars with warm, hand-knitted hats and scarves and hand-quilted blankets.

Two of Luke's brothers were courting wives, women they'd met in church. In the spring, at least one of them would be married. Luke was caught up between schoolwork and Daddy showing off the photos he took. For Christmas, Mama and Daddy even splurged on a new camera, and Mama made a fancy bag for it out of the scraps she used to make quilts.

Both Mama and Esther seemed worn down. Mama was pale and looked sick, but Daddy assured Luke she was okay when he asked. That was when Esther finally made time to sneak away with Luke. They ended up in the barn, sitting on a couple of old crates. Luke shivered and pulled his thick jacket tighter.

"Mama's depressed," Esther explained. "Like being sad all the time, but worse."

"Oh."

Luke remembered, sort of, when Mama had Johnny, and she was so sad for a while afterward. She hadn't looked so weak, though, not the way he saw her in his memory. He wanted to ask Esther more about it, but she wasn't paying real attention to him. Instead, she bit her nail the way she wasn't supposed to.

"Lukey?" She hardly ever called him that anymore. She'd said it was babyish and stupid.

"Yeah?"

He looked over at her. She had her knees drawn up to her chest with her chin resting on them. She wore blue jeans and a fuzzy Christmas sweater. Mama and Daddy weren't like some families where they expected all their girls to wear dresses. Besides, there were only two. Ruth was allowed to wear whatever she could handle on her sensitive skin, so Esther was too.

Esther didn't answer right away. She chewed her bottom lip and then frowned. Luke almost saw fire in her hazel eyes. She finally met his gaze.

"I hate Roman's future brother-in-law. His fiancée's brother," she added as explanation for Luke. "He's a pig."

Luke gasped on two accounts. "We're not supposed to hate anyone. Or call names."

She leaned closer to him, her hands curled into fists. "Go ahead. Tell on me. I don't care. I'll say it again to Mama's face."

Because of course Luke wouldn't dare tattle to Daddy. He hadn't been planning to tell Mama either, but Esther was scaring him. He backed down, afraid of her anger right then.

"Why do you hate him?" he whispered.

"I was at Roman's new house so he wouldn't be alone with Tabitha—you know the rules—and he came over. He said he had some stuff for them. When he saw me, I thought he was looking at me like I was something dirty. It made me feel like that time I accidentally rolled onto an anthill, only without the ants. Then he said they should make me dress properly."

"What's wrong with how you dress?"

"Everything, according to him. He said it wasn't right for me to be my age and still dressing like a boy."

Luke scoffed. "Girls at regular schools dress like you. I know because Sam Whelock told me. His dad is a teacher there."

Esther huffed. "I know, but we don't go to that school. Just hush so I can finish telling you."

"Sorry."

"Well, then Sam's brother came over with a welcome basket. Tabitha's brother caught him waving to me, and he said something about how he should leave me alone and it wasn't good for us to be friends."

"Sam's brother?"

"Yes! Seriously, Luke. I have to tell someone, okay?"

"Sorry again."

She cleared her throat. "He was giving me that anthill crawly look again. And..." She looked around and leaned toward Luke. She murmured, "He put his hands on me."

"Like...how?" Luke was confused. People in his family touched each other all the time. That didn't seem too strange.

"Not in places a grown-up man should be touching me."

Luke shivered. He still didn't exactly know what she meant, but it sounded bad. He was about to answer her when they both heard Mama calling. Luke hopped off the crate he'd been sitting on and dusted his rear end. Esther did the same.

"I'm glad to be back home," she said.

So was Luke, especially when Esther's story made him feel so funny.

Chapter 14

WHEN THEY STOP at a gas station an hour into Ohio, Jory takes off for the side of the building to smoke. Luke slides out of the RV while Connor pumps gas, and he meanders over toward the convenience store under the pretext of going inside. He hovers, though, watching Jory enjoy their cig. Luke could stare at them all day.

They aren't really like Jax, but they aren't unlike Jax either. Luke is fascinated in all the same ways. Thinking about Jax propels him forward the rest of the way into the store. He shouldn't be thinking about either of them, Jax or Jory. There is too much history with the former, and too much baggage with the latter.

Browsing the aisles takes his mind off it. They don't need any more food or snacks—Connor stocked up at the grocery store in Buffalo, so they have what they need for a while. Luke isn't going to buy anything; he needs the distraction of looking at neck pillows and energy drinks and air fresheners. Not to mention it's cooler inside the store.

While he's checking out a rack of baseball caps with corny sayings on them, he catches Jory out of the corner of his eye. They must've come in while Luke was in one of the aisles. He would have to pass them in order to exit the store. To avoid conversation, Luke beelines for the checkout and picks up a pack of gum he probably won't chew.

He's finishing up paying when a voice behind him says, "Hey." He turns his head slowly toward Jory. "Hi."

Jory has several packages of chips and a neck pillow. "Grabbing some stuff for the road."

"I see that." He waves at the snacks. "We have food in the RV."

"Yeah, well, I didn't want to count on you all being super generous about that, especially Connor. Is he always this much of a dick?"

Luke laughs. "Actually, yeah. Or he used to be, anyway, but he's finally figured out his filter most of the time."

"I don't think he likes me."

"He doesn't hate you."

Jory scoffs, but there's amusement hidden in it. "Is that supposed to make me feel better?"

"Not really."

"You're kind of a dick too, just less of one." Jory grins.

Luke hands over his bank card to pay for the gum, which is possibly overkill for something that's only a dollar. He steps aside to let Jory up to the register. No one other than Greg has ever accused him of being a dick before. Even Greg didn't exactly. He was more likely to call Luke a slut or a queen, and neither was meant as a sexy shared joke between lovers. He knew Adam thought mostly the same, but he was at least polite enough not to say so.

"I haven't decided yet whether I like you either," he tells Jory.

"Yes, you have." Jory winks.

Luke gives them a dark look he doesn't really mean and stalks out of the store with the sound of Jory's laughter in his ears. They're right, of course, but Luke is for sure not going to admit it. He shoves the gum into his jeans pocket and returns to the RV.

Connor has pulled over to wait for them, and he smiles at Luke when he approaches. Not once has Connor complained all the times he's had to wait for Luke in a travel plaza. It's a strange feeling, not being someone's burden.

"Get what you need?" Connor asks.

Luke pulls out the gum. "I guess. You want a piece?"

"Sure." Good thing Connor likes winter mint. "Everything's so close in on the east coast, so it's not that far to get to our next stop in Cleveland." He frowns. "I'm not sure what to do about Jory, though."

"What about me?" Jory pops up, seemingly out of nowhere. They're good at that.

Connor is trying to hold back, and Luke commends him for his restraint when he says, "We're on a trip to visit some of my family. I didn't tell them about you, obviously."

Jory bites their lip. "Oh. D'you think they'll mind?"

Connor's eyebrows draw together, and he catches Luke's gaze before answering. "I doubt it. I'm sure it's fine."

Jory's shoulders relax visibly. "Okay, then. But if you need me to, like, hide in the RV, say the word and I'm no more than a shadow."

Luke shivers at the way Jory says "shadow." He thinks they possibly have some experience with this. He doesn't comment, though, and the three of them get back into the RV. This time, Jory leaves the front passenger seat for Luke, who is about to accept but changes his mind.

"You okay if I stay back here for a bit?" he asks.

Connor shrugs. "Up to you. You okay if I put on music?"

"Up to you."

Connor's scrolling through his phone, and Jory peers over his shoulder. "This one. Gin Wigmore's 'Happy Ever After.'"

The music comes out quietly through the speakers, and Connor turns it up. Jory's singing along, and Luke bounces his leg with the beat. Zakhi and Rimona are pretending to dance in their seats. Even Connor's nodding in time as he pulls back onto the highway.

"Hey," Jory says, tapping Luke's arm. "You got any playing cards?"

"Yeah, I think so." Luke fishes in one of the cupboards until he finds a deck. He puts them on the kitchenette table between them. "I've never learned how to play, though."

"Here, I'll teach you Rummy." Jory nods at the other two. "You want in?"

"Sure," Rimona says.

Jory shuffles the cards, and they all pass the time with the music and the game while Connor drives.

****

"We're calling for a ride here," Connor announces. "Too much driving, and the people we're going to see don't have the time to shuttle us."

They've set up camp at an RV park outside city limits. It's still fairly early. Connor says they're heading for a place called Snowflakes, where they'll meet another of his father's cousins, who owns it with his partner. Zakhi and Rimona have met them before and are looking forward to reconnecting.

Luke wonders if what he's wearing will be appropriate. He doesn't have a lot of clothing. Sylvia let them throw a few things in with the family's laundry while they were in Buffalo, but Luke will need to find a laundromat soon. He thinks about the shirt Jax gave him. It's tucked away in his duffel, but he could pull it out for tonight.

Even though they were only in Pennsylvania briefly, Connor managed to find a couple of postcards while they were stopped earlier. Luke has them tucked into the first page of his scrapbook, and he looks at them now. One is a picture of Lake Erie; the other is a roadmap of Pennsylvania. He's not sure which one he will send to Jax and which he will keep.

He's about to go change, but he discovers Jory is already in the tiny bathroom. They glance over their shoulder at him, and Luke's mouth drops open. Jory has put on makeup, a full face. Their hat is gone, and their hair is gelled into stylish spikes. They've made their eyes smoky and sultry, and their lips pop with a deep purple matte lipstick. Only then does Luke notice Jory is wearing a short, pleated black skirt with a vividly purple button-up shirt, open far enough to reveal a tight, black shirt with a lace edge.

Jory tilts their head. "What?"

"You look...wow," Luke says.

Exiting the bathroom, Jory forces him to back up toward the bedroom. "Connor said we were going to a club. Figured I'd clean up a little." They frown. "You're still staring. Is something wrong, or did you think I was too butch for this?"

"No, I—" Luke swallows, his insides still humming with appreciation. "I assumed you were like my friend Jax." He doesn't add that he's been thinking of himself lately too and what his feelings about Jax mean.

"Your friend is gender fluid?"

"No, but they aren't a man or a woman."

"Gotcha. Well, you've got the pronouns right, but I like to mix it up some with how I dress." They do a once-over of Luke that makes him flush. "You might want to change too."

He doesn't want to admit to them he doesn't have much. He never bothered with anything fancy when he went out with Jax, unless Jax let him borrow something. He balls the racerback shirt in his fist, trying to hide it. He doesn't fool Jory.

"Lemme see," they say, so Luke unfolds the shirt. "Okay. Not bad." They narrow their eyes in thought. "Hm. C'mere."

Luke steps closer, and Jory takes his head in their hands. They turn it this way and that, examining him from every angle. Jax did that sometimes too. It reminds Luke of being younger and having his mother check his face for dirt before dinner.

Jory nods and lets go, as though they've settled something in their mind. Perhaps they have. They re-enter the bathroom and pick through the cosmetics strewn on the tiny surfaces of the sink and cabinet. At last they select several items and bring them over.

"You need a shave, and then come see me. We'll sit out there where there's more room and I can see better."

Luke figures he has no choice but to obey. He takes out the razor he left in one of the drawers and cleans up. Like Jory did, he turns his face this way and that, examining. He doesn't want to keep them waiting, so he throws on the shirt, tidies the small space, and exits the bathroom.

The two of them sit in the kitchenette, and Jory spreads everything out. Luke wonders how they fit it in their bag, but he doesn't ask. Instead, he studies the array. There's everything he needs to look...something. He's never had anyone do much before, not even Jax.

"What are you going to—"

Seemingly ignoring him, Jory says, "You'll look best in this silver-blue. Matches those pretty eyes."

Luke flushes again. Jory only smiles and lines up what they want. They set to work on his face. Luke has no idea what everything is, but Jory talks to him the whole time, explaining what they're doing. He's not sure he wants to look like Jory does, nor is he interested in how Jax always did their face, all soft and glossy. Suddenly, he wants to assert himself, to insist he have a style all his own.

"Hold still, will you?" Jory gripes. "Let me finish your eyes, at least."

It seems like forever later when Jory applies the lipstick. It feels weird and waxy. Even the one time Luke let Jax play with his face, they only did his eyes. Now he wants to smear it off, but Jory instructs him to pucker.

"Ugh, it's gross!" he complains.

"You'll get used to it. I didn't pick anything like what I have on. You look better with something neutral."

Luke scowls, but he doesn't want to mess up the rest of his face before he's even seen it, so he relents. He looks at the tube of lipstick, which is a pale pink-beige. Jax always liked something with a bit of red to it, and they looked fabulous. Jory looks good in the deep purple. Luke can only trust his gut that Jory knows what they're doing.

"Am I done?" he asks.

"Yeah. Go have a look. I can fix anything you're not happy with."

Slowly, Luke heads for the bathroom. He takes a second to compose himself before he looks. And...he stares. Everything Jory has done is subtle. Yes, it's obvious he's wearing makeup. But it's not heavy, making him look like an accentuated version of himself without being androgynous like Jax. Around his eyes, the silvery blue makeup shimmers. That's where Jory's done the most work. It does indeed make the blue of his eyes pop, drawing attention there. The lipstick isn't much different in color from his natural lips, maybe a shade darker, and it has a subtle shine without being glossy. Luke was afraid Jory covered over his real self, but they didn't. They've enhanced what was already there.

He's so blown away by what Jory's done that he's overcome. He holds it in, not wanting to ruin Jory's artwork. He returns to the kitchenette, where Jory waits expectantly. They look up and raise their eyebrows in question.

"Can you show me later what you did?"

Jory grins. "You bet. Should we go find the others and help them get ready?"

Luke laughs. "I can't imagine you'll get Connor to join the fun, but we'll see."

In the end, Jory convinces Connor to try out some black eyeliner. It gives him a dark, brooding look. He doesn't say anything about either Luke or Jory's appearance, but he keeps glancing at both of them out of the corner of his eye while he calls for a ride.

Zakhi and Rimona are ready too. Rimona looks great in a leather vest over their red shirt, and they have a matching cap and high, lace-up boots. They refused Jory's offer for makeup. Zakhi is trendy in black leather pants, a black T-shirt, and a gold-and-black paisley jacket. He, too, declines makeup, but he does accept help styling his thick, wavy hair.

The car arrives. Luke is hesitant about getting in with a stranger, especially with how he's done up. The others look like they're on their way to a rock concert, but Luke doesn't. The driver doesn't mention anything, though. He keeps up a steady stream of chatter about Cleveland's nightlife and other places to visit while they're in town. Connor maintains their side of the conversation, leaving the others to watch the scenery fly past on the way to the nightclub.

The driver drops them off in front of the club and gives them a cheerful wave. Connor turns to the rest of the group. "Ready?"

He pulls open the door without waiting for a reply.

Chapter 15

S NOWFLAKES ISN'T EXACTLY what it advertises on the package, at least on the exterior. It's a nondescript building on a street with several other similar places. It's not obvious from the outside that it's an all-inclusive queer bar. A little boxy, old, brown brick storefront, the windows blackened out. There's a red awning underneath an unlit—the place is closed—neon sign with the name and a stylized snowflake.

"This is it?" Jory asks, shooting Connor an incredulous look.

He glares at them. "What were you expecting? It's not open yet. I'm sure in—" he checks his watch "—two hours, it'll look different. We're here to see my cousin Hy and his boyfriend Moishe."

He pulls open the door, and they step inside one by one. It's dim inside, but Luke notes that everything looks brand new and up-to-date. The lights are mostly off, except for a couple in the ceiling and a row of white theater lights around the bar. The decor is silver, glossy blue, and black. He isn't sure what the name alludes to, since it doesn't at this stage appear to have a winter theme. He can't wait to see what the place is like with people there to dance and drink and let go for a while.

"We're closed!" calls a voice from in back of the bar, followed by footsteps. A glitter-encrusted pair of purple Doc Martens arrives at the foot of the stairs, followed by someone Luke can only describe as a color-swirled extravaganza. He has long, long legs, most of which Luke can see because his denim shorts are impossibly short, the same color as his shoes. His multi-colored plaid shirt is tucked in and unbuttoned to the waist to reveal the white A-shirt underneath. He's not wearing makeup, and his hair is lazily piled on top of his head, a cotton-candy-pink twist that bounces when he jogs the rest of the way down the steps.

He stops in front of the three of them. "We open at five-thirty."

"I'm not here for the club. Well, I suppose I am, but I'm Connor Wasserman. I'm here to see Hy."

"Oh!" The newcomer claps his hands, and his whole demeanor changes. "Wonderful! We've been expecting you. I'm Moishe."

He holds out his hand delicately to Connor, who takes it, blushing furiously. Luke exchanges an amused glance with Jory. Moishe drags Connor closer and air-kisses him on both cheeks.

"This is Luke, my traveling companion. I believe you've met Zakhi and Rimona before, and this is our...friend...Jory."

Luke supposes it's probably for the best that Connor didn't introduce Jory as the hitchhiker they picked up in Erie. That might not have come across so well.

"The more the merrier." Moishe grins as he echoes what Zakhi said when Jory joined them. "I was just getting ready for tonight. I'll take you upstairs to our apartment and introduce you to Hy. He'll be *so excited*."

Luke doubts anyone can top Moishe's enthusiasm, but he supposes it must be like everyone else in Connor's family so far. All of them have been ready to greet them with open arms.

They follow Moishe's sashaying ass up the steps. Somehow, it doesn't come as any surprise that they have to push beads aside in the front door. Moishe leaves them in a huddle and takes off into the recesses of the apartment, calling for Hy.

A couple minutes later, a man who has to be at least twice Moishe's age arrives in the room.

He's less colorful than Moishe, more smooth and suave, with silvery hair and beard. He almost glides over to take Connor's hands in his. "Welcome, welcome! It's wonderful to meet you. And Zakhi! I remember when you were this high." He holds his hand palm down at waist height. "One of Avi and Sylvia's foster boys, all grown up and married! It's been too long since our last visit to New York. Wonderful to see you both again." He turns his gaze to Luke and Jory, and Luke is put at ease by the warmth in his gentle brown eyes. "Make yourselves at home, and I'll fetch us something to drink." He gestures to the living room.

The five of them sit, but Moishe continues to stand, leaning against the arched doorway between the rooms. He crosses his legs, causing his hip to jut out. Connor keeps stealing glances at him while trying to cover it. Luke isn't sure why; Moishe is eye-catching, but Luke never realized this was the sort of man Connor was attracted to. It needles him, but he can't put a finger on why.

Hy brings a tray with glasses, a water pitcher, and a bowl of lemon wedges. He sets it on the coffee table then takes a seat on the sofa. Everything in the apartment looks like it belongs in a bygone era, except not all the same one. It has the appearance of being collected over decades. Luke's chair is an off-green, made of the type of slightly scratchy material he recalls from occasional visits to older people in the town where he grew up. He runs his hands over the arms.

There's a record player, but it looks new. The albums on the shelf next to it do not, though Luke can only see the first one. He supposes it shouldn't come as a surprise that it's Queen. The apartment itself isn't as colorful as Moishe, doorway beads aside. It's cozy and homey, and Luke likes it here.

"So, Connor," Hy says. "You're traveling across the country, eh?"

"Yes. My father didn't leave me much to go on except a handful of names of aunts and uncles. He was an only child, and my grandparents both died years ago. There's no one left in my direct family, so I'm looking for any cousins who might've known my father."

"I don't know how much help I can be," Hy confesses. "We weren't close growing up. Until he passed through here, I hadn't seen him since we were teenagers." He sighs. "I know it's at least partly my fault. I was wrapped up in my own life, and I cut myself off from our family for a while." He's lost in thought for a few minutes, but then he sits up and leans forward. "I believe I have something for you, but I'll have to dig it out. I'll find it for you before you leave."

"All right," Connor says. "And until then, what should we do?"

"Why, tonight, we celebrate, of course!" Hy's joyful grin is back. He throws his arms wide. "The club will be open, and you're all my guests. Moishe and I will take care of you."

Moishe unfolds himself and lopes closer. He's so sensual, even in what Luke suspects are his "casual" clothes. He eyes all of them in turn. Jory earns an approving thumbs up. Zakhi and Rimona receive nods. Connor gets a shrug but no commentary. Luke holds his breath, peering up at Moishe's narrowed eyes and pursed lips. He only exhales after Moishe gives him a wink.

"You'll all be fine, darlings, but if any of you need to borrow something..." He trails off with a flip of his hand. "Some friends of mine will be here tonight. I can introduce you, and I'll be around if you need anything." Leaning closer so his full lips are near Connor's head, he adds, "Anything at all."

"What about you?" Connor asks Hy. Luke sees the slight shift in his posture, and his face hasn't returned yet to its normal color.

"Oh, I'll observe from afar. It's Moishe who likes this scene." Hy smiles indulgently up at Moishe, then takes his hand and kisses the palm. Moishe's expression conveys return fondness. "Why don't we enjoy an early dinner in the meantime?"

He rises, and Luke notices the way he and Moishe move around each other in the kitchen with practiced ease. It's not a large space, but they don't seem to have any trouble navigating it. Even when Luke lived with Jax, they never had this kind of comfort. He certainly never had it with Greg. Not with AJ either, though they were only teenagers when they were more or less together.

Luke catches Connor out of the corner of his eye, his gaze still riveted to Moishe. Jory pokes Luke with one toe, and they share a secret smile before Hy turns to invite them to the table.

※※※※

The time has flown by, and Luke is awed by all the work the staff has done to turn Snowflakes from an empty, dark shell into a blue neon paradise. He sees now the way the walls light up, making it look like it's snowing indoors. The blue leather has become electric in the room's charged glow.

Moishe continues to surprise him. He directs the flow of employee traffic and answers questions with firm, practiced ease. Luke was under the impression Hy owned the club, but it's clearly Moishe who is in charge here. It's his playground, and there is no doubt he loves every second.

It's early yet, but there are a few people who show up for happy hour, including Moishe's friends. There's a heterosexual couple—Luke only knows because Moishe assures him it's so—and a geeky-cute man around Luke's age with his much older partner. The silver-haired man has to be somewhere in the neighborhood of Hy's age, and Luke wonders if that's how they all met.

He doesn't have a whole lot of time to dwell on it. While it's still quiet enough to talk easily, Connor shares the story of how they came to be on their trip. Luke tries to focus, but he's distracted by the atmosphere. It's very different from Thundershock, and yet somehow not. It's got the same contemporary club feel, but this crowd seems on average slightly older than at Thundershock. It's also less mixed company, despite being advertised as inclusive. Luke sees very few women aside from Moishe's friend.

Soon it becomes too noisy for much conversation, so Moishe's friends get up from the table to go dance. Zakhi and Rimona are already out on the floor, and Luke watches them for a bit. They're less affectionate than Hy and Moishe, but there's the same feel of ease between them. Rimona laughs as Zakhi twirls them, and Moishe's friends open their circle to let the new pair in.

Jory tugs on Luke's hand, and he follows. When he looks back at the table, he sees Moishe doing the same with Connor, who turns rosy again as he accepts Moishe's hand. Out on the dance floor, Luke tries to keep his mind—and his eyes—on Jory, but he keeps stealing glances at Connor and Moishe.

Eventually, Moishe notices. He shakes his head a little, tossing his glossy pink hair over his shoulder and giving Luke a sly wink. Luke swallows his discomfort. He's known many men who have open relationships, including Adam and AJ. But for no good reason, it bothers him to think of Moishe and Connor this way.

Moishe air-kisses Connor and sidles up to Luke and Jory. "I think it's my turn," he tells Jory, then turns his charm on Luke.

Jory grins and steps away. They head for a group of people by the bar. Luke returns his attention to Moishe and is surprised to see him standing with his hands on his hips, eyebrow arched.

"Uh...how about that dance?" Luke asks.

"No, honey. You're gonna come with me for a sec."

Moishe takes Lukes hand and marches him across the room. They slip up the stairs to the apartment, and Moishe silently holds aside the beads. Inside, he's shocked to see Hy, astride some young guy, his tongue deep in the man's mouth. Luke stares for a long, tense moment.

"Now," Moishe whispers, letting the beads fall back, "let's go."

They descend back into the club then outside. The sky is darkening, but it hasn't cooled off yet. The air is thick and humid. Moishe leads Luke around to the back, where he leans against the wall. Luke imitates his posture.

Moishe rolls his head to the side to look at Luke. "I saw how jealous you were when I was with Connor."

"I wasn't—"

"Maybe I read that wrong, but I doubt it. At the very least, you thought I was going after him and would cause some kind of damage." He snorts. "As if your friend isn't a grown-ass man who can decide for himself."

"That's not—"

Moishe waves a hand, his earlier sway returning. "Oh, please, honey. I know that look when I see it because I have some experience here."

"You mean because of Hy."

"Don't judge us, sweetheart. You think I care?"

"Don't you?" Luke is more than a little certain he would.

"I knew who Hy was when we got together. How do you think we met?" His smile is tight at the corners. "I was that pretty boy once, the one Hy brought up to the apartment.

149

His man always said he didn't care if Hy was fucking someone younger and hotter. But I was his last straw. He packed up and left." Moishe blows out a breath. "I stayed in his place."

"Why?"

Moishe shrugs. "You ever been in love?"

Luke doesn't know how to answer that. Maybe several times. Maybe none. He's never found whatever Moishe is talking about now. "I don't know," he says honestly.

"I knew Hy was the one. Not because he fucked me so good I saw stars, even if that first time came pretty damn close. No, it's everything else. He's the most wonderful man I've ever known. I don't care if he brings a dozen men a week into our apartment. You know why?"

Luke shakes his head.

"Because," Moishe continues, poking Luke in the chest with one finger, "in the end, I know all they are to him is sex. That's what his last partner didn't get. I'm the one Hy returns to. I'm the one he sleeps next to every night." He sighs. "At first, he would apologize. He'd bring me gifts or breakfast in bed, or he'd take me on trips and spend every night making love to me. I finally told him I was never leaving him unless he asked me to. I stay away on nights like this, when the club is full and he has his choice of barely adult men wanting to feel grown-up with him. When it's done, when we close, I'll be the one at his side."

Luke doesn't understand their arrangement or why it doesn't upset Moishe. Why Moishe isn't doing the very same thing as Hy. But when he looks at Moishe, all he sees is someone in love. He remembers the way Hy looked at him, the love and tenderness when he kissed Moishe's hand.

Moishe tilts his head, and it's clear he's satisfied that Luke comprehends at least to the point of leaving it alone. "What I did with Connor is only harmless flirting. It's fun.

I like people, and I love gorgeous, sexy men. But it's not going to reach the point of what Hy does. I'm simply not interested."

"Okay." The knot in Luke's belly over seeing them together has loosened. Moishe won't hurt either Hy or Connor, and that's all he cares about.

"Now." Moishe's infectious grin is back. "What do you say we pop back inside and have a good time?"

He doesn't wait for an answer, tugging on Luke's shirt. Luke has no choice but to follow and let his worries be swallowed up in the music and lights.

Then

THERE WASN'T ONE defining moment in Luke's young life when he knew how he felt about other boys. It could've been anything. He only knew that as he got older, the freedom he was once allowed was restricted. Instead of caring for the babies and helping Esther and Mama, he was expected to begin learning how to do the kind of work Daddy and the big boys did. No more staying out of their way as he took photos of the buildings.

It was during that time when Luke first connected the dots, all the bewildering fragments coming together into a whole picture. The summer after he turned eleven, Luke went to stay with Roman. Dad—it wasn't Daddy anymore—believed that would be the best way for him to learn. He sent Esther too, despite her protests that Luke wasn't a baby, didn't need her to look after him. But Dad was stern and said it would make life easier for Roman's family to have the help.

Mama still had bouts of what Dad called "sickness." She stayed in bed for days at a time, and Esther had to remind her to wash and eat. Luke looked after Ruth and Johnny, even though the grown-ups were strict with him that it was Esther's work and he shouldn't make trouble for her. Esther privately told him it was okay, so Luke did what he could.

Mama was doing a little better by summer. She said the warm weather helped. So that was when Dad said it was time to go to Roman's. Luke thought Mama needed Esther's help more than Roman's family did, and he tried to say so, especially after what Esther had told him about Roman's brother-in-law. But Dad cut him off and said she would only be there the first week. That seemed to satisfy everyone.

They arrived at Roman's house while he was still out on a contract. Tabitha settled them in and put Esther to work in the kitchen right away. Luke was free to wander. He went over every inch of the house, but there wasn't anything interesting to do. Tabitha finally had enough and sent him outside.

There were other kids in their neighborhood. It wasn't as out of the way as Luke's family homestead. Roman and Tabitha lived closer to town, and the street was full of boys and girls riding bikes or playing basketball in freestanding hoops. They all seemed to be in their own worlds, taking no notice of the new boy.

Except one. Sam Whelock from the homeschool co-op was on the front stoop of one of the houses, watching a group of kids spray each other with water guns. He looked bored. Luke stopped across the street from him. He stood and stared for a while, hoping Sam wouldn't catch him. Luke liked looking at Sam, and he usually didn't get such an unobstructed view.

Sam had shaggy, dark hair that almost covered one eye. He was forever brushing his bangs aside like his mother didn't take him for a haircut often enough. His brown eyes were twinkly when he was up to mischief, and he was always smiling. Sam was the happiest person Luke knew, bubbling over with life and energy, constantly in motion.

One time at the co-op, they were sitting at tables. Sam tried to turn himself upside down under the table while his mom was doing the lesson. He promptly fell out of his seat, and everyone laughed.

On the rare opportunities Luke had to watch him unrestricted, he got a feeling in his belly like it was full of prickly heat. Sometimes at New Year's, Luke's parents would let him sip the sparkling cider. It tickled going down, and it made him buzz. Sam was like the sweet-spicy cider, causing Luke to shiver when he looked for too long.

Now, Sam finally noticed him. Instead of seeming annoyed that Luke was staring at him like a fool, Sam stood up and waved. A splash of embarrassment and excitement hit Luke. In a moment, Sam was headed Luke's way. Luke thought about pretending he hadn't seen and heading back up the street, but Sam was already almost there.

"Hi," Sam said.

"Hi." Luke rubbed the toe of his sneaker in the dirt.

"How come you're here?" Sam didn't waste any time.

"My parents sent me to stay with my brother for a while."

"Why?"

"They want me to learn to do more boy stuff."

Sam wrinkled his nose. "Like sports or something?"

"No. Like fixing houses, the same as my dad and other brothers do."

"That sounds so boring." Sam bounced on his toes.

"Yeah. I'd rather take pictures." Luke finally looked up at him. "You look bored too."

"Those are my cousins." Sam jerked his thumb over his shoulder to indicate the kids with the water guns. "They're okay, but they don't like to do anything really fun."

"Oh."

"You want to hang out?"

Luke did. He wanted to spend as much time with Sam as he could. They hadn't really talked at the homeschool co-op, and Luke couldn't believe his luck now.

"Sure, okay."

Sam's eyes lit up. "You said you take pictures?"

"Um." Luke flushed. "Yeah."

Pointing to Luke's bag, he said, "You have a camera in there?"

"Yeah." Luke didn't seem to be able to say much else right then. His head felt like it might float right off his body.

"I have an idea."

Sam grabbed his hand and yanked, and Luke laughed as he was pulled along. The sparkling-cider feeling was back, and Luke understood suddenly that this was something he could never tell anyone, least of all Roman. Even Esther wouldn't be able to make sense of it. Luke tucked those thoughts away and followed Sam back to his house.

Chapter 16

ALL FIVE OF them sleep late the next morning. Hy said to meet him back at Snowflakes at ten because he has something for Connor. Luke is the first one up, and he's already showered and dressed when Connor emerges sleepily from their shared bed space.

"Morning," Luke says. He's amused by Connor's rumpled look, his hair askew and his eyes still half-closed.

"Ungh," Connor mutters. "Must you be so cheerful?"

"Must you overdo it the night before hitting the road again?" Luke replies, but he hands over the cup of coffee he's prepared.

"Don't remind me." Connor groans as he sits at the table. "I didn't even get drunk. I don't think."

"No, you were fine. But we were up late, and you definitely looked like you had more than usual." Luke realizes he has no idea how much Connor normally drinks.

"A bit, yeah. I thought I was spreading it out enough, but maybe not." He sips his coffee and sighs contentedly.

"It was fun anyway," Jory says, descending the ladder from the bunk over the cab. They look more bright-eyed than Connor, so either they handle their alcohol better or they had less. Luke's leaning toward a combination of the two.

Jory begins opening cupboards, and Luke and Connor stare at them, the way they make themselves at home. It takes a few minutes before Luke realizes they're about to cook. They have ingredients from the fridge lined up on the counters, and they rummage around to find a pan. In a moment, the RV smells divine.

"I seriously underestimated you," Connor remarks.

"Gotta earn my keep somehow." Jory stirs the eggs in the pan. "This'll help you feel better. Don't want to go out on an empty stomach."

They set down two plates, one of eggs and one of hash brown potatoes, and then slide into the crowded table next to Luke. As they serve up and begin eating, Connor says, "Are you coming with us?"

"Naw. This is your family history. Fascinating as that may be, I'm gonna go have a look around town while you're out."

Zakhi emerges next, almost as rumpled as Connor. "Bars are not my scene," he groans. "Oh, there's coffee. And... breakfast?" He grins at Jory. "You're a treasure."

Jory laughs. "You got me."

When Rimona climbs down the ladder from the double bed, they look like they tried to straighten themself out a bit. The huge yawn, though, gives them away. Jory provides plates for both Zakhi and Rimona and then for Luke.

"What about you two?" he asks. "Are you coming back to see Hy?"

Zakhi shakes his head. "We have some phone calls to make, and then we'll pick up a few groceries. Like Jory, gotta contribute our fair share."

Luke understands they don't want to intrude. He already feels like he might not belong there, even though Connor has said he wants Luke along. If it's anything like talking to the family in Buffalo, Connor may be in for a few more surprises.

"Hey," Luke says to Jory. "While you're out, can you pick me up a couple postcards?"

"What for?" Jory gives him a confused frown.

"My-my scrapbook." Luke flushes.

"Oh, okay. Yeah, no worries." Jory pauses. "You got any money?"

"What? I gave you some yesterday!" Luke scowls. "You spend it all at that convenience store?"

"Maybe." Jory lifts one shoulder. "Fine. No, I didn't. I'll use that. You happy?"

"Am I supposed to be?"

"Will you two cut it out?" Connor rubs his temples. "You're making my headache worse, with your childish arguing."

"Sorry." Jory has the sense to look guilty.

"Yeah, sorry," Luke says, more grudgingly than he means to.

"Great. Let's get our shit together and get out of here, then."

He stands and puts his coffee cup by the tiny sink. Luke sighs. He remembers Connor being prone to sloppiness when they briefly lived together. The others all disappear too, and Luke realizes they've left him to do the dishes. He rolls up his sleeves and gets to work.

✳✳✳✳

Connor and Luke arrive back at Snowflakes a few minutes before ten. There's a note taped to the outer door telling them to go right up to the apartment. When they arrive, Moishe greets them, a towel wrapped around his head, hiding his pink hair.

"Morning, you two. Did you already eat?"

"Back at the—" Luke starts, but Connor elbows him. That's when he notices the food out on the table.

Moishe laughs. "It's all right. Hy and I just finished, so I figured I'd offer. Let me put this away, and then I'll join you in the living room. Hy will be right out."

A few minutes later, the four of them are seated around the coffee table. Hy has an old shoebox with a sneaker logo on the side. He opens the lid to reveal a packet of letters.

"Saul left these with me."

Connor's mouth drops open. "When? I mean, when did he come see you?"

"Only once, last year. Said he was heading west and that I should hang on to these. I didn't know what to do with them. Hell, I'm not even sure what they all are. I assumed at first they were letters to or from your mother, but they're not."

Connor is still gaping, so Luke says, "They're not?"

"No. I didn't read them, only the addresses. Everything was meaningless aside from a few from our relations. Take them. Read them over. I hope they give you some clues about who your father was."

Now Connor finds his voice. "But can't you tell me anything?"

Hy taps his fingers together. "I don't know if what I'll say is what you want to hear."

Luke and Connor exchange a glance, and without thinking, Luke grasps his hand. They've already heard some things that surprised both of them. Whatever Hy tells them won't be any different.

With a sharp nod, Hy says, "All right. When he visited, I had the impression he was...confused or chasing something that didn't exist. I won't make commentary on his mental health because I don't know. But he kept talking about some wild theory of his. Something about a dream he had and everything being connected. He wanted to know what the dream meant, I think. Told me that's what he was going to find out."

Once again, Luke and Connor make eye contact. Luke is curious. He says, "Did he tell you the dream?"

Hy shakes his head. "I wish he had. Maybe I could've helped him more."

"Thank you," Connor says. "For everything. For this." He holds up the packet of letters.

"It's no problem. I hope you two won't be strangers. Any time you're in town, you're always welcome as our guests."

It seems their visit with Hy and Moishe is over. There's work to do at the club, and Connor isn't planning on another night there. He wants to be on the road as soon as they can, so he thanks Hy again and says he'll be sure to stop in next time they pass through. Luke wonders now if either of them will ever drive this way in the future.

They stand, and Moishe says, "We'll give you a ride back to your campsite."

Hy tosses him the keys, and he takes Luke and Connor by the hand. He squeezes affectionately and lets go.

On the way, Moishe tells them about the local culture and the food and the best places to go next time they're in town. Connor replies politely while Luke points his camera out the window and snaps a few pictures. When he closes the window, he turns to see Hy smiling. Luke smiles back and wonders what Hy is thinking, but he doesn't ask.

Moishe brings them right to the RV. They get out, and Hy leans against the car. Moishe hugs them each in turn. After he lets go of Luke, he hands him one of Snowflakes' business cards. "For that scrapbook Connor tells me you're making."

Luke only smiles and tucks it into his jeans pocket. He asks if Connor will pose for a picture with Hy and Moishe. The camera clicks, and this part of their trip is stored in digital memory. Luke already has some from the previous night.

With tears from Hy and blown kisses from Moishe, the two of them re-enter the RV. Hy and Moishe drive away, the sound of their car growing fainter as Luke and Connor watch them go.

*****

Inside the RV, Luke sits down at the table to put the business card in his scrapbook. Jory hands him the two postcards they picked up in town. One is a picture of a barn with some Ohio facts next to it. The other is the typical "greetings from" type, with CLEVELAND in large letters. Luke slides the greetings postcard back into the scrapbook and flips over the other one to write to Jax. He picks up the business card again and notices there's writing on the back.

Things aren't always what they seem. Love, Moishe.

There's a song written there too: "Shut Up and Dance" by Walk the Moon. Later, Luke will add it to their road trip playlist. He puts the business card in with the postcards and closes the scrapbook. Then he writes to Jax, telling them about their latest adventures. He pauses to glance at his phone, sitting beside his elbow. The itch to call Jax is strong, but he forces himself to focus on the postcard.

It's beginning to rain, big, splattering drops hitting the RV's windshield. Zakhi offers to drive, and Connor sits up front to navigate for him. Jory settles down at the kitchenette table with Luke, and Rimona joins them.

Up front, Luke hears Zakhi say, "Where to next?"

"Gary, Indiana," Connor answers.

Jory sings a few lines from the song, and Luke can't help giggling as all of them except Connor join in.

"Didn't know you liked musical theater," he says to Jory.

"I don't," they reply. "But who doesn't know that one?" They snort. "We gonna meet Harold Hill there or something?"

Connor groans. "No. Have I mentioned that you all are horrible?"

Jory looks back at Luke and grins. "Not in the last five minutes. See if you can make it ten next time."

"Who are we going to see?" Luke asks in the interest of breaking up a potential argument.

"My father's cousin Danya. She runs a publishing company, but she's also the one I contacted first about this trip. She's been keeping careful track of family records."

"Your family must be huge," Jory remarks. They turn to Luke. "How about you?"

"What about me?" Luke plays ignorant. He'd rather not have this conversation right now.

"Your family. I have the sense there's a story there."

Luke frowns and concentrates on the postcard, even though he's finished with it. "What makes you think that?"

Connor interrupts them. "Make sure you're buckled in. We're hitting Dead Man's Curve, and I want everyone to stay put."

"Yikes. That sounds painful. Aye aye, Captain." Jory tugs their belt to make sure it's tight.

The curve is nearly ninety degrees, Connor tells them. He's never driven on it before, but he made sure he knew the route before setting out. That stretch of road is one of the most dangerous on the entire trip, the site of far too many accidents. Zakhi sticks to the recommended speed limit, but even so, Luke feels as if his stomach has gone one direction while the rest of him travels the other way.

They're quiet the entire time Connor talks Zakhi through this stretch, but at last they're beyond it and back onto normal highway. Cautiously, Zakhi speeds up and takes them out past Cleveland limits.

Luke thinks it's safe to put things out on the table again, with less danger they'll slide all over. He hasn't yet begun work on the pages for his road trip, and he figures now is as good a time as any. He hesitates; no one here has seen him put together the pages in the scrapbook before. Sure, they all knew he had postcards in the album, but that's different from laying out the theme and design.

He glances at the others and makes a decision. If any of them have a problem with it, that's on them. He won't go back to hiding his scrapbooks, disguising them inside the covers of old homeschool texts. He takes out his new one again, along with some card stock and markers.

"You were about to tell me about your family," Jory says before Luke can begin work.

"I was?" He doesn't look at them.

"Or I was about to get you to talk."

"I'm from South Dakota. We're going to pass near my hometown, but not quite through it. Or we aren't stopping there, anyway." Luke nods to the map. "Connor's got a pin in Sioux Falls, which isn't where I grew up, but it's not that far."

"Yeah?" Jory folds their arms on top of the table and leans forward. "Go on."

"My family was...religious, but honestly, I'm not sure my parents were especially...strict. Not like some of the other kids I knew. I was homeschooled, but I ended up graduating from public school."

"How'd that happen?"

Luke wants to close his eyes so he doesn't have to look at anyone. He's never felt comfortable explaining to strangers that he left home at fifteen. But he wills himself to meet Jory's gaze. "I wasn't living with my family anymore."

As predicted, Jory's eyebrows shoot up almost to their hairline. "I don't suppose you want to tell me why not."

"Not really." Luke looks up front at Connor, whose eyes are on the road. Whether or not he's listening is anyone's guess. Luke sighs. "Fine. I left home on my own."

Jory nods. "I don't suppose religious families take too well to people like us." They shrug. "I wouldn't know. My family never had much of a problem with it. I had partners of all kinds, and no one made a peep."

Luke isn't sure why this surprises him. It's not as if he hasn't known anyone else queer whose family welcomed them. AJ's parents ran a whole charity to help kids like Luke. But Jory seemed like they were escaping something and as if life hadn't been easy, and somewhere in Luke's mind, he wondered if that was why.

"My family never even knew," he says. He can't help the sting behind his eyes. He's sure his mother wouldn't have cared, though he doesn't know about his father. "I'm sorry. I...can't."

"Hey." Jory puts their hand on Luke's arm, and he looks at them. "It's okay. I pushed, and I should've left it alone. Whatever happened, if you want to tell someone, I'm here."

"Yeah. Okay." Luke sniffles and wipes his eyes. "Hey, weren't you going to tell me your story?"

"Another time. Why don't you show me what you're working on instead?"

Luke has never purposefully shown anyone what he does, and this trip is the first time he's worked on it in front of anyone but Jax. Slowly, he turns the book so Jory can see how he's arranged the page, leaving room for when his photos are developed.

"Hey, this is pretty cool," Jory says, examining the page. They turn it so Rimona can see too.

Rimona adds, "It's amazing. I used to try to do this, but I have no eye for how to make it look nice."

"I, uh, have a book that's almost done," Luke says. "Do—do you want to see it?"

"Definitely!" Rimona says. "Maybe I'll get some ideas."

Jory is quieter. They tilt their head, smiling a little. "Yeah. I'd like that a lot."

Then

SAM WHELOCK KISSED Luke in the tree grove behind the church where they had their homeschooling co-op. It was squashy and weird, and Sam smelled like the tuna sandwich he'd had for lunch not five minutes ago. It turned Luke's knees to jelly and made his stomach do the sparkling-juice bubbly thing again. Luke gasped and then kissed back, which made everything okay.

And then Sam dragged his mouth away, pulled his fist back, and punched Luke so hard his head bounced off the tree and he saw stars. He knew his nose was broken by the way it bled freely down the front of his T-shirt.

"Oh! Oh, g-gosh. Luke, I'm sorry!" Sam stammered. "I didn't mean—" He backed away, gaping.

Luke wanted to demand Sam do something about all the blood. He tried to catch it in his hands, which only led to them being covered in it.

"I'll get help!" Sam took off, leaving Luke standing there staring after him with his nose still pouring like a red faucet.

It took forever—or possibly only five minutes—before Mrs. Whelock was there with a towel and some ice. No one asked any questions, including Luke, who wanted to know what in the world reason Sam had given for Luke's broken nose. Obviously, he wouldn't have said what they'd been doing beforehand, and he probably wouldn't have told her he'd hit Luke, either.

"You two shouldn't have been chasing each other in here. Sam tells me you crashed into the tree. Your mother won't be too happy about this."

That answered at least one question. "I doe," Luke mumbled through his pinched nose. His mother also wouldn't take him to the doctor or hospital. Mama had gotten funny about it ever since the doctor started asking what she thought were nosy questions about Esther. She didn't trust anyone except their pastor and a few of the people at the co-op. Luke wasn't sure she even trusted them.

He did, though. Mrs. Whelock was nicer to him than the other teachers. She let him stay in during lunch, even in the warm weather, to use the art supplies she brought every week. And she never, ever told anyone about the scrapbook she tucked in the bottom of the box for Luke to work on. He was long past the age where the adults thought it was all right. Every time he brought a finished book home, he took one of his old schoolbooks off the shelf. Carefully, he pried the cover loose and attached it to the scrapbook. If anyone looked at his shelf, they'd think he was an exceptionally dedicated student.

On this particular day, Luke had gone with Sam after lunch instead of staying inside. They'd been doing that for a while, eating and then escaping the others in the wooded area behind the playground. Mrs. Whelock hadn't said anything, and Luke had the impression she was glad Sam had friends.

Luke didn't remember how they started hanging out like this. Some of the other kids thought Sam was weird, but he fascinated Luke. He didn't have a name for the feelings he had about Sam, other than how much he liked being with him and really liked having a friend who was just his, not one he had to share with all his siblings or who was forced on him by his parents.

Sam sat with his back against a tree opposite Luke. He wouldn't look at him or his mother while she tended to Luke. Mrs. Whelock fussed over him. It was nice to have someone look after him who wasn't too busy with a hundred other tasks.

"Looks like the bleeding's stopped now." She withdrew the towel but instructed Luke to keep the ice on his face. She muttered, "Your parents really ought to have it seen to." Louder, she said, "How are you feeling?"

Sore, in more ways than one. Luke's heart ached almost as much as his nose. But all he said was, "I'm okay."

Mrs. Whelock stood and brushed off her skirt. "Sam, can you keep an eye on him? Let me know if anything else happens, okay?"

"Sure, Mom."

She left, taking the blood-soaked towel with her. Luke drew his knees up and wrapped his free arm around them. He waited for Sam to acknowledge him.

"I'm really sorry," he finally said, still not looking directly at Luke. "I didn't mean to hit you like that."

"Yeah, you did." Luke was surprised at his own boldness, but what Sam had said was a lie. He sure did mean to punch Luke, just maybe not to break his nose.

"I didn't mean to hurt you."

"Well, that's closer to the truth."

Sam looked up and glared at him. "I'm not a homosexual."

The word made Luke cringe. He'd heard it lots of times before, mostly yelled from the pulpit on Sunday mornings. He wasn't about to admit he probably was, not with Sam frowning at him like that.

"Me, neither," he said, forcing the words out.

"Good. Maybe we can be...not homosexuals, you know, together." Sam picked up a stick and drew a spiral in the dirt. "Like...that thing at church. What's it called? When you stop each other from doing sin?"

They didn't go to the same church, so Luke wasn't sure what Sam meant. "Prayer partners?" It didn't sound like a whole lot of fun, hanging out in the woods during lunch at co-op, praying. Maybe it wouldn't be so bad if it were with Sam.

"Um...kind of? I think we call it some other thing. Like, you see the person do a thing, and you just go, 'Hey, cut it out. That's sin.' Or something like that."

Luke snorted, and it made his nose throb. "That sounds stupid."

"It does, doesn't it?" Sam's quiet laughter made Luke's belly wriggle happily.

"Or we could just pretend that's what we're gonna do, and instead we can hang out back here like always."

"That definitely sounds better." Sam looked at Luke with troubled eyes for so long it made Luke squirm. "Maybe we can forget about today?"

It would be difficult, given Luke's swollen nose and black eyes. But he would do a lot to be able to keep spending time with Sam. No one else got it about Luke's being from a big family or having to do work he didn't like because "it's what boys do." Besides, it would be easy enough to convince at least his father to let him hang out with Sam outside of co-op too. Dad was always on Luke about spending too much time with the girls.

"Okay. Deal," Luke said. He stuck out his hand, and Sam scooted closer to take it.

Chapter 17

Now

I T'S LESS THAN five hours from Cleveland to Gary, even with a brief stop for lunch and gas. They make it to the campsite, and it's still raining. The sky is dark, and Luke can tell a thunderstorm is coming. He feels the crackling in the air when he steps outside the RV with his camera.

His heart thunders, and he's shaking. This isn't the first time he's tried to take photos of a storm, but it's the first time he's been back in an RV since the move when he was eight. He remembers now the way he and the others had to run for shelter and how he'd turned back to take those pictures. How proud Dad was he'd managed to get it on film so they could show the insurance company.

The sky lights up, and Luke counts the seconds until the clap of thunder. He's not sure if it's accurate or only an urban legend that you can tell how far away the lightning is by the time in between. It's comforting to know it's quite a while. Unless the storm moves fast, they're safe here. Besides, Old Tracey doesn't have all the fiberglass like in the RVs Luke's family used.

Luke's shaking stops, and he takes some photos. He manages to capture the next lightning strike. Then he returns inside the RV, slightly damp from the splashing rain. He changes his clothes and hangs the others to dry.

Everyone else is lounging around quietly. Jory is up in their bunk. Connor and Zakhi are listening to music, comparing concerts they've been to. Luke's only been to one concert in his entire life, years ago when they all moved for AJ and the others to go to college. They were back home for the summer, and AJ dragged Luke to see Green Day. Connor was there too, and Luke hears him mention it to Zakhi. When he does, he glances up at Luke and grins.

"Remember that?"

"Yeah."

Luke sits across from the two of them. He doesn't have a lot to say about the concert. It was overwhelming and exhilarating, like nothing he'd ever experienced before. It might have been the newness of it all, or it might have been that he smoked his first weed right before they went in. Whatever the reason, it all felt like magic to him.

The conversation has changed while Luke's been lost in thought. He hears Zakhi ask, "You planning on seeing any sights or just visiting family?"

"Mostly family," Connor says. "I hope we'll get to do a few other things, but the whole point is to talk with Dad's cousins."

"You said you felt there was something you needed to find," Zakhi remarks. "Any idea what your father might've intended?"

Connor shakes his head. "Not really. I haven't even fully read the letters he left me. They read like an unfinished manuscript. The writing is mostly poetry and very weird essays, some that sound like conspiracy theories. That's why we're going to see Danya. I guess he contacted her, but I'm not sure what about."

They fall silent, and Luke can hear the steady drips on the roof of the RV. The rain is letting up, but not enough to go out and make a campfire. Luke is slow and sleepy. Out of half-closed eyes, he sees Connor take out a book. Zakhi joins Rimona at the table, both on their phones. The peaceful atmosphere lulls Luke into a state between sleep and awake.

His phone buzzing in his pocket rouses him, and he sits up. "Hello?"

"Hi," a woman says. "Um, you might not remember us—"

A man cuts in. "From the bed and breakfast? We were on our honeymoon."

"Oh!" Luke smiles. He didn't have an address for them to stay in touch, so he gave them his phone number and told them to let him know how the pictures came out.

Missus says, "The photos are beautiful. I don't know how you did it, but—"

"—you got everything perfect," Mister finishes the sentence.

"It's like you knew us," Missus tells him. "But that's impossible."

"Anyway, we'd like to thank you. We can't let you have done this for us for free."

"Oh. Uh...I've, uh, never been paid for my photos before," Luke tells them. "You don't have to—"

"We want to," Missus assures him.

Luke feels awkward, wrong-footed and as if he shouldn't be accepting anything from them. It was a fun day on the beach, nothing more. He didn't do it for the money. He tells them this, but they insist.

"Please," Mister says. "It meant so much to us. I wish you could see them."

"Wait!" Missus says. "I transferred a couple to my phone so I could show my family. I'll send one."

There's a long pause, but eventually, Luke's phone buzzes with the incoming text. He pulls it away from his ear to look. He studies the couple. The woman is laughing as she tugs her new husband away from the splashing tide. Another text arrives, this time of the two of them looking into each other's eyes right before a kiss. The man's toes curl into the sand as he leans forward, and the woman's face is tilted up. Her hand is on the back of his neck.

Luke lightly touches his phone just beyond the edge of the screen. Warmth like sunshine flows through him. He can see how in love they are, how the two of them are facing a future they both desire. He knows nothing else about them, but he feels their adoration even through the glass.

He's quiet so long that Mister clears his throat. "So...about paying you..."

"Okay," Luke agrees softly.

"Great!" He can envision Missus bouncing a little as she speaks. "Tell us how we can get it to you."

"I've got an app. I'll text you the details."

He still feels strange, but he can use the money. He won't have to depend solely on Connor for the duration of the trip. He won't tell anyone, though. It's private, something he isn't ready to share even though he doesn't know why.

He says goodbye to Mister and Missus, and then he texts them. He saves the photos to his phone, although he isn't sure what he'll need them for. Maybe to remember them and know he made them so happy.

The rain has stopped, and the sky is beginning to clear. There are pops in the distance, but not thunder. Curious, Luke steps outside. The place where they're parked has a good view of the stars. In between the tiny, twinkling lights, a red firework lights up the night. Luke steps back inside to get his camera.

"Someone's setting off fireworks," he says.

"I'd forgotten!" Connor exclaims. "It's July fourth."

The others follow Luke out to watch. Whoever it is, they're giving a good show. Luke takes pictures of the rings, willows, and horsetails while the others *ooh* and *ahh* beside him. A warm breeze stirs Luke's hair, and he thinks tonight is another good night to be free.

****

In the morning, the five of them call for a ride and pile into the van that arrives to whisk them away. Danya Wasserman's office is on the top floor of a run-down building in a suburb of Gary. Judging by the chipped bricks on the outside,

Luke is expecting the office to be several decades out of date with dirty, worn carpeting and peeling paint. Instead, the entire floor must've been renovated recently because it has the smell of fresh paint and new furniture.

When Connor knocks on the glass-enclosed main office, Danya waves them in. She's shouting on her phone to someone, but more like she's excited than angry. After a couple more minutes, she ends the call and turns toward the newcomers.

"You must be Connor," she says. Her voice has a slightly nasal quality and the remains of an accent Luke doesn't instantly recognize.

"I think you might remember Avi and Sylvia's foster son, and these are my friends Luke and Jory. They're along for the ride."

Danya shakes everyone's hand and gives hugs all around. She's short and slim with thin, gray hair pulled into a clip at her neck. Her eyes are dark brown and sparkling. She motions for everyone to follow her out of her office and into a small conference room. On the way, Luke looks around. There are only two other people in the entire office, both working at their desks.

"It's so good to see you all!" Danya holds Rimona's hands. "And you're Zakhi's lovely spouse. So good to meet you finally. Sylvia has told me so much about you."

Rimona blushes. "All good, I hope."

"Of course, of course! Do you all want some coffee or tea?" Danya taps a single-brew machine on the counter. "Please, feel free at any time."

Connor accepts her offer—naturally—and Zakhi makes tea for himself and Rimona. Luke and Jory take only water from the canister by the door. They sit around the table, and Luke keeps his eyes on Connor, who tracks Danya's movements as she perches on her chair. Once they're all comfortable, Danya folds her hands on top of the table. There's a long silence, and Luke's finally had enough.

"What do you all do here?" he asks.

"We're a small publishing company specializing in Jewish-interest books. I took over from my father, and he took over from his, though it wasn't books back then."

"What was it?" Connor wants to know.

"My grandfather started a Yiddish newspaper here. When people began asking for it in English, he changed over. It ran until things turned mainly digital, and then my father began publishing books instead." She sighs. "It's...probably not sustainable. Most of my employees work from home now, and this isn't their only job. We're struggling to pay authors their royalties without compromising the editorial staff. And my COO has been...challenging, I suppose is the right term." She straightens her back. "But you came here to ask about Saul, so enough of my drama. What did you want to know?"

Connor looks at Luke and then Jory as if they might tell him what to say. When no one else speaks up, he says, "I lost touch with him before he died. I—" He purses his lips. "I don't even know who he was or why he wouldn't have tried to contact me. My mother is...challenging," he says, chuckling at the echo of Danya's words. "She won't explain it to me, maybe because she's not very accepting of who I am."

Danya's shoulders move with the deep breath she takes in. She lets it out noisily and nods. "I'll tell you anything I can, but to be honest, I hadn't seen Saul in quite a while either. He came to see me maybe six months before he died to let me know he was sick. It came as an incredible blow to him. He said something about being sure he'd done all the right things, so maybe G-d was testing him. I'm not sure if he was looking for a cure or some kind of reassurance or what."

Luke glances at Connor in confusion, so Connor explains, "My father had cancer. A form of leukemia."

Luke mutters, "Sounds about right." He pretends his scrapbook page is fascinating while mentally searching for ways to put Jory off.

They pick up one of Luke's markers and twirl it. "Why don't you want to talk about them?"

"Why don't you want to talk about why you were hitchhiking through Erie?" Luke snaps.

Jory grimaces. "Fair enough. Let's do a trade."

"I don't think we know each other well enough for that." Luke hasn't even told Connor. Jax and AJ know the most, and even they have no idea what happened to make him leave.

"Or I could make something up." Jory's toothy grin is wicked. "I could imagine a tragic backstory for you. Hmm... let's see. You got lost in the woods when you were three, where you were raised by wolves for two years before a hunter discovered you. It took you ten years to recover, and you came on this trip so you could finally find your real parents."

"That is incredibly...weird and not even close." Luke can't help laughing.

Rimona giggles, reminding Luke they're sitting at the table too. "I've got one. Your parents are wealthy, and they have their own island. You grew up helping them run a tourist resort there, where you learned to surf. You were going to become a champion, but a tragic accident left you hospitalized for months. Now you're writing a memoir about it."

Luke shakes his head. "Where do you two get this stuff?"

Jory taps the side of their head. "Right here. Now, are you sick of this and gonna tell us something real, or should we go on?"

Luke sighs and looks past Jory to the map on the wall. It's a long trip, and he figures he might as well give them something or he'll be stuck in the RV with them pestering him for miles and miles.

Danya continues, "About a year or so before that, he sent me his 'memoir.'" She uses air quotes. "It was..."

"Bad?" Jory suggests.

"Weird?" Connor asks.

"Messy?" Luke glances at the others when he says this.

"...messy. Yes. That's a good word for it." Danya nods at Luke. "It would take a lot of work to get it into shape, and I sincerely wasn't sure what I'd find when I read it in its entirety. Saul was prone to romanticizing everything, even when he was the one who had done wrong." She reaches out and takes Connor's hand, giving it a squeeze.

"Did you end up finishing it?" Luke surprises even himself when he asks.

"Yes." Now she pinches the bridge of her nose under her small, wire-framed glasses. "It was still a disaster in editing terms, but Saul had some remarkable insight into why our family acted in certain ways."

From Connor's expression, Luke can see he both wants to know and doesn't. He shifts so his leg presses against Connor's under the table. He feels the movement when Jory does the same on his other side.

Danya taps her fingers on the table. "This could take a while. Do you want to get some lunch and have a look at what he sent me?"

"All right," Connor agrees.

"Good. I'll have my assistant call for something and pick it up. She can join us too, since she knows as much as I do about the whole thing."

Danya rises from the table and exits the conference room, leaving the others to stare after her in silence.

✦✦✦✦

Half an hour later, they're all back in the conference room with sandwiches from the kosher deli around the corner.

Luke is about to reach for the only thing he recognizes—the pastrami—when Connor puts a hand on his arm.

"Try one of the others," he suggests as he nabs the pretzel bagel that looks like it has some kind of fish on it.

"Which one?" Luke asks.

Connor points to the toasted wheat bread. "That one. It's avocado, tomato, and tofu."

Luke pulls the wrapper closer. Jory's grabbed the pastrami, and Luke's not sure what's in the ones the others have taken. He bites into it, and he's instantly in heaven. He closes his eyes while he chews, only opening them again when he hears soft laughter. Flushing, he swallows and tries to smile.

"It's my favorite deli," Katri, Danya's assistant, says then winks. "It had better be, seeing as my parents own it."

Everyone laughs this time. Even though they have serious business ahead, it feels relaxed. Danya and Katri talk more about the publishing company and what's been happening, the "drama" alluded to earlier. Another publishing house has been angling to take them over and absorb their debt, which Danya's COO has been pushing for. Danya wants to work on better marketing and internal decisions.

"I don't want to be at odds with him," Danya concludes. "But we can't resolve it like this. I'm not sure what to do. All I know is that something feels off in the way he's pressuring me on this. But he hasn't done anything wrong, and I can't justify relieving him of his duties, temporarily or permanently." She crumples her sandwich wrapper. "All right. Let's get to work on Saul's manuscript."

She opens her laptop and pulls up the document. The first thing Luke notices is that it's formatted oddly. Even he can see it, and he doesn't have much experience. He wonders what else is in there that Danya would have to fix before it could be released to the public.

"Are you still planning to publish it?" Connor asks.

"I wasn't, no. I was going to try to contact you to see what you wanted to do with it. But you called me, so I figured we'd discuss it then. And here we are." She turns the screen all the way so Connor can read it. "It's written like poetry, for the most part, which is fine. I've had some excellent memoirs come through that way. We had one out last year that was entirely in verse form, and we had one that we turned into an audiobook right away because we didn't want to lose the spoken word rhythm. This, however, is not any of that."

Luke tries to make sense of what's on the screen, but it looks to him like Connor's father was mostly rambling. He sits back and lets Connor scroll through it by himself. Luke can't tell from Connor's changing expressions what he thinks of it, other than that his brows seem permanently drawn in as he reads.

"I don't know if I understand half of this," Connor says. "Some of it reads like his personal opinion on politics, and some of it is disjointed stories about his childhood. It's similar to what he left me, but not the same stuff."

Danya nods. "Do you know anything about our family history?"

"Only what I learned from Sylvia and Hy. Which is to say, not that much."

"It would probably help if I sent you some information. I'm not the family's archivist, and I'm also not the last person your father spoke to. Come to think of it, I'm not even sure who that would be."

Connor says, "I'm on my way there. I guess Dad took the same trip I did, sometime before he died."

"The nearest I can figure is that your father thought he was being watched. By the government? By someone else? I don't know. Before you ask, I doubt it's true."

"So..." Connor pauses. "You think he was paranoid?"

"Or confused or lonely and making things up. I honestly couldn't say. All I know is that I didn't publish this, and I'm not going to. He was angry with me, and he said if I wouldn't, he'd do it himself. He never got around to it, to my knowledge. I looked for it online, and I didn't find anything."

The room falls silent. Luke isn't sure what to say to reassure Connor, who looks upset. It's a lot to take in, and Luke wonders if he would handle things any better in the same situation. Before he can make a move, Rimona reaches out to put a hand on top of Connor's. They address Danya.

"Would it be possible to send this to Connor so he can read through it later? I'm not sure I'd be able to sort through all that in one short meeting, if it were me."

Connor's shoulders relax, and Danya agrees. She pulls her laptop back toward her, and a few clicks later, she closes it up.

"How about you let me finish out my day here, and then we can get together again for dinner? Our family is so scattered from one coast to the other that I've never met most of my cousin's children. I'd love the chance to catch up and find out more about all of you." She smiles and rises from her seat.

"Sure." Connor's return smile is tense, but some of the edge has disappeared from his expression. "You want to text me when you're ready?"

"Absolutely."

When Connor stands, Danya comes over and wraps him in a hug. She shakes hands with Luke and Jory, hugs Zakhi and Rimona, and then she and Katri head back to her office. Connor stands frozen, as if even the act of taking out his phone and calling for a ride is too much.

Jory holds out their hand. "If you give me your phone, I'll get us a ride."

Still mute, Connor does as he's asked then doesn't wait for the others before he heads for the door. Luke looks to Jory, who only tilts their chin to indicate they should follow.

Chapter 18

BACK IN THE RV, Connor begins cleaning. None of them have been particularly sloppy, with Jory keeping all their things in the upper bunk and Luke not wanting Connor to have to keep after him to pick up. Luke's not sure what Connor is tidying, aside from some stray wrappers that ended up on the floor after their last stop.

Rimona stops him and puts their arms around him. Connor leans in, and Zakhi comes to stand with them. Luke looks on, at a loss for his own role in this. He's startled by the hand on his shoulder.

"Your man wants some space," Jory murmurs.

"But—"

Jory pinches Luke's lips closed. "He'll talk to us. I mean, there are how many more miles we'll be riding together? He doesn't have a choice. Let him process this his own way. We'll go for a walk. He needs his family right now."

His real family. Not someone like Luke, who hasn't been close with Connor in years. Luke wishes he knew what it was like to have people like Zakhi and Rimona. He gives them all one last look, in time to see Rimona lead Connor to the kitchenette table. Then he follows Jory out of the RV.

Luke has no idea where they'll go. They're in a campsite, not the recreation area, and it's not as if there's a whole lot to do there. He did see a lodge store by the rental office, and the view is pretty along Lake Michigan. So he agrees to the walk, if for no other reason than that Jory wouldn't let him stay by the RV even if he argued for the next hour about it.

As they stroll, Luke says, "You know, in the last few days, I've seen three of the Great Lakes. That's three more than I've seen in my entire life."

"Seriously?"

"Yeah. We didn't travel a lot when I was a kid. Not more than a few hours to see family. When I came to Philadelphia, I hitched rides." He doesn't add a comment about Jory's travels.

"Huh. Well, I've lived in or near Erie for most of my life. I've been up to New York, but not much of anywhere else."

Luke kicks at a few stray sticks on their path. "I saw the Atlantic Ocean and Niagara Falls too."

"I've never been to either."

They're quiet as they follow the road around the loop toward the campground entrance. Luke figures that'll be his chance to get some new postcards. He's not sure what he'll write to Jax about this time. It feels too raw, not like the fun they had in Buffalo or Cleveland.

After a while, Luke says, "He's not my man, you know."

"Aren't you and Connor..." Jory twirls their hand in a way Luke understands to mean they're asking what kind of relationship Luke has with him.

"No."

"You were awfully quick to answer that. I mean, you're sharing a room and all, and I've heard some...sounds. At night. I guess I assumed a few things."

"Well, you were wrong," Luke snaps. He regrets it and tries to smooth things over. "I get dreams sometimes. Not good ones, but not always nightmares, not exactly. I don't want to be alone in a strange place."

"I see." Jory doesn't look quite like they believe Luke, but they don't ask.

Luke presses on anyway. "We sort of were. You know." He waves his hand in an imitation of Jory's "together" move.

"Gee, I'm shocked." Jory's smile is wry, and it makes Luke chuckle softly.

"It was a long time ago. Things are better this way."

"Are they?"

The question surprises Luke. He doesn't see anything out of place in the way he's renewed his friendship with Connor, but maybe it looks different to someone on the outside.

"Well, they aren't worse. There's nothing wrong with being close friends with someone."

"Fair point."

There's another long silence, during which Luke thinks it's taking longer than it should to walk out from the campsite. He fills the emptiness by asking, "What about you?"

"What about me?"

"Are you 'you know.'" Luke uses air quotes this time. "Someone you're on your way to see. Is that why you needed the ride?"

Jory stops walking abruptly. "Already told you I was getting away. The rest is none of your business."

The momentum carried Luke, so he's gone a few paces farther and has to turn around. "And you think it's your business to ask about me? Last I checked, we were just the people who offered to get you out of Erie. But you still haven't told us anything about where you're going or what you want from us."

"Nothing," Jory says. "I don't want nothing from you. I'll tell you what. You quit grilling me, and I'll leave it alone about what it sounds like you're up to behind that curtain at night."

"Nothing," Luke echoes. "Like I already told you."

"Then we're square. No one is doing anything. I'll let you know when we get where I'm going."

Luke sighs heavily. "Fine. Now, can we get to that convenience store? I need to see if they have postcards."

"For that cutie you keep writing to, right?" Jory winks, and Luke rolls his eyes.

"Yeah. They're the one. More nothing, as you said."

"Right." Jory grins now, the vague argument lying on the side of the road as the store finally comes in sight.

****

When Luke and Jory return from the camp store, the RV nearly sparkles with how clean it is. Connor's laptop is on the kitchenette table, but it's closed. He's on the bench seat, his arms folded next to the laptop and his head resting on them. He looks up when Luke sits across from him.

Jory is outside, smoking, after sending Luke in and inviting Zakhi and Rimona out. Jory wanted to give Luke and Connor some privacy. Luke's not sure Connor cares, but he appreciates the gesture himself. He puts his hand on Connor's arm.

"Are you okay?"

"I don't know." Connor's eyes are red, but he doesn't cry now.

Luke waits for a moment, but Connor doesn't say anything else. So Luke closes the emotional gap between them. "When I was eight," he begins, "I spent a summer with one of my older brothers. My mother was...sick. My sister came with me for a little while, but she went back home to help take care of the youngest two."

"Jesus," Connor mutters. "Remind me again, how many of you were there?"

"Sixteen all together, including my parents."

"And here I thought my mother's Catholic family was huge."

"You gonna let me finish?" Luke's mouth is dry. He's never told anyone about what happened to Esther. It felt like it would be a betrayal of her trust. He senses now that Connor needs something, though.

"Yeah. Sorry. Why were you with your brother?"

"My father believed it was time for me to start learning how to work in our family's construction business. Be a man." Luke says it as casually as he can, but he notes the way Connor finally understands. "I tried to keep them from sending Esther, which is why she went home after only a short time. Something happened to Esther once before, when she went to chaperone my brother with the woman he was courting. I think...she never really said specifics, but I think our sister-in-law's brother molested her."

"Fucking hell."

"I know. I didn't tell you that to get you worked up. I'm saying that she only ever told me, as far as I know, and she didn't give any details. I never told anyone because I was scared either she'd be mad or they would. Whatever shit you found out today, don't hide it."

Connor scrubs his face. "I always thought my father didn't want to see me, so I didn't make the effort either. When I read his garbage 'memoir,' there's so much I realized I never knew. He was scared. Like, all the time. Some shit happened when he was a kid, and now I know why he never let me go see his parents. They were older when he was born, and they both died by the time I was in high school."

"What happens to us when we're kids sticks with us." Luke sniffles. He doesn't mean to take anything away from what Connor's telling him, but he feels the pain of both his and Connor's histories acutely.

And then Connor's crying, his face in his hands. Luke slides closer and puts his arms around him, opening his own wounds enough for the two of them to weep together. They hold each other until the tears slow.

That's where Jory finds them a few minutes later when they re-enter the RV, smelling of the cigarette they've just consumed. Luke wipes his eyes with the hem of his shirt.

Jory wrinkles their nose and glances around until they spot a box of tissues. They politely place it on the table, and Connor takes three.

"You fellas all good?"

"No," Connor says. At least he's honest. "But I will be. Why don't you sit." He glances at Luke, who nods. "I guess I might as well explain it to you too."

"It's your call," Jory says, but they sit anyway.

"My father's grandparents left Germany in the thirties. People they knew were being sent to Dachau. It was harder and harder to leave the country, but they managed. I gather Hy's grandparents had to escape by hiding, but that was almost a decade later. My father's writings are jumbled, but he has all of that documented pretty clearly. It reads more like his notes than like a narrative, but it's in there."

"Go on," Jory says. They're leaning across the table, eyes on Connor, listening intently.

Connor runs a hand through his hair, curling his fingers around the strands. "They didn't do it on purpose, but they raised my father's father with a lot of fear. He did the same to his children. His mother grew up in a similar way. No one meant to hurt anyone else. It's generational trauma, passed from fathers to sons and mothers to daughters for decades. My father..." Connor stumbles, choking on his words a little. He clears his throat. "He tried his best to protect me. He wanted me to know the generous, loving spirit of his faith, but my mother wouldn't allow it. She..." He can't finish.

Luke reaches for one hand and Jory the other, the same way they'd pressed against him when Danya presented the manuscript. It doesn't matter that Connor is too upset to continue. They will surround him like a protective bubble until he's all right again.

Softly, Jory says, "I think that's enough for now."

Connor's body language agrees. "There's got to be more to his story than this. Something I'm missing still. He named the things in his life that led to leaving Mom and me, but he didn't explain what he did during his last years. And I still don't understand why Danya refused to publish it. His 'conspiracy theories,' as she put it, aren't exactly unfounded. He was raised to have a deep distrust of people's motivations."

"Maybe you could ask her more at dinner," Luke suggests. He pulls out his phone. "We're supposed to meet her in an hour."

"Shit!" Connor slides off the bench. "Well, let's get moving, then."

****

It's raining again by the time a car shows up. Zakhi and Rimona return from wherever they've been, but they decline dinner with the others. Luke suspects they need time alone, and he encourages Jory to join him and Connor.

When they return to Danya's office, she's with someone they haven't met. A man. They're arguing, but it doesn't seem hostile, only passionate. Luke, Connor, and Jory wait politely in the main part of the office for them to finish in Danya's private one.

Katri pops out of the kitchen with a trash bag. Luke hadn't noticed much about her appearance before, but he has a better look now. She's a petite, curvy woman with long, dark hair braided down her back. She has a septum ring and one in her left nostril. She's in all black, with impossibly high heels. He wonders how she functions at work in them.

Her bright-red-painted mouth curves into a warm smile when she sees them. "Hi, guys!" Her gaze lingers on Jory.

Luke stifles a laugh when he returns her greeting. The others do the same, and Katri leads them to a small lounge to wait for Danya. In a few minutes, Danya arrives, looking ruffled.

"Sorry to keep you waiting. I was talking with my partner in crime." She laughs, but it's thin and tired. Putting up her hand before anyone can comment, she says, "We'll work it out. We always do."

"Good thing, or none of us would be able to go home at night." Katri appears to ignore the ferocious glare Danya gives her.

"What do you mean?" Luke asks.

Katri looks at Danya, who gestures for her to go ahead. "Running a publishing company takes a lot of work. Sometimes it can end up feeling as if it's all we do."

"What she's trying to say is that she's on Karl's side. We need the help, and merging with another company could be the leg up we need."

Connor says, "But you don't agree."

"No. But I can tell you about it over dinner."

Danya has chosen a place in a different part of town, one where the buildings are less worn and there's more traffic. It's cozy inside the little Italian restaurant, warm and inviting. Luke inhales the scent of garlic and tomatoes and smiles. It reminds him of AJ, who learned to cook from his Nonna. Luke's happiness fades when he thinks about those long gone days. Another person in his life who has moved on to the next thing.

Connor bumps Luke's shoulder with his own, and Luke snaps out of his haze of memories. The host seats them, and they chatter about nothing important while they peruse the menus.

Once they've ordered, Danya folds her hands on the table. "I promised to explain everything, but I think that might be too much. My publishing company has a long history with the one that wants to take us over. We were rivals back when my father still owned it. Eventually, we negotiated, at my request. Karl was supposed to do it. In fact, he was the one

Dad originally had planned to take over the business. But I went in his place, and he's never quite gotten over it."

Luke studies Danya, considering. "What aren't you telling us?"

Danya laughs. "Karl's my brother."

"And Katri..."

"Is my wife."

"Well, now everything makes much more sense," Jory says.

"Right. Anyway, Karl's probably right. Katri too. But I swore if it was the last thing I did, I would never let anyone make us fold. So here we are, at an impasse." The server sets glasses of water on the table, and Danya takes a sip. "But we aren't here to discuss my business woes. You wanted to understand more about why I rejected your father's manuscript."

Connor purses his lips, leaning back in the booth. His gaze doesn't leave Danya's, and Luke can't tell if he's challenging her or merely thinking how to answer. Jory is looking at her napkin, and Luke bounces back and forth between Connor and Danya.

At last, Connor says, "No. It's your decision whether you want to publish something, and I don't need all your reasons why. My trip was for the purpose of understanding who my father was. I hardly knew him, other than all the times my mother yelled at him on the phone, blaming him for..."

He doesn't finish the thought, but Luke knows. Connor has said it before. Once, when they were back in high school, Connor almost boasted to AJ about his mother calling him hateful names. The depth of Connor's pain terrified Luke then.

Danya says, "I think it would help you if I explained." She reaches out for Connor's hand, and he hesitates but takes it.

"Go on," he says.

"His parents were assimilationists. Do you know what that means?"

Connor nods. "They thought their best chance of survival was to blend in."

"My parents disagreed. They loved our culture. I won't spread fear that, underneath, carries the view it's our own fault for being too different. The way forward isn't to hide in our anger but to do something about it." She pauses, and Luke can see there is more she wants to say but either can't or doesn't know how.

"You think he was hiding?"

"No. His parents were the 'suffer in silence' type, and I don't know if he ever learned to express himself better."

"He did, though," Connor tells her. "When I was little."

"Life doesn't always follow a straight path. Who knows what happened?" She raises one shoulder slightly and takes a sip of her wine. "Karl and Katri both wanted to publish it. Katri does our acquisitions, and she saw something in it that I somehow am failing to."

There's an extended silence after that, during which the server brings their food. They eat, and no one speaks for so long it becomes uncomfortable. Luke shoves the food around on his plate, wishing there were something he could do for Connor. They've had such different lives. He wonders if Connor feels he's gotten his answers or if there's more out there he can learn.

Connor is finally the one to speak, echoing what Luke has wondered. "Do you think this is all there is for me to learn about him?"

Danya sets down her fork. "Only you can answer that. I've told you everything I know."

"If you're not going to publish his book, do I have your permission to do what I want with it?"

"Of course. I can even give you that in writing if you like."
She pauses. "But, Connor, if you can unlock its secrets, then
come back and see me. We'll talk."

"Sure." Connor glances at Luke and Jory. "That's enough
of the heavy stuff. Why don't we relax, and you can tell us
more about yourself."

Danya smiles. "Well, if we're not talking about my job—
and I'd really rather not—how about I tell you how Katri
and I met?"

*※※※

They lie in bed later, side by side with the small space in
between them. It feels like a cavern. Luke thinks about Jax,
picturing their beautiful face. The ache is even stronger after
today. He's turned on by the memories of the last time they
were together, tangled up on the floor among the boxes of
Jax's belongings. He slides his hand down, gently pressing,
not rubbing. It's been ages since he masturbated, given the
lack of privacy. It feels strange to rub one out with Connor
two feet away.

With a muffled grunt, he rolls over to face away from
Connor. Sleep won't come, whether due to arousal or the
parade of thoughts in his head. He misses Jax, and everything
about Connor's family history is sending a current of anxiety
through Luke about his own. He still hasn't told Connor or
anyone else the truth, and every mile of roadway brings them
closer to finding out. Luke squeezes his eyes shut as if that
might turn off both his brain and his penis.

There's a soft sigh behind him. "Lukey?"

"Yeah?" he tries to sound sleepier than he feels.

"You awake?"

"Sort of." He mumbles it into the pillow.

"I...can we put the extra mattress thing between
the beds?"

Luke turns over. "Why?"

"Just...please?"

It takes some shifting, but they finally have the bed arranged as a queen size instead of twins. When they settle back in, Connor shifts closer. Without thinking, Luke reaches for his hand as Connor turns off the flashlight.

It's hot in the RV without the air conditioning. This park doesn't have electric, so Connor's using the battery. To save energy, he's only running what's necessary. It's a good battery, souped up over the years his family used it. But Connor's wise, and he prefers to conserve. The result is the two of them are now sweaty from rearranging the bed.

Luke kicks the sheet down, and Connor does the same. Their hands are still joined, even though Luke is sure his palm must feel clammy. Connor's, in contrast, is cool and dry.

"Thanks," Connor says.

"Was it a dream?" Luke thought Connor was asleep before, but now he's not sure.

Connor pulls his hand away. "I was going to lie and tell you yes. The truth is, I don't know what's wrong with me."

"It's okay." Luke wishes he had something more profound to offer, some words that will make Connor feel better or have a different outlook on how the day went. Instead, he inches closer.

Connor's huffed breath sounds like he's letting out the rest of his anguish. He rests his head on Luke's chest. Luke pauses then hesitantly reaches up a hand to run his fingers through Connor's thick, dark hair.

Luke's turned on again but for different reasons now. They didn't touch like this back when Luke had those nightmares. Connor was so careful with him. Now he's reaching out to Luke, and he isn't hesitating to rest in Luke's arms. Unthinking, Luke angles to press a kiss to Connor's head.

Connor looks up, his mouth a startled O. There's a pause, during which something shifts. His gaze turns pleading, and Luke can't help it. Too much time has passed since he's been with anyone, and his body hums with sensory starvation.

If he blinked, he'd have missed the instant they both moved. They're kissing now, fierce and hungry. Luke's trying to keep the sound low, even though this is what Jory already believes they're doing. He both wants more and he doesn't. They never made it past this stage when they were together. Connor was so careful, so gentle. Never pressing. Never allowing them to release their collective pasts.

Connor's tongue in his mouth feels good the way it rubs against his. Luke gasps, pulling Connor closer. He feels as if he's been parched, and all of a sudden, someone's given him water. It's a flood, and he's being pulled under. Connor makes a small, needy sound, and then his lips are by Luke's ear.

"God, Lukey." His gasping breaths puff against Luke's cheek. "Jesus."

Luke tries to find Connor's lips again, but Connor remains where he is, his face turned just out of reach. He kisses Luke's earlobe and retreats so their eyes meet. Luke puts a hand on Connor's face, his beard rough under Luke's fingertips.

"Are you okay?" he asks.

"I'm sorry," Connor says, and he does sound genuinely regretful. "I can't do this."

Luke huffs. Connor has every right to decide this isn't what he wants, but Luke can't help wondering if it's more of the same bullshit left over from Greg. "It was five years ago. I'm not going to break," Luke says.

Connor rolls over and tugs on his hair. "I know that."

"Then what's the problem? Is it Jory? They already think this is what we're doing."

"No." Connor snorts. "And of course they'd think that. We share a bedroom, and we were doing so even before they were here."

"Don't change the subject."

Connor sits up. "Luke, you have no idea how much I want to. But not now. Not here, like this, when..." He shakes his head. "I don't want to have pity sex."

"What if it's not? What if it's, you know, sex between two people who haven't had any in a few weeks?"

"Months," Connor mutters. "At least on my end." He draws up his knees and rests his chin on them. "I mean it's a bad idea because I'm a wreck after today. I don't want to use you to avoid my problems, and I don't want you trying to comfort me that way." Softer, he adds, "We're not a couple."

Luke understands at last why Connor wouldn't even try after Greg. It was never about Luke but about Connor's own view of what would be healthy for himself. "What do you need?"

"You," Connor says. "Just you. Here with me."

They lie down again, and Luke wraps Connor in his arms. It's still too warm, but Luke doesn't mind. Rain drums on the roof, lulling them both to sleep.

Then

IT TOOK SAM a while before he kissed Luke again. He asked this time. What he actually said, while they lay on their backs looking up at the changing foliage, was, "I'd like to kiss you."

Luke turned his head and discovered Sam was watching him. He was tilted slightly away, as if afraid of Luke's reaction. Instead of doing what he probably should have and saying no, Luke nodded.

It wasn't that he didn't want to. He'd wanted to try it out since the time Sam broke his nose, but he was neither brave nor stupid enough to bring it up. He settled for living with the sparkling-cider feeling when in Sam's presence and promised himself it was plenty. It was not.

Lately, he'd been thinking about it at night as he lay in bed, the most secret of his thoughts hidden from everyone else. And now here he was, leaves in his hair and his back smudged with dirt, and Sam inches away from giving him what he'd longed for. So of course he said yes.

The kiss was sloppy, neither of them sure what they were doing. It was also one of the most wonderful things Luke had ever experienced. They practiced for a while, getting better at it. The sparkling-cider feeling made even the tips of Luke's fingers and toes tingle now.

When Sam pulled back, he grinned. "Wow."

"Yeah." After a pause, Luke said, "You're not gonna punch me again, are you?"

Sam's soft chuckle was awkward. "No."

Luke took his camera out of the handmade bag he still carried everywhere. He aimed up into the trees, capturing the blue sky between the branches and the red and gold leaves. Beside him, Sam sat up.

"Lemme see that thing."

"No!"

"C'mon, please?" Sam reached for it, laughing.

Luke held it out of reach. "Why d'you want it?"

"I'll show you."

Sam waited with his hand out, and Luke hesitantly put the camera in it. Sam shifted away and focused the lens on Luke. He snapped a picture. Luke covered his face with one hand and held the other out to block the camera as Sam took another photo.

"Stop!" Luke cried, but he was laughing now too. "What'd you do that for?"

"Wanted to remember this forever," Sam said. He shrugged like it was casual, but there was something far away in his tone.

"Okay." It made sense to Luke.

When he got the pictures back, he would give these to Sam. Luke didn't need them for his scrapbooks, and it was Sam who'd said he wanted to remember the day.

"Better than the first time," Sam muttered. He glanced sideways at Luke, who put a hand over his nose.

"Definitely."

"Gotta get back. I think lunch is almost over."

Sam scrambled to his feet and hauled Luke up. The cool, autumn breeze ruffled Luke's hair, and Sam pulled a leaf from it. He handed it to Luke. Putting it in his pocket, Luke decided this would go in his scrapbook. No one would question an ordinary boxelder leaf. They walked back to the co-op, bumping shoulders and brushing hands.

Chapter 19

NEITHER LUKE NOR Connor says anything in the morning about the kiss the previous night. It's left in the RV campsite along with their tire tracks. Connor checks them out, and the others all stay in the RV. Jory is looking out the window and with a small jump, they yank the curtain closed.

"What?" Luke asks. He's writing his next postcard to Jax, having left it last night because he was too tired after dinner with Danya.

"Nothing. Just got surprised by a...bee."

Jory is already weird enough that Luke doesn't feel a need to ask more questions. He finishes the postcard and tells them he's going out to mail it at the store. When he steps down from the RV, he catches sight of a person through the trees. Their eyes lock, and Luke shivers. It reminds him of his brothers chasing him through the woods behind the homeschool co-op.

Once he's mailed the postcard, he turns to look at the scenery. He's already taken a picture of Lake Michigan, but now he takes one of the campground. Something to remember where he's been.

Connor emerges from the camp office, and the two of them enter the RV again. Luke is restless, and there's an undercurrent of tension now between himself and Connor that wasn't there before. He doesn't know what to do with it. They have no privacy to talk, not with three other people along. Luke huffs. He's not sure it would be any better to be alone with Connor anyway.

"Where to now?" Jory asks, breaking Luke out of his funk.

"Chicago. It's only an hour or so from here, but we'll be meeting my father's cousin Wade and bringing Zakhi and Rimona to their new home."

They pull out of the RV park and head for the highway. Jory's offered to drive, so Connor sits up front. He still doesn't entirely trust Jory. That leaves Luke in the rear seats with the others. He works on his scrapbook, aside from adding the photos. Connor is flipping stations on the radio, and Luke chuckles when he hears both Connor and Jory singing along to the Rascal Flats version of "Life Is a Highway." They are more alike than either of them wants to admit.

Luke tunes out for a bit, looking at the map on the wall. Connor forgot to change the Indiana peg, so Luke gets up and does it. He settles back into his seat and listens in on the conversation in the front now that the song is over.

"That makes no sense," Jory says. "They're underwater. How in the world does it make sense to have a fucking bonfire?"

"It doesn't have to make sense. That's not the point. It's about the commentary, not the laws of science or whatever."

"You can have social commentary and humor while still obeying basic principles. Next you're going to argue about how it's fine that a character doesn't need pants but does need to cover his nonexistent genitals with a towel because it's 'social commentary.'"

Connor huffs. "Keep your hands on the wheel, and yes, I think that is saying something about our society."

Luke is about to return to his scrapbook when Connor yells, "Look out!"

Clanging metal. A bump. The RV swerves toward the shoulder. They've hit something, but Luke has no idea what. Jory pulls all the way into the shoulder.

"What was that?" Luke asks. His stomach is still in his throat.

"No idea." Connor's shaking. "Something was in the road."

"Is everyone okay?" Jory asks.

Luke is unsteady, but everything seems to be intact. He wonders how much damage there is to the RV. Connor unbuckles and goes to check, Zakhi in tow. A few minutes later, they're back.

"Busted tire—must've run over whatever it was. Some dents. Otherwise, it looks okay. I'll call for some help—"

"You don't know how to fix the tire on one of these?" Jory asks.

"Not by myself, no."

They roll their eyes. "Seriously? I'll help. Come on." They motion to Zakhi.

"How in the hell do you know how to do this?"

"Wouldn't you like to know? Just come with me, and we'll fix it."

The three of them jump down, and Luke sits back in his seat. He feels useless. It's the same old story, the way he can't figure out how to do things the right way round. The way his father described him: all thumbs, couldn't hit a nail if it was a mile wide, no useful skills without a camera in his hands. He frowns.

Then his gaze rests on his scrapbook. He pulls out the old one, with all the photos in it, and flips through the pages. He smiles. There are a lot of Jax, which isn't surprising. Jax is incredibly photogenic. They're smiling in almost all of them, unlike most of their professional portfolio. In many of Jax's posed photos, they were instructed to look sexy or brooding. But in Luke's pictures, they're relaxed and happy, so much like their real self. Luke can see the ones where Jax was being playful, a teasing tilt to their head or the way their eyes focused. In others, Jax is shy—like the one where they're laughing but have their hand up as if to block the camera.

"Who's that?" Rimona asks. "They're beautiful."

"My friend Jax. We lived together for a while, and now they're in Boston to be a professional dancer."

Luke rotates the book so Rimona can see better. His throat is tight as he turns more pages. There are older ones of AJ and a few from after he met Adam. There's a year missing when AJ was going through a hard time after a messy breakup with an abusive girlfriend. Luke didn't even ask to take photos then, but part of him wishes he had for AJ's sake. The ones after he met Adam are happier, but Luke can still see the reservation in his posture.

He's looking at the wedding photos when Connor, Zakhi, and Jory climb back into the RV. They're disheveled but otherwise, they appear to have bonded over the tire incident. Zakhi takes over the driving. Luke's about to close his book when Jory sits down.

"Whoa, did you take those?" They point to a page of photos from the reception.

"Yeah. Is the tire all good?"

"It's fine now." Jory waves dismissively. "Tell me more about this." They tap the book.

Luke glances past Jory to where Connor is giving Zakhi directions. "Um...it's a scrapbook."

"I don't mean that. These pictures are gorgeous. You have a real eye, you know that?"

"I guess." Luke wants to pull the book closer, to hide it. He doesn't like anyone else to see his work.

Jory doesn't miss a thing. "I'm sorry. I shouldn't have butted in on your personal stuff." They push the book toward Luke. "If you make some space, we could play cards."

"Okay." Luke closes the book and takes out the Uno deck. He's not in the mood for something he has to think too hard about.

"Hey, Connor!" Jory yells as Luke begins to shuffle the cards.

"Yeah?"

"How long do you think it'll be?"

"Dunno. Forty-five minutes or so? Wade said when I called just now that he's on his way to a protest, and we can join him there if we like."

"A...protest..." Jory mutters. "Yeah...I'm gonna stay away from that mess."

Luke wonders why but doesn't ask. "That could be interesting."

Connor laughs. "Only if we get arrested. But sure, we can go see what it's all about."

With that, he focuses on the road, and Luke turns his attention to the game.

❊❊❊

It turns out that by "protest," Wade—whoever he was—didn't mean an event where they chained themselves to a building or blocked traffic or resisted arrest. He meant a rally in the park, where a guest speaker is at the microphone, talking about climate change. There probably aren't more than a hundred and fifty people here, although Luke considers it a good turnout, given how it's started to drizzle. He's glad Connor made sure everyone had umbrellas before they left the RV park.

They stand in the rain for fifteen minutes while Connor texts with Wade, trying to figure out each other's locations. At last, Connor shoves his phone in his pocket and motions for the rest of them to follow him.

Wade is not at all what Luke is expecting. He supposes when he heard Connor say he's an environmentalist, he envisioned someone like the pictures of Jesus in his old schoolbooks. He knows that's a stereotype, but he can't help it. The image is shattered the instant Connor spots him and waves.

The man who waves back is big and burly with a head full of curly, black hair. He does indeed have a full, black beard, which parts as he grins to reveal straight, white teeth. He's wearing tan cargo pants and a forest-green polo shirt. The moment Connor is close enough, Wade grabs him in an enormous bear hug, tight enough Connor lets out a grunt.

"Connor! Welcome!" Wade turns to the others. "You must be Luke, who Connor told me about on the phone. And...well, my goodness. Zakhi!" Another round of crushing hugs, then he addresses Jory. "And you...I don't recognize."

"Just a friend," they say. "Grabbing a ride with these guys on my way out west."

"You missed the keynote speaker, but there will be music and more later," Wade tells them. "If you're game to stay, I'll help you get Zakhi and Rimona settled in their new digs, and then we'll talk. I hear you have some questions for me, and I might have something for you as well."

"Oh?" Connor's interest is clearly piqued.

"Later, later," Wade says, laughing. "C'mon. They're going to talk about responsible purchasing, and there are some booths set up with local goods. Zakhi, Rimona, you'll be interested in this."

Luke has no idea if they will or won't be, but Wade is nothing if not enthusiastic. He leads them to the booths, all the while explaining to them what it is he does with this group. Apparently, he's one of the organizers for the event. Luke looks around at the crowd, and for the first time, he notices that it's mainly youth. There are some adults, many of whom seem to be group leaders. It's an interesting mix. There are some religious groups of various types, bearing symbols of their faiths on their posters. Others have the name of their organizations, like Youth for a Clean America, on banners.

They're not right in the middle of Chicago but instead in one of the surrounding suburbs. It's not far from where Zakhi and Rimona will be doing their future work. They're now explaining it to Wade, and Luke senses a similarity in their approach. It makes him wonder about the ways families are alike and if it's possible there are things written into one's genetic code or if it's primarily through nurture. Wade and Sylvia are blood relations, but Zakhi became part of their family in a different way. Perhaps it isn't blood but something else entirely that draws people to the same goals.

Luke doesn't have time to wonder more about it because somehow, he's become separated from the others. It's not that large a park, and there aren't so many people he wouldn't be able to spot them again if he tried. But the fact that he hadn't been paying attention to where they went and now has to search makes him panic.

He turns on the spot, but all he sees are strangers. His heart hammers, and he tries to squeeze out from between the people who are pressing in on him to get to the booths. At last, he wriggles his way out on the far side and cranes his neck. He still can't see the others.

It might be better to stay put and let them find him, but he isn't thinking clearly now. He darts away from the crowd toward a grove of trees. From there, he hopes to be far enough away to look without being in anyone's way. Before he can do anything, he feels a hand on him and whips around to stare right into the dirt-streaked face of a kid.

"Don't even try it," Luke says. He knows this kid's game. "I don't have anything you want anyway."

"Fuck you," the kid spits. "Wasn't doing anything."

"So you weren't going after whatever you think's in my pocket. Okay, fair enough. Then what do you want?"

The kid's demeanor changes to something approaching charm but not quite hitting the mark. "Maybe I wanted to offer you something."

"You're not old enough," Luke tells him. "And I'm not buying. Look, I'll give you some money, but you're better off if I take you somewhere you can get what you need."

"No. Been there, done that, got the scars to show for it." The kid cranes his neck around Luke. "They have food there. Buy me something, and I'll forget I saw you."

Luke laughs. "You'll forget. Right. Because you weren't the one trying to take my shit." He nods at the booths. "It's vegan, so if you're game for a tofu burger or whatever, I'll treat you."

The kid shrugs. "I'm not picky."

They head back toward the booths. There are two food vendors, and Luke picks the nearest one. While they stand in line, he wants to ask the kid about what made him hide in a park, stealing from people. He could've told the kid he was once in the same position, although he was never bold enough to lift anything right off someone's body. He knows about making offers to strangers too, or simply having them take what they wanted and leaving him with a handful of cash and a lot of regrets.

By the time Luke buys the kid a tofu hot dog with everything, he finally spots Connor and waves. He's about to say something else to the kid, but when he turns around, the kid and his tofu dog are gone. Luke wishes he could've done more or at least given the kid a bit of life advice from one former runaway to another. He figures the kid would've ignored him anyway, so maybe it's just as well.

"There you are!" Connor says. He glances at the food truck and the wallet still in Luke's hand. "You got hungry?"

"No, I..." Luke doesn't want to tell Connor about the boy, but he isn't sure why. "Yeah. I'm starving."

Connor looks confused, but he doesn't question Luke. "Let's eat, then, and Wade's enlisted our help for the afternoon events."

"Cool," Luke says. "Let's do it."

They stand in line again, and Luke can't help looking around to see if he can get one last glimpse of the kid. He's long gone, and Luke's heart squeezes as he wishes the boy well.

Chapter 20

ZAKHI AND RIMONA'S new home is on the opposite side of town from Wade. The houses are smaller and closer together, and there are a lot of rent-controlled apartment complexes. The two of them will be living and working in a row of townhouses similar to Avi and Sylvia's. Inside, it's crowded with boxes and furniture.

For the rest of the afternoon, they help set up the townhouse. By the time they finish, the furniture is in place and the remaining unopened boxes stacked neatly in the table-less dining room. Wade invites everyone to join him at his house afterward. They all pile into his van and hit the road.

Wade lives in an old farmhouse on the far edge of town. He doesn't do any farming, however. He's an art teacher at a local high school, which explains how he knows so many teens. When they step inside, Luke gasps in awe. It looks like every spare inch of the house is hung with paintings. Many of them have abstract nature themes: green things growing up from soil and plants with mouths and vines wrapped around unidentifiable masses. There are also sculptures made from recyclables.

"Did you do all this?" Zakhi asks, sounding as stunned as Luke feels.

"Most of it," Wade says. He waves his hand at a couple of pieces. "Some was done by my students or kids from the climate change group. Go ahead and look around while I get something for us to eat."

As he heads for the kitchen, Luke explores the house. Wade has never married or had children, so there are no photographs of smiling preschoolers or trips with a spouse to tropical destinations. Instead, there are many pictures of Wade with his colleagues, friends, and students. One room of the house is devoted to walls of these memories, photo collages of Wade's life saving the planet and painting his world.

Luke pauses to use the bathroom, and he thinks he shouldn't be surprised that this room, too, is a work of art. It's a mural, a celebration of the cosmos in deep blues and purples and greens. Twinkling lights are built right into the wall, and they are what illuminate the space. The walk-in shower is tiled to match the paint, forming a picture of the planets. It reminds Luke of a sliding puzzle.

He returns to the others and finds dinner is ready. Wade has laid out a simple meal of homemade bread, tomato bean soup, and locally grown fruits and vegetables. They bring their meal to Wade's back porch, large and enclosed with two wooden picnic tables.

Once they're seated, Wade says to Connor, "You said you wanted to know more about your father and the trip he took. What have you found so far?"

"Not as much as I'd like," Connor replies. "I have two fragmented pieces of his writing, and I'm not sure if or how they fit together. Danya thinks he was confused or having a mental breakdown. Avi and Sylvia told me he was homeless for a while but that he was a good and generous man. Hy didn't give me much at all."

Wade nods. "I think he showed each of us a different aspect of himself. After dinner, I have something for you. Meanwhile, I don't know how much help I can be. He stayed here for a couple of months." At the surprised expressions all around the table, Wade shrugs one shoulder. "It happens.

People feel at peace here. I give them time to heal and hope. Sometimes they need to hear something stronger, and that's what I told Saul. I said eventually he would need to move on. Not because I didn't want him here but because I sensed something holding him back. He kept saying he wasn't ready, but I pushed. Maybe I shouldn't have. I don't know if he ever accomplished what he set out to do."

"That's what I'm trying to find out," Connor says. "Did he reach his goal? And what even was it?"

They leave the dishes because Wade is anxious for Connor to see whatever he has. Everyone follows Wade upstairs. Like the rooms Luke has seen so far, these are all full of artwork. He would suggest it's like a museum, except it isn't. There isn't the sterile feel of preserving the work. These are meant to be explored, touched, and known. Wade encourages this as they go, suggesting they feel the paint on the stairwell walls, run their hands along the carved banister, pick up the small figurines in the guest room.

This is where Wade stops. He turns on the light, and they all look around. There's no theme to this place, and some of the paintings are stacked along the wall with old sheets in between them. There is a shelf full of sculptures, carvings, and ceramic figures. On the other side of the room, there are larger mechanical structures on the floor.

"This is work people have done while they lived with me," Wade explains. "Most take it with them, but sometimes they leave it here. I keep it in case they come back for it. After long enough, I find a new home for it, either here or with someone else."

He crosses the room to where an easel is draped with a sheet. He pulls it back to reveal a painting of the solar system. No, Luke realizes on closer inspection. Not this solar system but another one, with two brilliant blue suns. A comet soars at the top. The colors are so vivid, Luke feels as if he could reach out and be pulled into the picture to explore other worlds.

"It's his," Wade says, his voice low.

Connor steps closer but stops as if the painting's suns might burn him. Saul wasn't Luke's father, but even so, Luke feels as if he's standing on the edge of understanding something. If only he could reach a little farther and grasp it. Connor's expression tells Luke he's in the same place.

"I wish I knew what it meant," Connor says.

Wade puts out his hands, palms up. "Who can say? Sometimes the things people let out are obvious." He gestures to a sculpture of a person doubled over in pain. "Other times, not so much. He never explained it to me, but I suspect he intended you to understand it."

Connor stands still, staring at the painting. There's a slight shift in his posture, enough that Luke knows he's on to something and needs time. Luke's about to suggest leaving Connor alone to think about it when Connor snaps out of his trance.

"I'll give it some thought," he says abruptly.

Wade nods. "I thought you might say that. The painting is yours to take. I'd have given it to Saul if he'd returned. Instead, you should have it. I'll wrap it for you."

"Thanks," Connor says absently.

They leave the room, the mood substantially more subdued. The evening is coming to a close, and they need to say goodbye to the others. Wade drives them, leaving Zakhi and Rimona at their new home first.

There are tearful hugs and farewells and see-you-soons on all sides. Rimona holds Luke for a long time, and when they let go, they put their hands on his face. Leaning in, they say, "Take care of him. He needs you."

They slide a paper into Luke's hand. It's an address and phone number, along with another song to add to their playlist: "For Good," from *Wicked*. Luke smiles. He knows that one. Jax used to sometimes sing along with the soundtrack to their favorite musical. Luke likes that Rimona has that in common with Jax.

Wade leaves the rest of them at the RV campsite. He helps Connor find a place to store the painting, and then he too is wishing them well. He tells them not to be strangers and that his place is always open for them to come and find rest. Then he's gone, driving away into the night and leaving Connor, Luke, and Jory all with their own quiet thoughts.

One by one, they enter the RV, Luke last. He pauses at a rustling in the bushes, shuddering and feeling grateful not to be sleeping in a tent. Who knows what wildlife is lurking around. With that thought, Luke steps in and closes the RV door behind him.

❖❖❖❖

It's strangely quiet in the RV as they pull away from the campground. Luke is driving again, and Connor guides him back to I-90 from the passenger seat. Jory is stretched out behind them with a book Luke thinks they got from one of Connor's bins. Connor hasn't even turned on the music.

Luke misses the conversation and card games with Zakhi and Rimona. Without them, the three remaining travelers are at loose ends. It doesn't help that so many things happened in such a short span of time. Connor's hardly paying attention to navigating, staring out the window. Luke isn't sure whether it's good or bad that there's endless roadway ahead of them until their next stop.

He tries once asking what their destination is, and Connor only grunts a response about La Crosse. It's not far, less than five hours' drive. Enough time for one stop to eat lunch and fill up the RV's gas tank. Possibly not enough time for Connor to work through whatever's on his mind.

The rain has started again, the type that spits and splatters and is too much to leave the windshield wipers off but not enough for them to be truly useful. Luke is about to ask Connor to put on the music, if for no other reason than to break the painful silence. Before he has a chance, Connor angles toward him.

"When I was little, my father used to tell me stories," he says. "Stuff he made up, not out of a book. Your family ever do that?"

"No," Luke says. "We read Bible stories and ones about missionaries."

Out of the corner of his eye, Luke sees Jory shift and knows they're listening in. He wonders what sort of childhood they had.

Connor continues. "I suppose it's unusual. I don't remember my mother doing it. She didn't read to me, either. I think...something happened, and she...struggled. My father did a lot of those things."

Luke nods. "My mother was like that after..." He's never explained it before, and somehow, he feels as if he's betraying her to say it now. Still, he wants to know what Connor's thinking, so he says, "My youngest sibling was stillborn. I don't know any more than that, but my mother wasn't the same after."

"I'm glad I'll never have to be pregnant or give birth," Connor remarks. "Seems like it's no picnic. Anyway, maybe something like that happened with Mom. Whatever the reason, it was Dad who told me bedtime stories."

This was going somewhere, but Luke sensed he should poke a little or Connor might stop talking. "What kinds of stories?"

"I don't remember most of them. But there was this one, and I used to ask him to tell me more. About a planet with two blue suns."

"So the painting was for you after all?"

Connor shakes his head. "I don't think so. But I don't know what it means."

They fall silent again, and Luke concentrates on driving. He's grown used to maneuvering the RV now and doesn't require much direction from Connor. The only words they exchange are when Connor tells Luke to pull into a gas station with RV pump access.

It's still raining. Jory disappears behind the convenience store, presumably to smoke. Connor shows Luke how to put gas in the RV and then leaves him, entering the store. While he uses the pump, Luke people-watches. The gas station parking lot is half full, but with the rain, most people are ducking in and out of the store or staying inside their cars.

Because he's distracted, Luke almost misses the movement inside the RV. He catches it briefly out of the corner of his eye, and his heart rate increases. Have they unknowingly brought some kind of wild animal from the last RV park? Luke takes a few deep breaths and replaces the gas pump. He closes the tank and steadies himself before walking toward the store. He doesn't want to enter the RV without backup and possibly a baseball bat.

Connor is emerging from the bathrooms when Luke intercepts him. "Something's inside the RV."

"What do you mean?"

"I saw it moving around."

Jory joins them. "What was moving around?"

"I don't know!" Luke is shaking with both frustration and anxiety. "An animal or something. In the RV."

"Are you sure?" Connor looks skeptical. "I think we'd have noticed if we brought a raccoon with us from the campsite."

"Maybe it's a stray cat," Jory suggests. "Probably would've stayed hidden."

Luke relaxes. They're both likely right. If it's a cat, maybe that's not a bad thing. Luke's never had a pet before, but he likes cats. Convinced by the others it's nothing to worry about, he follows them back to the RV.

Connor turns to them. "On the off chance it's something less...innocent than a cat, we should go in carefully."

He opens the RV door inch by inch. It creaks, and all three of them jump. When nothing happens, Luke breathes a sigh of relief. Maybe it was his imagination after all. They all climb in and then freeze.

There's a boy who looks all of fourteen standing in the kitchenette with a package of cookies in his hand. He's slightly crouched as if he was about to sneak off when the others arrived. Luke stares at his dirty face until awareness dawns.

"You!" he exclaims.

Connor and Jory both turn to Luke. Connor says, "You know this kid?"

"Not...not really, no. He was at the park where we met Wade. I bought him some food, that's all."

"Hey, kid," Jory says. "How'd you end up here?"

The boy scowls and crosses his arms. He's clearly giving nothing up, not even the cookies he's still clutching.

"That's it," Connor says. "We're taking him back." Under his breath, he mutters, "And losing two hours to do it."

"You can't!" the kid blurts. "I won't go."

Connor gestures around him. "We're at a rest stop on the highway. How are you going to keep us from driving you back to Chicago?"

The kid backs toward the RV door. "I'll find another ride."

Jory blocks his path. "Not until you tell us what's going on and how you ended up in here. And how the hell you hid from us for however long you were in here."

"Luggage compartment," the boy says with a one-shoulder shrug. "I..." He looks at each of the others and then his shoulder slump. "I lifted a guy's wallet and followed you all back to the camp. Thought maybe I could find some vacationers to give me a ride. When I saw you were leaving, I hid."

Luke has a feeling that isn't quite all, but he doesn't press. "We can't keep you with us. You're underage."

"I'm sixteen." The boy straightens up. "I know what my rights are, and I can consent to whatever I need."

Connor scoffs. "Try again."

"What?" The boy glares.

"No way are you that old."

"You need to see my ID or something? I'm telling you the truth. I'm just short."

Luke steps closer. Of the three of them, he suspects he has the most experience here. He examines the kid's face, and he sees what made Connor assume the boy was much younger. It isn't his height, though that's probably a factor too. It's how the kid has no facial hair, not even the budding of a caterpillar on his upper lip. He does, however, have a few stray pimples on his forehead and nose. His voice doesn't seem to have begun to change either.

The boy is wearing a baggy T-shirt and sagging cut-off jeans. His dark-brown hair is wild and wavy, sticking up in every direction and badly in need of a trim. His small, bright eyes are the most unusual color Luke has ever seen, amber and framed with thick, dark lashes. He has silver tunnels in his earlobes.

"He's telling the truth," Luke says.

Jory looks the boy up and down. "I'd say so too."

Connor glances between them and then back to the kid. "Fine. Doesn't solve what the hell we're supposed to do with him."

"Take me with you," the boy begs. "I promise, I won't be trouble."

Luke snorts. "You stole someone's money. I would say you're already trouble."

"I only took the cash! I left the rest where someone will find it and return it."

"That's still stealing!" Connor says. He throws up his hands. "I'm leaving it to you other two. Sort this out. I'll move the RV so we're not in the way."

He turns his back on the rest of them and plunks himself in the driver's seat. Without further warning, he starts the RV and begins to move. Luke, Jory, and the kid all dive for seats so they're not pitched onto the floor.

Connor doesn't turn around after he parks, so Luke knows he's serious. He expects Luke and Jory to decide. It annoys Luke. This is Connor's trip and his RV. If he has an opinion about what to do, he ought to share it. But he's not engaging with them at all. Luke sighs.

"Let's start with your name," he says.

For a moment, it looks like the boy isn't going to answer. Finally he says, "Kem."

"Okay, Kem. Where are you trying to get to?"

Another long pause. "Home," he whispers.

Then

LUKE AND SAM were late coming back to co-op classes after their lunch break, barely getting their shirts tucked back in before they entered the church. They rushed into the Sunday school classroom, where they received a stern look from Sam's mother. She didn't say anything, just went back to scrawling equations on the whiteboard. Luke and Sam exchanged a glance, thinking the same thing: how much trouble they'd be in later when the rest of the class left.

Mondays and Thursdays at the co-op were usually the only time they saw each other. Sam was busy with his family's new homestead, and Luke was bravely trying to learn how to do general home repair. His father and brothers had figured out—finally—that he was not going to be any use with building or roofing work. Dad had the brilliant idea Luke might be able to manage the indoors. So far, he was equally terrible, but he'd picked up a few useful skills. He'd put them to work at home, which made Mama happy and Dad less grumpy.

Luke's homeschool cohort had dwindled from a dozen students to five. The rest had either gone to public high school or had aged out or quit the co-op. It was now Luke, Sam, and three girls. Sam's mother still taught them math and science, and the girls' mothers rounded out their studies with other subjects. The co-op had small groups of younger students as well, mostly siblings of the teens or each other. It was less vibrant than it had been even a few years ago, but they still made it work.

After class, Mrs. Whelock held the boys back. Luke looked anxiously out the classroom door, expecting Mama to worry when he didn't come right away. She liked to get Ruth and Johnny home as soon as school was done. There was no one waiting, though, so Luke obediently sat at the table with Sam and his mother.

Mrs. Whelock faced them, her hands folded on top of the table. Luke glanced at Sam, who was staring at his lap, and then back at Mrs. Whelock. This wasn't the first time they'd been late, and Luke knew they shouldn't be disrespectful of lessons. But with a limit to how much time they could be together, they took full advantage. It was a wonder no one had caught on to what they were up to in the woods that ran between the co-op and the back of the Whelocks' homestead.

"Sorry we were late again," Sam mumbled.

"Yeah." Luke coughed. "I mean, yes. We're sorry."

Mrs. Whelock sighed. "I know you think I'm old and clueless, but I assure you, I am not."

Sam's head snapped up. "What do you mean?"

She put one hand on Luke's and reached for Sam too, but he refused. "You two have always been very close. I've kept my mouth shut, mostly because I have a very good idea how some families might react. But surely you understand I don't miss a whole lot of what goes on under my watch."

Luke swallowed. His face was hot and his hands clammy. She knew at least part of the truth. Maybe she didn't know the reason they were late was that they'd been half undressed, kissing and getting off together under the big boxelder by the creek. But she certainly knew there was something different from friendship between them.

"It's not what you think," Sam argued.

"Oh?" Mrs. Whelock raised her eyebrows at the same moment Luke's stomach plummeted.

"We lost track of time. It won't happen again."

"I'm sure it won't," Mrs. Whelock said briskly. "That's all. Sam, go wait for me at the car." Luke started to rise as well, but she held him back. "Stay for a moment. I want to talk to you about your homework."

Sam scowled and slouched out of the classroom. Luke remained in his seat, confused. He'd been conscientious about his work, so he couldn't imagine what was wrong. To stop his hands shaking, he folded them and pressed them between his knees.

Mrs. Whelock rounded the table to sit next to him. "I can't speak for Sam, and I'll talk to him later. I assume you need me to keep this quiet?"

Luke nodded, his cheeks burning again. He couldn't utter a word, afraid of what he might reveal.

"I hope someday you can talk to your family," she said. "Your mother is a good woman, and I don't believe she would reject you the way some families do."

Luke thought about the time his mother had whispered to him to ignore the preacher's hate-fueled words. He also thought about the way Dad kept trying to make him in his own image and about the stern way his older brothers spoke to him about how he'd someday have a wife, and how would he support her if he didn't learn their business?

"I know she wouldn't," Luke whispered.

Mrs. Whelock leaned forward. "I won't either. When you're ready, I will stand up for you. Until then, you have my word I won't tell a soul. Now, go on, go find your mother."

He almost bolted from the table. It didn't make sense that Sam was so adamant he wasn't like Luke, not when Mrs. Whelock was so willing to accept them both. What made Sam so fearful?

Luke didn't see Mama in any of the classrooms, so he went outside. It was cool enough now for a light jacket. Luke pulled his sweatshirt hood over his head and looked around for his family. He saw the car, and he was about to head for it when a hand shot out and grabbed him. Luke grunted but let Sam drag him into the shadow of the building.

"We can't meet up like that at lunch anymore," he said.

"But—"

"My mom knows, and that means someone else probably figured it out too."

"Your mom said—"

"I don't care!" Sam hissed. "I'm not a homosexual, and I don't need rumors about me."

"Nobody knows, and your mom said she wouldn't tell."

"What about you?" Sam tilted his chin at Luke.

"Who would I tell?" He didn't mention that he'd been thinking about talking to Mama. Sam wouldn't understand how sick of hiding Luke was.

"I don't know, but don't you dare."

Luke trembled. He didn't want to lose Sam, but it wasn't up to him what Sam did or didn't do. An idea occurred to him. "Esther," he said.

"You want to tell Esther?" Sam sneered.

"No. Well, yes, sort of. I mean, we can keep hanging out, but not at the co-op. I'll get Esther to set it up so she can bring us. She drives now."

"And what are you gonna tell her so she'll do that?" Sam's words still had bite, but now he sounded more curious than angry. Good.

"I'll think of something. Besides, that way, she can see Tristan. He's not on the 'approved' list, but you are because my family doesn't know anything. I'll tell everyone we're doing a project for the co-op."

Sam sighed and ran a hand through his hair. "Fine. Set it up. But you'd better come up with an actual project so we have something to show them if they ask."

"Your mom would help us," Luke muttered. He thought Mama might too, but he decided against it, given Sam's need for them to keep it secret. Mama had enough to deal with.

"No." Sam was clearly still angry with her.

Luke brushed it off. "Okay. I'll tell you on Thursday. I'm not risking a phone call about it until we have everything we need."

Sam didn't respond. He pushed past Luke and stalked to his mother's car. Luke went the opposite direction. When he got in the passenger seat, Mama eyed him, but she didn't ask any questions. Luke turned partially around so he could see Ruth and Johnny, and he spent the whole ride home listening to them talk about school.

Chapter 21

CONNOR TAKES THE wheel after their stop, and Jory and Kem are playing cards, so Luke occupies himself. He alternates between staring out the windshield and flipping through a magazine he bought at another rest stop. Connor's picked the music this time. Luke doesn't know the band, but he likes the singer's voice. Gritty, raw. Her lyrics are brash, too.

Luke turns a page, and there's a black-and-white ad for a helpline. The photo is a closeup of a face, half in shadow with a tear running down one cheek. Luke shudders. He's reminded briefly of Greg, and then his memories turn to Sam. The summer Sam broke his nose wasn't the last time a boyfriend—or a pseudo-boyfriend—punched him that hard.

It wasn't even the last time Sam hit him. They fooled around in the woods plenty of times, mostly chasing after each other or looking for interesting things buried in the leaves. They recoiled from the exposed needle, kicked at the empty chip packets and coffee cups, and giggled endlessly at the used condoms. But occasionally, they found something interesting, like a discarded coin purse or a pendant or some loose change.

It was one of those times Sam kissed him again. Luke remembers the way it set off fireworks in his belly. For months they were happy like that, sharing their secret only with the trees surrounding them. It lasted all the way until Sam's mother caught on. After that, Sam changed.

Over and over, the same story. "I'm not a homosexual," he said, right before putting his tongue in Luke's mouth. Or "I'm not one of them, you know," just as he put a hand up Luke's shirt. And "I ain't gay," while sliding his fingers under the waistband of Luke's hand-me-down jeans. For a year, every time ended in Sam shoving Luke and walking away.

Luke always says AJ was his first, and in a sense, that's true. AJ was the first boy Luke actually *made love* with. The first person he took off his clothes and slid under the covers with. He's the one Luke wants to remember, not the boy who strung him along and taught him that a push or a slap was an expression of love.

He hurries to flip the page, tearing it a little as he does so. Connor glances over, but Luke doesn't think he sees what was there. He turns back to the road, and Luke tries to read an article about skin care. It's a model who reminds Luke of Jax, and sure enough, as he reads on, it's a gender-fluid makeup artist. They're paler than Jax, with lighter hair. Luke touches the glossy page with his fingertip. He thinks he might cut this picture out and put it in the scrapbook.

Thinking about Jax makes Luke's heart ache. He hasn't quite adjusted to Connor's company and the ways it's different from Jax's. Connor doesn't always understand Luke's need for quiet and thinks he needs to cheer him up. But it's not the same as when Jax used to drag Luke out for the evening, dressing him up and gelling his hair.

Luke runs a hand through his blond locks. He had his hair cut before the trip, and it's at his favorite stage. The part where the stylist used clippers has softened but hasn't yet become shaggy. Jax used to like playing with it, running their fingers up it the wrong direction or sliding them through the longer strands in front. They always said Luke's hair was like cornsilk.

They were never anything more to each other than best friends who sometimes messed around. So why does Luke miss Jax so deeply? And why does the thought of Jax's hands in his hair send a shiver of anticipation and lust through him? He swallows and turns to look out the window, closing the magazine.

"There's a place to camp near our next stop coming up," Connor says. Luke turns toward him. "Sorry. I didn't want to interrupt while you were reading."

"No, I..." Luke glances at the glossy cover.

"I don't want to wait until after dark. It's harder to get things set up."

"Yeah, okay."

"We stopping?" Jory asks, looking up from their game with Kem.

"Maybe ten miles," Connor says.

Kem has drawn his knees up and is resting his chin on them. Luke wants to ask about what happened and why Kem wants to go home, but he doesn't. He knows at that age, he never would've answered adults, not even ones he thought seemed safe. It gnaws at him, though. Something about it seems important in a way he can't explain.

Luke turns back to the window and puts it down. This stretch of road is bordered by grassy hills dotted with clusters of trees at intervals. Luke points his camera and snaps a picture that captures the exit sign. He puts the window up in time for them to pull off the highway. At Connor's request, Luke switches from music to GPS. He glances back at Kem again before turning his attention to navigating for Connor.

*****

The four of them finish setting up the site in record time, leaving a little while before Connor's family arrives. Kem has picked up the magazine Luke was reading, and Connor is rearranging the cupboards. Luke washes the few dishes they used at lunchtime.

At the sound of a vehicle pulling into the campsite, they all look up. The horn toots, and a moment later, a beat-up van comes into view between the trees. Connor steps out of the RV, and the others follow.

There are two women in the van. As soon as they park, they climb out. The shorter one is compact and muscular. Her brown hair is streaked with gray and white, pulled up in a wild mass on top of her head. She's wearing a long, loose skirt and a sleeveless blue blouse. There are laugh lines around her eyes, and her skin is deeply tanned and dotted with sun freckles.

The tall woman has smooth, medium-brown skin. Her short locs are tipped with red, and when she smiles, there's a gap between her front teeth. Tattoos wind their way up her bare arms. Her white A-shirt is tucked into her faded jeans, and she has a wide, studded belt. She puts her arm around the other woman as they walk toward Connor and the others.

Jory exchanges a raised-eyebrow glance with Luke. He isn't sure what Jory was expecting, but obviously, these two women are not it. Luke isn't sure what he was expecting either. He wonders what Connor knows about the women.

"Connor?" the woman in the skirt says. When he nods, she continues, "I'm NaeNae, and this is Ruta."

Connor points at each of the others in turn. "Luke...Jory... and Kem."

"Awesome!" Ruta says. "Get in, and we'll take you back into town. I think you'll like what we're gonna show you."

Intrigued, Luke follows Connor to the van. Jory and Kem haven't moved, though. NaeNae leans out the window and yells, "C'mon, folks!" After a moment's hesitation, they climb into the van.

It's about a twenty-minute drive. Ruta tells them the air conditioning is broken in their ancient beast, so the windows are rolled down. It's hot even with the wind whipping Luke's hair. NaeNae insists Connor tell them about the trip so far and where they've been, so he does, leaving out some of the details.

"Oh, I'd have loved to see Avi and Sylvia's kid all grown!" NaeNae exclaims. "I remember him as a young'un, barely. I was newly an adult when he came into the family."

Luke finds this interesting. He has brothers he barely knew as a child because they were so much older. Roman was seventeen when Luke was born. Although Connor's father was an only child, his cousins are numerous and spread out in age.

They arrive in town, and NaeNae parks the van outside a strip mall. She leads them into a store on the end of the row. From the outside, it looks like a small shop selling used games. When Ruta opens the door, a bell tinkles. Cool air hits Luke's sweaty skin, bringing relief and goosebumps.

"Welcome to paradise," NaeNae says.

She waves to a teenager behind the counter and leads the others through the store. It's far larger than it looks from the sidewalk. Not only do they sell video games, both new and old, they have supplies for tabletop role-play, board games, card games, and more. Luke sees a few private rooms on their way to the back.

Ruta notices him looking and says, "You into gaming?"

"Not much," Luke admits.

"Those rooms are for live games. There are free events, and people also pay to book rooms here. We've even had a few kids do birthdays."

NaeNae takes out a key and unlocks the room at the back. Luke can see this is different from the other private rooms. It's full of glass cases displaying collector's items. There are vintage board games, handmade chess sets, and pewter figurines. NaeNae stops beside one of the cases.

"This is what I wanted to show you," she says.

Connor peers inside, and Luke comes to stand beside him. Inside, there are hand-painted figurines arranged against a detailed backdrop. Luke is mesmerized by the tiny scene, and he thinks he could look at it for hours and still not see everything.

"I...I remember some of this!" Connor says. "My father worked on it when I was growing up. He kept it all in a cabinet in our family room." He snorts. "I also remember my mother complaining that it took up too much space and too much of his time."

"He entrusted it to us," NaeNae says. "It was unfinished, but one of our staff took on the responsibility of following Saul's detailed notes."

"Notes?"

"Yes. He had something he wanted to do with it, but he never told us what. The only thing he said was that we were to show you if you ever came this way. Until you called, I figured there wasn't much chance of that."

"Wow," Jory says. "This is incredible."

Kem looks somewhat bored, so Ruta says, "Why don't we leave the others to talk, and you and I can check out the rest of the store?"

"Can we?" Kem's face lights up.

"Sure thing!"

Kem follows Ruta out, and after they're gone, NaeNae says, "There's more, if you want to see it. Saul left something for you."

"He did?"

Luke thinks Connor shouldn't be surprised anymore. He's collected his father's childhood memorabilia, a manuscript, and a painting. Why would it be shocking that there's more in store for him?

NaeNae opens a closet at the back of the room and pulls out a wooden box. The top is painted like a chessboard. Inside, there's another set of figurines. On closer inspection, Luke sees it is indeed a chess set, with pieces hand-painted to resemble the ones inside the glass case.

Connor's hands shake as he takes the box, and Luke reaches out to support the lid. The pieces are beautiful. There's something tucked underneath them that piques Luke's curiosity.

"We have no idea what that means," NaeNae says. "It's some of Saul's writing, but it's hard to understand. When he was here, he talked about a lot of things we couldn't follow. The main idea seems to have been a belief that some kind of destructive force was coming. He saw it as his responsibility to deliver the message." She sighs. "We could never figure out if he always believed that kind of thing or if it was because of his illness. In any case, he said we have a responsibility to help put things right. If you can make sense of it, more power to you."

Connor shrugs. "It seems to be the same story in every place we search. So far, I haven't been able to put the pieces together, but that's what this trip was for."

NaeNae nods. "Why don't we go have something to eat, and we can talk about it. Maybe it'll help to bounce ideas around between us."

"Sounds good." Connor looks around. "Where'd the others disappear to?"

"I think Ruta took Kem back out into the store. Knowing her, we could be waiting a while. Want to take a look around?"

They follow her out of the room, and she locks it back up. Ruta and Kem are at the counter, talking and laughing with the teenage employee. NaeNae tells them to go ahead and browse, so Luke follows Connor to look at gaming dice.

"You play?" he asks.

"No. Just needed some space."

Luke puts a hand on Connor's shoulder. "Are you okay?"

"I guess. Something's bugging me about this, but I don't know what. Not about the store or Ruta and NaeNae. About Dad." He shakes his head. "It's probably nothing."

Luke wonders if Connor is right about that. It's been on his mind too, but he doesn't know how to help Connor solve the mystery. "Maybe something will turn up," he says.

"I hope so. Come on, Let's go back to the others. I'm hungry."

****

Ruta and NaeNae drive them back to the campsite after dinner. They've made several purchases at the game store to pass the time on the road. Luke squeezes into the far back seat with Connor, and Kem sits with Jory in the middle. With Ruta's tendency to push the speed limit, they're back in no time.

"You want to stay and hang out for a bit?" Connor asks. "I think we've even got some marshmallows to roast once we get a campfire going."

"Sure," Ruta says.

Connor pulls the camp chairs back out, and NaeNae grabs the ones they keep in their van. It's almost dark, and it's cooled off. Jory tosses blankets to everyone, and they lounge comfortably around the fire pit. Jory is teaching Kem how to build a fire. Connor and Ruta talk quietly, but Luke is busy observing NaeNae. He thinks she's older than she lets on, and he wonders what the story is between the two of them.

NaeNae catches him looking and smiles. Luke is startled to discover he's more intrigued than embarrassed. Her nose stud sparkles in the light from the lantern suspended from the pointed peak of the RV's awning.

"I have a feeling you want to ask me something," she says.

"It's probably not what you think it is," Luke tells her.

"Try me, then. Go on."

"I was wondering how you and Ruta met." It's close enough.

Her eyebrows arch, and the corner of her mouth lifts in a half-smile. "You're right. Not what I was expecting."

"Are you going to tell me?"

"Hm, I may need Ruta's help on this one." She reaches out and touches Ruta's arm. "Babe, Luke wants to know how we met."

"I take it you want to tell him something besides 'on the army base.'"

NaeNae laughs. "I was hoping to, yes."

Her face serious, Ruta leans forward to address Luke. "She was my mother-in-law."

Now that, Luke hadn't anticipated. He chokes a little before he can answer. "I'm sorry, what?"

"I was married to her son. Listen, she was young when she had him, okay?"

NaeNae breaks in. "My turn." She picks up the story where Ruta left off. "I was seventeen. My boyfriend was enlisted, and I planned to join him a year later. Never happened. I got pregnant the night before he left. Well, I was so sure he was gonna be that type of guy, you know? The ones who don't stick around after they make you a baby. Only he wasn't. He wrote me every single time he got the chance, and the second he found out we were about to be parents, you'd've thought it was his own birthday." NaeNae smiled. "He loved being a daddy, right from the first time he held his son in his arms."

Ruta takes her hand. "They were both something special."

"They sure were." NaeNae squeezes Ruta's fingers. "I got surprised by how much I loved being a mama. We got married as soon as he was back stateside. We moved around a lot those early years, so I never went to college after all. It was all right. We did okay with me being mostly home. Soon as he was old enough, my son joined up too, and he met Ruta."

"Oh, this is where I come in," Ruta says. "So of course, I married him."

"This is the wild part," NaeNae says. "They were in the same unit, along with my younger son. It's unusual, but it happens on occasion. Not as uncommon as people might think. They loved serving together, and because of their relationship, my husband was sort of 'dad' to the other guys, too."

Ruta continues the story. "And then they all promptly get sent overseas. Well, the two of us and Nae's other daughter-in-law took care of each other that whole time." She closes her eyes briefly. "They never came back. It wasn't even proper war or anything. It was a stupid accident, something that shouldn't have happened but did. They fed us some bullshit about the explosion meaning it was over quick, but who knows? I don't think they'd tell us, 'Oh, by the way, it took them hours to die, and they suffered horrible pain the entire time.' Easier to let us believe it happened in a blink."

"And...you two got together?" Connor's brow makes a puzzled V.

"Not exactly." Ruta laughs ruefully. "It took time. We comforted each other, spent time together. When it came time to leave, seeing as we were on a military base and our husbands were dead, we went together. The rest of the spouses all left, except for me. NaeNae tried to tell me to get out there on my own and leave her to figure things out, but I couldn't do that."

"The game shop was my husband's baby," NaeNae explains. "He and our sons planned to open up once they were out of the army. We decided to see their vision through."

"And that's when we ultimately fell in love." Ruta smiles. "All that work and time together, how could we not?"

They're quiet for a while, the story sinking in. Jory and Kem have gotten a decent fire going, and it crackles and pops, the sparks rising into the darkening sky. Luke draws his blanket closer around him and leans toward the heat.

Connor says, "Tell me more about my father coming to see you."

NaeNae nods. "We expected it. I got a call from Danya. She and I were close growing up. When Saul visited her, she was confused about what it meant." She pauses, chewing on her lip. "I think it would be best if you visited our family historian for some context, to be honest."

"You're talking about Jens, right?"

"Yes," NaeNae confirms. "He's collected a lot of information. I know Saul went to see him too. Our history is complicated. In any case, Saul kept talking about needing to set things right." She leans forward and braces her elbows on her knees. "Any idea what he meant?"

"Not at all," Connor admits. "He didn't contact me even once before he died, other than to leave me this weird trail of breadcrumbs. My mother thinks he was delusional."

"I don't believe that," Ruta says. She taps her lips with her finger. "He wasn't talking about conspiracy theories, or not the way most people do. It was the other way around, actually. He felt we were in danger from our collective actions."

"And he saw it as his job or whatever to warn people?" Connor's brow is furrowed with incredulity.

"Maybe?" NaeNae shrugs. "I don't honestly know what his plan was."

Connor sighs. "I feel like every place I go, I only end up with more questions."

"Talk to Jens," NaeNae urges. "At least some things should be more clear. As to why your father was seemingly on

227

a mission, I can't answer that. I hope one day you uncover the truth."

"Me too," Connor says.

They fall silent, surrounded by the sounds of the fire and the natural world, all of them lost in thought about what NaeNae has said.

Then

LUKE POINTED HIS camera at the thick greenery, sliced through with the rushing creek. He loved this spot. Mama had brought him with her and the younger ones for a picnic. Esther, at seventeen, said she was too old. Luke suspected she was using it as an excuse to go see Tristan, but he kept it to himself.

Mama needed a lot of help with the younger ones, so that left it to Luke to go along. Dad still kept saying she was "sick," like she had a cold or something, but Luke was old enough now to understand what it really was. He liked that on good days she could still find the strength to bring them here. It almost made up for the worst days, when Mama didn't even come out of her room.

Ruth was sitting on the blanket, playing with a pair of hand-me-down fashion dolls and singing quietly to herself. Johnny had butt-scooted closer to the water and was drawing in a notebook. He went through several of them a month. One of the older women at church had given him a real sketch pad, and he'd filled it with doodles. He'd been careful with that one, even without being told. Something in him obviously knew it was precious and he should use it sparingly.

Luke put his camera away and came to sit on the blanket. He braided Ruth's hair. Even Esther thought it was silly for him to still like playing with the silky strands. But he enjoyed it mostly because it helped both Ruth and Mama. Ruth's hair tended to get tangled and end up in her way, and Mama got tired of fixing it all the time because the hair tie slipped out— or Ruth pulled it out, whichever the case happened to be.

"Did you get some nice pictures?" Mama asked as she set out their food.

"Uh-huh. Want to see?"

"Of course I do!" She offered him a smile, something which had become more and more rare over time.

He wound the elastic around the end of Ruth's braid, and she reached back for it. Luke gently moved her hand away before shifting closer to Mama. He took his camera from around his neck. This was the new one, which Mama had saved up every penny to buy for him. She must've hidden money a little at a time for a year. Once, Luke had found some folded bills under the cushion in the sofa. Another time, he'd spotted them in one of the houseplants. He still wasn't sure why she would need to keep it a secret even from Dad, but he'd left it alone. At the time, he couldn't imagine what she was doing.

Then came the camera. It was long past when his father had let him take photos of the work he and the big boys did. Anything Luke did with his pictures was simply not discussed anymore, as if it didn't exist. When Mama gave him the camera more than a year ago, she'd said he mustn't make a big deal of it. If he said nothing, Dad wouldn't pay attention to the fact that it was a lot nicer than the old one. It was similar enough, and Luke and Mama were the only ones who would understand.

So he took pictures mostly when he was on his own free time, away from school and his older brothers. Like now. He shifted so he could show Mama the window and scroll through the images. He smiled when she made delighted sounds.

"You have a real eye, sweetheart. These are lovely. What do you think you'll do with them?"

"I have a scrapbook," he told her. "I got it from the dollar store, so it's not real fancy."

"Will you show me sometime?"

"Okay. I'll get some of these printed and add them too."

Mama reached up and brushed Luke's bangs away from his right eye. "I know the others sometimes tell you that you should learn how to do what they do. But don't stop taking your pretty pictures, sweetheart. Don't you ever stop. Someday, you'll be glad."

Luke folded his knees up and crossed his arms. He rested his chin on them and thought about what Mama said. He was already glad he took photographs. A person could learn so much from one, often as much about the photographer as the image. Luke loved the big History in Pictures books in the oversize section of the library. He'd already studied things like the presidents of the United States and the civil rights movement. There were images that made him feel like he was really there, seeing what happened.

Mama knew he liked that section, and she never minded hearing about what he learned. There was one book he didn't share with her. He didn't know if she would be all right with it. He'd learned a lot about other people like himself and Sam and about important times in their history. Mama still didn't have any idea something was going on between them. If he took pictures of Sam, would anyone understand what they meant? Would someone with a good eye spot a hint of emotion in the way he angled the camera or the way Sam smiled?

"What are you thinking about?" Mama interrupted his thoughts.

Luke wriggled his toes inside his sneakers. "I was wondering if there was anything in those library books you might get mad at me for reading."

Mama laughed. "Where in the world did that question come from?"

"The pictures. I was thinking about how much you liked these, and I remembered about going to the library last week to look at some."

"Well," Mama said, looking thoughtful, "I suppose it would depend. There might be some subjects I wish you would be older before looking up, and there might be some I think invite sin. The first ones we can talk about. The second I don't think the library has."

Luke was pretty sure he knew what kinds of books were in the second group, and he blushed. No, the library didn't have any. He'd thought about trying to find photographs like that. Sam was allowed to watch and see things Luke wasn't. Mama and Dad had different ideas about that. Dad was harsh, saying it was just plain wrong and God didn't approve. Mama said some kinds of things weren't kind or loving, and God wanted everyone to be respectful to others.

"The first kind," Luke told her. "It was people doing protests and things. Some of them..." He swallowed, not able to continue.

"Oh." Mama put a hand on his knee. "You wonder if God is all right with those kinds of protests?"

"I guess."

Mama looked thoughtful again, and Luke tried to read her expression but couldn't. "Your father and I might not agree with all the opinions people have when protesting things. But one thing he and I do agree on is that everyone has the right to do it. If you don't learn about those things in the library, where there are books with words and pictures to explain, then you'll learn somewhere else. So if that's all you were worried about, then it's perfectly fine for you to research those things." Her arched eyebrows indicated to Luke she thought there might be more.

He blushed again. "I know our church doesn't agree with some of the things they were doing." He didn't mean only the protests, but he wasn't sure how to explain without telling Mama everything.

Mama took his face in her hands. "Sweetheart, you will do things someday—maybe even today—that I don't agree with or Dad doesn't like or our church believes are wrong. But not one bit of that changes how much I love you. All right?"

"Yes, ma'am."

She smiled at his politeness. "Now. Go help Johnny while Ruth and I clean up."

Luke went over to where Johnny was still sitting in the grass, doodling. "Mama says I should help you."

"Okay." Johnny turned the notebook. "Wanna see what I drew?"

Luke wasn't sure what was typical for a seven-year-old, but he thought the drawing must be pretty good if the river and the trees and the picnic grove were all recognizable. "It's really cool," he told Johnny, earning a grin.

He helped Johnny stand. His walking had steadily improved, and the crutches made it possible for him to keep up with the others. Luke wondered what he would do when he got older. Maybe Luke was biased, but he liked to think Johnny was brilliant. He could do whatever he wanted, and it wouldn't have to be learning how to put on a new roof or install drywall.

"Ready?" Luke asked, and at Johnny's nod, they returned to Mama and Ruth.

Chapter 22

I'T'S QUIET IN the RV. Jory is driving, and Kem is in the front seat talking with them. Connor has retreated to bed, but Luke doesn't think he's sleeping. While the others are occupied, Luke pulls out his latest postcards.

He wants to write to Jax, but he's at a loss for what to put on the card. Not for the first time, he's lonely. All the people missing from his life have left a gaping hole. He wishes Jax were with him, and then he feels guilty because that would mean Jax giving up their dream. Luke picks up a pen, but he still doesn't know what to write.

A light, misty rain is falling. Luke is distracted, watching droplets as they slowly collect and roll down the windows. At their next stop, he's going to call Jax. He's made up his mind, at least for the moment.

Jory pulls into a gas station, and Connor climbs out to pump so Jory can go have a smoke. They disappear around the side of the building. Kem slinks into the store, and Luke gets out under the pretense of making sure Kem is okay. He checks to see if Connor is looking—he isn't—before rounding the building the opposite direction of Jory.

Luke pulls out his phone. He knows he's not supposed to call Jax, that he has a whole drawer full of unsent postcards because he stopped writing days ago. The reception is good here, though, so Luke uses that as his excuse. He needs to hear Jax's voice and be reassured they're okay.

"Hello?" Jax sounds distracted, and Luke can hear some noise in the background. There's crackling on the line, and then some shuffling.

"Hey," Luke says. "It's me."

"Lukey! Oh, my god! Hey. Sorry about that. I had to go where it's quieter."

"You're out with friends." Luke's disappointed, but he understands.

"Nah. Just a rare night everyone is home at the same time. We were finishing up dinner."

Home. They've used the word so casually, already settled in with this new group. "I'm sorry I interrupted."

"It's fine. What's up?"

"I—" Luke isn't sure what to say. That he misses Jax? That he wishes he could go there right now and spend the night talking and just being together? "Figured I'd check in with you, that's all."

"How's the road trip? I haven't gotten a postcard in a while. You must be pretty busy." Jax's tone is teasing.

"It's okay. We've met a lot of Connor's family. They seem nice."

"Yeah?"

"Uh-huh. Oh, and we have a couple of stowaways."

"Like, you picked up hitchhikers?" Jax sounds alarmed.

"Kind of, but it's okay. Jory's cool. I told you about them from Erie, right?"

"Oh! Oh, yeah. But you have more people along?"

"A kid. We're taking him home to somewhere in Minnesota, I guess. Not too far from here." Luke giggles. "He tried to lift my wallet at a protest in Chicago."

"Luke!" He can picture Jax's horrified expression.

"It's fine. I caught him at it. He wasn't real happy, but I bought him some food. Then he snuck out and got in the RV. We were already on the road when we found him."

Jax sighs, but it turns into a light laugh. "That sounds exactly like something you'd do, Lukey." There's pride in their tone, and it warms Luke.

"How's everyone there?"

"Good." Jax pauses. "What's really going on? I don't think you called only to tell me about hitchhikers or ask about my roommates."

"I, uh, missed you." Luke's face is hot as he says it.

"Oh. I miss you too," Jax says, but it sounds far away, like they're repeating the words without filling them with any meaning.

"I...when this trip is over..." Luke has no idea how to express what he wants to say or ask what he needs.

"Oh, Luke."

So he doesn't need to explain after all; Jax catches on. There's a long silence, and Luke knows it doesn't mean anything good. Jax won't be responding in kind with the same level of commitment.

"I'm sorry," Luke says.

"So am I." Jax clears their throat. "I feel like I'm breaking your heart here. I didn't know you thought there was anything more than us being roommates."

"I didn't," Luke says. "I thought maybe...there could be."

"I can't," Jax says. "Not when I'm starting school and everything is changing so fast. You understand, right?"

"Of course I do," Luke answers, but inside, he's shriveling. Jax wasn't using him, but they never took into account the ill-defined relationship and what would come of it. He clears his throat, his eyes burning.

"Lukey, listen to me," Jax says. "I know you. Don't cling to the past, okay? Keep moving forward. Something good is out there for you. Don't miss out because you're wrapped up in memories."

Luke brushes at his eyes. It's exactly what Jax has done. They never look over their shoulder at what was or what might have been. It's how they were able to press on until they achieved their dream.

"I know..." Luke trails off. "Is that why you wanted me to come with Connor?"

"Yes," Jax confirms. "I wanted you to see what else is out there. You've been so sheltered, even with your life. I wanted you to see there's more than a dinky, gross apartment and a shitty job."

"You made our gross apartment a home and made up for my shitty job."

"And that's why I knew you needed this. Lukey, I love you so much. Maybe not the way you hoped, but it's true. You gotta trust me, okay? And trust Connor." They pause. "Maybe not every stranger who asks for a ride, though."

Luke laughs and wipes his eyes again. "Jory's okay. So's Kem."

"See? And I trust you enough to believe you. Go have fun with them. Take some pictures. How about you send me some of those instead of the postcards?"

"Okay."

"Bye, Lukey." Jax makes a kissy sound into the phone.

"Bye, Jax."

He ends the call and stuffs his phone back in his pocket. When he returns to the front of the building, he sees the others converging on the RV from different directions. Before he joins them, Luke steps off to the side and takes a photo of the countryside. Everything is green, the grass swaying in the light breeze. When he checks the photo in the camera's window, he's pleased. The colors pop due to the overcast sky, and he's captured a fantastic shot of the horizon.

He re-enters the RV, taking his turn at the wheel. Connor slides into the passenger seat and queues up the playlist.

He's added a couple of NaeNae's suggestions, and The Head and the Heart's "Rivers and Roads" plays through the RV's speakers as Luke pulls out of the gas station.

✳✳✳✳

"Where are we going next?" It's Jory's go-to question, and they're all used to it at this point.

"Not too far from the South Dakota border." Connor, now back in the driver's seat, glances over his shoulder at Kem. "Is that right?"

Kem nods. He looks tense, sitting in one of the rear seats with his hands between his knees. They're maybe an hour or so from their destination. Connor has agreed they'll take things slow, setting up camp before making their next move.

There isn't any particular family in the area, but Connor knows from his father's notes that he's stopped somewhere nearby. He plans to look for clues once they arrive. Meanwhile, Kem still hasn't said much about his family or what he's going to do when they reach his hometown.

Jory searches Connor's playlist and makes a happy noise at finding the song they want. They don't hesitate to sing loudly on the chorus of "Take Me Home, Country Roads." Luke enjoys surprising the others that he does, in fact, know all the words, even the verses. It's still raining, but somehow, that seems less important than the road ahead of them and the music filling the RV.

It's still a ways down the road, so Luke settles in to look through his photos. He had the first few printed before they left Cleveland, and he sifts among them to find the ones he wants. He's making the scrapbook pages for their last couple of stops. He smiles at the photo of Moishe making a kissy face at Connor outside Snowflakes. That one will make a nice centerpiece for his pages of Ohio.

Jory and Connor are talking up front, but Luke only catches a word here or there. He half listens while he arranges the photos. He's not making it look like those fancy pages his mother used to create. She had bins of paper and embellishments and other art supplies to turn each page into a three-dimensional photo collage. Luke has his own way, more about the photos and which ones go together to tell the story. Sometimes he adds journal entries or mementos to the page, like the wedding invitation from Adam and AJ.

They stop to eat, and there's a ravine behind the gas station. Right at the edge is a flat, white rock. It's huge, big enough to sit on, and covered in signatures of people who have sat on this rock before. Some of them might even be from before Luke was born. Sure enough, he sees initials and "1989" on one corner. He wonders about the people who left their mark.

The writing and doodles on the rock aren't the only thing back there. It's a graveyard for empty liquor bottles. Luke wonders about those too, who was back here and why they simply left the bottles instead of throwing them out properly. He supposes someone did it once and everyone else followed along after.

Connor comes to join him on the rock. The rain has slowed to a light drizzle, and Luke likes the way the cool mist feels on his skin in contrast with the heat of the day. Connor bumps his shoulder.

"Ready when you are," he says.

"It's up to you." Luke tries to get a read on Connor's mood. He seemed happy in the RV, but this trip has been different from everything he expected.

"Maybe in a few minutes." Connor looks down into the ravine, and as he does so, he spots all the whiskey bottles. "Wonder who left these all here."

"Dunno. Are you okay?"

"I guess." Connor shrugs. "There's this whole other side of my father I never got to know. But he was also paranoid and running away because he was so sure someone was chasing him. I don't know what to think." He reaches down and picks up a bottle. "I went on a trip once at one of my schools. There was a spot like this."

Connor picks up a rock. He hurls the whiskey bottle into the sky, takes aim with the rock, and hits it squarely. The bottle shatters. He does it again before indicating Luke should do the same. They stand and spend the next several minutes searching for just the right bottles to throw. The damp air becomes saturated with the heavy scent of the whiskey left in some of the bottles. It mingles with the aroma of wet earth and cooking from the convenience store's restaurant.

After a while, Jory joins them. Without a word, they pick up a bottle and a rock and smash them the same way Luke and Connor have been. Luke sees Kem watching them and beckons him. Kem silently crosses the parking lot and follows suit in smashing a bottle. It's satisfying, emptying themselves of whatever's become lodged inside them along the way.

When they've purged the unspoken emotions, they troop back to the RV, a little wetter and a little lighter than they'd left it.

***

Kem is always quiet, but he's hanging back now, away from the others. He's angled away from Luke in his seat, staring out the window. Connor is driving, taking them to the RV park. On their way to the turn, Jory laughs, and Luke can only stare.

"Uh..." Connor says. "Kem? What the hell is *that*?"

Kem finally seems to come back to awareness of his surroundings. "Oh, the Jolly Green Giant?"

"That's certainly a statue," Connor says. "Yep."

"Seriously, why?" Luke asks.

"Are you kidding?" Now Kem is a bit more animated. "I can't believe you all didn't know about it."

"I had a sheltered childhood," Luke says with a shrug.

"I'm from the east coast," Connor tells Kem. "I've never been this far west."

"But...but...like, the vegetables, right?"

"I guess?" Connor laughs. "But a huge-ass statue? I don't get it."

"I think it was to attract tourists," Kem says. "There's even a museum."

"Pull over!" Luke says. He takes out his camera.

"What? Why?" Connor glances over his shoulder, but he slows down.

"We need a picture with that thing."

"I don't think you'll get more of it in than its feet," Jory remarks.

Connor turns onto a road, and Luke snickers at the sign: Giant Drive. After locating a place to leave the RV, the four of them head for the statue. Luke can only stare for a moment. He finally turns on his camera and makes the other three pose for a photo op. When they're done, Jory reaches for Luke's camera.

"Give me that thing."

Luke holds it out of their reach. "No!"

"I won't break it. You need to be in a picture too. Go on, stand next to Connor."

Reluctantly, Luke hands over his camera and takes his place beside Connor. Kem opts out of this one, saying the memory belongs to Luke and Connor. Luke thinks maybe later, he should explain to Kem they're not a couple.

When they're through—they don't visit the museum after all—they return to the RV. Connor heads for the fairground, where they'll be camping for the next couple of nights.

"Oh, my god." Jory is still chuckling as they enter the campground. "That was wild."

Connor stops at the main building to check them in, and Jory ducks out for a smoke, leaving Luke and Kem alone. The amusement of seeing the fifty-foot statue has faded, and Kem's gone back to silence. Luke wishes he were the kind of person who knew what to say. He did all right when he caught Kem trying to steal his wallet, but this is different. Without knowing how Kem ended up so far from home, Luke doesn't have anything to go on. There's still a mystery there, but Luke isn't sure Kem will ever explain it.

The others climb back into the RV, and Connor heads for their campsite. "This is the halfway point!" he says cheerfully.

"Halfway..." Jory prompts.

"Our road trip is half over. This the exact midway point of I-90."

"Whoa," Luke says.

While they set up, Connor explains the purpose of this part of their trip. "My father left notes about this being the midpoint," he says. "It meant something to him. His father's cousin lives here, and he's the family historian. I'm hoping he can shed some light on things."

"Blue Earth," Jory muses. "Didn't you say there was blue something-or-other in your father's writing?"

"Blue suns," Connor replies. "It was a story he used to tell me. About a..." He scrunches his face, trying to remember. "A utopian society, I think. It's been a long time."

"It's not that great here," Kem mutters, but then he sighs, and his shoulders slump.

"Hey," Luke says. "We'll get you home, okay?"

Kem nods, but he's still holding back. Luke understands. Some things aren't meant to be shared with strangers. Maybe they aren't even meant to be shared with friends. He wants to tell Kem he knows what it's like, but he suspects Kem's story isn't the same as his.

"Hey," Connor says, breaking into Luke's thoughts. "Wanna give us a hand with some dinner?"

Luke drops the idea of talking with Kem for the moment. He'll talk when he's ready. For now, they'll enjoy the food and the quiet sounds of nature around them.

Chapter 23

L UKE WAKES UP to rain pattering on the RV's roof. He sighs and rolls over, yanking the blanket over his head. He's tired of wet weather, and he'd much rather stay in bed for the foreseeable future. He lies still for a few minutes, but he can't get back to sleep. He cracks one eye open and peers at the other bed. Connor isn't in it.

It's quiet in the RV. Luke has no idea what time it is. He squirms until he can reach his phone, and he's surprised to discover it's already nine. He listens hard, but he still doesn't hear anyone else moving around. Shoving the blanket down, he stretches and yawns.

It takes a full ten minutes before he has the motivation to leave his bed. Connor and Jory are nowhere in sight, but Kem is at the kitchen table. Luke stops short when he sees what Kem's doing. He has Luke's scrapbook out in front of him, flipping through the pages. It's not the new one Luke's been making for their trip nor the recent one with AJ's wedding pictures; it's his old one, the one he started after he left home.

The first few photos are the ones from Luke's old disposable camera. When he bought it, Sam and Esther had messed around with it, snapping a couple of pictures for fun. There's one of Esther making a face and one of Sam in a tree. After that are the pictures of the fire. Luke taped in the memory card he rescued from the dirt, never having had the courage to find out what was on it. His brothers were sure they'd destroyed it, but when Luke picked it up, he saw they'd only shoved it into the dirt rather than breaking it.

"What are you doing?" Luke demands, hurrying over to the table.

"I-I...n-nothing!" Kem stammers. "J-just looking. I found this in the drawer when I was looking for a spoon."

"So you thought you could just, what, search through my things?" Luke flips the book closed and takes it back.

"It's not like that!" Kem's lip trembles.

Luke backs off now he has his book. "You should've asked," he says, trying to calm down. His heart is still racing. How much did Kem figure out from the pictures?

"I know. I'm sorry." Kem won't meet his gaze. "I didn't know it was private."

Luke sighs. He didn't hide it because Connor already knows about it, and he didn't think Jory cared. They don't seem the type to be interested in something like that. He should've known better, given Kem's age, curiosity, and tendency to put his hands on things that aren't his.

"Wh-why do you have that anyway?" Kem asks.

"It's a long story." Luke puts the book away and sits across from Kem. "I don't usually let anyone see it."

Kem looks up. "Who are all those people? And what was that huge fire?"

Luke wonders how much to tell Kem. Not even Connor knows. On the other hand, maybe it'll jog something in Kem, and he'll begin talking. "The girl is my sister, and the boy was her boyfriend. He...um, he died. In that fire."

"She doesn't look like you."

This is true; Esther has a darker, rosier complexion, and her hair is brown. Luke never thought about it much before. There were so many siblings, and people tied them together mostly because they knew their family.

"Did she die too?" Kem asks.

"No. I think she ran away, like me. M-my brothers set the fire."

243

"Why?" Kem stares at him in alarm.

"They thought her boyfriend hurt her."

"Did he?"

"Not at all." Luke thinks he'll give Kem one more detail. "That's when I ran away. I saw what they did, and I was scared of them."

"So it wasn't because—" Kem cuts off.

"Because I'm gay? No. I'm pretty sure they didn't know for sure, but I have no idea if they'd have cared. They thought I was a spoiled brat, but not for that reason."

"That's not why I ran away either," Kem says. "Well... I'm not really gay. I'm pansexual. But it's still not why. My parents were okay with that."

"And okay with you being trans?"

Kem nods. "Mostly. It was weird at school for a while, but it ended up fine, I guess."

"So then—" Luke starts to prompt Kem, but the door to the RV swings open before he can finish.

"Hey, you two!" Jory says. "Rain's letting up. Connor says we should get going and eat so we can see whatever relative he's visiting today. We should also get Kem home."

"Right," Luke says, glancing at Kem.

"Right," Kem echoes faintly.

*****

Connor decides to rent a car for the day. They call for a ride, and then they pick up a blue compact car. Before taking care of Connor's business in town, they drive Kem to his house.

Kem sits up front, clenching and unclenching his fists as he gives Connor directions. They pull into a townhouse complex, and Kem guides them to the correct one. Connor parks, and all four of them climb out to say their goodbyes.

Connor and Jory each give Kem a brief hug. When it gets to Luke, he first holds Kem at arm's length, studying him. He regrets he never learned more about him along the way, but Kem was too closed off. Luke pulls him in and holds him, wishing again he had the right words.

Kem stands for a moment outside the door, looking back at all of them. He sniffles a little, nods, and opens the door. They watch him disappear inside, and the door closes behind him. It feels like the unsatisfying end of a book.

A drop of rain lands squarely on Luke's nose. He sneezes and brushes it away. Connor laughs, breaking the tension. They head back to the car and drive off toward the retirement home where Connor is meeting his family.

It takes about thirty minutes before they pull into the parking lot of a sprawling building. The walkways are tree-lined, and there's a large expanse of grass with a pond in back. Summer flowers bloom everywhere along the perimeter of the building. Connor checks his information and parks near the south entrance.

The retirement community isn't so different from the row of townhouses where Avi and Sylvia live or where they dropped off Kem. It's more like a cross between apartments and a hotel with outdoor entrances, although only a few of the units have an exterior door or a balcony. There's a main foyer, and when they step inside, Luke can't help staring.

It's elegant, all cream and gold tones. There's a small fountain inside the entryway. Luke wonders if it's meant as symbolism, like the fountain of youth or some such. It bubbles merrily into a pool that's lit from underneath. Luke sees the loose change previous visitors have tossed in. He pulls a coin from his pocket and flips it into the water. It splashes, earning a tiny giggle from Jory and a stern look from the woman at the desk.

She peers over her half-moon glasses at them. "Can I help you?" She sounds as if she hopes their answer is no.

Connor steps up to the desk and says, "We're here to see Jens Vaserman. He's expecting us."

The woman's expression relaxes. "Of course." She taps an open notebook. "Sign the visitor log, and I'll get you your badges."

Connor writes his name, and as he passes the book to the others, he tells them, "Jens lives in his own apartment. There are assisted living units, but he's self-sufficient."

Once Jory, Luke, and Connor have all signed the book and affixed visitor stickers to their chests, the woman at the desk gives them detailed directions through the winding passages to the apartments toward the back. These are the ones that have exterior doors as well as interior, and there are parking lots behind them for the residents. At last they arrive, and Connor knocks.

"Come in!"

Connor opens the door, and Luke is instantly in awe. Jens Vaserman's apartment is a colorful sensory extravaganza. He has shelves and shelves of books, spilling over everywhere. Luke is sure he's never seen so many, not even growing up in a homeschooling household with numerous siblings. He's delighted to see an entire bookshelf, floor to ceiling, devoted to what look like photo albums or scrapbooks. He's a guest, so he remains silent, but he wishes he could ask about them.

Besides the books, the apartment is quite a mix of mismatched furniture and handmade quilts and painted pottery. There are paintings on every wall in different styles. In the midst of it all sits Jens himself. He has a long, thick beard, and both it and his hair are so white it's nearly blinding. He's wearing a purple silk shirt, pressed orange-and-teal-striped trousers, and—despite the heat—a hand-crocheted scarf that ties it all together.

He looks surprised at first that Connor has brought so many people along, but a moment later, his lined face breaks out into a wide, welcoming smile. "Hello, friends!" He stands, and although the motion is silent, it's slow enough that Luke imagines the sound of his joints creaking.

Jens totters closer with the use of his cane. He holds out his free hand to Connor, who takes it. Jens presses his lips to it and then draws Connor into a hug. He pulls back and looks Connor up and down.

"My goodness, but you do look like Saul's side of the family. Come sit and tell me how they're doing." He gestures to the couch.

Connor exchanges a glance with Luke and Jory. He and Luke perch on the couch, which is covered in plastic. Luke's afraid he might slide off it. Jory takes a plastic-sheathed chair, and Jens returns to his recliner.

"Mr. Vaser—" Connor begins, but Jens interrupts.

"Please, do call me Jens. Mr. Vaserman sounds so formal." He chuckles. "I'm eighty-five years old, and I still think that sounds strange."

"All right. Jens, I don't know if you'd heard, but my father passed away a few months ago."

"Ah, I'm so sorry."

"Thank you. Anyway, I..." Connor clears his throat. "I never knew much about his family, and I was hoping you could fill me in." What Connor doesn't say is that he doesn't know much about his father, either.

"Hm," Jens says. "Well, our fathers were cousins. Our family is large, and we came to this country in waves. Some of us were here from the end of the nineteenth century. Some came over after 1933. That would be our branch. Saul's father was one of ten children. My parents arrived here in 1943."

"Oh, that's why you spell your name differently." Connor nods. "You came at separate times."

"Right. I'm surprised you found us, actually, given all the different circumstances. We were lucky. There were already people here ready to welcome us. But it was difficult for Germans of any kind to find safety in those years." He points to the shelf of albums. "Bring that here, the third one from the top on the right. Yes, that's the one," he says when Luke hands him a brown-and-gold book. "I was eight years old when we made the trip."

They spend the next hour gathering stories from Jens about what it was like to come to America as a boy and how his family acclimated. As he grew, Jens took a special interest in collecting the family's data. Over his lifetime, he reached out to all the various branches. On request, Connor hands him another album, this one full of family trees dating back to 1899.

"Did you show all this to my father?"

Jens nods. "He contacted me and asked for it, mostly so he could track down family members who had spread out. When he arrived here, he spent hours poring over the documents and reading anything I'd collected. If you like, you're welcome to do the same. The albums are full of all sorts of things, from newspaper clippings to birth and death records. When I'm gone, this will all pass to Danya, as she's the only one interested in record-keeping."

Jens explains that before Saul arrived, he hardly knew him, but he did remember him as a boy. "Smart, inquisitive... prone to getting himself into trouble." Jens laughs. "Did you inherit any of that spirit?"

"Maybe a little."

"Hm. I could tell you a story about what Saul did at his bar mitzvah." There's a mischievous smile playing on his lips.

Connor cringes visibly. "If it's anything like what I did at mine, I can only imagine how that went over."

Luke looks at him. "You had a bar mitzvah?"

"Yeah. Why?"

"I always thought...well, because of your mom. I assumed she'd had you baptized Catholic."

"Oh, she did, but we never told the rabbi that part." Now it's Connor's turn to laugh. "My parents thought if they raised me with both, I'd one day magically pick one. Only I ended up more confused." His smile falters. "That was the last time I did anything big with my father."

Jens reaches out and pats Connor's knee with his wrinkled hand. "Well, then, let's catch you up with some family stories, eh?"

*****

Jens offers them brunch, and they sit around his kitchen table enjoying the food he's prepared. He's made some kind of whole grain pancakes and spicy eggs, and there's also fresh fruit. Luke listens closely to what Jens tells them while they eat.

"Connor, do you understand generational trauma at all?" he asks.

Connor shakes his head. "I think I get the concept, but it's not something I've ever given much thought to."

"I believe this was the monster your father was fighting." Jens sets down his fork with a sigh. "We grew up in a very different time. It isn't that the horrors have gone away. They've only gone underground. But we didn't properly learn—or teach—how to manage."

"What do you mean?" Connor asks.

"Your grandparents tried to force your father to blend in, not to make any waves. To hide who he was. For a long time, he was apathetic. If he was to blend in, then he would go all the way."

"So that's why he married my mother." Connor nods.

"Probably not entirely, but yes, in part. I don't think he knew who he was back then."

"You're saying he figured it out?"

Jens shrugs one shoulder. "It seems he did, but perhaps too late to do more than spread his message."

"I don't even know what message that was!" Connor bangs his fist on the table, making Luke jump.

Lightly touching Connor's hand, Jens says, "You work in healthcare, yes?"

"I'm a nurse practitioner, yeah," Connor replies. "What does that—"

"And what do you do when someone comes to see you for an illness or injury?"

"I give them medicine or instructions on self-care, of course. I still don't—"

"That is what your father was doing. He finally learned the meaning of being a mensch."

"An honorable man," Connor says. "In what way?" He sounds bitter.

"It is not our job to simply receive G-d's blessings. We must *be* blessings to our neighbors, to strangers, to the world. That is what it meant to your father, and that is the message he sought to pass on."

Connor's hand trembles, and he withdraws it, folding them both in his lap. "I wish he would've told me."

"I know," Jens says. "He believed you were on the same path, but he assumed you wanted nothing to do with him after the way he behaved."

"I didn't," Connor admits.

"He left you something."

Jens rises from the table and retreats into his bedroom. Several minutes later, he returns with a wooden cigar box. He places it on the table beside Connor.

"You don't need to open this now. I suggest you take it back with you. Do some reading on what it means to be a blessing." Jens turns to the others. "I don't have anything tangible for either of you, but I do have something." He smiles at Luke. "For you, a picture. Connor tells me you're a photographer."

Luke tries to protest. "I'm not—"

"Come. Let's take that photo."

Jens sits in his chair, and they arrange themselves around him. Luke sets the timer on his camera. After, he checks the window to see how it came out. He's pleased with the results and shows the others.

"Perfect," Jens agrees. He turns to Jory. "And for you, a song." He hands them a slip of paper.

Jory opens it, and Luke peers over their shoulder. *"With a Little Help from My Friends," Joe Cocker.* Jory gives Luke a puzzled look. It might be a message for both of them; Luke isn't sure. He's also not sure how much he believes it. He's managed on his own since he left home, and he suspects Jory is much the same.

With a small shrug, Jory slips the paper into their pocket. It's time to go. Jens stands and takes each of their hands in turn. Then he closes his eyes and recites a prayer.

"Y'hi ratzon milfanekha A-donai E-loheinu ve-lohei avoteinu she-tolikhenu l'shalom v'tatz'idenu l'shalom v'tadrikhenu l'shalom, v'tagi'enu limhoz heftzenu l'hayim ul-simha ul-shalom. V'tatzilenu mi-kaf kol oyev v'orev v'listim v'hayot ra'ot ba-derekh, u-mi-kol minei pur'aniyot ha-mitrag'shot la-vo la-olam. V'tishlah b'rakha b'khol ma'a'se yadeinu v'tit'nenu l'hen ul-hesed ul-rahamim b'einekha uv-einei khol ro'einu. V'tishma kol tahanuneinu ki E-l sho'me'a t'fila v'tahanun ata. Barukh ata A-donai sho'me'a t'fila."

"The wayfarer's prayer," Connor murmurs. "My father used to make us say it in English every time we left for vacation. I can still recite the whole thing in both English and Hebrew. 'May it be Your will, Lord, our G-d and the G-d of our ancestors, that You lead us toward peace, guide our footsteps toward peace, and make us reach our desired destination for life, gladness, and peace. May You rescue us from the hand of every foe and ambush, from robbers and wild beasts on the trip, and from all manner of punishments that assemble to come to earth. May You send blessing in our handiwork, and grant us grace, kindness, and mercy in Your eyes and in the eyes of all who see us. May You hear the sound of our humble request because You are G-d Who hears prayer requests. Blessed are You, Lord, Who hears prayer.'"

Jens smiles. "I am glad your father left you with some good things from his childhood. You are no longer strangers but friends. My home is open to you should you travel this way again."

"Be a blessing," Connor says. "Well, you've certainly done that for us. Thank you."

"You are most welcome. Now carry it forward, young man."

They return to the rental car, each of them silently pondering the gifts and the blessing Jens has given them.

Then

LUKE CAUGHT THEM kissing. At least, that's how he categorized it in his mind. He knew there was more to it than that, and more to it than a single incident. Nothing started overnight; he would know.

He was surprised at how little it hurt, but he wasn't shocked that it happened. Sam was a full year older than Luke, and Esther had only just turned eighteen. Luke knew Tristan lost interest in her ages ago and was busy with college and work at the gas station. It made sense for Sam and Esther to find each other in the mess everyone had created.

Sam was as keen to keep her a secret as he had been Luke, and this time, Luke was on board. Esther was supposed to wait for someone their parents approved of to start courting.

They wanted her to find someone—or they wanted to find someone for her—who already had his life in order. Neither Tristan nor Sam qualified.

It was raining that day, a cold, pelting rain that slapped against the windows and came with a wind that roared around the house. Luke wasn't sure when they'd had time to mess around without him there. Might've been while he was focused on finishing some of his schoolwork, exactly as he'd promised his parents he would. He wasn't one hundred percent sure Sam wasn't trying to make him angry or jealous. All he knew was that they'd disappeared, and when he went to look for them, Esther was in his bed.

"Shut the door!" Sam yelled, yanking the blankets up.

"There's no one else here, and I've seen it already," Luke snapped. "Shut it yourself."

He left the door wide open and stomped down the stairs. He wasn't mad at them for being in bed together. He was mad that they hadn't said anything to him. Over the weeks they'd been working on their project, he and Sam had stopped fooling around. They didn't even sneak off to the woods during co-op anymore. Everything had cooled off as soon as Mrs. Whelock had made it clear she knew—and didn't disapprove of anything except their tardiness. Maybe it was the lack of excitement, or maybe it was the relief of having someone else who understood. Luke didn't feel tied to Sam so much anymore, whatever the reason.

A few minutes later, Esther came downstairs. She was flushed, but she'd put her clothes on and smoothed her hair. She sat at the Whelocks' kitchen table. Luke waited for her to explain.

"Are you upset? I know he was your friend first."

Luke wanted to tell her the truth, but that would've meant exposing the secret Sam was determined to carry to his grave. "No," he said, and he was being honest. "It's a little weird, but I don't care."

"You won't tell anyone?"

"Why would I?" Luke demanded.

She lowered her head slightly, making her gaze intense. "You could threaten to tell our family to keep me from telling them about you."

Luke sat back in shock, but he tried to cover it. "What about me?"

"I'm not stupid, and neither are you. I hate the way they control us. As soon as I figure out how, I'm getting out of here. Paul's new wife is a sweetheart, and she's helping me. Paul is too. He says times are changing, and our family is stuck in the past."

"So...you know. About...my thing."

"Well, I don't know what word you're using, no. But Sam... I'm sorry, Lukey. He told me. He says it's not the same for him as for you, and he doesn't know what to do."

"Not the same?"

"He likes me. Not the way Tristan used to have a crush on me, but the way a boyfriend likes a girlfriend."

"Oh." Luke frowned. That did sound different than himself.

"I wish our parents thought it was okay to talk about this. I had to go to the library to find out all the right sorts of words."

Luke's mouth dropped open. "They have that kind of stuff?"

"If you know where to look." Her face fell. "They had some stuff to explain our family, too. Our parents shelter us, and that's why we have no idea about a lot of it. Anyway, Sam's gonna tell his parents, but he'll leave you out if you want."

Luke shook his head. "His mom already knows. Not about you, though. Not yet."

"She will."

Sam walked into the kitchen, stopping their discussion. He looked between them, and Luke slid out of his chair. He draped an arm around Sam's shoulders, intending to reassure him.

"All good?" Sam asked, hope all over his tone.

"Sure. Listen, I'll keep this from my parents. I'm pretty good at secrets." Luke glanced sideways at Sam, who blushed but laughed.

"Yeah. I'm sorry to ask you to do it again. I'm..." His eyes misted over, and Luke squeezed his shoulders. "I really like Esther. I'm gonna talk to my parents about all this. I'm so sorry I messed it all up so bad."

"It's okay." Luke let go of him. "We had fun, but I'm only stuck here a little while longer. When you guys get out, send for me. There's something out there for me too."

They hugged again, the three of them, holding on as if sheltering each other from the wind and rain.

Chapter 24

I T'S RAINING. STEADY and soothing, as if it's in no hurry to get anywhere. It's neither a mist nor a thunderstorm. The rhythmic drumming on the RV's roof is calming. Luke wakes slowly, still sleep-warm and lulled by the sound. He curls up under the blanket, and for some reason it brings up a memory of his mother reading Robert Louis Stevenson's poem, "Rain." He still knows it by heart.

Luke's drifting in and out of sleep, and his mind is fuzzy. It alternates between present and past as he hears rattling in the kitchen. There are low voices and then the delicious smells of breakfast. He knows he should get up and help—cooking has been mostly his way of pitching in when they stop—but he doesn't want to move. The blankets are too cozy, and the rain is too comforting.

That's what finally makes him stir. Instead of triggering a flood of terror, he's enjoyed the pattering droplets. He's safe here with Connor and Jory, warm and dry inside their temporary home on wheels. He stretches then slides out of bed, wrapping the blanket around himself.

Connor turns toward the sound of the bedroom curtain, and his grin makes Luke happy. "Morning, sunshine!" Connor singsongs cheerfully.

Luke laughs. "You've seen outside, right?"

"I wasn't talking about the weather. Wanna come give us a hand?"

"Sure. You didn't burn anything this time, did you?"

"Shut up." There's no sting in Connor's tone, and he elbows Luke good-naturedly.

The three of them eat breakfast squashed together at the tiny table. They talk about nothing, about Connor's playlist and a story about a camping trip from Jory's childhood and about when Luke learned to make authentic tacos from his former employers. They clear the dishes, and Jory takes out a magazine from their last rest stop. They lounge in one of the seats, their leg over the arm rest.

Luke has more photos, having printed them at a chain drugstore at their last stop in Minnesota. He spreads them out, considering which ones to use and how to lay them out with the new postcards and other souvenirs. It's quiet in the RV aside from the rain and the occasional rustle of Jory's magazine.

Connor stands at the window. It's open a crack to let fresh air in. With the awning out, the rain can't sneak inside. A cool breeze wafts in, ruffling Connor's thick, dark hair. He's still in his pajamas, a ratty, red sweatshirt, and a pair of worn-thin flannel pants printed with Captain America's shield. His feet are encased in white socks, and he's holding a fresh cup of coffee as he stares outside, one arm braced above the window.

He turns then to smile at Luke, and a flood of affection washes over him. Luke only had a vague idea what to expect about this trip, but quiet, holy mornings with no plan and the day stretching out in front of them weren't part of it. He thought they would spend all of their time tracking down the people and places Connor's father once knew. Yet here they are, relaxing and staying dry.

It lasts all of fifteen glorious minutes before Connor's restless energy kicks in. He finishes his coffee and washes the cup. That appears to have done nothing but make Connor eager to do something. Luke is perfectly content to stay and work on his scrapbook, but Connor is pacing.

"Jeez," Jory remarks. "Dontcha ever sit still for five?"

"I did that already," Connor answers, though he does stop wearing a groove in the RV floor.

"Well, take five more, then." Jory shakes out their magazine and buries their nose in it.

"I don't see why it matters to you anyway," Connor mutters.

The warmth and friendly atmosphere from earlier dissipates, fizzing like rain on a hot sidewalk. Luke sighs. He's going to have to do something or risk being stuck there with the other two at each other all day. The rain isn't looking like it will clear up any time soon.

"What's there to do here?" he asks. "Maybe we can catch a car into town or something."

Connor shrugs. "You would know more than I do. Haven't you been here?"

"Not for more than ten years." Luke doesn't tell Connor that traveling even to somewhere nearby wasn't common.

"Fine. I'll look something up."

They're a little way outside Sioux Falls. Luke's never been to this particular place, but it's nice. They're in a tree grove, and there's a—now very wet—picnic table outside the RV. Connor knew what he was doing when he planned the trip, though Luke reflects it must've cost him a fortune to book all the places they've stayed. He never talks about it, so Luke wouldn't know for sure.

There are guide books in the crate under the map, one for each state they've visited. Luke thinks once they reach Seattle, he'll have enough road experience to cross several goals off his nonexistent bucket list. He moves his photos aside to make room for Connor, who now has the South Dakota guide book and is flipping through it.

"Lots we could do if it weren't for the damn rain," he says.

"Nothing if we're stuck in a storm, huh?"

Jory peers over the top of their magazine. "We could see a movie."

Connor scoffs. "Shouldn't we do something, you know, more touristy?"

"Why?" Luke wants to know. A movie sounds good on a wet day. "Check the weather. Is it supposed to be wet the whole time we're here? And what exactly are we doing here anyway, other than stopping?"

"That's pretty much it," Connor admits. "This was one of the places Dad visited in his last year. So I'm here too. Like in Pennsylvania, he didn't have family. He obviously had other plans, or else this was to break up the trip into smaller chunks."

Luke reaches across the table to put his hand on Connor's arm. The fabric of his old sweatshirt is soft under Luke's palm. "We'll get to see some of it. The rain can't last forever."

"Or it can," Connor gripes. "It's rained for over half this damn trip." He looks at the window and barks, "How about some fucking sunshine?"

"The weather is ass," Luke agrees. "So let's do something fun instead of being stuck here complaining about it. Gimme." He stretches out his hand for Connor's phone, and Connor reluctantly delivers it. "Okay, cool. There's a vintage theater showing old stuff. See?"

Jory tosses their magazine aside and comes to join the others at the table. "What's playing?"

"They're having a 1980s fantasy film festival." Luke turns the phone so the others can look.

"I've never seen any of those," Connor says.

"Me neither," Luke admits. "Besides those being before I was born, I didn't see a lot of movies or television as a kid."

Jory frowns. "Why the hell not?"

"My parents were...kind of protective."

Connor snorts. "You mean super religious, right?"

Luke shrugs. "I'm not actually sure. We—" He stops short. This isn't part of his childhood he's told them about, and he feels strange, protective of his family in spite of what happened.

"How can you not be sure if your family is religious?"

"I mean, we were, yeah. But...I don't know. Not like that. My parents didn't let us watch a lot of stuff because they thought time in front of a screen meant we weren't being active or reading books." He smiles, remembering one thing he loved about his parents' house. "We had a lot of books. My sister once said our parents sheltered us, and maybe they did, kind of. But they let us read literature of every kind." He giggles. "They had it sorted by age, though. Stuff they thought we were ready for, and stuff they thought was too grown up. We were homeschooled," he clarifies.

"Aren't most people who do that, you know, really strict?" Jory wonders.

"No. My best friend's family did it because they had three boys who couldn't sit still. Like you," he says to Connor, who is pacing again.

Connor stops. "You've never told me any of this." He sounds disappointed.

"I don't tell a lot of people, no. I left home when I was fifteen, and...I haven't been back."

"We're close to there now, aren't we?" Connor asks. Luke doesn't like the excitement in his voice. "We could go see your family."

"No!" Luke snaps. He turns the phone over and leaves it on the table. "I'm going to go get dressed."

He feels the others' eyes on him, but he doesn't turn around. The last thing he wants is to go see any of them. He's wondered sometimes what happened to Esther and to Paul and his wife. He thinks about the younger ones and wonders if they'd even recognize him now. He doesn't dress or do his hair the way he did when he lived at home. But if he never sees the rest of his brothers, it'll be too soon.

When he emerges from the room, Jory's gone back to reading, and Connor's gone back to brooding about the shitty weather. Luke knows he's disappointed because he'd expected this trip to be good weather at least some of the time. Sunny days have been few and far between since they left Erie.

Luke eyes the photos on the table, and his heart squeezes when he thinks about Kem discovering his old book. He knows he should have at least Kem's amount of bravery, the courage to face his family. Luke can't muster it, though. The past is behind him, and he doesn't want to revisit it. What his brothers did will haunt him forever, and no amount of time will heal the gaping wounds.

Still, Luke thinks he may have been too hard on Connor. At some point, Luke will explain why he can't do what Connor's asking. Now is not that time, but he can at least make it right for being harsh. He comes up behind him and puts a hand on Connor's shoulder.

Connor half turns around. "I'm sorry. I know better than to be pushy." He runs a hand through his hair. When he drops it, he holds Luke's gaze. His dark eyes are searching, and Luke couldn't look away if he tried. Yet Connor's expression is tender, asking and not demanding the truth.

"What?" Luke asks.

"I wish...I wish I understood. That's all."

Luke decides it's all right to give him something. "I'm sorry too. I shouldn't have snapped. But you're not missing out by never meeting them. They're not kind people." His chest tightens. That's not entirely true; Mama always was, and Luke misses her with a ferocious ache he hasn't felt since he was a teenager, lonely, scared, and cold in a strange city. Esther and the babies, too, for that matter.

Connor raises his hand as if to cup Luke's cheek, but he changes his mind at the last minute and drops it to Luke's shoulder instead. "I don't understand how unkind people could've made someone like you."

He turns away again, and Luke has to swallow several times to clear the lump that's formed in his throat. He's never thought of himself as anyone special. No different from anyone else. But the way Connor was looking at him makes him feel as if he means something.

"Hey." Connor interrupts Luke's thoughts. "I'm gonna get dressed, and then let's call for a car and go see those movies."

****

The movie theater is nearly empty except for the three of them and a handful of people a good two decades older. Jory laughs softly, and Connor coughs. They are at a 1980s film festival after all.

The theater is nice, so Luke assumes they otherwise do good business. This film festival has been going on for several days, and it's the middle of the week, so it's possible that's the reason for the quiet. The next movie doesn't start for twenty minutes, so they have time to look around.

Luke loves it. There are movie posters from the past six or seven decades, in all genres. He admires the glossy old-fashioned ones, with dapper gentlemen and beautiful ladies. Then there are the more modern ones, sometimes with car explosions. They fascinate him. It's not that Luke hasn't seen any movies in the dozen years since leaving home. It's more that he's mostly seen them in someone's home rather than a theater, and he's never seen so many posters at once from so many eras.

Jory and Connor flank him, and they stand there looking until a voice behind them says, "Hi, guys. What can I do for you?"

They turn around, and instantly, Luke's mouth is dry. The man in front of them isn't much older than they are. He's got a long, faded scar that runs down one cheek and onto his neck. One of his eyes is cloudy, and he lists slightly to the right as he approaches them. Regardless of his decade-old injuries, Luke would know him anywhere. He tries to shelter himself behind Connor, but it's too late.

Tristan Whelock stops short, his scarred mouth hanging open. He tilts his head, and it's obvious he can tell Luke is trying not to be seen. He doesn't give anything away, just closes his mouth and smiles crookedly at them.

"Are you all here for the film festival? There's a list of each day's movies up at the front, and you can stop by for half-price popcorn today."

"Thanks," Connor says. He glances over at Luke, puzzled.

"Right," Tristan says. "Well...I'll be up there if you want tickets. Unless you'd rather look at the movie posters. I'll have to charge you after an hour, though." He laughs when the others stare at him in shock. "Kidding!"

His limp reminds Luke uncomfortably of the way Adam's gait is unsteady after being attacked by Luke's ex. Luke knows exactly how Tristan sustained his injuries, and his heart hurts. Connor suspects something, but Luke isn't ready to explain. He trails after the others to the ticket counter.

Tristan collects their money and hands Connor the tickets. The others head toward the snacks, but Luke hesitates. He hangs back, waiting until Jory and Connor are out of earshot.

Leaning forward, Tristan says quietly, "You disappeared."

"I know. They were after me. They thought I was going to go to the police."

"Were you?"

Luke nods. "I had it on my camera. Every second, from the fight to the fire."

Tristan puts out a hand and traces Luke's scar, the one that almost matches his own, with his fingers. "How'd you get away?"

"Ran. Sam helped me."

"He would've."

Luke doesn't know what that's supposed to mean. "Of course he would."

"No, I mean that sounds like what he'd do." Tristan purses his lips. "He was so in love with you."

"He wasn't," Luke argues. "He was the one—" It's not Luke's story to tell, but with the others gone, he supposes there's no reason to hide anymore. "He was the one who got Esther pregnant."

Tristan's face registers his shock. "Sam? No."

"They were planning to save up to leave," Luke says. "I was the only one who knew except for Paul and his wife. It's why Paul tried to stop the others. They were so sure it was you, but he knew the truth. Sam couldn't go with her because he was too young. And now he's—" Luke chokes up, unable to say it.

Tristan stares at him. "Wait. Sam's what?"

"D-dead," Luke stammers. "In the fire."

"What the hell are you talking about? Sam didn't die in that fire."

"What?" Now it's Luke's turn to stare. "Then he's still—"

Tristan shakes his head. "He's not still in our hometown. I haven't seen Sam in ten years. I thought he'd left to find you."

"If he did, he never got in touch. What about Esther? I heard she'd gone to Seattle. I kept in touch with Paul for a couple weeks, and she left right after I did."

"Don't know," Tristan admits. "She disappeared around the same time as Sam."

Luke's heart sinks. When he first saw Tristan, he didn't want to talk to him. Now that he has, he wishes Tristan had more news for him. He won't ask after the rest of his family. He doesn't want to know. "How did you end up here?" he asks, shifting the conversation.

Tristan grins. "I manage this place!"

"You do?" Luke stares at him. "When did that happen?"

"I went to school for media, but there weren't many jobs. Mom's health wasn't too good for a while, so I had to stay close by, especially after Sam took off." He smiles again. "She'd like to see you, you know."

"Maybe next time I'm in town. So what happened?"

"Got a job here, and I took over when the previous manager retired. It's fun. I love thinking up new film festivals. They always draw a big crowd on weekends. Summer too, usually, with kids out. I'm surprised it's quiet in here today, especially with this lousy weather."

Luke's about to answer him when Jory and Connor show up with three drinks in a carrier and some popcorn. Jory looks from Luke to Tristan, but Connor is staring hard at Luke.

"We wondered where you'd got to," Jory says.

"I—" Luke considers lying, pretending he doesn't know who Tristan is. Or making something up, introducing him only as someone he vaguely knew a long time ago. But he can't. He won't keep hiding things from Connor. "This is Tristan," he says. "We were friends when we were kids. Um..." Luke's knees shake. He needs to explain, but he's run out of words.

Tristan says, "My brother was his best friend."

"M-more than that," Luke corrects. "We never said, but... yeah. We were a thing." He's not sure if Tristan knew for sure, but he does now.

Jory comes to the rescue again. They put an arm around Luke and absorb his continued trembling. "It's nice to meet you." They hold out a hand to Tristan. "I'm Luke's friend Jory."

Connor imitates them, and Luke is grateful no one is asking any other questions. There will be some later, but he can handle that. He leans into Jory's side, and they pull him in a little before dropping their arm.

"I don't want to hold you up from the movie," Tristan says. He squeezes Luke's upper arm. "It was good seeing you."

Luke doesn't want to leave it there. He pauses then opens his arms to hug Tristan. He can feel Tristan's relief, and they hold each other for what feels like a long time but probably isn't. Eventually, they release each other.

"Good seeing you too. Um, I could leave you my number, in case you need it." He doesn't add anything about Esther or Sam, just accepts the paper and pen Tristan hands him.

He passes the paper back to Tristan, and then he and the others turn around. Luke likes when Connor slides a protective arm around him on the way toward the theater.

Chapter 25

THEY RETURN TO the RV after the movies and grocery shopping, all three of them loaded down with bags. At the store, they were talking about the films—Luke was a bit over-awed—and joking good-naturedly about dinner plans and what they needed to stock up on. Connor filled up the extra gasoline can, given the long expanses of road with few stops. He isn't complaining about the rain anymore either, though it's still drizzling.

Now, back at the RV, things are quieter as they fill the cupboards and refrigerator. Jory hums softly, something Luke doesn't recognize but Connor obviously does because he joins in with the words. Luke pauses shelving things to listen, a soup can still in his hand.

"What is that?" Luke wants to know when they finish.

"Wait," Jory says. "Not only haven't you seen most movies, you also don't know anything about Broadway?"

Luke rolls his eyes, but he laughs. "Are you suggesting I should because I'm gay?"

"No, I'm suggesting you should because musical theater is popular. That was 'For Forever' from *Dear Evan Hansen*."

"Oh," Luke says. "I mean, I've heard of it, but I've never seen it. We didn't exactly go to see shows all the time." Or ever, really, but Luke doesn't want to admit he's never seen live theater.

Jory shuts the fridge with their foot and turns to put a box of pasta on the table. "Not even after you left home?"

This is going a direction Luke doesn't like. "With what money? I left when I was fifteen and was homeless until

I went through a series of shitty foster families. Then I followed my friends to college, where they all got fancy-ass degrees while I worked because that's how I was able to stay alive. Well, that and the asshole who used to use me as his personal punching bag." Luke sets the soup on the shelf harder than necessary and slams the cupboard door.

He heads for the tiny sleeping quarters for some privacy, but Jory stops him with a hand on his arm. "I'm sorry."

"Fuck off." Luke shrugs their hand away.

He can't go anywhere because Connor is blocking his path. "You didn't like it when we were bickering this morning about the rain, so I'm telling you now, both of you back off."

"I don't need you to nanny me," Luke snaps.

"Enough." Connor isn't yelling, but his voice is firm. "If you don't want to talk about it, that's up to you. But I doubt this is about your lack of cultural education."

"You want me to talk?" Luke is shaking, but Jory poked the bear, and there's no going back. "Fine. The truth—all of it."

"You don't have to," Connor says, more gently this time. "We're not owed an explanation."

"Yeah, you are." Luke deflates. "I let everyone think my parents kicked me out because I was gay. That was a lot easier than explaining what happened."

Connor frowns. "I did actually think that, yeah."

"Everyone does. It's probably not fair to my parents. Or my mother, anyway. I have no idea if my father knew or cared."

"So...you ran away?" Jory asks.

"No. Um...maybe we should sit."

Dinner can wait. They arrange themselves around the table, with Luke in the middle, as always. He feels as safe as he ever does, but it doesn't stop his limbs from feeling like jelly or his stomach from cramping with nerves. He takes several deep breaths, but they don't help. This is the part of his story he's never shared.

"My family was...religious, as you've probably guessed. But not bad, like some families. I mean, my parents clearly did not believe in birth control. They weren't necessarily against anyone being gay, either, I guess. The only two times my mother said anything about it were once in church when she told me not to listen to the pastor going off about it. The other is murkier. She once said birth control wasn't natural, and people should never go against what God has created in them. She said it in a way I thought she might've meant me, but who knows."

As they did with Connor before, the others connect to Luke like a circuit. Jory clasps one hand and Connor the other. The breathing helps this time, and Luke continues.

"You met Tristan today. He was sort of courting my sister Esther, I guess, but because his family was a different kind of Christian, my parents weren't happy about it. His mother was on her own and divorced—another no-no—and they didn't have a lot of money. She worked nights and homeschooled them by day. We lived outside the nearest bigger town, and the schools were far away and not great. Anyway, homeschooling is how I met Sam."

"Sam..." Jory muses. "Oh, you told us he was your boyfriend."

"Sort of," Luke agrees. "He kept telling me he wasn't gay, even though his mom was completely fine. She caught us once. We used to sneak away during lunch at the homeschool co-op. We'd been, uh, kissing. And things." Luke knows his ears must be red because he feels the heat.

"'And things.'" Connor lets go of the others to make air quotes. "Yeah, sounds about right."

"Okay, well, if you want me to spell it out, we'd had our hands down each other's jeans in the woods behind the church where the co-op met."

"Didn't need details," Jory says, but they grin to show they don't mean anything by it.

"Right. Well, Sam's mom promised not to tell my parents. She let us do a fake project at her house so we could see each other, and Esther supervised us. We cooled off once we had permission. I don't know...something about being the only two gay kids we knew made us stick together, but we really weren't made to be boyfriends. He and Esther..." Luke trails off.

"Wait," Jory says. "So Sam really wasn't gay after all?"

"No," Luke says. "We weren't exactly sheltered—or he wasn't—but even then, I don't think most of us knew there was much besides gay or straight. Sam and Esther fell pretty hard for each other."

"Jesus, I'd have been so pissed off," Connor remarks. "Were you?"

"No," Luke says. "Well, maybe a little, at first. Mostly because they didn't say anything, and I caught them in Sam's bed. Esther had her shirt off. I think they'd have had sex then if I hadn't walked in. After that, it became me covering for them instead of Esther covering for Sam and me."

He can't continue right away. Everything is rushing back: Esther's confession, their older brothers finding out, the convenience store where Tristan worked, the fight and the fire. He's gasping for breath, and he feels lightheaded.

Connor angles so he can take Luke's face in his hands. "Breathe with me. It's okay. You're safe. Whatever happened, it's in the past."

Jory still has hold of Luke's hand, and they press tightly, an anchor. Luke opens his eyes to look right at Connor. There's something soothing in the way Connor is holding him, the same way he held Connor the night after they read Saul's memoir. Inch by inch, Luke comes back to the present, his panting slowing to normal rhythm.

"It was bad," he says, as if the others couldn't have guessed.

Then

LUKE WAS IN the Mobil convenience store. He'd finished his chores, and he was supposed to meet Sam as soon as Sam finished mowing the lawn. Only a few of them knew about Esther's baby. After the initial surprise, they had some planning to do. Paul was going to take her in for a while and let Dinah care for her until they figured out what to do. Sam was still underage, technically, even though there were only two years between them. Not to mention Mrs. Whelock wouldn't stand for Sam quitting school over it. She would sooner take Esther herself, but they hadn't told her anything yet.

Privately, Luke thought they should have. He didn't believe his parents would disown her or anything, but they sure would be mad. Luke had to admit he was a little mad at the two of them himself. He couldn't understand, after all Esther's talk about looking everything up in the library, how she hadn't figured out what to do.

He had asked her if she was going to go off to one of the bigger cities like Sam said some girls did. It sounded so old-fashioned to Luke, no matter how he imagined the situation. Esther could sneak off, away from their families, and get it taken care of. Or she could get sent to Paul's house to hide until the baby was born. Luke thought it was all stupid.

So here he was, waiting for Sam so they could decide on a better solution. Luke was going to convince Sam they should tell his mother at the very least. He wondered if they should tell Luke's parents too. He had an idea—if they went that way, it might soften the news for him to confess everything about himself at the same time.

Inside the store, he browsed the shelves, hidden toward the back near the coolers of soda and water. He picked out a pack of bubblegum and a bag of pretzels. He had his camera around his neck, since he'd been out taking pictures to use for another project. He was going to go next door to the strip mall and print them at the drugstore if he had time before Sam showed up.

Tristan was working at the register. He looked bored. An older woman paid for her gas and left, and Tristan made himself busy—or made himself look busy; it was hard to tell which. The bell over the door chimed, and in walked five of Luke's older brothers.

Luke frowned. There was no reason for them to be there, not all together like that. Unless Dad had some job they were on, and they were all taking a break to buy drinks. Luke didn't think so, though. They had a serious look about them, as if someone had died.

Tristan was unprepared for the first punch.

Mark had him over the counter and in the middle of the group before Luke could say a word. He pulled out his camera and made sure the flash was off so it wouldn't alert them. He wasn't big enough to stop them, but he sure could capture every second of it. He snapped as many pictures as he could while his brothers pummeled Tristan.

The only thing Luke caught was that they believed he'd raped Esther. How they could've figured that was anyone's guess, and they were as far from the truth as possible. Once they knew what really happened, they would go after Sam next. Luke gasped, then held his breath to see if the others noticed. He ducked behind a shelf and peered around.

Matt looked up and frowned, but then he went back to their fight. It wasn't a fair one. Tristan was pretty fit, and he wasn't small, but five adults against one eighteen-year-old would never work out to his advantage. Luke had seen enough; he knew he had to find a way to get out the door and get help.

He crept around the displays, crouching down so he was below the height of all the shelves. His heart thundered so loud he was shocked his brothers couldn't hear it over their angry shouting. He heard Tristan's faint protests, but he also knew if Tristan figured out what was going on, he would do everything in his power to protect Sam. That made it all the more important Luke get someone quickly. When his brothers were done with Tristan, they'd go find Sam.

Luke looked up at the bell over the door. Once it jangled, he would have only a few seconds' head start over his brothers. He wouldn't fare any better against them than Tristan. Worse, maybe. Tristan was muscular from working on the farm. Luke was a skinny fifteen-year-old whose primary skill was with a camera.

He eyed his brothers and then the door one more time before he drew in his breath and made a dash for it. He crashed through the door, slamming it open so hard the bell only made a feeble attempt at ringing. From there, he ran. He didn't look back, despite the shouts behind him. He had no idea where he was going. He first thought of Sam's place, maybe, to find him and his mother and a phone. Or to Paul and Dinah's house. Both of which were somewhat stupid—he would need a car. It was too far on foot.

Luke changed course and ran for the adjacent plaza. There would be someone in the pharmacy who could call the police. He ducked inside, his ears ringing from the sudden silence. No one was at the front counter, so he threaded through the aisles to the pharmacy. He spotted both the elderly pharmacist and her young assistant.

"Hey!" Luke yelled. "Please. I need help!"

At first, the pharmacist only looked over her glasses at him. He wished she would hurry up and decide he was sincere already. Unhurried and unaware of the commotion next door, she came out from among the rows of medication bottles.

"Yes?"

"Please," Luke begged. He panted, bracing his hands on his knees. "My brothers...they're... They have Tristan Whelock next door and they're hurting him." He gasped for breath. "Call someone. Please."

He was crying now, so wound up from what he'd seen that he couldn't get hold of himself. The pharmacist nodded at her assistant, and he grabbed the phone. Luke couldn't hear what he was saying. The pharmacist came out from behind the counter. It seemed like it took all her emotional energy to put her arm around Luke in an attempt to comfort him. She wasn't especially effective, but he was grateful she was trying.

He heard voices and tensed, his insides coiled like a spring. Had they come for him now too? A moment later, James and Jude appeared. Luke almost sighed with relief. He could tell them what the others were up to, and they would help.

"There you are!" James said. "C'mon. Mom needs us to get home."

Luke frowned. Something didn't feel right, but he was too upset to figure out what. He nodded and stepped away from the pharmacist. She glanced at his brothers then peered at him over her glasses again.

"You should stay here and wait," she advised. She addressed James and Jude. "Why don't you let your mother know he's here. He'll be needed for a while."

"What for?" Jude demanded.

She straightened her spine and looked Jude dead in the eye. "This young man witnessed a crime. The police will need to hear what he has to say."

"Then they can call us," James said. "You can't force him to sit here. He's underage."

For some reason, the way James said it made Luke shiver. He didn't like the way Jude and James were speaking to the pharmacist. But he suspected he wouldn't have a choice in the matter. They would take him by force if he didn't willingly come. No doubt someone else had managed to get the police there already, and the only thing Luke could hope was for his brothers not to have killed Tristan. Surely even they wouldn't go that far in broad daylight in a public place.

"Right now, Luke." Jude stepped forward, his arms crossed.

Meekly, Luke inched toward him. He saw the pharmacist's disappointed expression, but he couldn't worry about that now. The only thing on his mind was making sure Esther and Sam were safe. James and Jude turned and walked away once they were convinced Luke was following them.

He considered running back. They were facing away, and he would be able to sneak off without notice. He only had a few seconds to decide. Jude turned his head, and the moment was gone. Luke trailed out of the pharmacy behind him.

Outside, James roughly shoved Luke into his truck. Jude hopped into the bed, and they took off. It was about five minutes before Luke realized they weren't going home. He peeked at James out of the corner of his eye, but James's eyes were on the road, his expression hard as steel. Luke gazed down at his lap, keeping his mouth shut.

They were at the edge of the woods behind the homeschool co-op, the ones that butted up against the Whelocks' property. Luke's head shot up when he saw. It wasn't as if there were a lot of places they could go that weren't out in the open, but Luke had no idea what they were doing there.

His pulse raced as Jude yanked him roughly from the truck. James shoved him hard in the back. Luke tried to ask what they were doing, but Jude slapped him.

"Shut your mouth, mama's boy. You know some things about this, and you're gonna tell us or we tell her we all know what you are."

A flash of anger raced through Luke like lightning. "And what is that?"

James punched him in the gut, making Luke double over. Leaning in, James murmured in his ear exactly what he meant.

"She...wouldn't...care," Luke gasped.

Both James and Jude laughed at that. James said, "That's what you think. Move." He shoved Luke.

He could never say for sure what the next sequence of events was nor why his brothers made the choice they did. The five who had gone after Tristan were waiting for them, and Luke saw now how mean they looked. He wished he knew how they'd found out about Esther and why they'd hurt Tristan instead of taking some other path.

It no longer mattered. One of them—he thought it was Tim—grabbed his camera and smashed it. He pulled out the memory card and stomped that too, leaving it in the dirt. Titus, the biggest of them, punched Luke in the nose, re-breaking it. He slammed Luke into a tree, causing ripples of pain up his back.

Matt grabbed Luke by the bloody collar of his T-shirt. "We're telling our parents everything. You know something about it? Now's the time to come clean."

Luke shook his head. He wouldn't sell out Sam like that any more than Tristan would have. He would rather die with the secret than tell his brothers anything at all.

Mark scoffed. "Ma was always too soft on you. The babies too. And now look at you. If she hadn't played favorites, you'd be more of a man, not some weakling homo brat."

Luke wanted to tell Mark that he was the strongest of them, the only one who knew what real loyalty meant. They thought it meant protecting their family, making sure no one would ever suspect them of bringing shame on their parents. Luke knew it meant saving loved ones in the face of pain.

"If you won't tell us, then we'll make sure you can't go home and tell stories. You didn't see anything, you understand me?" Titus said. He stepped toward Luke with a menacing glare.

"I get it."

"You'd better run."

Titus hit him once more for good measure. After he let Luke go, someone hurled a knife. It sailed close enough to strike Luke's face before landing somewhere behind him. That was when Luke ran.

※※※※

The knife barely missed doing serious damage to Luke's face. As it was, the blade grazed his cheek as it whistled past to land at the foot of the tree behind him. He heard someone shout "Run!" It wasn't directed at Luke, but he obeyed the command anyway.

He dashed through the grove. His brothers surely hadn't intended for him to be lost in the woods, given how small and easy to navigate they were. But neither did they intend for him to return home. Whoever threw the knife—probably Titus—could've done serious harm, but that hadn't been the intent either. It was a message, a warning. What they'd done to Sam Whelock's brother, they'd do to him in a heartbeat.

It didn't matter that Tristan Whelock was as innocent a bystander as Luke was. He'd been in the wrong place at the wrong time, and Luke's brothers didn't know he wasn't responsible for Esther. Only Luke knew the truth, and he would take it to his grave. If he'd had any idea Titus would lead the others down this path, he'd have found a way to stop them. Instead, he'd done the only thing he could: document it all.

They'd destroyed his good camera, but what they didn't know was that they hadn't succeeded in ruining the memory card. They also didn't know about the disposable camera he had in the bag's inner pocket. Anything he saw, he could still capture on film. That was why he was headed in the opposite direction they'd intended.

He was alone, racing through the trees in hopes of finding someone who would get him anywhere but there. The last of the dead autumn leaves crunched under his feet. He didn't stop, not even when his legs began to ache and his lungs burned and he had a sharp pain in his side. He would run as far and as fast as he could away from his brothers.

The trees thinned, and he slowed. He'd never been on this end of them on foot. This was the far side of the Whelocks' property. He hadn't meant to go this way, but here he was. And right there, mowing their yard, was Sam. Luke pulled up short, panting.

"Sam!" he yelled.

Sam looked over, and his mouth dropped open. He rode the mower around until he was next to Luke, where he cut the motor. He jumped down and approached slowly.

They hadn't spoken since what happened with Esther. Even now, Luke was taking a risk. He was sure Sam hadn't heard yet what Luke's brothers had done; if he had, he wouldn't be casually mowing the lawn and stopping to talk to Luke. He would be rushing at Luke and pummeling him the way he deserved.

"What the devil happened to you, Luke?"

"My...I..." Luke stared at Sam. A lie would do just as well as the truth, especially a believable one. "They chased me off. Threatened to tell our parents I'm...you know."

"Aw, hell." Sam reached up as if to touch Luke's cheek, but he withdrew his hand at the last minute. "Here." He pulled out a wad of tissues and handed them over.

Luke dabbed at his cheek, wincing at the sting. "I gotta get out of here."

Sam glanced behind him and then peered over Luke's shoulder. "They after you?"

"Naw. But they will be." That part was the God's honest truth if his brothers found out where he'd gone. "I know it's a lot to ask, but can I hide out here?"

Sam shook his head. "This is the first place they'll look for you. We both know that." Another glance around. "There's this old man, lives up back of our place on the other side. He can arrange a ride for you." Sam cleared his throat. "You didn't tell them about Esther, did you?"

"No. I wouldn't do that to you. You know that."

"Yeah, okay."

Luke heard shouts then, and he froze. Surely they hadn't followed him. It took him almost a full minute to figure out the shouting was from the other side of the property, toward the house. A full minute in which he should've been already on his way as soon as Sam gave him directions.

Sam heard it now too, and he turned around. "Goddamn. Luke, get out of here. I don't know what's going on, but I'll take care of it." He looked back at Luke. "Do they know about us? Is that how they—"

"No, and I'd never tell them that either." Luke swallowed the lump in his throat. He wished Sam couldn't still make his stomach tight with need. He wanted to drag Sam with him, to kiss him and make him promise they could get through this. Only he couldn't, and he was running out of time.

"I gotta go. I'll—" He was going to say "write," but he wouldn't.

"Get," Sam said.

Luke ran again, this time around the perimeter of the property. There was an entire cornfield, and he could hide behind it. He crossed and uncrossed his fingers seven times, just like he had when he was little. He didn't know why his brothers were going after Sam when they'd already had a go at Tristan, and he was afraid of what their anger would do. Sam thought he was protecting Luke, but Luke hoped he knew how to protect himself.

When he got to the back of the big house, he looked past it to the next field. Sure enough, there was the homestead Sam mentioned. He paused to catch his breath, and that was when he made the mistake of looking back. He saw the flash and then heard the bang before Sam's house was engulfed in flames. Luke screamed.

His heart thundered as he pulled out the disposable camera. He would take the pictures and then run, sending them to the police later. Sam was gone, maybe his mother and Esther too, if she'd been at his house. There was nothing Luke could do to bring any of them back. His best shot was to get out of there and make sure someone knew the truth about his brothers.

Luke tucked the camera away. He had precious little time to make it out in the open before he was discovered. He put his head down and ran as fast as his skinny legs would carry him.

Chapter 26

L UKE FINISHES HIS story and slumps over the table. He can't look at the others. What if they think he's a failure because he left Tristan like that? He doesn't know what happened after he ran. Until today, he was convinced Sam died in the fire. Luke never tried to contact Esther, though he knew from a single phone call with Paul that she was safe. Nor did he go to the police after all, too scared to try. He puts his head in his hands.

Connor's hand on his back is warm and comforting. "None of this is your fault, Lukey." He's resorted to the old pet name, and for some reason, that too is reassuring.

He knows it's not his fault, but he also knows he shouldn't have let fear stop him from doing what he could to protect the others. "It was my job to keep Esther and Sam safe. I didn't do that. I don't even know where they are now."

"Why don't you find out?" Jory asks.

Luke stares at them. "How would I do that? Even Tristan doesn't know. He said so."

"He also suggested you visit his mother," Connor says gently. "I overheard."

"If she knew anything, then Tristan would know too." Luke shakes his head. He figures Tristan probably wants Luke to have the answers, but if no one has seen Esther since Luke left, then it means she doesn't want to be found.

"It's your choice," Connor says. "But I'll tell you that tracking down my family was worth it. I don't yet know

281

everything about my father, but I don't care. He didn't do a lot to support me, and he didn't even try to find me before he died. But his family? They've been amazing."

Luke thinks about that. Mrs. Whelock was kind to him at a time when he was afraid of the consequences of being himself around his own family. She never cared that he and Sam were trying to discover who they were. There must have been others at the church where he grew up, kids who heard the pastor's messages and whose parents agreed. Did they have anyone like Mrs. Whelock?

"I don't know," Luke says. "I really don't."

Connor leans his head against Luke's. "It's all right. You don't have to decide right now."

The three of them slide out from the table and begin making dinner without speaking. Luke marvels at how easily they move around each other in the tiny space. It almost feels like home, even though Luke knows they won't stay in the RV forever.

It's not late, but the sky is darkening. The on-and-off mist turns to rain again, and the wind picks up. It whistles as it blows around the RV, an eerie, tuneless melody. Luke shivers, knowing there's going to be a thunderstorm. He's grateful now that he and Connor chose to add the extra piece between the beds. He hates admitting it, but he doesn't want to be alone right now.

They eat at the small kitchen table. Afterward, while the wind rocks the RV and the rain pelts the roof, they clean up and play cards until long into the evening. The rain lets up, and the sky is smoky gray-black. The air is so dense with moisture that everything feels damp and heavy.

There's no discussion about their sleeping arrangements, but somehow it's decided they'll all share sleeping space. Luke wants to object at first, but the rumble of thunder and flash of lightning in the distance change his mind. They'll be warmer together, and Luke won't feel alone.

He falls asleep that way, cocooned in the blanket and flanked by Connor and Jory. His dreams are troubled by a mixture of memory and unconscious fears. There's a monster with seven heads and a dense forest and a baby in a clearing who tacks a message to a tree. None of it makes sense to him. Eventually, he wakes to gray light filtering in through the gap in the bed space curtains.

He wonders where Connor's gone. Luke's alone, which doesn't feel so bad with the sky growing lighter. It's still cool, but it feels as if the wet weather has lifted. He slips out of bed.

Connor is at the kitchenette table, the still-unopened box from Jens in front of him. Jory's bed is empty, the curtains open. It takes Luke a moment to recall that Jory joined them last night. They aren't in the kitchen with Connor or lounging in one of the cushioned seats.

"Where're Jory?" Luke asks as he sits down.

"I though they were still asleep."

"Nope. Maybe they went out for a smoke and a walk."

Speaking of which, Luke feels the need for air himself. He steps outside the RV. The welcome scent of fresh earth greets him. This RV park is gorgeous, tucked away so they can almost pretend there's nothing nearby. There's no rush to be out of there any time soon, which will give them time to process everything that's happened before taking the next leg of their journey.

Luke looks around, expecting to see Jory come strolling out of the woods. He's puzzled when it remains quiet at their campsite. He doesn't smell Jory's cigarettes, either. Jory's never told them where they're headed, so he supposes it's possible they've gone wherever they planned. They never said goodbye, though, and Luke thinks that's not much like them.

While he's standing there pondering it, Connor steps out. "Luke? I think there's something you should see."

Luke follows Connor back inside, shivering a little. Connor points to the open drawer where Luke's been storing his scrapbook. The new one with all the postcards is still there, but the old one is gone. In its place is an envelope marked with Luke's name. Luke picks it up. Inside is a single sheet of paper, which he pulls out.

I haven't been much use to you all so far, but now there's something I have to do. I'm going to help you, I promise. I won't keep hiding the truth.

"What the hell is that supposed to mean?" Connor asks.

"I don't know." Luke crumples the paper.

Jory took his scrapbook, the one Luke's been making for years. What use would it be to them? It's full of the only pictures he has of Esther, memories of AJ during college, and some photos of Jax. A lot of photos of Jax. Is that where Jory went? To find Jax and bring them here, to this RV park? That seems unlikely. So what—

"Wait." Something in Luke's brain is turning over. "The memory card. The one my brothers thought was gone." Luke looks up at Connor, horrified. "They've taken it to find my family."

****

They're outside Mitchell, almost to Liberty Station, the small town where Luke lived for less than a third of his life. Luke can tell by the exact way the road bends, the sharp angles up into hills and back down again. If they keep going, they'll be right into Luke's hometown. The land flattens out into farms as they approach.

There are rises in the road, but they're longer and more sloping. Luke has to breathe slowly as they pass the spot where he was almost found and returned to his family. First, they pass the house where a group of kind strangers located a ride for him. Next, he recognizes the white house with the blue trim and wonders if the older woman who lived there is still around. Would she remember the skinny teenager who knocked on her door? Or the phone she promised him only to deliver a call to the cops?

"Hey," Connor says. "You okay?"

"Not really," Luke admits. He points to the white farmhouse. "The woman there, she called the police when I stopped for help. I had to hide from them."

"Jesus," Connor mutters. "What was wrong with your family?"

"I honestly don't know," Luke replies, but part of him does. He remembers the proud way his father used his photographs for the insurance company when they claimed storm damage on the RVs. He also recalls how he was allowed to do what Esther did, until he was old enough his father bowed to pressure to make him more like his brothers. Matt and Mark in particular were always angry with him then.

"I get that," Connor is saying now. "I've never really figured out what made my parents act the way they did. My mother used to tell me I ruined her life. My father disappeared. I don't get why families do that shit." He stares ahead at the road for a moment then continues, "They weren't like that when I was really young. I feel like there's this missing piece, something I'm this close"—he pinches his thumb and finger together—"to grasping and can't quite get."

"So, in all our traveling to see your family, you're still not sure?" Luke thought Connor might've found his answers somewhere in his father's memorabilia, but it seems not.

Connor shakes his head. "I wish. What I want to know is why he left, and what made my parents end up so angry with each other. And with me." He says the last part more quietly, like a secret wish.

"My brothers always thought my parents loved us young ones better. I mean, not the oldest ones. They were adults with kids by the time I left. I have one brother who was seventeen when I was born. I barely know him. My father sent me to live with him for a summer. That's about when they figured out I was one hundred percent useless at their home building and renovation business."

Connor's eyebrows shoot up, and he looks like he's trying to hold in his laughter. "I can see how they might decide that, yeah."

"Shut up." But Luke smiles.

There's a sign ahead, one announcing the town of Liberty Station. It's white with gold lettering, and it looks as if it's been repainted recently. It no longer has the population count on it; perhaps that's not a point of pride for the town any longer. Connor pulls the RV into a turnaround area off the shoulder of the road.

"Why don't you take a picture?" he suggests.

Luke isn't sure why he would want to remember this specific moment, but he does as Connor says. He pulls out his camera and steps down from the vehicle. First, he takes a photo of the sign. Then he points the lens toward the edge of town, down the hill where they're parked. He can make out the first gas station and convenience store, right next to the auto shop. Farther along, one or two houses are set back from the road. It looks like almost every other small town they've seen on this trip. Nondescript until one enters the town properly, with an empty strip of state road, a store that sells Pepsi products, a diner, and three or four random houses.

He shows Connor the picture in the preview window on the camera, and he can tell Connor is thinking the exact same thing. What he actually says is, "It's...like a postcard?"

"Nah," Luke says. "Those at least tell you something interesting about the town." He tucks the camera away. "Liberty Station isn't even interesting enough for a postcard."

"We'll see," Connor tells him.

They buckle in and head right into town. There's no official campground here for the RV, but there's a hotel that allows RV parking. No water or electric, and the cost overnight is the same as a hotel room. Luke hopes they won't be here that long, but he doesn't know what they'll find when they get here.

It's familiar and not. The main street is lined with historic houses, and those are all kept in pristine condition. They belong to the very few wealthy families living in Liberty Station. Some have patriotic flags out front. One has rows and rows of windows, and Luke remembers the owners had candles in every single one. If they still do, he can't tell in the daylight.

There's a town hall and a small library, both of which also have patriotic flags. They pass a couple more houses, and then things begin to spread out again. The school building has been updated. They have an electronic sign now, and the school boasts a population of nearly 300 students. Luke never set foot in any of the classrooms as a child. He was in the gym once or twice for events, but that's about it.

There's a couple of newer neighborhoods near the school. Luke's brother Roman lived in one of the ones closer to the building, but the housing developments have expanded since then. He wonders if Roman is still there or if he's moved to another neighborhood or even out of the town entirely. With a jolt, Luke realizes Roman's oldest child would've graduated high school by now.

"Where to?" Connor asks.

"I'm...not sure." Luke looks around. "My family used to live out past all these places. We didn't have a farm, but we lived on a pretty big tract of land. There's a church with woods behind it." He swallows. "Sam lived on the other side of those, closer to the town center. Let's go there first. Tristan said his mom would like to see me, so I assume she still lives there."

Connor continues past the newer neighborhoods out to where the homes are older and where gardens and farmland begin. Luke has no clue what he'll find, but he assumes the Whelocks must've had their house rebuilt after the fire. When a light-blue house comes into view, Luke is overcome with relief.

He has to take several calming breaths before he can say, "There."

They follow the curve of the road, and Luke notes that the pavement is new. It used to be a gravel road. Connor pulls in behind a black sedan; the driveway's been paved over too. Luke remains seated when Connor kills the engine and unbuckles. Without a word, Connor hops down and comes around to Luke's side. He opens the door and offers a hand.

"I'm right here," he says. "Exactly how you've been for the last few weeks."

The words give Luke new courage, and he releases his seatbelt. He accepts Connor's hand and jumps down. Together, they walk up the driveway and to the stone path leading to the front porch. There's new landscaping, and Luke sees the farmland has been divided up. Of course, Mrs. Whelock would be older now, and so would her parents, who helped her care for their property. He wonders if any of them are even still there in the house or if they've all left, the house and land passing to someone else.

Luke rings the doorbell. It's a while before a woman answers. She looks surprised and then puzzled. "Can I help you?"

"I was looking for Elaine Whelock," Luke says. The woman looks vaguely familiar, but she wasn't the parent of any of his homeschool peers. She's far too young.

"Oh!" The woman smiles. "We bought this place from her about four years ago. She lives in town now. I can give you an address and phone number. She's such a lovely person. Hold on a moment while I go get pen and paper."

Luke's nervous energy returns, but he's also relieved in a way. This woman seems kind, exactly the sort Mrs. Whelock would've liked to sell her house to. A moment later, the homeowner is back with a page from a notepad, lined and with a strip of dancing Santas across the top. Luke glances at it and badly suppresses a giggle.

The woman laughs outright. "Not quite appropriate for the season, but it's what I had." She holds out a hand. "Dinah Spier."

Luke's hand shakes, and he drops the paper. Connor picks it up and then has to support Luke's weight as he slumps. He can't breathe. Which of his brothers is married to this woman? It's not as if his surname is unusual, but this was—and still is—a very small town. The majority of people bearing that name are relations of his, owing to his large family. He struggles for an answer and then hits it: Paul.

"Oh, god," he whispers.

"Are you all right?" Dinah is now out on the porch, fanning Luke with the notepad she still has. She looks to Connor. "He's all flushed. Must be the heat. Come in, and I'll get you both some water."

Connor has to shove on Luke to get him to comply. The last thing Luke wants is to enter this woman's home, but he has no choice. Both she and Connor think he's having some kind of heat stroke. Connor probably hasn't made the connection yet, or if he did, it isn't of much significance to him. Luke finally caves and lets them take him inside.

Dinah shows Connor to the couch, and he helps Luke stretch out. Luke thinks this may be a good thing, given he's still on the verge of passing out. The initial shock is wearing off, though, and he has enough presence of mind to look around. The house obviously looks nothing like when he was last there. Everything is new, and the decor is rustic and homey. Different from Mrs. Whelock's old-fashioned elegance.

In a few minutes, Dinah is back with two glasses of water. She hands one to Connor, and Luke sits up to accept the other. He sips slowly and takes deep breaths in between. He'll have to say something eventually, but the drink gives him time to stall and study Dinah.

She's pretty in the way of a glossy online photo. Shiny. Her hair is long, golden brown, and silky smooth, framing her heart-shaped face and her green eyes. She's feminine in that sort of modest way that's so prized among families like Luke's. Conservative dress: flared, white capri pants, a coral-colored straight-neckline tank top, and a patterned shirt—matching the coral, of course—over the top. She has a single thin necklace with a cross pendant and tiny earrings that catch the light. Her makeup is soft and subtle, only enough to accent what natural beauty she possesses. Luke sees how she ended up married to one of his brothers in the first place. He shudders but reminds himself Paul wasn't one of the ones who dumped him in the woods and forced him to run.

"Feeling better?" she asks. When Luke nods, she says, "I think you were about to tell me who you really are and why you showed up on my porch."

Luke's mouth drops open, and he catches Connor out of the corner of his eye, wearing a similar expression. How Dinah figured it out is a mystery. To deflect, Luke asks her about it.

"How did you know?"

She sighs. "You really don't remember me?"

Luke shakes his head. "I'm surprised you do remember me."

"You look just like my son. Genetics are a funny thing."

Luke knows he doesn't look much like most of his brothers. There's some resemblance, but he and Johnny were more alike than either of them were like the others. They were the only two with blond hair and blue eyes. Luke grew up wondering if they'd been adopted, though he vaguely recalled Johnny's birth, and Mama always corrected him that she had very much been there when he was born and would've told him if she hadn't. He trusted her because she said she didn't believe in keeping that sort of secret. Now it's a relief to know someone else in the family has his unusual looks.

"I shouldn't have come here," Luke says, struggling to sit all the way up.

Connor stops him. "Maybe we should hear her out."

Dinah smiles at him, and it's full of warmth and the same sweetness she projects. Luke has the sense it's all earnest, not put on for show like some of the women at his church growing up. She can no more change who she is than he can change himself.

"I like your friend," she says to Luke. "He's right. Don't go yet. I think we might have some catching up to do."

"They can't find me here," Luke blurts.

Dinah's eyebrows shoot up. "Who, your brothers? If you were looking to hide, maybe coming to a small town and finding your boyfriend's mother wasn't the best idea." She puts up a hand at Luke's budding protest. "Nope. Don't even try it. Several of us knew, including your mother. We respected your privacy until everything that happened."

"He wasn't really my boyfriend," Luke mutters. It doesn't matter anymore whether or not he protects Esther and Sam. He doesn't even know where they are.

"Hm," Dinah says. "I'll let that one go because it sounds like there's a story there. If nothing else, we knew you were reaching out to each other." She leans forward and puts a hand on Luke's knee. "Most of us thought it was a good thing. Your family has different views on what is and isn't right. Maybe we chose wrong by not telling you, but we thought silent support was the right thing to do at the time. We had no idea you would take off like that."

Luke frowns at her. "No, that's not what happened."

"We all assumed you left because of Sam. You mean you didn't?"

He's reluctant to explain about Esther, but he also doesn't want to protect the people responsible. "I left because seven of my brothers chased me through the woods with a knife and threatened they'd kill me if I came back. I was the only witness to their crime. But what would it matter? They destroyed the evidence."

It's Dinah's turn to stare in shock. "What crime?"

"They beat Tristan Whelock nearly to death in the convenience store. They thought he raped Esther."

Now Dinah can't hold back. She's crying, and Luke feels terrible for having pushed this far. He reaches for Connor's hand and grips it tightly.

"We—Lydia and Leah and I, your other brothers' wives—thought Esther was protecting you and Sam. The two of them left after you did. Paul and I were going to help her after she said she was pregnant. She said she couldn't live with knowing her job was to someday be married and have a dozen children in the name of the Lord."

"I don't know where Esther is," Luke says. "But I do know she and Sam were the ones I was protecting. He was the one she was with, not Tristan. I never found out if she decided to have the baby or not."

"My guess is probably not," Dinah says, confirming what Luke mostly suspected. "So it was Sam's baby? Same as everyone else, we assumed Tristan was the father, but he didn't go with them. Now it makes sense why."

They talk for a while, with Luke catching her up on some of what happened after he left. He doesn't tell her everything; it isn't all for her ears. But he does tell her about the road trip and how they're looking for their traveling companion.

"They took off from Sioux Falls, where we saw Tristan," Luke says. "We had an idea they would come here because..." He flushes. "I've been avoiding it."

Dinah puts her hand on his. "I understand why."

"You won't tell anyone I'm here, will you?"

"Not unless they ask me directly. I won't lie if that happens, but I won't bring it up." She squeezes his hand and lets go. "I think you should tell them yourself. It's only a few of us left anyway."

"I'll think about it," Luke agrees. She's probably right, and he doesn't want her to have to carry his secret to her grave. But he's still not sure he wants to see his family.

They rise from the couch, and Dinah gives them both warm hugs before sending them on their way again. With that, they're back in the RV and headed toward town. Silently, Luke passes over the slip of paper with the address and directions. Then he takes his phone and taps in the number, his heart hammering the whole time.

Chapter 27

CONNOR HAS TO park at the back of the townhouse lot because there's no room to fit the RV anywhere else. Fortunately, no one else is back there. The two of them lean against the RV. Luke's phone is still in his hand.

"Just to make sure, she said it's okay to park here?"

"Yeah."

Luke doesn't want to talk. He needs time to think, to process what's about to happen. If nothing else comes of it, he at least wants to make sure Esther is safe. Guilt gnaws at him for not trying harder to find her after he left. It wasn't only fear of his brothers driving his avoidance.

"I still don't understand why you never said anything about all this," Connor says. "I've known you for years, and I had no idea."

"Why would I tell anyone?"

Of course Connor doesn't get it. He wouldn't ever have had a need to hide from anyone, to make sure no one ever found out who he was. He left a trail of fake names with the people who gave him rides. The homeless shelter never asked questions, and he made it clear he wasn't going back regardless.

"Because we're your friends," Connor replies.

"Would it have changed anything?"

Connor is considering the question. Finally, he says, "No. It probably wouldn't."

"Then there's your answer. I never wanted this part of my life to return."

Luke pushes off from the side of the van, and Connor follows suit. The townhouse where Mrs. Whelock lives is new, in a row that looks like tiny cottages. There's little in the way of landscaping, only whatever tree growth has occurred in the previous few years. Luke comes to a stop in front of number six, and he halts so abruptly that Connor stumbles into him from behind.

It takes a moment before Luke can knock. He feels like his veins are full of fizzy liquid, and his hands are shaking so much he shoves them in his jeans pockets to stop them. It only takes a moment before the door opens.

There's a fraction of a second between when Mrs. Whelock appears and when Luke reaches out for her. He can't help it. Her presence is so familiar and comforting that all he wants is to be held. She obliges, folding him into her arms and standing on her stoop, rocking him like he's a young child.

Luke finally breathes again with relief. He hasn't had to say anything; Mrs. Whelock absorbed it all without either of them uttering a single word. Luke steps back and looks at her at last. She's aged, of course, but otherwise, she looks much the same as the last time he saw her. There's a bit more gray in her brown hair, and there are a few more lines around her eyes and mouth. Not much else is different.

"Why don't you come in?" she offers, peering around Luke to where Connor stands awkwardly off to the side. "Both of you."

They enter, and now Luke sees the familiar cozy cottage-style decor he remembers from visiting Sam when they were younger. She indicates they should sit while she gets some drinks, so Luke and Connor sit on her sofa, touching shoulder to hip. Luke thinks about how many people's homes he's been in on this trip, every single one different.

Mrs. Whelock returns with not only drinks but food as well. "Help yourselves. You'll need your strength, Luke, because I have a lot of questions for you." She peers at him over the top of her glasses, her gaze stern but kind.

"I know," he says. "I'll do my best to answer them all." He plucks a sandwich from the top of the pile.

"Where on earth have you been these last...what is it, a dozen years?"

"Thirteen," Luke says. "Almost, anyway. I lived in Philadelphia for a while, then I went farther south. Followed some friends to college, but I didn't finish school."

"Well, now, that sounds like it's hovering somewhere in the middle. Why don't you start at the beginning."

So he does. He explains about his brothers and hitchhiking and failing to get to New York City. About the foster families and AJ and Greg. About coming back north and living with Jax, though he leaves out some parts of their relationship. About taking the road trip to find Connor's family. He's not sure how long he's been talking, but somewhere in there, Mrs. Whelock paused him to bring out more food before allowing him to continue. Everything she served is gone, the three of them having worked their way through it while Luke poured out his story.

"It's remarkable," Mrs. Whelock says, "that you are here now, able to tell me about all of this."

Luke nods. He knows how lucky he is, even if sometimes he can't feel it and even on days he wishes some of it were different. "Can I ask some questions now?"

"Of course." She smiles. "You saw Tristan, I understand. He called me."

"Yes. That's why we came. He says Sam left right after I did, but he never told me what happened."

"Your brothers happened, is what."

Luke swallows. "I thought he died in that fire."

"No, but it was close. He heard the gas explosion and had only enough time to get as far away as he could. He figured out fast he'd better not get caught up in things. It took him a long time to contact us."

"Where is he now?"

"He was in Seattle."

Luke stares. He wonders why Tristan didn't know that and why the two of them are estranged. "*Was* in Seattle, you said? And Esther?"

Mrs. Whelock shakes her head. "He took her with him, but we lost track after that because, well, you recall how Sam was. He never shared anything he didn't need to, and even then it was minimal. He gave me a mobile number, but he won't give details on his location. I don't know whether they stayed together or where she might've gone if they didn't. I think you would need to ask your mother if you want to know."

Luke definitely doesn't want to do that. If he goes to see her, he will also have to face his father and possibly his brothers. There's so much he feels he's missing, though. It's like putting together two jigsaw puzzles at once and realizing some of the pieces have been swapped.

"Esther told me at the time that she and Sam were planning to leave together eventually. She said my brother Paul was helping them. I'm only here because I went to your old house and found out he and Dinah bought it."

"That's right. I had to sell when my parents got too old to help take care of the property. They're in the independent living center, and I moved here. I don't know if Tristan told you that I had cancer a few years back."

"He said something about your health not being good."

Mrs. Whelock pats his hand. "I'm doing well now, just slower than I used to be."

Luke chews his lip. "I wish I knew what to do."

"Go see your mother." Mrs. Whelock gives him a pointed look. "She believes you to be dead. I always held out hope you were out there somewhere, mostly because Sam assured me you were alive when he last saw you. After he let me know he was safe, he said he tried to find you and couldn't. But he believed you were okay."

"And I am."

"He'll want to know that." Mrs. Whelock reaches for a pad of paper. "This is his mobile number. Usually, I have to wait for him to call back, and sometimes he doesn't. I think he'll respond to you, though."

Luke accepts the paper, and he thanks her for the meal and the conversation. He tells her he will see Mama, but he's not sure yet. He senses she knows this but doesn't try to push him. She never did. When they say goodbye, she holds him for a long time and tells him not to be a stranger now that he's come back. Luke doesn't let on that he thinks it might be the last time he returns here, this time for good.

❊❊❊❊

As they pull out of the parking lot, Luke wonders again where Esther went. Did she stay with Sam? He stares at the paper in his hand with Sam's number. He wants to call him before he visits with Mama. Another thought occurs to him.

"She didn't mention my father," he says out loud.

Connor glances over. "Is that strange?"

"Yeah, of course it is. Everyone knew Dad. He had the largest building and repair businesses in the area. Not only our town but for several nearby. Do you suppose he could've died?"

"I wouldn't know, but I figure she'd have said if he did. Which makes me wonder what's up."

"No kidding. It's weird."

Luke sits back. Talking about his father distracted him from Sam temporarily, but now he's back to internally waffling on calling. He makes the decision quickly with his gut before his brain can catch up and talk him out of it.

He catches Connor eyeing him, but he doesn't explain what he's doing as he hits the numbers.

It rings twice before someone—a feminine voice—says, "Hello?"

"Um. Hey, this...this is Luke Spier. I'm looking for Sam Whelock?"

"Oh. Oh, my god. Lukey?"

"Yes. Who is this?"

"Honey, it's Esther."

Luke almost drops his phone. "Esther?" he repeats in a whisper.

"Yeah. Listen, it's complicated, but I'm here visiting, and Sam asked me to grab the phone. I'll let him explain."

There's some shuffling, and then Sam's on the line. The moment he says hello, Luke's crying. And then he can hear Sam crying. It's a long time before they're composed enough to have a conversation.

"I saw your mom, and she gave me your number. But she didn't think Esther was with you."

"She is and isn't. I mean, she doesn't live with me. We left together, but neither of us felt safe telling anyone she was here."

"So, you're still..." Luke isn't sure what they were in the first place. "...in a relationship?"

Sam chuckles. "It's complicated."

"That's what Esther said. She told me you'd explain it."

"I suppose you guessed she didn't have the baby after all."

"Yes," Luke tells him. "I figured as much, and Dinah confirmed she assumed the same."

"Right. Well, we do actually have kids. Twins!" He laughs.

"Okay..." Luke is still confused.

"My husband and I. She's our girls' mother. She and her partner co-parent with us."

"Partner?"

"A man. Don't get your hopes up that she's one of us."
He laughs again.

"I wasn't!" But Luke laughs too. "So the four of you are
a family."

"Yes. Maybe not the most conventional, but our daughters
won't lack for love." He pauses. "The thing is, my mother
doesn't know about the girls. We still won't go back there,
and I don't even feel safe with anyone in town knowing
where we live or about my family." Another pause. "You said
you saw her? I really have to know how that came about.
I figured you'd never go back either."

"I wasn't going to. But things happened, and...well, I'm on
a road trip with my...friend. Connor. It's a freaking long story.
I...can we come see you?"

"Now?" Sam sounds as confused as Luke had been earlier.
"I mean, you're welcome any time, but aren't you a long way
from here?"

Luke looks to Connor. "We're on our way to Seattle.
We'll figure it out."

"Your... 'friend,'" Sam says, and Luke can definitely hear
the air quotes. "Is he your boyfriend?"

"No," Luke rushes to say. "Someone I've known since
a few months after I left."

"Okay." Sam laughs. "Well, he's welcome too, of course.
I can't wait for you to meet my husband." Luke hears the
blush in his voice, and he can't help smiling. He's glad Sam's
found happiness. "Listen, I have to go, but I can put Esther
back on if you want."

"Sure."

A few seconds later, Esther says, "Hi again."

"Hey." The well of emotions that's been filling threatens
to overflow. "Um. I know you haven't been home in, like,
forever, but...do you know anything about Ruth or Johnny?"

Esther sighs. "No. Well, I did manage to get a letter to Johnny a few years ago, and he wrote back to say they're okay. I think he's been helping to take care of Ruth, but he was going to school too, so I'm not sure exactly."

So Esther didn't take Ruth with her, then. Luke makes another decision that he won't go back on. He has to go home. If Johnny's going to school, he'll be back for the summer, unless he's moved away for good. Luke suspects not, especially if he's caring for Ruth. But he has to know for sure, and the only way to do that is to talk to Mama.

"I'm going home," Luke tells Esther. "I have to find them."

There's an extended silence before Esther says, "Be very careful."

"I've already talked to Dinah, and she gave me Mrs. Whelock's address. It'll be okay." He's not sure if he's trying to reassure her or himself. "Hey, one more question."

"Go for it."

"Do you know anything about Dad? I mean, Mrs. Whelock didn't say, but...something didn't feel right."

Esther sighs. "Not over the phone. All you need to know is that you won't have to worry about him or the big boys right now."

"Did something happen?" Luke can't stop the way his voice rises in alarm.

"Lukey." Esther's tone is firm. "Not like this. I'll tell you more when I see you, I promise." She sighs. "I hope you know what you're doing. Just...Lukey?"

"Yeah?"

"Please don't say anything about us, okay? We've made a life here, and we don't need trouble."

"I know. I promise, I'll come see all of you soon. Those are my nieces you're raising there."

She laughs. "True enough. Love you, Lukey. Take care, and call us again when you're here."

Luke ends the call and sits with his phone still in his hand, resting in his lap. He isn't sure what to say to Connor, who probably doesn't understand the conversation. He would only have been able to hear Luke's end, for the most part.

Sure enough, Connor says, "What just happened?"

"I talked to Esther. My older sister."

He explains as much as he can, ending by telling Connor he wants to go see them. Naturally, Connor agrees. They'll be headed there anyway for the last part of Connor's trip. Come to think of it, Luke doesn't have the specifics about Connor's last stop. He hasn't been clear about it.

"So," Connor says, "are we going to go see your mom?"

"Yeah. Let's go. But first, I want to stop in town. I need a few minutes."

With Connor's agreement, they head out on the main road into town.

Chapter 28

IN TOWN, THEY stop at the gas station to fill up. The convenience store is the same one that was there when Luke was last home, but it's a different brand of gasoline. The store's logo has changed too, and everything looks updated. He has little nostalgia for the way things were, and he's glad the town appears to be growing and moving forward, even if it's somewhat surprising.

While Connor is pumping gas, Luke gets out of the RV. He doesn't want to go into the store, even though he's sure no one he would know is working. He was sheltered enough as a child that his only peers were from church or the homeschool co-op. He wouldn't have known many from the local school. Still, he can't bring himself to see the same place where he witnessed his brothers' crime.

Instead, he wanders toward the strip mall. The pharmacy is now a chain store, and everything else has become something different from what it was. The ice cream stand all the way on the end, separated from the stores by a car-width alley, is deserted. Not that Luke wanted ice cream, but that's one thing he wishes were still open.

Connor calls to him, and Luke indicates he's going inside the pharmacy. He's not sure what he's looking for. It's likely the pharmacist is someone else now, given the change in brand. But something compels him to wander inside. He steps up onto the curb and pulls open the door.

Inside, it's cool, a relief from the heat rising off the pavement. It's getting late in the day, and they'll have to find somewhere to park the RV soon. Their trip to see Mama might have to wait until they've had some rest. Luke's starting to think that might be for the best.

He wanders up and down the aisles, not really looking for anything in particular. It's all arranged differently from the old pharmacy. The shelves are high enough he can't see over them. This is one place—his hometown—he thinks it would be nice to send Jax a postcard. There's a section with all types of greeting cards, but he doesn't think they'll have what he wants there. Not in a chain store.

While browsing the displays, he hears a soft voice beside him say, "Anything I can help you with?"

Luke looks up to see a face so strikingly like his own that he drops the card he's holding and backs up three steps. The young man leans down and plucks it off the floor to hand to Luke.

"I-I'm sorry," Luke stammers.

"It's fine." The young man smiles, and it makes Luke's insides shake with nerves.

"J-Johnny?" he asks. "Johnny Spier?"

"No one's called me Johnny in years. It's John now. But how do you know who I am?"

Luke's begun to recover and has some time to think. He says, "It's a long story, and I'd be happy to tell you. When do you get off work?"

John pulls out his phone. "About an hour. It feels a little weird to agree to a meeting with a complete stranger, but you want to catch up over burgers and fries at LuLu's Diner? It's—"

"I know where it is," Luke interrupts. He suggests a time, and John agrees before they part ways.

Still reeling a bit, Luke exits the pharmacy and heads for Connor and the RV. Connor is leaning against the side, flipping through what looks like a travel brochure. Luke can't help finding it funny because he wouldn't describe his hometown as a tourist attraction. Maybe things have changed in the last thirteen years.

"What's up?" Connor asks, closing the brochure.

"Get in, and I'll tell you." Once they're buckled up, Luke says, "We're going to LuLu's Diner. It's right by the motel, so we can check in first. I just saw my youngest brother."

Connor gapes. "The little one? He was, like, seven or eight when you left, right?"

"Eight. He's twenty-one now. My younger sister would be twenty-three. He didn't recognize me, or not immediately. I don't think he'd have agreed to meet a stranger for dinner, except he can't have missed how much the two of us look alike." And how little they both resemble all the others.

Connor doesn't question any of it, just pulls out onto the road and heads for the motel. Luke silently watches out the window as the town passes by. He doesn't know what tonight will bring, but he's prepared to ask some important questions that might provide an explanation for what's happened with his family while he's been gone.

***

Luke thought before he had everything sealed up, that he had a plan for meeting with Johnny—John. He has to remember this isn't the same little boy he left all those years ago. He crosses his fingers that his confidence, which has evaporated in the face of having to explain to his brother who he is, reinstates itself soon because he has a thousand questions. He hopes John can see past the hurt to understand why Luke left and why he hasn't been back.

He and Connor enter the diner and tell the host they're waiting for a third. It's starting to fill up, but John's definitely not there. They would spot his white-blond hair a mile away. They take a seat on the bench in the waiting area outside the bathrooms.

More people enter, none of them John. Luke periodically pulls out his phone to check the time, thinking John might've gotten held up at work. Connor fidgets, plays solitaire on his phone, or stares out the large window behind them. They don't talk to each other. Luke is half relieved he doesn't need to think up chitchat topics and half annoyed because he wishes he had a distraction.

Eventually, Connor puts a hand on Luke's arm. "He's probably decided it's not a good idea to meet a stranger for dinner, not even in a public place. We should go."

"We can at least have something to eat. It's kind of rude to sit here for forty-five minutes and not pay for something."

"Okay. Whatever you like."

They tell the host they're not waiting for anyone else now, and the young woman seats them. She leaves menus on the table. Luke picks one up and notes that it's yet another thing in town with an update. He opens the menu and gazes at it without really seeing it. He knows it's not his fault and that it makes sense John wouldn't trust him, but he's heartsick anyway. He sniffles and brushes at his eyes.

"Hey." Connor's palm is warm on the back of his neck. "It's okay to be disappointed, you know. You don't have to hide it from me."

"I'm not trying to." Luke dabs his eyes with his shirt and whispers, "I'm trying to fucking hold it together in public."

"Oh." Connor glances around. "I don't think anyone cares."

They probably don't. Luke looks up, and no one is watching them, not even to notice Connor's hand still on him. Luke fights down more tears and sits up. "I really want some French fries. Is that stupid?"

"Why would it be?"

"It's my go-to sad-about-shit food." Luke laughs weakly. "French fries with tons of extra salt and no ketchup."

"French fries it is. I think the chocolate pie looks great. I saw it in the case on the way in."

"If they still make it like they did when I lived here, then yeah, it's amazing. You're not gonna get after me about eating junk, Mr. Nurse Practitioner?"

"No. For one thing, you're a grown-ass man. You want fries, eat them. For another, who the hell cares? Desperate times call for desperate measures."

They order when the server comes over, and then Luke says, "I had it kind of planned what I'd say to him. But when we got here, all I wanted to know was something that might help me make sense of what happened."

"I totally get it. I wanted to find out who my father was and why he left. I'm not sure I'll ever get exactly the answers I wanted. Maybe I hoped there was some concrete reason he took off and slowly cared less and less as the years went by. But I didn't find that."

"Maybe I was wrong to have left," Luke says. "What if he's angry with me and thinks I should've tried to do more?"

"We still have time," Connor says. "Screw the schedule. Let's figure this out together."

"And then I promise we'll find your answers too," Luke replies just as his phone buzzes. "Hang on. Hello?"

"You might want to meet us somewhere." It's Jory, and their voice sounds dark.

"Who's 'us'?" Luke demands. His heart pounds.

"John and me."

Now Luke's angry. "Did you freaking kidnap my brother?"

He hears Jory's loud, angry huff on the other end. "What, exactly, do you take me for? No, he's here of his own free will. But I think there's some things you'll want to hear."

The server arrives with their food, and Luke tells him they'll take the food to go. The server shrugs and walks away as Luke returns to the phone call. Connor gestures that he doesn't understand, and Luke puts up a finger to hold him off.

"Where are you?" he demands into the phone.

"We're at his house."

Luke frowns. "Is my mother there?"

"Not yet. If you want your answers, you'll be here within the half hour."

"That sounds like a threat."

"Take it however you like, but get your asses here."

Jory ends the call, and Luke sits with the phone in his hand, staring at it so long Connor taps his wrist to get his attention. Luke looks up just as the server deposits the check and two food boxes on the table with an eye roll. Connor sneers at his back.

"Dick," he mutters. "What was that all about, on the phone?"

"Jory is at my mother's house with John. That's apparently why he never showed up. We're supposed to go there as soon as possible. Something about getting my answers." Luke shakes his head. "I don't know what's going on."

"Then let's get out of here so we can find out."

****

The motel doesn't offer RV hookups, so there's nothing to connect or disconnect, and they don't have to find another way of getting to Luke's old house. Connor makes sure he knows which site is theirs before they head back out. Luke gives him directions, but otherwise, they ride in tense silence.

Luke swallows his nerves when they pull up to the big, pale yellow house with white trim. Connor stares at it like he's never seen anything like it. Luke supposes it's impressive, as houses go. It's three stories with a giant wraparound porch. When he was growing up, there weren't many other houses nearby. They had a decent size plot of land, and the rest was largely undeveloped. Now there are neighbors within easy walking distance.

They climb out of the RV and walk slowly up the stone path. Luke has to take a few deep breaths before ascending the porch steps and knocking on the front door. It takes a minute, but it's Jory who answers. They drag Luke and Connor in and shut the door.

"What—" Luke tries, but Jory silences him with a glare.

"Sit," they tell him. "It's about time you got the truth out of someone."

That's the moment Luke realizes Jory's not angry with him but on his behalf. He thinks they're wrong, but he appreciates that someone is looking out for him. He sits on the couch, and Connor joins him. It feels formal, and Luke is struck by how strange it is to be a guest in the home where he lived from the time he was eight.

John is already there, slouched in a plush chair that wasn't there the last time Luke was in the house. He doesn't look afraid. A little confused, yes, but also determined. Luke is reassured that John isn't in any kind of danger, and he feels guilty for thinking Jory would do harm to him. They'd gone ahead of Luke and Connor, presumably to draw out the same answers Luke's about to get now. He faces John.

"Jory says you can tell me what's going on."

"I'm sorry," John says. "They got to me first." Luke doesn't miss John's use of Jory's correct pronoun, and out of everything he's seen and experienced, that puts him more at ease than anything else. He won't have to hide himself from John.

"Yeah, I can see that." Luke glances to Jory. "And I assume they'll fill me in on how that happened and why. For now, I'm not sure what it is you know that I don't."

"We don't have a lot of time," John says. "This isn't how I want Mom to see you again for the first time in thirteen years. She thinks you're dead, and it's only because of Jory that I have any idea at all you're not."

"Then start talking. Where is she, by the way?"

"Probably getting Ruth from work and going for dinner at her boyfriend's house."

"Uh." Luke can't fathom Ruth being an adult, let alone with a job and in a relationship. Not because of her disabilities but because she was a little girl the last time he saw her. Given she's twenty-three now, he supposes none of it should be a shock.

"I know!" John chuckles. "Even I can't get over the whole 'boyfriend' thing, and I live here. Anyway. Jory gave me the condensed version of what you went through, and I'm sorry. Still kind of pissed off, but I get it. That's why I think you should know more than whatever it is you believe about our family."

"Uh," Luke says again. His tongue feels stuck.

"Right. Did you ever ask yourself why there are, like, a million of us but no cousins? Why we're so isolated?"

"No," Luke replies. He honestly hasn't wondered. Mama said she was an only child, and Dad never talked about it. Luke had the sense there was some kind of falling out, but he isn't sure what and doesn't care.

"Maybe you should have." John runs a hand through his fine, blond hair. He meets Luke's gaze and holds it. "You definitely should've been asking why you and I look like twins but don't resemble anyone else except Mom."

Luke wants to correct him, to get John to stop calling her Mom instead of Mama. To go back to calling himself Johnny. It all feels stiff, as if they never knew each other. Instead, he says, "Genetics are weird? That's what she told me when I asked why Esther and I don't look alike."

"Mom hated that life," John says. "She didn't want to be stuck taking care of the house and the garden and the kids forever. That's why she was so miserable when we got here.

She'd hoped what happened before we left Seattle would be her ticket out, but it wasn't. It only got worse for all of us."

"I'm beyond confused."

"You and I...we have a different father."

Luke's head is spinning. He can't grasp what John's telling him. While his brothers are still his brothers, Dad is not, in fact, his actual father. Luke isn't sure what to make of that. Dad treated him like a son, at least to the degree he treated any of them that way. He was exasperated sometimes at Luke's lack of technical skill, but he never raised a hand to him or behaved in a manner that indicated he thought of him differently. And there was yet another man entirely in there?

"You should probably start at the beginning," Luke tells John.

"There isn't time for that. I can explain more later, but all you need to know right now is that Mom didn't plan on the life we had. Our father..."

Jory is watching them, and Luke thinks they're the key to all of this somehow. They know something, and they aren't saying it. Luke's mouth is dry, and he feels sick. He wants to ask a million questions, but his tongue is still immobile.

There's a crunch of tires on the gravel driveway, and everyone freezes. John's already pale face goes almost stark white. Jory stands and grabs Luke by one arm and Connor by the other. They march the two of them upstairs.

"John's got this," they say. "You come with me. Luke, you can show me your old room."

"I doubt it's been preserved."

"I don't care!" Jory hisses. "Just move it."

Luke takes the others down the hall to his former bedroom. He nudges open the door. Unsurprisingly, it now looks like any bedroom. The predominant color is blue, including the quilt on the bed. Everything is in pristine condition, as though they'd redecorated after Luke left and then didn't touch the room aside from cleaning it.

What does surprise Luke are the framed photos on the wall. They are Luke's work. He was only thirteen or fourteen when he took the pictures, and his amateur skill shows. But he's startled to find his style is similar to how it is now. He likes to imagine what's under the surface of what's visible in his subject. Every one of his old pictures does the same. He remembers when he took these. The kids in town had pictures done at the public school, and one year, Luke said he wanted to do them for his siblings. It's only Matt, Mark, Esther, Ruth, and John, but they make Luke smile.

Connor elbows him. "Did you take these?"

"I did."

"How old were you?"

"Middle school, probably, because there's pictures of Matt and Mark but no one older."

Jory tilts their head. "Shh."

Annoyed by Jory's attitude, Luke slips past, ignoring Jory's glare and attempts at grabbing him again. He sneaks to the top of the stairs to listen. Connor follows, and Jory seems resigned to letting them go. Luke sits on the first step and strains to hear.

"...doing parked in my driveway?" It's Mama's voice. "Is someone else here?"

"Just a friend, Mom. Can we sit? I have something to tell you."

"That's ominous," she remarks, but she doesn't sound either worried or upset.

"Is Ruth here too?"

"She's coming. Getting her things from the car."

The front door opens and closes. Luke can't see it from where he's seated, nor can he see Ruth. Like with everything else today, it makes him feel lightheaded and bubbling over with nerves. He wants so badly to dash down the stairs and wrap her in his arms. He hears John ask her how work and dinner went, but he doesn't catch all of her answer. He remembers that she didn't usually have a lot to say, and she's always been soft-spoken.

"John says he's brought a friend home," Mama says. Luke smiles because he can hear in her voice the mild chastising.

"I'm getting to that," John says. "We really should sit down."

There's a long pause, and Luke tries to hold his breath but finally has to let it out. Jory glares at him. He puts a hand over his mouth. Jory steps around him, and Luke is about to ask where they're going. They put a finger to their lips and shake their head, so Luke slouches back down.

"I was at work today," John says, "and...someone came in. I..."

"I wasn't concerned before, but now I am. Is everything all right?" Mama's voice is gentler now, so much like how Luke has chosen to remember her. He can't help the gasp that escapes his lips. Connor puts a comforting hand on his shoulder.

"There's a lot I didn't know about our family," John says. "People I've never met. Things you should've told me yourself. I've been doing some searching, and it turns out there are people who were looking for me too."

Luke is utterly confused, especially as he watches Jory descend the stairs. He wishes he could see what's happening. Instead, he has to imagine the scenario. He knows Jory has stepped into the living room because he hears everyone else talking at the same time. John whistles, and the talking stops.

"Mom, this is Jory. They're my—"

His what? Luke wishes someone would explain.

"I know who this is," Mama snaps. "I can see they look like him. The question is, what are they doing here? And how did they find us?"

"Well, now, that's a whole other story."

"I can explain," Jory says. "But first, I want to show you two things."

Luke starts to stand, wanting to know what's going on, but Connor drags him back down with a hissed, "Wait."

"My God," Mama says. "Where did you get these?"

"The first one I've carried with me for most of my life. The second I acquired early this morning."

"Whose is it?" Mama demands. "And how did you come to possess it? That's impossible."

"It's very much possible. I'll prove it to you. But not until you can tell me the original owner will be kept safe."

"From what?"

"From the people who led you to believe he was dead."

Chapter 29

THERE'S A LOT of shouting after what Jory's said about keeping Luke safe. He wonders how Jory managed to get to town in the first place and what they did in the time between then and when Luke and Connor arrived. Clearly more than Luke realized.

He's still confused, too. How did Mama know who Jory was? And what did Mama mean by "they look like him"? There are so many things Luke can't figure out. He strains to catch anything important in the chaos of everyone talking over each other.

"HEY!" It's Ruth, yelling above the other voices. Luke is proud of her; he never heard her raise her voice in the years he lived at home. When everyone is quiet, Ruth says— loud enough for Luke to hear—"Somebody tell me what's going on!"

"Good idea," John says. "Jory?"

"I have something else." There's a pause, and Luke assumes Jory is showing them whatever they have.

"What's that?" Ruth asks.

"It's a camera memory card and insurance you'll protect the person who took these photos. I'm not telling you anything else unless you can convince me you won't call your older sons."

"It wasn't all of them," Luke mutters, but he's glad Jory's looking out for him. He never tried the memory card, but there's a good chance it still works. Good thing he saved it.

Mama says, "They don't speak to me, for the most part. Not the ones you're talking about."

"Then I think there's someone else you need to see."

A moment later, Jory's at the foot of the stairs, beckoning Luke and Connor. They descend the stairs and round the corner into the living room. Mama's jaw drops, and Ruth's eyes are wide. Luke doesn't think Ruth remembers him, not really, but he didn't think John did either.

It takes exactly three seconds for Mama to fly across the room and wrap Luke in her arms. She's crying, and then Luke's crying, and somewhere in there he thinks he hears the others sniffling. As much as he wants to stay there forever, once Luke has calmed down, he has more questions than he can organize in his mind. He pulls away.

"I have to know," he says. "Everyone keeps saying there's more to what happened than I'm aware of, so you all need to explain it to me."

"First, you're going to introduce me to this complete stranger," Mama says, wiping her eyes. "I know who everyone else is, but not him."

"This is my friend Connor," Luke tells her. "We've been traveling together all summer. We met after I left home, and we've known each other since then."

Mama studies them both. "Not like Sam?"

"No." Luke flushes, and Mama gives Connor a long look up and down.

John brings in more chairs, and everyone sits. Luke stays next to Mama, with Ruth on her other side. She keeps peering around Mama to stare at Luke. He finds it funny, and it warms him because her expression is curious rather than distrustful.

"Where should we start?" Luke asks. "I have a feeling my story and all of yours are tangled together."

"Why did you go away?" Ruth asks.

As good a place as any to start, so Luke tells them as much as he thinks is all right. He won't tell them where Esther went, but he does explain that his brothers blamed Tristan and chased him away when they found out he'd seen them. John frowns, and Luke is puzzled as to what he might be missing.

"Where'd Esther go?" Ruth wants to know when he's finished.

"I can't tell you that," Luke replies. "She's still afraid."

Mama sighs. "There's nothing for her to worry about. Most of them are gone. Not dead," she quickly adds. "Times here have been hard on them. The town has grown, but some of them haven't been the most responsible. Your father's long disappeared too, and he took some of them with him."

"I know he's not my father," Luke says quietly.

"He's as much father as you ever had," Mama answers, but there's an edge in her voice, something that tells Luke she doesn't fully believe what she's saying.

"He raised me, and he wasn't generally terrible. But I think this is where I need the rest of the story."

Mama looks defeated. "I suppose if someone's filled you in about the man you called Dad, then you know how he and I met."

"Not that part, no."

"Did you ever wonder why we never saw my family? Why you only met your father's parents?"

"I guess I thought I didn't have anyone on your side."

"No, that's not it at all. I met your father when I was in college."

Mama has a college degree? Luke is embarrassed that he never knew. "Then what happened?"

"Average things. We got married and had children. Two wonderful little boys. I'm not going to get into everything about the dynamics. It's enough to know things changed after that. His family was more strict than mine, but not to the point they demanded we live a certain way. My family never warmed to him, though. They thought he was controlling me. That wasn't it at all, not in those years. I made choices I thought were right at the time.

"He had certain beliefs, one of which was that we should not stop ourselves from having the children God ordained for us. The idea never bothered me—I wanted lots of children." She smiles. "I loved all of you. And then..." She stops and reaches out to take Luke's hand. "This won't be easy for you to hear. I should never have hidden the truth from you, but your father...I mean..."

"He's my father," Luke says, contradicting what he said earlier. "It isn't as if there's someone else I ever called Dad."

"Right," Mama says. "I accepted things as they were, thinking I was doing the correct, godly thing. I didn't count on meeting someone else. Or re-meeting, I suppose. He was the real reason we left Seattle. Your fa—my husband thought if we were away from him, we could pick up our lives and move on."

Luke wonders if Mama ever tried to find him. He can't wrap his mind around all the secrets his family held on to for so many years. "Re-meeting?"

"Before your father, he was someone I knew from school. We weren't right for each other at the time. But things happen, and we found each other again by chance. When I became pregnant, there wasn't any way to know for sure until after you were born who your father was."

"But then John—"

"I knew that time. I put an end to the relationship. After that, we started making plans to move. Your fa—my husband didn't ever want you or Johnny to know."

Luke looks between John and Jory. They both know something else, and Luke wants to demand they explain it. Jory hasn't said a word since Mama and Ruth came home. They stand and pace, twisting their lip and avoiding eye contact with everyone. The room has fallen silent.

Finally, Jory turns around, looking defeated. "I was adopted," they say. "I always knew. No one hid anything from me. Until my eighteenth birthday, my parents had an agreement to send an annual letter to my birth mother." Their lip trembles, and they brush at their eyes. "I'm so sorry, Luke. I wish I could've told you the truth sooner, but I didn't have any proof. It was only coincidence that you happened to be the ones to stop in Erie."

"Tell me what?" Luke's heart hammers, and he wipes his clammy palms on his jeans. He suspects what Jory is about to say. Is he ready for it?

"We have the same father. I didn't know for sure until the day Kem had your scrapbook out. I saw the pictures, and..." Jory reaches into their pocket. "About a year ago, my birth mother sent me this. She hasn't had any contact with him in years, but she gave me a name and a face. I found him, and I was trying to find a way to get across the country to meet him."

They hand Luke a photo. There's no mistaking it; the man in the picture bears uncanny resemblance to both Luke and John. Luke looks a little more like Mama, but otherwise, the two of them are the spitting image of the person in the picture. Luke stares at it, his hand shaking until he drops it as if it's on fire.

"No..." he says.

John retrieves the photo and hands it to Mama. "This is him?"

"Yes," she confirms. "Dustin Sewell. No question."

Luke still can't grasp it. "But how—"

"I'm older than I look," Jory says. "My birth mother worked for him." They pause. "In his photography studio."

"His..." Luke feels faint.

"Genetics are weird," Jory says, echoing what Luke said when he was still in denial.

They're all quiet again for a while, absorbing the information. Jory is on their way to meet this Dustin Sewell. Does Luke want to meet him too? He doesn't know. He can't even say for sure if the man knows about him or John.

Mama breaks the tension, turning to Luke. "I know you must have a lot of questions. I'm happy to answer them all, but maybe over dinner. Will you stay?"

Luke looks to Connor and Jory, and they both nod. "We'll stay," he says.

****

Luke stirs when the sun comes up. It's still too early to be out of bed, so he pulls the blanket up under his chin and thinks about the previous day's events.

It was late into the evening when they returned to the motel, and Jory joined them in the RV again. They were all too tired for much conversation. Jory turned over Luke's book to him with an apology, but that was all any of them had energy for. The three of them collapsed into bed soon after. Luke was too exhausted to make sense of what happened.

Now he has some time, with the others still peacefully sleeping. He still isn't sure he believes everything. How could Mama have kept something like that from him? And how had he never figured it out himself? He still doesn't have a clear answer to whether he wants to meet his biological father. The man doesn't sound like anyone Luke wants to know, not if he was so willing to have children he cared nothing for. On the other hand, Luke doesn't know if Dustin Sewell ever knew any of them were genetically related to him.

The rest of what Mama told him doesn't surprise him. The ones responsible for Tristan's beating and the fire were caught and spent time in prison. Some of the oldest brothers moved away, perhaps to find better work or to distance themselves from what the younger ones did. The strain of it all made Dad bitter and angry, and he finally left too.

Ruth and John, however, are both happy and thriving. Even Mama seems more at ease.

Luke dozes off with these thoughts swirling in his head. It's much later when he comes fully awake to the sound of Connor and Jory talking. He rises and drags on a T-shirt before joining them in the kitchenette.

Jory's backpack is by the door, and Luke guesses before they speak what's going on. "You're leaving."

They nod. "Your mother helped me so I could fly out there. John's driving me to the bus station in Mitchell, and from there, I'll head back to Sioux Falls." They smile. "You two still have a ways to go. I'd have stuck around, but this is faster. Besides, now I'll have at least a little time to get to know my youngest half-sibling."

Luke is surprised by how torn up he is. Jory's been with them for a good part of their trip, and he'll miss them. They eat breakfast together, and it's almost possible to pretend it's not the last morning the three of them will have like this.

When it's time to leave, Luke doesn't want to let Jory go. He's only recently found them, and he wishes they had more time together. Connor checks them out of the motel, and they drive Jory back to Mama's house. John is waiting for them on the porch.

There are tearful goodbyes all around. Luke doesn't want to leave John again either. He promised Connor, though, and it isn't as if he can't go back after they reach their destination. He hugs John again and tells him he's proud of the man he's become.

John slides into the driver's seat, and Jory stands beside the car. "I guess this is where we part ways," they say. They put a hand on Luke's shoulder. "I have two things for you. One, a song. Add 'Fifty Ways to Say Goodbye' by Train to that playlist of yours."

Luke giggles. "Seriously? I wouldn't have figured you were a fan of Train."

"I'm not, but I like that song." Jory shrugs. "The second..." They pull out their phone and tap something in.

Luke's phone pings, and he pulls it out to read the text Jory sent. "This is..."

"Yeah. It's Dustin Sewell's phone number. If you need it. I won't tell him about you, but you now have the option of telling him yourself. Something to think about, anyway."

Jory turns to leave, but Luke says, "Wait!" He ducks into the RV and emerges a moment later. "You can tell him if you want, or not. But this is for you."

He hands Jory one of the pictures from the scrapbook. It's not a great photo. Esther took it, and she didn't know what she was doing. But it's the only picture Luke has of himself and John.

"I can't take this," Jory says.

"You can. We're family, right?" In more ways than blood, Luke thinks, recalling the hundreds of miles they've traveled together.

Jory nods and tucks the photo into their bag. They get into John's car, and with a wave, they're off in the opposite direction Connor and Luke will take.

"And then there were two," Connor remarks. Luke can only nod in response.

They re-enter the RV, and Connor checks everything to make sure they're ready. Their next stop is in Wyoming, and it'll be a long drive. Luke offers to take the wheel first. While he's adjusting the seat, he catches a glimpse of Connor fiddling with his phone. He's adding the new song to the list and queuing it up. Then they're off, heading out of town and back to the highway with the music playing through the speakers.

Then

THE TEMPERATURE HAD been unseasonably warm the day Luke ran through the woods and away from his brothers. Now it was chilly, a function of the ups and downs in the weather that autumn. He only had the light jacket he'd worn when he left to go to the convenience store, and otherwise, he was in a long-sleeve T-shirt and a pair of worn work jeans. He had sneakers but no boots.

He also had no idea where he was supposed to go. At first, he'd stayed in the barn of the neighbor Sam had sent him to. But the farmer didn't seem to quite buy Luke's story, and he'd only let him stay a couple of nights before urging him to go back home to see if things had blown over. Luke couldn't convince him it was more complicated than that.

They didn't live near any larger towns, or not any that would be easy to get to on foot. Luke could probably walk for a hundred miles and not see anything bigger than where he lived. There was a bus station, but Luke had nowhere near enough money for a ticket.

He'd thought about heading for New York, but it wasn't as if he had any idea how to get there. He was alone on a strip of state road, and the only thing nearby was a farmhouse that might've been a mile and a half away. There was nothing for it except to go that direction and hope it led somewhere afterward.

Luke didn't even have someone he could call. Everyone he knew lived in his hometown. His own family made up a large chunk of the population. For whatever reason, he had no contact with any aunts or uncles. He wasn't sure if he had none or if his parents simply didn't keep in touch with them.

Two cars passed him on his way to the farmhouse. One of them blew by without any indication they'd seen him. The other driver honked and made a rude gesture out the window. Luke ignored the person and kept moving, one foot in front of the other. He'd already been walking for hours, and his feet hurt.

At last, he reached the farmhouse, a big, white two-story with a blue door. He knocked, and when no one answered for several minutes, he put his hands in his pockets and turned to go. Just as he was about to step off the porch, the door opened.

"Can I help you?" asked a short, plump woman with her curly hair pulled on top of her head.

"Um." Luke poked the step with his toe. "I'm...lost." It was close enough.

"Lost," the woman repeated. "You need to use the phone?"

"Um." Luke scrambled for something believable, but he came up with nothing. "Yeah, okay."

The woman eyed him up and down, and Luke felt like he was being thoroughly inspected. "I'll bring it out to you."

She closed the door and left Luke standing awkwardly on the porch. He waited for a while, but he didn't hear any sounds from inside the house. The woman didn't appear to be returning, so Luke retreated from her porch. He wandered up the road, glancing back occasionally. He still didn't see the homeowner, so he determined she'd intended him to go away.

He only made it about halfway to the next house, which he could see over the rise of the hill. His feet hurt, so he sat down on the side of the road. He heard a car coming from the other direction, slowing as it reached the house Luke had left. He squinted, and his heart hammered when he saw it was a police car.

No way did he want a run-in with the local cops. They would surely take him back, and he was afraid of what his brothers would do to him then. So he crouched low and crept farther off the road, rolling once he got to the slope. There were some bales of hay dotted around the field, and he hid behind one after another until he felt he'd put sufficient distance between himself and the house. Then he ran.

It didn't matter how much his feet hurt. That was nothing in comparison to what he faced if the police officers found him out there. It took what felt like forever, but he finally reached the next house. In fact, there was a line of homes closer together once he was past the farm. Luke hid behind the shed and peered out.

The police car was now moving slowly along the road, so Luke scrunched himself as small as he could and pressed up against the shed wall, not daring to look out again in case the cops saw his face. He held his breath, too, but that was useless and only made him lightheaded. He stayed still for a very long time.

A rustle nearby almost scared the pants off him. He held in a shriek and waited until his pulse slowed before he looked around. Two little kids were peering up at him.

"Whatcha doing?" The pigtailed girl had a pail in one hand and a trowel in the other.

The boy didn't say anything. He looked quite a bit younger than the girl. He had messy brown hair and a dump truck wrapped in a pink blanket like a baby doll. Despite the situation, Luke had to work to keep from laughing. They were both adorable.

"I'm...playing hide-and-seek," Luke told the girl.

She giggled. "We found you."

"So you did. Is there a grown-up home at your house?"

"Yeah. We're here visiting our auntie and uncle." She lowered her voice. "They're not really actually our auntie and uncle. They're Mommy and Daddy's friends, but we call them that."

Luke didn't need the specifics. He only needed to find adults because two small children, only one of whom could talk, were not going to get him away from here. "Can you take me to them?"

"Sure."

He followed the girl, and the boy trailed after them. She led Luke to the back door, and they went inside. She reminded him to wipe his feet on the rug by the door.

Four adults were seated at a round table, teacups in front of them with the sugar bowl and cream pitchers in the center of the table. They were talking and laughing, but the moment Luke and the children entered, they went silent. Luke fought the fidgets and stood still with his hands at his sides, just as he'd been taught when meeting someone new or important.

"Who's this?" one of the women asked.

"I found him by the shed," the girl declared. "He was playing hide-and-seek." She seemed so proud of herself that Luke felt bad the adults weren't giving her more credit.

The other woman said gently, "Why don't you take your brother and go play upstairs."

The girl glanced at Luke. "Can we watch a movie?"

After looking to the other adults, the woman said, "Just this once." When it was obvious to them she thought Luke was supposed to come too, the woman shook her head. "Your friend stays here for now, okay? You can talk to him later."

Luke almost breathed a sigh of relief. They weren't immediately assuming he was dangerous. But would they call the police like the last homeowner had? How safe was he here with these strangers?

One of the men pulled up another chair, and the other set a fresh cup in front of Luke. He poured some tea and pushed the sugar and cream closer to Luke. After adding what he liked to his tea, Luke wrapped his hands around the cup. He hadn't realized his fingers were so cold.

"Now," the first woman said. "Why don't you tell us what brought you here?"

Chapter 30

THE ROAD THROUGH Montana is bendy, and there are a few spots where Luke thinks he may have lost a few years off his life. The miles stretch out in front of them. The trees are thinner here, but the hills are thicker. He's gotten more comfortable driving the RV, though he could do without some of the more precarious sections of highway. He's particularly dismayed when Connor reads him a statistic about I-90 being one of Montana's most dangerous roads.

To distract him from his fears, Connor explains the situation they're walking into. Two of Connor's father's cousins were in some kind of feud over the land they live on. There doesn't seem to be a clear reason for whatever it was, but it only ended recently and the truce is tenuous. When they arrive, they will have to exercise caution.

Luke laughs. "That sounds like something out of an old western or something."

"Right?" Connor chuckles. "I gather it's a difference in philosophy. Ike's a musician, and he wanted the land for tourism and travel. He has a setup for local concerts. Eli's a rancher, and he wanted a peaceful stretch of land for raising sheep and crops."

"And those two things can't coexist?"

"I guess not. Or at least, the two of them seemed to think not. I doubt the real argument is over any of it. I do wonder what happened recently that they were able to reconcile, though."

"I suppose we'll see, eh?"

Connor wasn't kidding when he said it was hilly where they're headed. Once they're off the main highway, the road rises and falls at irregular intervals. Luke feels like he may never remember what it's like not to pitch side to side in his seat. He fervently prays the RV holds together on their way up the side of one hill. The road narrows, only barely big enough for a car to come the other direction. Luke wonders if there's even room for that. There's no shoulder to pull over, with shrubs on one side of the road and a steep drop-off on the other.

They turn onto a dirt road and begin a climb up what Connor says is a driveway. He's maneuvering the RV well, but even so, Luke can't help the rising panic that they're going to careen off the road. At last, they reach the top, and a house comes into view. Luke loves it at once: it's like a modernized log cabin, with multiple stories and a balcony on each one. It's strung with colored lights even though this is summer and nowhere near Christmas. There are planters hung from the balcony and flags made of scrap material.

There are gardens surrounding the house in every direction. Some have flowers, and others are obviously for growing food. It's chaos, but there's an organization, a flow to it. The people who live there are less concerned that everything be tidy than that it be both functional and welcoming.

When they park and exit the RV, Luke hears music coming from somewhere. The song sounds familiar, though he can't place it. A woman steps out onto the porch and waves to them before descending the outdoor stairs and coming down from the house to where they parked. She has the same structured chaos feel to her as the property, but Luke can't quite summarize what it is. He only knows he likes her before he's even met her.

The woman's hair is a wild mass of gray-streaked brown curls, pulled back from her face with a clip. She's wearing loose jeans, a sleeveless, flowered blouse, and leather sandals. When she spots Connor, she flies over to him and wraps him in a big hug.

"Oh, my word. It's so good to have you here!" She pulls back to assess him. "You look like you could use some home cooking. Come on in the house, and we'll take care of you." She pauses and turns her attention to Luke. "I'm so sorry. I should've introduced myself. I'm Miriam Woods." She clasps Luke's hands in hers before letting him go and heading for the house.

They follow her up. Luke murmurs, "Is she another one of your father's cousins?"

"No, Ike is her partner. They have a third, Tam. She's probably in the house."

The inside of their home is as interesting as the outside. The walls are stained wood, and every bit of furniture is covered in handmade quilts. There are houseplants everywhere. The entire second floor is a balcony, and Luke can see it doubles as a music room. There are several guitars, a keyboard, and a number of music stands.

Miriam is already in the kitchen, pulling out dishes and serving things from three crockpots bubbling on the counter. Another woman, considerably younger, is sitting on a stool in the corner and mending a curtain. She looks up when Luke and Connor enter.

"Hey, fellas!" She slides off the stool and sets the curtain on a mostly empty counter. "I'm Tam, and it looks like you've met Miriam. Ike's in town, getting supplies."

Miriam sets the plates at the table. "Eat up, boys," she says.

Luke's mouth waters. The food they've eaten on the road has been fine, but this is better than anything they've enjoyed since leaving Avi and Sylvia. While they eat, Miriam sits with them and fills them in on what she knows.

"Saul came to see us not too long before he died. He was in rough shape by then, but it seemed to revive him a bit to be here." She smiles. "Must be the good country air, I expect, and maybe a fair bit of Ike's cooking."

"What did he want?" Connor asks.

"Rest, I suppose. And to leave something for you. Ike taught him a little about how to play guitar. He said it was important. I'll let Ike explain that part when he gets home."

As if on cue, the door opens and a man enters. He gives Miriam and Tam each a kiss. "You've met the women, I see."

Ike has a lot of laugh lines in his deeply tanned face, and his clothes are work-worn. He takes Connor's and then Luke's hands in turn. Luke is overwhelmed by his presence. Ike dishes up some of the food and joins the others at the table. Tam has gone back to her mending. They make small talk for a while before Ike gets down to business.

"How much did Miriam tell you?" Ike wants to know, so Connor fills him in. "All right, well, I'll tell you one other thing. His reason for the guitar lessons was to have some help writing a song. I'll show you later. Wild stuff. He left that and a book for you. Dunno why he thought you'd get it in your head to travel, but I guess he figured we'd send it to you if you didn't show up."

Tam looks up, her needle on pause. "It was Saul who made things right between Ike and Eli."

Connor's mouth drops open. When he recovers, he says, "I sense there's a story there."

While they're eating and talking, the door opens yet again, and in walks someone who takes Luke's breath away. They're compact, muscular and tan, as if they've spent the better part of their life working outdoors. They have dark hair gelled into spikes and small, oval glasses with rainbow-patterned frames. The minute they're inside, they're full of spitfire.

"I cannot take even another minute of Daddy's attitude!" they declare. "Enough is enough, and if you two don't make this right, I'm gonna have to up and leave here. He's saying now he doesn't want me to come over here for lessons. Can you imagine? I'm not a child, I'm twenty-three!" They throw their hands in the air. "He can't stand it that I don't want anything to do with his godforsaken ranch." They pause for breath and finally notice Luke and Connor. Quieter, they say, "Oh, hello there. Who're you all?"

"I'm Connor, and this is Luke. My father was your Uncle Ike's cousin."

"Jewel." They offer their hand.

"This is Eli's youngest," Ike explains. "Being honest, the relationship between our kids was the real trouble with us. Saul sussed it out and got us to a better place. But that doesn't mean we don't still have a moment or three slip in there."

Connor laughs. "I can see that. Guess I'd better have whatever my father left for me and get a sense of how that fits into the picture, then."

*****

Ike takes Connor somewhere to show him whatever it is his father left there. Jewel is still in the kitchen, having helped themselves to some of the food. Luke is still fascinated by them. They have a tiny stud in their nostril and one in the shell of their right ear, as well as black plugs in their earlobes.

Jewel catches Luke staring and winks. "Didn't go with them to hear about Cousin Saul's visit?"

Luke shrugs. "Connor will fill me in later."

"Uh-huh. How'd you get roped into this trip, anyway?"

"Connor asked. I said yes."

"Obviously." Jewel laughs. "I meant why."

That's too long a story for a stranger. Luke is at a loss for how to answer the question without all the details, so he goes with, "I was the only one who was free."

"Okay." That seems to have satisfied Jewel. "You like music?"

"I guess? It depends on what it is. Connor has this playlist we've been using for our trip, but I don't even know half the songs on it."

"Mm. What are you into, then?"

"Uh..." Luke searches for something to tell Jewel. "I take pictures."

"You're a photographer?"

He laughs. "Not exactly. I mean, I'm not a professional or anything."

Jewel taps their finger on the table. "You have a camera?"

"Sure, of course I do."

They slide off their chair and hold out a hand to Luke. "Come with me. I can show you a great spot."

Luke takes Jewel's hand and allows Jewel to pull him up. They let go, and Luke follows them through the house. In the living room, Jewel points to a painting-sized photo on the wall. It's a black-and-white image capturing ranch life, with a gentle-eyed sheep right in the foreground. Luke admires the angle and lighting. Whoever took it was skilled.

"That's my cousin Ash's work," Jewel says. "A big part of the problem with our families has been who owns the land and who will have it when the previous generation is gone. Uncle Ike was the first one to say he had no interest in raising sheep. It made Dad angry because he didn't want the responsibility all to himself. The problem was never really about borders or even use of the property. It was all about Dad feeling like he'd been the responsible one, and Uncle Ike was unreliable with his 'fake hippie' ways." Jewel makes air quotes.

"So what happened?"

The two of them begin walking again, and Jewel continues. "I did, and so did my cousins. Both of Auntie Miriam's kids loved life on the ranch. Me, I couldn't wait to get away. They took off for college to study engineering and environmental science. Came back to put their smarts to work on Dad's ranch. I went to school to study music."

"I have a feeling someone wasn't happy about any of that."

Jewel laugh-snorts. "Got it in one. Nobody was happy with us, except all our mamas. I'm an only, so it was assumed I'd want to be the first non-male to own that land. Ha! No, thanks. Give it to my cousins. Meanwhile, neither of them had any sense of rhythm, let alone ability with a guitar, and they didn't want to. Pissed Uncle Ike right off, at least in part 'cause he wanted to rub Dad's face in it."

"What did you all do? Wait, hang on a sec."

They've reached the RV, and Luke ducks in for his camera. He follows Jewel's lead, and they head for a spot overlooking the valley below. The view is breathtaking. Luke can see the ranch from there, and he supposes this is why Jewel brought him this direction.

"You asked what we did," Jewel says. "Nothing but fight until Cousin Saul showed up. He asked us all a lot of questions, mostly about what started the fight. He was an interesting man. I think he had some odd theories, and I know he blamed his cancer on 'toxins.' I never did figure out whether he meant in the environment or the struggles between people. Maybe both. Anyway, he helped us make peace. No, scratch that. He demanded we do it. Said life was too precious to waste on petty squabbles. I didn't understand him, honestly, but he said it was his purpose to be a blessing—to bring light into the world before he died."

Luke mulls that over. "It sounds like there's still some tension, though."

"Well, you don't fix everything overnight. We started over, and it's mostly good. My cousins love what they do. Cousin Saul was way into protecting all life, including the land and the animals. He brought some fresh perspective, and they've taken his suggestions seriously." Jewel laughs again, and Luke notes the musical sweetness of it. "They're science nerds, so it's right in their wheelhouse."

"And you're learning music with Ike?"

"I am! Well, new music. I sing. Got my fancy-ass degree from a respected conservatory. Uncle Ike's kind of a local celebrity. He does this style of folk-pop-country people just love. Learned everything I know from him."

"Maybe you'll sing something for us later?" Luke suggests.

"Maybe I will," Jewel agrees.

They stop talking, and Luke drinks in the sight. He raises his camera and takes a few shots. When he gets the chance, he'll send some to Jax. They've never been anywhere like this. Luke thinks they'd love it.

"Come on," Jewel urges. "There's a bunch more places I can show you. Let's make you some memories."

Chapter 31

AFTER THEIR FEUD ended, the brothers and their families planned a party to celebrate. They called as many of their collective neighbors as they could as well as friends from other parts of the town. Connor and Luke are fortunate enough to be there when it happens. The revelry lasts all night up on the hill, with music and dancing and beer and weed.

Connor's gone with some of the younger guys, and they're laughing and drinking beer by the fire. When the music starts up again, a few of the guests start dancing. Connor is pulled in by an older woman in a long, flowing skirt.

Luke is high. Not to the point of losing track of time or his thoughts, but enough for a pleasant buzz. He's lying on a blanket, away from the crowd, looking up at the sky. It's so beautiful and unobstructed here, so much like his family's homestead. The stars whirl a little in time with the spinning in his head. He feels warm and safe.

Someone comes and lies next to him, elbowing him. He looks over and smiles. It's Jewel. They look fantastic tonight in jeans and a leather vest with nothing underneath. They're not wearing any makeup aside from black eyeliner. Their plugs are silver, etched with a tree of life. They're wearing a silver medallion on a black cord, a tree of life that matches the plugs in their ears. Not the Jewish kind like on the album Connor bought but the Celtic type. Without thinking, Luke reaches over to trace the pendant. Jewel's fingers are warm when they touch Luke's, stopping his motion.

"How far gone are you?" Jewel asks quietly.

Luke gazes up at them through his lashes. "Enough to feel good, not enough to forget where I am."

"Fair."

Jewel closes their eyes and drops their hand, letting Luke continue to explore the tree pendant. He reaches its roots and rests one finger there before hesitantly moving it to feel the buttery leather of Jewel's vest. He hears Jewel's sharp inhalation and pauses again. Jewel moves their hand to Luke's neck and rubs the short hairs there.

It makes Luke's body hum, and not only from the fading effects of the weed. He wonders briefly if Connor's still by the fire, but the thought flies out of his head as quickly as it enters. Whatever is happening here with Jewel is more important.

Luke lowers his mouth at the same time Jewel arches up. They're kissing, and the relief of contact with another person is so great that Luke's afraid it won't take much for him to reach a different kind of high. Before he can think about it, Jewel's rolled him over and is straddling his hips. They're pressing into him, and now Luke knows he won't last long.

"Fuck..." he mutters. "Hold on." He pushes a little.

"You okay?" Jewel sits up, still astride him.

"Too fast."

Jewel slides backward, their ass rubbing along the way and making Luke groan. They reach down and squeeze him. "I want you to fuck me. But I thought you were only into boys."

"Mostly," Luke agrees, now that his head is slightly clearer. "More like not into women."

"Mm. Well, I fit that restriction, then." They reach into their pocket. "I've got stuff on me."

Luke glances around them, but no one is nearby. They're on the other side of the RV from the party, and even Connor still isn't back. Luke hesitates anyway, even knowing they're going to fuck.

"You gonna get all weird on me? I'm fucking horny, and if not you, I'll find someone else or do it myself."

For whatever reason, the idea of Jewel fingering themself does it. Luke grabs the condom. "I want to."

He's shaking as he takes off his clothes and watches Jewel do the same. He thinks their body is perfect, and he's more than ready. They collapse back on the blanket and join their bodies. Luke is carried away by the weed and the moonlight and the relief of being inside someone else. Jewel rides him, their hand between their legs, until they're coming. Luke isn't far behind, his ass rising off the blanket as he finds release.

Afterward, they lie naked on the blanket, rumpled now from their coupling. Jewel has a glass pipe, and they sit up to take another hit. Luke joins them, resting his arm against theirs for warmth and solidarity. It feels better than he imagined to fit his body with another person's again. He blows out a cloud of smoke, closing his eyes and reveling in the relief.

"You look like you needed that," Jewel remarks, lying back down.

"What, the weed?" Luke hands them back the pipe, and Jewel sets it aside.

"No." Jewel snickers. "The sex, babe."

"I didn't mean it to be over so fast."

"Hey." Jewel adjusts to lie on their side, propping themself on their elbow. "It's fine. We were both pretty worked up."

They move to half lie on top of Luke, and then the two of them are kissing again. It isn't like any of the other people Luke's kissed. He likes comparing them, thinking of them each in their own ways. It's exciting to be with Jewel, even knowing it's going nowhere beyond this blanket and this expanse of glittering stars. He's hard again, and he feels Jewel moving, rutting against his hip.

They join their bodies again, this time using hands and mouths and ending by rocking together until they're both sweaty and spent. Luke feels boneless, awed by how satisfied he is. Jewel has given him a gift, the joy of pleasure beyond his neediness with Jax. He doesn't know if it's the weed or the moonlight or the miles of road behind them, but he doesn't have words to express his gratitude.

He doesn't have to. Jewel brushes his bangs off his forehead and kisses him there. He squeezes his eyes shut against the sting of unshed tears. Jewel rests their head on his chest, and Luke holds them. He feels less alone tonight than he has in many months.

****

Luke wakes, freezing cold and with his head throbbing. He slept outdoors on the ground, and the only thing covering him is a thin blanket. He's not sure who put it there. The last thing he recalls is falling asleep with Jewel pressed up next to him.

He looks around to see what woke him, instantly sorry he does. His neck hurts like hell. He's spotted the source of the noise, though. One of the revelers is pissing not twenty feet from Luke's makeshift bed. The guy finishes, groans, and yaks onto the puddle of pee he just left. Luke turns away, disgusted.

He's not entirely pleased with himself, either. At least he's not fully exposed to the elements. He remembers the previous night, how it felt to have skin-to-skin contact again. He didn't mean it to happen, not with Jewel and not at a wild, weed-infused party under the wide expanse of Wyoming sky. But it did, and now he has to deal with the consequences— including his sore muscles.

Luke rises from the ground, wrapping the blanket around him. He tries to be quiet, but Mr. Hangover spots him. The man waves and yells a good morning.

"Looks like you had a good night!" The guy is grinning.

All Luke can muster is a half-hearted wave before sneaking back into the RV. The door creaks, and he freezes, waiting for Connor to wake. Not a peep from him, so Luke closes the door behind him and tiptoes through the kitchenette. He's almost to the back bedroom when someone behind him clears their throat. Luke turns around slowly.

"I'm sorry I left you like that," Connor says. "I didn't want you to get too cold, so I found an extra blanket."

"You could've woken me."

Connor taps his fingers on the kitchenette table. Luke can tell he's pissed and trying not to show it. "Better to let you sleep and sort it out in the morning."

Luke frowns. "What do you mean?"

"I saw you and Jewel."

"Oh, god."

"What the hell were you thinking?" Connor shakes his head. "I mean, I can guess what part of your body you weren't thinking with."

Connor wouldn't know it was nothing more than two people, both high and horny, needing to get off and allowing the moonlight and the weed to guide them. He would've felt left out of the loop, as if Luke were hiding something from him. That couldn't be farther from the truth. If he wanted to keep it all a secret, he'd have found a better way than fucking out in the open like that.

"It's not your place to babysit me." Luke knows it's more complicated than that, but he won't let Connor off the hook. "Besides, wasn't that you last night, getting drunk and dancing around the fire?"

Connor scoffs. "That's not the same, and I wasn't drunk. Which you should be able to tell by my distinct lack of hangover. You, on the other hand, look like shit."

Luke reaches up to touch his hair. It's a mess. He's sure the rest of him doesn't look any better. "It wasn't that big a deal."

"Are you serious?" Connor makes an exasperated noise. "I hope you were at least careful."

"I'm not a child. I'm fully aware of what condoms are and how to use them."

"Yeah, just not always aware of how to make good decisions."

They stand in the kitchenette, glaring at each other with their arms crossed. Luke won't back down. He has never once needed his friends to parent him. And yet they persist, especially since Greg. One bad decision in his life, and no one will let it go. He left on his own, struggled on his own, and would have continued even after Jax left.

"Stop fucking treating me like I'm a baby. You always do this."

"Do what? Look out for you? In case you'd forgotten—"

"Forgotten what? What am I forgetting about my own goddamn life? This is why I almost didn't come with you. Everyone acts like I'm some helpless child who needs you all to protect me. I thought I'd left this 'for your own good' bullshit behind when I aged out of foster care, but obviously not. Ten years on, and I still have you treating me like I'm always going off on impulsive whims. Aren't you the one who couldn't handle your own problems?"

Connor reels back like he's been slapped and stares, mouth open. "What did you say to me?"

"You heard me the first time or it wouldn't have upset you. Here's the short version—Fuck. Off."

Luke turns and heads for the bathroom. He pisses, brushes his teeth, and fixes his hair. He needs to go for a walk to clear his head and get away from Connor for a while. He knows they'll be all right, but for the moment, it's better to give each other space.

Other guests are beginning to stir in their tents and campers, packing up their gear to head out. In a little while, Connor and Luke will do the same. Luke looks at his phone. There's enough time for him to put in a call to Jax, if for no other reason than to be reassured it'll be okay. The thought of talking to them makes Luke feel better. The guy from earlier offers Luke a cheery wave on his way past, and Luke can't help grinning and waving back.

****

Luke is disappointed when Jax doesn't answer. He doesn't leave a message. What would be the point? Still, the time spent finding a quiet spot and making the call have given Luke an opportunity to cool off from his argument with Connor. He's about to head back to the RV to help get ready to leave when he bumps into Jewel.

"Hey, stranger," they say, smiling. "How're you feeling this morning?"

"Okay," Luke says. "I got kind of cold last night, but I feel better now." He rolls his shoulders. The stiffness there is gone too.

"Good, but that's not what I meant."

"I know. And..." Luke sighs and runs a hand through his hair. "Connor wasn't happy about us."

"Not his damn business, but I guess I can see why."

"Me too. But I don't regret it."

"I'm glad. Hey, you all want some help?"

"I think we've got it. We'll stop by the house later before we leave. I wouldn't want to piss Connor off even more."

"He's got a bit of a temper."

"Not as bad as he used to, and not the kind of temper that hits people." Luke swallows.

"All right, then. Hey, I got something for you." Jewel hands him a slip of paper, kisses his cheek, and disappears inside the house.

It's starting to drizzle, so Luke shoves the paper in his pocket to keep it dry. He returns to the RV. Connor's mood seems to have lifted, and the two of them pack things away for the next leg of their trip.

Connor's left his new treasures from his father on the kitchenette table. There's a stack of music notation paper and a book on environmental justice. Connor still hasn't opened the box he received from Jens, and that's there too. Luke doesn't press; he figures Connor will do it in his own time.

"You ready?" Connor asks.

"Whenever you are."

They make their way back up to the main house. The family is all in there, saying goodbye to a stream of other guests who wanted to wish them well before leaving. Connor and Luke wait their turn.

Miriam grabs them both in a fierce hug. Ike, Eli, and the cousins shake hands, and Tam gives them gentle squeezes. Jewel offers Luke a secret wink. There are a few tears and a lot of "don't be strangers" and offers of food to take with them. Connor accepts a cloth bag with some lunch in it, and Miriam tells him not to worry about returning the dishes.

And then they're walking away, back to the RV. Connor takes the driver's seat, and when Luke sits on the passenger side, his pocket crinkles. He remembers the paper Jewel handed him and pulls it out. It's two songs. One is a duet by Ike and Jewel. The other is Tom Petty's "Time to Move On," which makes Luke laugh.

Connor eyes him, sees the song, and then laughs along with him. "Add it to the list," he suggests.

So Luke does, and then he plays it as they head down the narrow driveway toward the main road.

Then

LUKE'S HEART RACED as he climbed up the tree and scooted across to AJ's window. AJ's parents wouldn't have a problem with Luke being there, but his foster family sure would. What they didn't know wouldn't hurt them.

AJ helped haul Luke in and brushed him off. Luke dropped his backpack on the floor. There wasn't much in it, only a change of clothes and a book. They'd been planning this for a while, so Luke knew AJ was prepared. Besides, his father ran the homeless youth shelter. AJ had access to anything he needed.

They stood there awkwardly for a minute or two. Finally, AJ said, "Hi."

"Hi."

After another pause, AJ put his hands on Luke's shoulders. "Um. Can I...can I kiss you?"

"Okay."

AJ was more careful than Sam had ever been. He always asked, every single time, about everything. Luke wasn't sure if it was what he'd been taught or if he was nervous. It didn't matter. After the long, awful trip from his hometown, Luke was grateful for every bit of caution.

It was a wonder the two of them were standing there in AJ's bedroom. Luke recalled when they'd first met, the day he showed up at the shelter. AJ gave him warm clothes and hot soup. There was another boy there too that day, a kid with brown hair and a slight sneer. He seemed to have this bubbling anger under the surface.

That was Connor. He went to the same Catholic school as AJ and sometimes hung out with AJ's group of friends. Even though Luke was with AJ, something about Connor fascinated him. He'd changed a lot since the winter. Less angry, more confident. Luke liked the difference.

But he was in AJ's bedroom, not Connor's. Luke had the good sense to know AJ was a better choice. They weren't exactly boyfriends. AJ was like Sam—he liked girls, too. Or something like gender didn't really matter. When Luke met him, he'd had a girlfriend. Luke gathered something happened between them that AJ didn't want to share. It was enough that he wasn't cheating on her when he invited Luke to hang out after curfew.

Luke would've gladly spent time with AJ after school, but his foster family kept a tight leash. Maybe they were scared he would run away again. He'd already left home and one previous foster family. This one was nicer, but they didn't trust him at all. Not that he'd exactly given them reason, but he thought it was more about making sure he stayed on the straight and narrow. Especially the straight part.

AJ was taking a risk too, having someone his family had helped under their roof without their knowledge and without the foster family's permission. He was just as anxious to figure things out as Luke was, though.

"Um," AJ said again, pulling back. "I...I don't know what I'm doing." His cheeks turned scarlet. On him, it looked hot. "The most I ever did was feel up my girlfriend."

"And me," Luke reminded him.

"Well, yeah. But...like...I've never—"

"Me neither." That was kind of a lie, but Luke didn't want to get into how very not-consensual his technically real first time had been. He also didn't want to explain about Sam.

"Okay. Well...maybe we should sit on the bed?"

They sat. And then they kissed again and fumbled and finally managed to more or less work out what they were supposed to be doing. It was nice. Not life-changing. Maybe not even quite as good as a decent hand job from Sam. Nice nonetheless.

Afterward, they lay together under the covers. This was the easier part, talking about the day-to-day ordinary things like school and what classes they were going to sign up for next year. Nothing about future plans or their relationship or Luke's past. It was something Luke liked about AJ. He valued their friendship more than the things they did in bed.

A while later, they fooled around a little again, nothing serious. Not as far as they'd gone before. Then Luke got up and put fresh clothes on. AJ dragged on pajama pants and helped Luke escape back out the window. He took off into the night, not sure if he felt more grown up or less than before.

Chapter 32

Now

THEY REACH THE campsite, and Luke feels the weight of the previous week pressing down on him. He's tired, and he can tell Connor feels the same. It takes them an eternity to set up for the night, by which point the only thing on their minds is sleep. They have time; Connor has no family in Montana. The only purpose of this stop is to rest.

In the morning, Luke stirs from a dream, vague images of flames. He's hot, as if he's suffering with a fever. He opens his eyes, and the night has given way to a gray dawn. Something isn't right, and he sits up.

His head aches, and he feels heavy. The dream might've had some reality to it because he feels awful, his throat raw and his eyes itching. He knows instantly he's sick. Probably nothing more than a cold, but it doesn't make it any better knowing it's not likely serious. He's risking making Connor sick as well.

Luke coughs to clear his throat and crawls out of the bed space.

Connor is slumped at the table, his head on his arms. Luke gently taps him, and Connor looks up. His eyes are glassy, and he coughs in the same way Luke did.

"I've got some cold medicine," he says, and Luke can't help chuckling despite his achy limbs.

He grits his teeth; it hurts to make noise.

"Tea," Connor mutters, standing and going over to raid the cupboards. "We need tea."

They sip their hot drinks, and Luke swallows a couple of tablets at the same time Connor does. They listen to the birds chirping, and Luke is happy to see the sun coming out. He feels better by then, less uncomfortable. The combination of tea and medication has helped, and he thinks some fresh air will be good for him.

The RV campsite has a gorgeous, unobstructed view of the vast expanse of prairie grasses and wildflowers. The sky has brightened to blue, and only a few wispy clouds remain. Luke takes another mug of tea and stands by the three-trunked tree next to the RV.

It isn't much like either of the places he lived before he left home. It's certainly nothing like what he remembers of their outer suburb near Seattle. It's not like Liberty Station, either, which had more tree groves. It feels enormous to Luke. He knows there are other guests nearby, but the quiet makes it feel as if he and Connor are the only two people left at the edge of the world.

After a few minutes, Connor joins him. They stand side by side, the sun warming their skin and the tea warming their insides. Despite still feeling sick, Luke thinks this might be the most relaxed he's felt since they left Massachusetts. Later, he'll send Jax another postcard.

That delivers a pang of both regret and guilt. He hasn't written to Jax since before they reached his hometown. So much has happened, Luke didn't think to fill Jax in on any of it. No time like the present. He returns to the RV to gather what he needs.

On the way in, he spots his scrapbook, returned by Jory. He misses their company and hopes they're all right. Luke picks up the scrapbook to use as a lap desk while he writes and returns outside. He settles into one of the camp chairs. He'll include the postcards with the letter, of course, but there's too much for a single, small rectangle. Luke takes out a fresh piece of paper and begins to write.

*****

Illness sidelines them for a couple of days. Connor pays for an extra night in the RV campsite, and they take turns to brew tea and cook light meals. At last, they're both down to a nagging sniffle, and Connor tells Luke it's time to leave.

They spend the rest of the day making sure the RV is clean and ready to go. Checkout is at noon, so they secure everything and pack up the rest of the campsite. Because of the rain overnight, they already put away their chairs and other gear. That makes it easier. By the time they're done, they still have almost two hours left before they have to leave the site.

The sun is shining through the trees, and the day is warming up. Luke still feels sniffly, and he judges Connor must be feeling the same given how many tissues he goes through while they pack and the way he sinks into one of the seats and groans.

"Just what we need, on top of everything else," he mutters.

Luke knows how he feels. So far on this trip, they've endured days and days of rain with few breaks, unexpected stops, mud, running out of supplies, and now battling head colds. It hasn't been the vacation Luke expected. Still, he's grateful. They have warm beds and cupboards newly stocked with soup. The rain is gone, and they're on their way to the last two parts of their journey. Just one stop in Idaho, and then they'll finally be in Washington.

Unfortunately, thinking about that leads Luke to wonder whether Jory's made it to their destination yet. Luke's glad they had a safe way to travel. When Jory disappeared the first time, Luke worried for them. He knows what it's like to try finding someone to take a hitchhiker, and some of them have a hefty price tag on their services. He shivers when he recalls the man who drove him to Philadelphia after long months of moving one town at a time. The one thing Luke swore he'd never do was sell his body for food or a ride.

Jory's an adult, though, not a terrified fifteen-year-old whose parents have no idea where they disappeared to. They don't need Luke's fears. They probably don't need his sentimentality, either. Luke misses their good-natured ribbing and the extra company on long stretches of roadway. He wonders if they'll ever see each other again. Thinking about it reminds him of the number he has in his phone.

"Hey." Connor is at Luke's side. He clasps his hand. "You okay?"

"Thinking about Jory," Luke admits. "Wondering if they're right and I should try to find my biological father."

"Do you want to?"

Luke shrugs. "I don't care. It won't do any good. What would I even say to him?"

Connor's quiet for a moment. He looks out the window, and a single tear slides down his cheek. He swipes it away. "You still have the chance to say whatever the fuck you want to him."

Luke folds Connor into his arms. The trip has taken its toll, and both of them are feeling it. Connor leans into Luke as though he wants to absorb all his energy. He's not crying, but he seems weary and frustrated. Luke searches for actions or words that might comfort him, might make this easier for them both. But there is nothing to soothe either of them.

Connor pulls back, and he's searching Luke's face. For what, Luke isn't certain until Connor's leaning in and kissing him. Luke's tired of being pulled back and forth by him and determines it's time to do something about it. Connor said he didn't want pity sex, but that's not what this is, and Luke is about to make that clear. They still haven't talked about the night Luke and Jewel fucked under the stars, but this is not the moment. They need each other, and their time is limited before they have to be on the road again.

Luke backs Connor up against the side of the RV and presses against him. Connor is broad and muscular, bigger than Luke, but he doesn't make a move to stop what's happening. Luke can feel that Connor's hard, so he roughly yanks on his belt, unbuckling it, pulling it through the loops, and tossing it aside. The buckle clanks against the kitchen table. Connor doesn't protest this time, doesn't try to convince Luke it's only about escaping his pain. Maybe that's what he wants, or maybe what they're doing isn't an escape after all. Luke doesn't care.

They pull off their clothes, barely separating from their searing kisses. Luke's headache and Connor's sniffles are forgotten in their rush to feel each other's skin. As soon as they're naked and breathless, Luke backs up. He tugs Connor into their shared sleeping space and pushes him onto the bed.

"Is this what you want?" he asks. He won't fuck someone who is ambivalent.

"God. God, Lukey. Yes. Please."

Connor seems both shocked and enthralled by the way Luke takes charge. Aside from Jax and Jewel, both more equitable, Luke's always been with men who preferred he submit to them. But this feels natural, right. It makes sense for him to stop waiting for Connor to move and simply be the one driving. The way Connor relaxes and allows Luke to call the shots fits perfectly.

"You're gonna tell me exactly what you want," Luke says. "This only works if you're clear. Got it?"

"Fuck. Yes," Connor tells him.

And he does. He pleads for everything he wants from Luke, and Luke has to hold back because the way Connor opens up to him is so beautiful that Luke wants to pray at his altar forever. He wants to worship Connor's body with his hands and his mouth, to feel every bit of him. He knows now they never could've done this all those years ago, not before Luke was ready to treasure Connor the way he deserves. Not before Luke realized he didn't need to wait for someone else to tell him what to do.

Connor is picture-perfect. He isn't flat-bellied, but he has muscle underneath the flesh. He doesn't strip his hair, either, not the way Luke carefully sculpts. Instead, Connor's chest is covered in thick, dark hair descending over his stomach and down to his wild, wiry pubes. Luke runs his hands through it the wrong direction, and they shiver together.

"I want to take your picture," Luke murmurs in his ear. "Not now, but someday. I want a record of how hot you are." Connor only whimpers, followed by a loud moan when Luke slides his hand back down.

Somewhere deep in the recesses of his sex-saturated brain, Luke wonders if anyone else can hear their lovemaking. Mostly, he doesn't care, only wanting as much of Connor as he's allowed to have in the short while before they both wake up and begin their journey again. The moment will be forgotten then, and Luke wants to hold on to as much of their precious time as he can.

They move together, uncoordinated at first but with growing confidence. Connor begs for him, demands Luke be inside him. Luke is more than happy to comply. They're wound around one another, pushing, thrusting, chasing after mutual pleasure. Luke thinks there's never been anything as wonderful as this holy moment. In all his years trying to understand what it meant to have faith, he never grasped it until now, leaping over the edge with no idea what's on the other side.

He clings to Connor as they both cry out, one after the other. And then all is still.

****

When Luke stirs from the light doze he's been in, he panics for a moment. They were supposed to be on the road, and he has no idea how long they spent making love or sleeping nor what time it is now. He sits up, making Connor groan. The sound is touched with pleasure and joy.

Connor promptly sneezes. "Shit. I'm still sick."

Luke laughs, but he has to turn his head when it triggers a coughing fit. He recovers and bends to kiss Connor's bare shoulder. "I'm good, but I'm not a miracle worker."

With a snort, Connor rolls over and smacks him. It turns into more kissing, but it's too soon for anything else no matter how much Luke would love to remain in bed and spend the next forever making out and fucking and sleeping in between. He thinks he could stay here for hours if they had the time, doing nothing but gazing at Connor's flushed, sexy body. His skin is golden, touched with a faint orgasm pink that hasn't yet faded. They haven't been asleep long, then.

Luke rises, and Connor groans again, this time with less happiness. "I'm fucking sticky," he complains. "And I already unhooked the water."

There's bottles in the fridge, but Luke thinks it would be unpleasantly cold to use that to clean up. He steps into the bathroom and plucks out the box of wet wipes, tossing it onto the bed. Connor scrunches his nose at it, but he takes a couple anyway.

"Could be worse," Luke remarks as he puts himself back together.

His phone says it's still only a little after eleven, so they have time. Connor gets out of bed and dresses. The two of them don't say anything else about what happened. It feels strange to Luke to have been in control like that. He eyes Connor, and his face heats when he remembers some of the things he said. About wanting to photograph Connor naked. His flush deepens when he realizes it's still true.

Connor offers a small smile. They move around each other the same way they always have, but there are little things in the way they brush against one another casually, as if they are both wanting and fighting constant contact with each other. Luke supposes that too will wither and die, the product of their need today and replaced with more pressing concerns tomorrow.

They're ready to leave, and Connor does one last sweep before settling into the passenger seat. Luke buckles in behind the wheel, and they head for the camp office. Luke buys that day's postcards while Connor checks them out. He tucks the cards into his scrapbook. Pointing his camera out the window, he takes a photo of the campground from that angle.

In a moment, Connor's back. Luke starts the engine and looks at him. "I have no idea where to go, so you need to tell me."

Connor pulls up a map and sets his phone in the cup holder. "Coeur D'Alene, Idaho."

They head out onto the road, and Connor fiddles with his phone to both listen to his playlist and have the map ready. Lynyrd Skynyrd's "Sweet Home Alabama" comes on, and Luke slouches in his seat, scowling. Connor only laughs.

"You wouldn't find it funny if you had to hear this song all the time at work," Luke grumbles.

"Sure I would. I mean, okay, we didn't really listen to the radio, but..." He pauses. "Nah, you're right. I'm sorry."

"Whatever." But Luke smiles at him.

They don't talk for a while, listening to the songs on shuffle. It's a gorgeous day, with blue skies and a stray cloud or two. In fact, this is the most sun they've had in a while, save for a few random days. It's hotter, too. The sun beats through the windshield, and Connor cranks the air conditioning.

They've been driving for at most twenty minutes when Connor breaks the silence again. "Are we gonna talk about it?"

"About...what?"

Connor sighs. "Never mind."

Luke peers at him sideways. "No, you brought it up. Whatever's on your mind, just say it."

Picking up his phone with one hand, Connor runs the other through his hair and tugs. "We had sex, Luke."

"I was there. I remember."

"Can you not? This is important."

"Why?" Luke demands. "Because we had a moment? We both needed it. That's all. I know you said you didn't want pity sex, but who says that's what it had to be?"

"It wasn't pity sex, for chrissakes. I know that. But what does it mean for us?"

Luke stares out the window. He doesn't want to look at Connor when he says, "It doesn't have to mean anything. I fucked Jewel too, and that wasn't any more than we were both high and horny."

"So you said." Connor's gripping his phone so hard it looks like he's going to break it.

"Why does that make you so upset?"

"I don't know why you're telling me, that's all." Connor's shoulders are stiff.

"Because you asked me what this morning meant."

Luke doesn't want to think about that question. He's not ready. They're heading into the last part of their trip, and Connor wants to have a deep discussion about the emotional impact of a single, physical act. He doesn't know what it meant because they never reached a point in their prior relationship of defining what they were to each other.

"Between us," Connor says, interrupting Luke's train of thought. "I wanted to know what it was. I guess you've answered me."

Luke sighs noisily. If Connor had some idea what was supposed to have transpired between them, he should've made it more clear. Luke keeps his eyes on the road, refusing to acknowledge Connor. This is what they do. They fight. Once upon a time, Luke thought Connor was there to comfort him. He remembers the last night he spent with Greg, the third time he had his nose broken.

Greg stole from him. He took every last penny Luke so carefully saved and stored in his socks. That was the money Luke was going to use to leave him. When Greg found out, he went apeshit. Luke managed to get to AJ's apartment, where he stayed until he could safely escape. Luke still blames himself for Adam getting in the way when Greg went hunting for him.

There was a night when Luke lay on AJ's couch, wondering what kind of future he had anymore. He dozed, his head in Connor's lap and Connor's fingers in his hair. Luke thought then that Connor would be his safe place to land. Instead, they couldn't make it work. Connor was always on eggshells, and Luke was restless and anxious. They never made it past holding each other in Connor's apartment. Luke's not sure their friends are aware of that.

He finally sneaks a glance at Connor, who hasn't turned the playlist back on. Something has broken between them, maybe the trust they've both worked hard to build along this trip. Luke doesn't know how to mend it.

"I'm sorry," Connor says after a while. "I shouldn't have pushed."

"No, but..." Luke chews his lip. "Your question wasn't exactly unfair. I just...don't know how to answer it."

Now Connor glances sideways at him. "Why not?"

"Because," Luke says with a shrug. "It's never been important before now."

"I don't understand."

How to sum up the last five years? Or the last ten? Luke is at a loss. "It's never felt like it needed to have some deep explanation. It's...I feel it with my heart. I don't know how to say it any better."

"Like...being in love? But then what about Jewel?"

Luke shakes his head. "I don't mean that. I guess every time, I've known it was the right moment. Things worked the way they were supposed to. Like with Jewel. We were celebrating, and it seemed exactly like what was intended to happen. Or with AJ. We were kids, and we both needed it for different reasons. He was trying to work out who he was. I already knew, but I wanted the comfort of someone I didn't have to be afraid of being with. When Jax and I fucked, it was functional and part of our friendship. I think they were defying expectations, and I wanted something to keep me from feeling alone." Luke eyes Connor, curious. "Isn't it like that for you? You do what's natural when the time is right."

"No," Connor says. "I was stupid when we were kids. I tried to kiss AJ, but even I knew it was kind of like kissing my nonexistent brother. The one thing it did for me was made me see I couldn't live with all that anger. After that, I didn't go around kissing boys unless we were both into it and both wanting it to go somewhere. Not the bedroom but an emotional space."

"Oh," Luke says. "Like a relationship."

"Well, yeah."

Luke has never been with someone in that way. Things fizzled with Sam, and they were never meant to go anywhere with AJ or Jax or the people Luke sometimes hooked up with. Greg was using him, but Luke supposed he might've been using Greg too, in some sense. Greg had roped him into a domestic setup Luke wasn't prepared for, and then he spent the next two years trying to control Luke's every move.

What would it look like to be with someone who isn't doing that? Someone who doesn't expect Luke to play house? Someone who wants him in that way? He thought maybe he and Jax could have that after all, but Jax set a clear boundary.

"Are you saying," Luke asks, searching for the right words, "that you want us—you and me—to have that...together?"

When Connor doesn't answer right away, Luke turns his attention fully to the driving and watches the scenery go by. It's just as well, he thinks, not to have to worry about protecting his heart again.

Then

THE BAR HAD promised "a friendly, welcoming atmosphere and hot cowboys and cowgirls." It sounded all right to Luke. He was bored out of his skull. He'd had two hundred and fifty percent as much as he could take of watching Connor and AJ go on about their classes—how tough certain professors were, who had a harder curriculum, staying up all night quizzing each other out of their notes. They weren't even in the same department.

And there was Luke, alone again unless he wanted to sit around with them. He wasn't taking classes at all. He'd tried, but he'd never been much use at what he still called "regular school." Come to think of it, he hadn't been great even back when he was homeschooled. He'd much rather have taken off with his camera. No good at fixing things, poor at academics, and uninspired about what he wanted to study. In other words, not anywhere near AJ's or Connor's league.

Here he sat, in this country-western bar, sipping his first ever beer. He'd had alcohol before. On his twenty-first birthday, AJ had bought a bottle of sparkling wine. It tickled Luke's nose and made him feel bubbly and warm all over. He liked it, but it wasn't something he wanted to do all the time.

Not that he was enjoying the beer, either. He had no concept of how to order one or what he might like. This one smelled like watered-down piss, and he imagined it tasted about the same. He sighed. At least the music wasn't too bad, and the bar definitely delivered on its promise. He loved watching all the different kinds of people, especially during the line dancing class they were currently offering. Luke wasn't much of a dancer, content to sit on the sidelines and enjoy the show.

The class ended, and he still hadn't even made it a third of the way through his beer. He couldn't stomach it. He turned around and set the bottle back on the bar, wishing he'd ordered anything else. He didn't have money to replace the shit with something better.

"Hey there," said a friendly voice to his right.

Luke turned to look, stunned by the handsome face of the man next to him. He was rugged but not too much so, broad-shouldered and dark-haired with a bit of stubble on his chin. His cheeks were flushed, obviously having come from the dance floor.

"Um." Luke cleared his throat. "Hi."

"Didn't see you out there on the floor, but when I spotted you, I knew I had to come over. Name's Greg." He held out his hand. "I'm one of the instructors tonight."

"Oh. Uh...I don't...really...dance." Luke's face was hot.

"Nah, this is easy stuff. You just need some practice." Greg nodded to Luke's beer bottle. "That stuff's nasty. Listen, I'll buy you something better if you give me your name." He grinned.

"L-Luke."

"All right, Luke." Another charming smile. "What'll you have?"

"I don't know. I don't drink much."

"Aw, no worries, then. I'll get you something you'll like." He grabbed the bartender's attention and ordered something with a fancy-sounding name.

When it arrived, Greg pushed it over to Luke. He took a sip, surprised at how sweet and pleasant it was. "This is good!"

Greg laughed. "I knew you'd like something like that. Listen, I know you said you don't dance, but how about you finish that up, and I'll take you for a spin? I promise, I won't drop you."

"O-okay." Luke still felt too warm and off-kilter with this man, but something in him liked it. He enjoyed the attention, at least.

He finished the drink and went to stand up, wobbling a little. Greg grabbed him around the waist and held him upright.

"Whoa, there. You're definitely a lightweight, eh? Well, come on. Let's dance, and you'll shake it off in no time."

Luke was really only a little tipsy, but he decided it wouldn't hurt to play it up if it meant he could keep feeling Greg's arms around him. He couldn't believe his luck. All he'd wanted was something to take his mind off feeling left out, and here he was, already being swept away by Mr. Handsome. Might as well make the most of it. It had been far too long since he'd relaxed like this, and the others were always telling him to get out there if he wanted to meet someone. No time like the present, especially with someone as attractive and friendly as Greg.

Luke smiled up at him. "What are we waiting for? I think you promised me a dance."

Chapter 33

CONNOR RETURNS TO the RV after pumping gas, and Luke looks up from what he's doing. He's rummaging in the drawer where Jory took his old scrapbook. The new one is in there, finally up to date after Luke printed photos of their trip. That's not the one he wants. He pulls the old book out and flips it open on the table.

"We have to find them," he says out loud.

"Who?" Connor comes over to the table and looks at the book. "May I?"

"Jory, and yeah. I thought you might like to see it."

Connor sits and begins flipping through slowly. He smiles at one page, and runs his finger over the plastic on another. "This is amazing." He looks up at Luke. "Don't get mad, okay?"

"Why do you always say that like you think everything you say is gonna piss me off?" Luke sighs heavily and sits next to Connor. "Jesus. You all think I'm so fragile."

Connor's mouth drops open. "Oh. Uh, well, I guess we always did, yeah. It seemed like life sucked for you, especially after Greg." Luke is certain he hears Connor mutter a rude name.

"Greg was definitely an asshole. But don't we all have shit to deal with? You remember how AJ was after what's-her-name assaulted him. He was a wreck, and he wouldn't tell anyone but me. And you..." Luke doesn't want to hurt Connor,

359

but he remembers him as an angry teenager and again how hurt he's been this trip.

"And Jax. Their parents sort of came around, but not enough to make them go back home. Okay, I get it." Connor looks down at the book again then back to Luke. "So you won't be upset if I ask you why you never ended up becoming a photographer?"

How to tell him? "I was going to," Luke admits. "My father gave up on me as useless. I couldn't do anything with a hammer and nails or electrical wires or even a damn bucket of paint." He giggles. "They tried. I spent a summer living with my oldest brother. Know what I did with that time?"

"I can't even guess."

"Sam used to visit his cousins there. I spent my days handing tools to Roman, and then I'd go hang out with Sam whenever he was there. I was pretty sheltered, I guess, compared to a lot of kids. But I wasn't totally ignorant. I knew what it meant if I liked him *like that*. Or not really him specifically, I guess." Luke props his chin on his hand. "Funny, I still feel really weird about saying I'm gay. I know I shouldn't. You didn't have any problem announcing it to the entire fucking universe." He laughs. "And I can say 'fuck'! It's like I'm still stuck there in some ways."

"Are you?" Connor asks, startling Luke.

"Am I what?"

"Gay."

"Well, sure. It's like I told Jewel—they were surprised too, I think—we had sex while they were masc. It was a little different with Jax, but they aren't a woman, so it never especially made a difference other than that I didn't like it if they had lipstick on."

Connor studies Luke until it makes him flush. "It doesn't matter. I was only curious because..." Now it's Connor's turn to blush.

"You're assuming a lot about what's under their clothes. But I will tell you that regardless of Jewel's or Jax's bodies, nope, that isn't what I care about. Um, I didn't have a ton of experience before AJ, aside from Sam, and we hardly did much. I guess bodies fascinate me, but I really only want to be with people who aren't women. Does that answer your question?"

"Maybe? It does make me feel a little like I'm being too picky or judgy. I've never been with anyone except cis guys."

"Would you reject someone who wasn't?"

It takes a moment before Connor answers. "No, I don't think so."

"Then it's a matter of opportunity more than being an ass on purpose." Luke runs his finger over the edge of the book while he studies Connor, who isn't making direct eye contact.

"Uh-huh."

Luke frowns. There's something Connor's getting at, but it might take some creative workarounds to arrive there. "Look, everyone has limits to what they find attractive. Mine are maybe a little more flexible than some. I'm open to possibilities, and I find lots of different kinds of things interesting or exciting."

"Okay." Connor clears his throat. "What would you say if sometimes I think about it? About being not a cis guy. I mean, uh, I'm not a woman, but...I dunno. I haven't figured it all out yet."

Luke takes his hand, and Connor finally meets his gaze. "I would say be yourself, and don't worry about what I think. But if you need my vote of approval, you have it." He kisses Connor's fingers.

It's the first time either of them has acknowledged what happened between them since their argument. Luke hopes he's offered the right amount of support. There's a fraction of a second when something passes from Connor to Luke and back, but whatever it is, neither of them takes advantage of it. Connor's phone alarm rings, and he drops Luke's hand and looks at his phone.

"That's our cue. We should head out so we're on schedule. This is really the last of my relatives to visit, but we need to make a stop near Seattle because it's where my father ended up."

"I'm ready," Luke says. "Want me to drive?"

"Sure."

They switch places, and Connor fuels the drive with the music on his playlist. The sun is shining, and for the first time in a while, Luke feels entirely at peace. When he glances over at Connor to ask directions, he senses a similar feeling from him. Whatever lies ahead, at least they're facing it together.

****

Jeremy Wasserman is a college professor. He invites Luke and Connor into his study, where he offers them water with lemon. This is the last relative they need to see, and Luke hopes for Connor's sake that he holds the last pieces of the puzzle.

His study is, as expected, lined with floor-to-ceiling bookshelves. Everything is arranged both by topic and alphabetically by author. Luke wonders what he teaches. There's an interesting collection of science fiction literature, everything from Isaac Asimov to N.K. Jemisin and dozens in between. There are other materials too, like science journals and books on environmental science. On one shelf are various items that look like they belong in a lab: a Newton's cradle, a block puzzle, a beaker full of blue liquid, and something pickled in a jar. There's an old-fashioned scale and a microscope with a box of slides. Another shelf has a number of figurines from popular science fiction television and films. Even Luke recognizes a few of them. He smiles when he sees something from one of the old movies they watched at Tristan's theater.

"No doubt you're wondering what Saul came to see me about," Jeremy says. "I think I can answer that fairly quickly."

He pulls out what looks like a star chart and spreads it on his desk, facing Connor and Luke. It doesn't look familiar, but Luke doesn't recall much from science class. It could be another galaxy from their own, or it's possible he was a poor enough student he never properly learned much.

"What does it mean?" Connor asks. "This isn't our solar system, is it?"

"Not at all," Jeremy confirms. "He wanted help drawing this. I have no idea what for, but I was happy to help. I've done similar projects for my work."

"Your work?"

Jeremy rolls his desk chair so he can reach a book on the shelf. He slides it across the desk to Connor. Luke sees J.M. Wasserman on the cover, and he assumes Jeremy wrote it.

"I teach several kinds of literature, but my real passion is for science fiction." He gestures at the shelves. "I spend a lot of my free time reading and writing it. For this novel, I had to design a star chart."

"Why in the world would my father need something like that?" Connor asks.

"He didn't say," Jeremy replies. "Only that he wanted to make it as a gift for you. I assume it must have some significance."

Connor looks at the chart again, and he sucks in his breath. He elbows Luke. "Look at this. It's like that painting he made."

"The dual suns. I remember."

"Painting?" Jeremy asks.

Connor tells him, "When we visited Wade, he gave me one of my father's paintings. It's from a story he used to tell me when I was little."

"He also left you this," Jeremy says. He reaches into his desk and pulls out a very small envelope.

Connor takes it and opens it. It's a key and some information about a safe deposit box at a credit union in Seattle. That explains what Connor's father was doing at the end of his journey, and Luke hopes it's the last clue Connor needs.

"Thank you," Connor says.

They spend a few minutes talking to Jeremy, but he isn't the warm sort. He isn't exactly asking them to leave, but he doesn't seem interested in much conversation. He does tell Connor to keep in touch and ask questions if he needs to, but Luke thinks Jeremy is the least likely candidate for Connor to make a repeat visit.

On their way to the campsite, Connor is quiet while Luke drives. After a while, he says, "I don't get it. I have no idea what it was my father was doing. Everyone seems to have a different opinion, and none of them quite match up. What kind of man was he? And why didn't he tell me any of these things while he was still alive?"

Luke thinks about his family. There were so many secrets and lies, including Mama believing him to be dead. If Connor's parents are anything like that, it's no wonder his father didn't try to communicate directly.

"I wish I could tell you," Luke says. "I wish I could solve the mystery for you."

Connor sighs. "Maybe whatever's waiting in that safe deposit box will explain it all."

They set up at the campsite and enjoy a quiet evening. Jeremy has given them a copy of his book, the one with the star chart. Connor reads to Luke as the sky darkens. When he reaches a good stopping point, he sets the book aside and they make love. Afterward, Connor settles with his chest to Luke's back.

In the morning, they'll start the last part of their journey. What it will bring is anyone's guess, but Luke hopes mostly for peace and resolution for them both.

Then

LUKE RAISED HIS hand to knock again, but the door opened before he needed to. Jax was only wearing a tight pair of shorts and an A-shirt, and they looked sleepy.

"Luke, right? What in the world are you doing here?"

"You're the only person I sort of know here anymore," Luke said. "I hate to ask, but...can I stay the night? I promise, I'll find somewhere in the morning, but nothing's open right now. I don't want to blow all my money on a motel."

"Okay. I mean, any friend of AJ's is welcome here."

Jax stepped aside and let him in. Luke barely knew them, aside from Jax being the younger sibling of one of AJ's friends. Donny, the one who was super into sports. Luke remembers Jax used to do dance, but for some reason, their parents made them stop.

"You want some tea or hot cocoa?" Jax asked.

Luke shrugged. "Okay."

He looked around the apartment. It was small and shabby, which wasn't a surprise. Jax was barely eighteen, and this was probably what they could afford. Their parents didn't quite disown them, but Jax wasn't welcome there anymore. There wasn't much furniture—a ratty sofa and a folding table with two chairs. Luke wondered if Jax had a bed.

"I'm sorry I don't have anything more comfortable," Jax said as they set two steaming mugs on the table. "That sofa isn't bad, though. It looks worse than it is. There's some spare blankets in my bedroom."

"Okay," Luke said again. He didn't care as long as he didn't have to sleep on the street.

Jax sat and invited Luke to join them. "You wanna tell me what's going on? I thought AJ said you were doing good."

Luke stared at his mug. It had been over a year since he left Greg, and he'd tried. He'd spent one semester in school, only to find it still didn't suit him. Besides, he still didn't have any idea what to do with himself. He was going to learn the hospitality business, maybe do more for the Guzmans. Even those classes felt wrong somehow. And then there was Connor.

"I don't think I was ever good," he said. "Functioning, maybe."

"Why didn't you tell the others?"

"Because..." Luke chewed his lip. Should he explain? Would Jax understand? "Connor."

"What about him?"

Luke put his head in his hands. "I dunno. He says he loves me, but...I can't be with him."

"Why not?" Jax's question wasn't pushy, only curious.

"I'm not ready."

There was so much more to it. Luke was afraid Connor was trying to rescue him or make up for something, possibly for not protecting him. Which Luke thought was silly. He'd made his own choices. He rescued himself too. It wasn't Connor's place to feel either guilt or protectiveness. That wasn't the whole reason Luke left. It was everything, far more than he can sum up in one night and one cup of cocoa.

"You don't owe me an explanation," Jax said. "You can stay here, but if it's longer than a couple days, we gotta get you added to my lease. Get a job, pay some rent. Those are the terms."

"Not a problem. If you want me gone tomorrow, I will be."

Jax rolled their eyes. "I never said that. Were you listening? I could use a roommate to help pay the bills. I was gonna start looking anyway. Now I might not have to."

"The minute it's not working, I'll go."

Jax's eyes were on him, and Luke felt as if they could read his soul. They were assessing, feeling him out. He wondered how much Jax had guessed from the little bit of talking they'd done.

"Anyone else know you're here?"

"No, and I want to keep it that way. It's better for now if I cut ties for a while." Maybe give Connor a chance to find someone who could love him back in the way he deserved. When Connor was happy, Luke might not feel so guilty about what he'd done.

"I won't say anything, but maybe you should at least let one of them know you're safe. I could talk to Donny—"

"No!" Luke says. "I'll tell AJ. He won't say anything if I don't want him to."

Jax scooped back their long, black hair. "Good. Listen, I need to get some rest. I have an interview in the morning."

"I can get myself settled."

Luke was relieved Jax wasn't the caregiver type. He would leave Luke to do a hard reset on his life without passing judgment or trying to solve everything for him. That was what he needed right now. Anything else could wait until he'd had enough time to get himself together. One day, maybe he would be able to prove to the others he could take care of himself. Until then, he had a place to stay. He might not have had a plan, but at least he knew what he had to do.

He could make it work. He had to.

Chapter 34

BEFORE THEY REACH the campground, Connor asks, "How far is it from here to where your sister lives?"

He's stalling, and Luke knows it. Connor has spent all summer gathering clues to the person his father was, but he can't bring himself to put them all together. Luke understands.

"Um, I think it's about a half hour or so."

"Then we should probably rent a car. There's a place to park at our campsite, and that means we can do all the other things we need to while we're here."

"Such as?"

"Didn't you say you wanted to find Jory? Or what about your biological father?"

"I hadn't made up my mind about that yet. It would be nice to see Jory, though, before I have to go back east."

"Great!" Connor's tone has brightened considerably, and it almost makes Luke laugh. He'll apparently go to any lengths to procrastinate.

"Lemme give Esther a call, okay? I can do that while you're renting the car."

"Sure. You think you can handle the RV, then?"

"After all this way, I'd better be able to. I'll follow you to the campsite."

They stop at a rental office, and Connor ducks inside. Luke pulls out his phone. He's known this was coming, and unlike with seeing his mother, he has no fear of what it will bring. There's only a low hum of excitement in his gut as he makes the call.

"Hello?" Esther says when she answers.

"Hey, it's Luke. We're camping about thirty minutes from you, and Connor's getting us a car so we can play sleuth with the last of his father's business."

"Cool! You want to meet up tomorrow? I have some time free, and I'd love to see you."

"Perfect. Give me your address, and we'll find you."

She recites it, and Luke scribbles it on an old receipt he finds in the glove compartment. He wants to ask about Sam and his nieces, but he doesn't. Instead, he wishes Esther a good afternoon and ends the call. He's not sure he'll be able to sleep later, far too excited to see her after all this time. It'll give Connor the excuse he needs to bow out of checking that safe deposit box for another day.

Connor's still filling out paperwork, so Luke opens his contacts. His finger hovers over Jory's number. Should he call? Will they want to hear from him? He wonders if they talked to their shared biological father yet. In the end, he touches the number before he can back out.

"Hey-o," Jory says. "Luke?"

"Yeah, it's me. We made it safe and sound to Seattle."

"Same here. Hey, there's something I want to talk to you about. But first, someone wants to say hi."

"What? Who?"

There's no answer, and Luke hears some shuffling before a slightly familiar voice says, "Hi, Luke. It's me, Kem."

"Kem? What—"

"It's kinda a long story. Maybe you and me and Jory can, like, meet up or something."

Luke frowns. That's odd. Kem didn't mention Connor, and Luke doesn't think it's a mistake or because he doesn't like Connor. There's something about it that makes Luke's palms sweat.

369

"Okay, sure. Connor's getting us a car so we can drive around. Are you free in a bit? I don't know where you all are."

"Lemme give Jory the phone. They can tell you."

More shuffling, and then Jory's back. "Oh, man. Luke, you aren't gonna believe what we found out. Listen, you gotta come see us, okay? We're staying at this cute little motel. I'll give you the address. Got something to write with?"

"Wait a sec. Why is Kem there with you? What the hell happened? And why do we need to talk?"

"Luke. Chill." Jory laughs. "It's nothing bad, just a real freaky coincidence. Come on over, and text when you get here."

They end the call, and Luke sighs. A moment later, Connor raps on the RV window with his knuckles. Luke opens it.

"All set. You talk to Esther?"

"Yeah. We're meeting her tomorrow. I called Jory too, and they want us to meet up now. Something happened, and Kem's with them."

"Kem?" Connor frowns. "How is that even possible? Never mind. I guess they'll tell us, right? Follow me out, and we'll check in first. Then we've got the car, so we can go see them any time."

Luke can't shake the bad feeling he has about all this, but he says nothing as he closes the window. He trails Connor, all the while wondering what new secrets they'll expose this time.

****

An hour later, they pull into the motel parking lot. Luke has hardly hit send on the text to Jory when they and Kem come rushing out to meet them. Jory suggests they head over to the all-night diner next door, so they leave the car and walk.

Once they're seated, Luke can't hold back. "Someone fill me in on what's happening before I explode."

370

Jory chuckles. "Which part do you want first? Kem's story or mine?"

"Kem's," Connor suggests.

Kem nods. "I couldn't stay at home, so I tried to find one of you to help me. I only had Jory's number. Turns out that was the best possible thing." Kem's giggle is nervous. "Maybe I should start all the way at the beginning."

"Good idea," Luke says.

"Remember how we met in Chicago? You probably want to know how I got there, right?"

"Go on," Connor says.

"A while ago, I started doing some stuff with, like, these kids at school. Environmental justice. You know, protests and stuff, like the one you were at. My parents weren't super happy, but they didn't make too big a deal out of it as long as I didn't get myself in trouble with the law.

"There was this guy who showed up. He kept talking about how he believed we could learn to do better about taking care of our world. He was...amazing. That's the only word I can use. We started hanging out at the local co-op to hear him talk about stuff he'd learned. I guess he'd been kind of traveling, maybe talking about this stuff. Like how we should be looking out for each other. I don't know. I'm not as good with words. He didn't just say this stuff, though. He would, like, tell stories. Folk tales, I guess.

"In the meantime, I was having a rough year. I mean, it wasn't as bad as it could've been, but it was super hard coming out at school and all that. I wasn't getting along with my stepdad at all. Not because of that. Normal stuff, I guess. One night, I yelled at him that he wasn't my real dad. Basically, Mom let me have it, in two ways. First, she yelled her head off about how ungrateful I was. And then she said if I was so desperate for a 'real' father, maybe I should look up mine sometime. She did say I'd regret it, but I didn't believe her.

"Anyway, I got all caught up with the environmental group. There were some people who said they thought we should make a huge problem to get noticed and make changes. They lied, by the way. But I believed them, and somehow, they convinced me and a couple others to take off with them to Chicago, where they said there was a bigger event happening. Please don't tell me how totally stupid I was. I already know."

"No promises," Luke says, but he smiles at Kem.

"Yeah, well, obviously, that didn't work out so well. This bunch of people only wanted some kids to help scam people. The others took off, and I ended up stranded there until you found me." Kem groans. "It turns out sometimes going home isn't the best idea. My parents were convinced I'd been, like, radicalized or some shit. They made a lot of really uncomfortable rules. I told them to stuff it, and that's when I called Jory."

Luke studies Kem for a few moments. He seems all right, despite what happened with his family. In fact, his happiness is almost tangible. He'll have a long road ahead of him; Luke knows firsthand. But for now, Kem is content. Luke sees no sign in him of the distress he remembers from their first meeting.

"So here's where my part comes in," Jory says. "I managed to scrape together some money and send it to Kem. I chose not to ask what other means he used to get here." They eye Kem pointedly. "I happened to mention I was going to go see my biological father."

Kem nods. "I said Mom told me mine probably still lives in or near Seattle too, so I figured, hey, why not?"

"And here's where it gets super, extra weird," Jory says.

"No, there's a weird part before that," Kem corrects them. "I don't think I said who the environmental guy was."

"No fucking way," Connor mutters. "Saul Wasserman."

"Yep, that's the one. Okay, now the best part."

"Kem's our brother," Jory says.

"Jesus!" Luke exclaims. "You can't drop something like that on me with no warning!"

"Sorry!" But Jory sounds about as far from sorry as possible.

"That dude got around," Connor remarks. "How the hell many children does he have?"

"Who knows?" Jory says. "A lot, probably. I think it'd be real fun if one day, we all showed up on his doorstep at the same time."

"What makes you say that?" Luke asks.

"Remember how I told you my biological mother did some modeling for him? Turns out it's the same story with Kem's mom. I'm willing to bet there are more."

"Shit. So he's preying on young women? Or at least he was."

"Sounds about right. We decided not to meet him," Kem tells Luke. "I can't do it. I mean, I only found out hours ago that you all are my sibs. It's a whole lot to take in. Maybe someday, but not now."

"I feel the same," Jory says. "Something isn't sitting right. He probably doesn't have any idea how many of us there are. I'm thinking about putting his name out there somehow and trying to figure out if there are more of us. Or maybe I'll stick with taking care of this twerp here." They ruffle Kem's hair, earning a scowl.

"You're going to stay with Jory?"

"I may change my mind," Kem says, crossing his arms. "They're making me go back to school."

Luke is temporarily stunned into silence. He can't believe he's sitting here with the two of them, for one thing, and for another, he's still reeling over their connections to each other. He doesn't think he can take any more surprises, at least not today.

"I know it didn't work out to meet our father," he begins. "But tomorrow, do you want to meet my sister? I know she's not really kin..."

"Of course!" Jory interrupts. "Think she'll be all right with it?"

"I'll ask, but I don't see why not."

Over dinner, they finalize their plans for meeting up in the morning before heading to Esther's house. Luke can't imagine what will come of all this, but he's optimistic for the first time in a while. Kem's story shed some light on Connor's father as well, which with any luck will spur Connor on to do the last bit of work piecing it all together. Under the table, he secretly takes hold of Connor's hand and squeezes. Whatever happens, he hopes Connor knows he can count on Luke.

*****

In the morning, they pick up Kem and Jory and drive out to Esther's house. It's a pretty, white two-story with blue trim and a row of evergreen shrubs out front. It reminds Luke of the house they lived in until moving to Liberty Station. There's a stone walkway lined with brightly colored flowers, and the lawn is freshly mowed. In the front yard, there's a kids' pool surrounded by squirt toys.

Up until this minute, Luke's thought he was prepared. Now the moment has arrived, he's not sure. His stomach is in knots. He doesn't know what he'll say to people he hasn't seen in almost fifteen years. Something of his fear must've shown on his face or in his posture because Connor rests a hand on his knee. Luke relaxes a little.

The four of them climb out of the car and follow the stone path to the door. Luke stands there for a minute, trying to collect his thoughts. He rings the bell and holds his breath.

When the door opens, he lets the air out in a forceful exhalation. He can't speak, too afraid he'll simply start crying. It's his Esther, the sister he thought he'd never see again. She looks almost exactly like he remembers her. It takes precisely six seconds before she steps forward and wraps her arms around him.

"Lukey," she murmurs into his hair. "Oh, my god. I've missed you so much."

He can't help it. His eyes are spilling over, and he's shaking in her arms. He's always held out hope she was okay, that she made it out safely and forged ahead with her life. In his wildest dreams, he's never imagined he would see this moment.

After a while, she lets him go to wipe her eyes. Luke does the same, and he can see the others are struggling to keep it together for his sake. Esther invites them all in, and Luke introduces them one by one.

"The others will be home later. It's my day off, so I've got the girls. They're upstairs napping, but you can meet them in a bit. For now, let's go have something to eat and talk about the last...what has it been, thirteen years?"

"About that, yeah," Luke agrees. "I don't know if I can condense it into something short enough to tell over lunch."

Esther laughs. "It's all right. I'm hoping we have more than one day to get to know each other again."

"We have as much time as Luke needs," Connor tells her. Luke doesn't even care if he's using this to stall again.

They sit around Esther's large kitchen table, and she sets some light food in front of them. No one eats much, too busy catching up and becoming reacquainted. Luke begins by filling her in on their summer travels, ending with what he learned about his biological father and Jory and Kem.

"That's incredible!" Esther says when he finishes. "How in the world did you all find each other?"

Jory explains their meeting, and then Kem does the same. He says, "You know, I only talked to you because you looked so similar to the photo Mom gave me. I knew you couldn't possibly be him, but it's how I convinced myself you were all right."

"After you tried to steal my wallet," Luke reminds him, and Kem cringes visibly.

"Isn't it funny?" Jory says. "I mean, most of that man's kids are queer, at least the ones we know of."

"John isn't," Luke says. "I don't think so, anyway. Which reminds me, Esther, what happened with you and Sam?"

She sighs. "I'm sure someone told you that I didn't have the baby. Which is a little funny now, considering we have twins together. I don't know how we all survived that awful time. Paul and Dinah helped us as much as they could. We were together for a while, but it was clear it wasn't going to work out. I wanted to get an education, and Sam still had to finish high school. We did the best we could, but we lost track of each other for a short time."

Luke listens to her talk about the years she was missing from his life. It wasn't any easier on her than it was on him. He wishes they could've stayed, but he knows his brothers would've tried something else. He counts himself lucky he's still alive and so is Esther.

Eventually, she departs to check on the girls. In a few minutes, she's back, her two-year-old twins in tow. Luke sees immediately they're not identical. One of the girls is the spitting image of Esther, and the other looks much more like Sam. Luke wonders again about their arrangement, but he supposes these girls are the luckiest he's ever met, with four doting parents.

It's almost dinnertime when the men arrive. Esther's partner, Gabe, comes home first. He's a warm, friendly man with a wide smile and a hearty laugh. Luke is genuinely happy for his sister that she's found someone who loves her as much as this man obviously does.

When Sam arrives, there's another round of hugging and crying. He holds on to Luke for a long time. Out of the corner of his eye, Luke notices Connor shifting uncomfortably, and he pulls away. He's the same old Sam, the first person Luke ever loved. Only when he looks at him, he doesn't feel the sparkling-cider bubbles in his stomach. Now it's only affection for the boy he once knew.

Sam looks him up and down the same way Esther did, shaking his head in disbelief. "I can't believe it's really you. After all this time."

"I was sure you were dead," Luke replies. "I saw the explosion."

"Give me some credit!" Sam shakes his head again. "I could say the same, though. Everyone thought you were. Your father even tried to have you legally declared deceased, but your mother refused. I only know because I heard it from the one or two people I managed to keep in touch with."

"I'm still here," Luke says. "And I can't wait to meet that husband of yours."

"Will you two save it?" Esther says. "Catch up over dinner. I'm expecting anyone who stays to eat to help out. Come give me a hand in the kitchen, and we'll finish talking then."

※※※

They've spent most of the week driving out to Esther's place so they can be together and finally fill in all the years they've been apart. Too soon, it's time to say goodbye—for now. Luke can't let Connor avoid forever the last business he has with his father, and Esther can't take more time off work to visit.

At the end of the week, Luke and Connor help the others clean out their motel room. Jory, like Luke, doesn't have anything to go home to. They've been on the road, with and without Connor and Luke, almost all summer. Now they have family, both biological and chosen. They'll be staying with Esther for a while to get back on their feet. Her family has an in-law apartment, and they're allowing Jory to rent from them until they find a more permanent solution. Kem will have some stability to finish school, and Jory can work to save up money. They've already found a job with a local grocer.

It doesn't escape Luke's notice that this is how he'll be with Adam and AJ in another couple of days, but he'd rather not think about it now.

"That's the last of it," Connor says, setting Jory's bags and the extra things he and Luke have given to them on the front stoop of the in-law apartment.

Connor's already making his rounds of goodbyes with Esther and the others. Now it's Luke's turn. He holds Esther close, and he feels the joy radiating from her. She's found many people these last few days whom she'd thought lost to her forever. Luke knows how she feels. When he lets go, he feels the paper slide into his hand. He'll examine it later, but he's sure by now he knows what it is.

Finally, he reaches Jory. "Here," he says, handing them the new scrapbook with the etching on the cover.

Jory gapes. "Luke, I can't keep this. It's yours, to remember your trip. All the precious things in here..."

He shakes his head. "The photos are on my camera, and I put most of them on Connor's laptop too. I'll make another one later."

"What about the postcards you collected? Or the other things from our trip?"

"You need them more than I do. Show Esther and the girls." He smiles and uses his thumb to brush away the tear tracking down Jory's cheek.

"I love it. Thank you."

They wrap their arms around him and rock him almost like a parent. Luke can't bear the grief of leaving them. He will call and write and find them on the internet, but just as it was with Jax, he knows without a doubt this is the last time he will see them. He fights off the tears, knowing that for the little family here in this house, it's a season of finding and welcoming in contrast to his season of letting go and loss.

Jory, too, puts a paper in his hand, and Luke smiles despite the ache. They and Esther are more alike than they know. Luke hopes now that they will learn these small things they have in common and delight in them.

"Take care of yourself," Jory whispers.

Luke knows what they mean, but he isn't ready to plan that far ahead. "I will."

Kem is watching them from the side, and Luke peers around the other two. He beckons for Kem to join them in their group hug. Kem's family didn't care about who he really was either. Like Luke's family, the problem was rooted in something deeper. Of all of them, he might be the one who best understands the complexities and burdens of doing the right thing against the family's wishes.

Luke and Connor climb back in the rental car, and Luke opens his hand. The first paper, with Esther's scrolling cursive, reads, "America" by Simon and Garfunkel. He smiles. It means many things now that he's seen a lot of what's between the coasts.

The second song puzzles him. "Ob-La-Di, Ob-La-Da," the Beatles. It's a cute song, but what in the world does it have to do with either their road trip or his life? He shows Connor, who laughs.

"I love that song," he admits. "Should we add it to the playlist now?"

Luke agrees and pulls up the list on Connor's tablet. He downloads it, and they drive away from Esther's house singing along. Connor knows all the words.

And then they're off, Luke and Connor without the others. It's time to do the last thing on Connor's list: the safe deposit box. It's at a small credit union in the town near where they're camping. Connor drives in silence, and Luke hopes with all his heart it will be okay.

There's only two items in the box, a letter with Connor's name on it and a small box. They take them back to the RV. It's finally time to lay out all the pieces and try to make sense of them. Connor sets the letter and box on the kitchenette table, and then he retrieves all the other things he's gathered from his father's cousins. There's the original writings he began the trip with, plus the ones he's collected along the way and the various trinkets and books and artwork.

Connor examines each one, and then he opens the box from Jens. There's another manuscript and an extensive family tree. Connor frowns at it for a moment before laying it aside. He picks up the envelope and turns it over in his hands.

"I'm not sure I can do this," he says.

"Go on," Luke urges. "I'm right here."

Connor's hands are shaking as he withdraws the letter. He clears his throat and begins to read.

> *Dearest Connor,*
>
> *The letter you're holding contains my final words to you.*

Connor pauses and laughs. "So dramatic."

> *I hope you've discovered all the clues I left you along my route. I would've contacted you directly, but I wasn't sure you'd want to see me after everything that happened. I heard you'd become a nurse practitioner. I'm really proud of you.*
>
> *I'm not going to tell you what you should do with most of what I've left you. When the time is right, you'll figure it out. I trust you. The only thing I'd like you to do is find somewhere for my ashes other than an ugly urn on a shelf.*
>
> *To be a blessing is not to give a gift or do a favor. It's a moment in time in which your meeting with another changes you both for the better. May everything I've left you become the tools you need to be a blessing, my son.*
>
> *All my love, Dad.*

Connor looks up at Luke. "I wonder what he means."

"Hm?" Luke heard what Connor read, but he's become distracted and has to recenter himself.

The family tree from Jens's box is puzzling Luke. It doesn't have any of the names of Connor's relatives. In fact, many of the names are strange. They sound like something made up. Luke's heard his share of odd names before, but this is different. He pushes the document toward Connor.

"Do any of these mean something to you?"

Connor's face pales. "These names..."

Suddenly, he's grabbing the various manuscripts and scanning them. He seems agitated, frantically searching the pages. Luke tries to remain calm for his sake, though he's anxious for Connor to explain what's been revealed.

After a long time, Connor sets the pages down. "These manuscripts...they're not my father's bizarre conspiracy theories. They're not even real life. He's written down the stories he used to tell me, but in a different format. Somehow, he's taken everything he's passionate about and poured it into this. The reason it didn't make any sense was that everyone had an incomplete part." Connor chuckles. "Well, also the fact that my father was a terrible writer. But with a little spit and shine, this thing could be incredible."

"Are you going to do it?"

"Not a chance. I'm an awful writer myself. But I think I know someone who could do it, someone who is passionate about the same kinds of things."

"Who's that?"

But Connor doesn't answer. He steps aside and pulls out his phone. "Hello, Jeremy? This is Connor..." He listens for a moment then puts it on speaker phone so Luke can hear too. "Listen, I found something I think you should know about. It's my father's writings. There's no way I can figure out how to make these notes and scribblings into anything decent. I think you could, though."

"A manuscript? For a science fiction novel. Hm..." Jeremy pauses. "Well, now you may be speaking my language. What's the catch?"

"None, really, except I want you to give Dad credit for the ideas." It's the first time Luke's ever heard Connor refer to his father as "Dad."

"That's it? I can do that, of course," Jeremy assures him.

"One more thing. I want you to send it to your cousin Danya to publish. A lot of these stories are rooted in Jewish folklore, but with a definite futuristic twist. Her company's in some trouble, and I have a feeling this might help her out. You're not exclusive with your publisher, are you?"

Jeremy scoffs. "I'm self-published, so I think I can clear it."

"Good. I'm going to call Danya and explain to her that what she gave me wasn't random. She was interested in figuring out the mystery as much as I was." Connor ends the call and hits Danya's number, still keeping the phone on speaker.

"Hello?" she says.

"Danya, it's Connor. Remember that manuscript you gave me? I think I've finally solved the puzzle, and I might have a proposition for you..."

Chapter 35

TONIGHT IS THEIR second to last night at an RV park and their first alone in a week. They're subdued as they hike the trails through the park and find places to scatter Saul's ashes. Afterward, they cook dinner together and then watch the stars pop out while they warm themselves by the tiny fire Connor's made. He brings out two steaming mugs of cocoa and two soft blankets, and they relax together with no real need to talk. Luke knows Connor understands how he's feeling now. Spending the summer becoming reacquainted has honed Connor's skills, returning them to how they were in those early days after Greg.

Connor reaches for his hand, and Luke closes his eyes with his fingers linked with Connor's. This moment is all theirs, the stress and strain of the road behind them now and the future stretching out ahead. It feels so full of promise that Luke brings Connor's hand to his lips to kiss it. Connor turns to him, and the look on his face is irresistible. Luke stands and pulls Connor up too.

They don't talk as they step inside the RV. This time, there's no fumbling or desperation. This is slow and sensual as they undress with only the light of the electric lantern on the counter behind them. Luke takes his time to map every detail of Connor's body with his hands and lips. He draws a route from Connor's mouth down his chest, making brief stops along the way. Connor's gasps and groans make the trip a delight for Luke.

They are one again and again in the dim light and the heat of the RV. Time no longer has any sway over them;

it stands still while they satisfy each other through the summer night. Over and over, they succumb to the tides of pleasure and release until all they can do is doze, sated, in one another's arms.

The gray dawn wakes Luke, but he doesn't want to leave the safety of Connor's side. He snuggles down under the blanket, the overnight chill making him grateful for body heat and nothing between them. Connor stirs slightly but doesn't wake. Luke wonders if he'll be stuck waiting a while for him. He's forgotten to put the last few photos on Connor's laptop like he told Jory he would, but it's all right. He can do it before they leave. He has time.

He'll be glad to get out of the confines of the RV and be in more open accommodations. It hasn't been bad, and it was definitely better than searching for places to stay. Besides, they would never have met the parade of guests they did if they'd stuck to motels and hostels along the way. Even so, Luke is beginning to feel cramped.

He is both desperate for his own space and heartsick over all the people he's going to miss. He'll be flying out tomorrow to Adam and AJ's home. He knows Connor has to sell the RV first, but Luke is hopeful they'll meet up again once he's done with sorting out his affairs and his father's. He isn't sure how long it will take because they haven't discussed more than when Luke will be leaving.

When Connor finally wakes, Luke figures it's as good a moment as any to ask about the timeline. "Hey," he says.

"Mm." Connor pulls him closer, and Luke temporarily forgets his question when confronted with Connor's wandering hands and renewed desire. The rest can wait. He can hardly believe they're functional to make love again already, but even that concern fades out of existence while they enjoy a round of tender, lazy morning sex.

Some time later, lying pressed shoulder to ankle, Luke finally gets around to asking. "How long do you think it'll be until you make it out to Adam and AJ's?"

Connor doesn't speak for so long Luke is alarmed. He nudges Connor with his toe. Slowly, Connor turns his head. "I'm...not going."

"What are you talking about? Are you going back to your mom's place?" Luke shudders.

"No, of course not. Lukey," Connor says, turning to face him. "I thought it was understood. I'm not going back."

"Not..." Luke breathes deeply. "Why?"

"I have a job. I don't know how you mistook what was happening, but the reason I drove all the way here was so I could have a place to stay until I found somewhere local. I'm headed to a place to live out of the RV for a while after you fly out."

"Staying." The word tastes ugly to Luke. "You were going to let me leave like that? Without even talking to me?"

Connor sits up. "I was sure you knew and..." He puts his head in his hands. "I assumed you wanted to go back east, or I'd have asked."

"Asked what?"

"For you to come with me." Connor takes Luke's face in his hands. "I want you to, Lukey. I love you. I have for years. In my head, I had it all planned—that I'd get myself an apartment, sell the RV, and bring you back here. I just wanted to have everything taken care of." He's full of excitement now, and he rises onto his knees. "You can take photos. All those beautiful ones you have from our trip, the way you see people for who they are. You could do it. I know you could! And I'd be here to help you."

Luke turns away in shame. He won't be kept by someone ever again. Greg was one time too many. What was Connor thinking? He can't expect Luke to pick up and move all the way out here, not when he's got his own ideas of how he wants to live his life. It isn't fair of Connor to do this without asking first.

Connor's hesitant hand on his shoulder brings Luke out of his mute shock. He says, "No."

Now it's Connor's turn for confusion. "But I thought—"

"You fucking thought wrong," Luke snaps. "I didn't even have time to think it over. You sprang this on me less than a day before I'm supposed to fly out, and you want my answer now."

"I don't need you to tell me yet," Connor says, and it's obvious he's trying to keep his voice steady. "You could spend some time with our friends thinking about it. Talk to them and whatever you need to do."

"They know too?"

"I mean, yeah. That's why I assumed you did. This is a great opportunity for me. You wouldn't be as far from family..." He trails off when Luke shoots him a dark look.

He needs to be done with this trip and maybe even with Connor. "I want you to take me to a motel tonight. I need some space."

"Okay." Connor sits back. "I understand, I really do. But please think about it, all right?"

"I need time," Luke tells him, even though he doesn't think all the time in the world will be enough.

∗∗∗∗

The airport isn't busy. Even Luke finds it hard to believe he's made it to twenty-eight without ever having taken a trip by plane. He hefts his duffel onto his shoulder, the sum total of his existence packed into one space. It's lighter by one photo album, the memento he's given Jory for their time together. He's glad they and Kem have each other, and he's happy Esther and Sam will be there to take care of them too.

"Are you sure?" Connor asked Luke when he dropped him off at a nearby motel. No, in all honesty, Luke isn't sure at all that what he is doing is the right thing. But he didn't want to see the look in Connor's eyes when they called his flight, so he told him he was fine.

He's not fine.

He chose not to check his bag. It's small enough they said he could carry it on, although they did rifle through it at security. He sits in one of the hard, plastic seats at his gate, checking and re-checking his phone for the time. A text pops up, but he ignores it. Jax. Luke doesn't want to talk to them any more than he wants Connor there. He has to leave most of his old life behind. Again.

Luke has plans. He'll go stay with Adam and AJ for a short time, and then he'll move on from them too. The last time he left them, he had Jax as a safety net. This time, he will be alone. He can't keep relying on one person after another to make his life happy.

His camera is around his neck. Lifting it, he takes a picture of the planes through the enormous window. One last photo in this place. He doesn't know where life will take him next. He feels the weight of the camera in his hand and thinks about what it would be like if he could do this all the time. It's what Connor said, what Jax said, even what Jory said.

Someone sits down a couple seats away, and Luke cringes. He can tell she's the cheerful, chatty sort, the kind of person who carries on half a conversation without realizing the person she's talking to has no interest. The woman has on a wide hat, the type women of a certain age wear to protect from the sun on the beach. Definitely on her way to somewhere for vacation because this is not exactly a spot for tourists in beach hats.

"Where are you off to?" she asks Luke as she fishes for something in her bag. She pulls out a pack of mints and offers one to Luke. He politely takes it as she continues, "I'm going to go visit my children in Charlotte. Well, my son and his wife. I think of her as my own."

"Cool," Luke says, not sure how to respond.

"They made me this playlist of songs to listen to on the flight. I've never heard of half of them, and it's not even that long!" She laughs. "Here."

She holds out her phone, and Luke takes it. He smiles when he recognizes a number of the ones on Connor's Ultimate Road Trip Playlist. Softly, he hums one of the songs, and the woman's eyebrows rise.

"You know this one?"

"I know most of these, yeah. It's a good list." He swallows around the lump rising in his throat, and he has to look away so the woman doesn't see the tears forming in his eyes.

She's rambling on, something about how she'd have waited for the holidays later in the year, but her daughter-in-law is having a baby and blah, blah, blah. Luke isn't focusing on her story. His mind is miles away, wherever Connor is now. It's on the endless roadway they traveled together over the last forty days, on the music and the adventures and the lovemaking. He thinks now about Connor going back to an ordinary life, one in which he'll be working at his new job a long way from the painful memories and the people who hurt him. That list includes Luke.

He can't help it. The tears are spilling over. He draws up his knees and folds his arms, still trying to hide his sorrow from the stranger three seats away. He's likely failing, unless she's too wrapped up in her story, but he doesn't care anymore. A warm arm slides around him, and before he can think about it, he's leaning on her. She's stopped talking, and now she holds him in silence the way only a mother can.

Luke tries to pull himself together. He sits up straighter and wipes his eyes on the cuff of his sleeve. "I'm so sorry," he says.

"Honey, it's fine. You want to talk about it?"

"I..." He gulps. Will she understand? He sniffles and then tries again. "I spent all summer with someone, and now we're both leaving. He asked me to stay, but I said no because I was stupid and stubborn. He's already gone on to his new job, and I'm supposed to stay with our friends and just...move on. But I can't because I—" He can't finish.

"You love him." It's not a question. Not for her and not for Luke either.

"Yes."

"Well, honey, why don't you tell him?"

"It's too late."

"What on earth do you mean? It's never too late. You have heard of cell phones, right? I may look like the grandma I'm about to become, but I do at least know your man is only a phone call away. Unless you deleted him from your contacts?"

"No." Luke chuckles weakly. "Of course not."

"Then go call him. And don't you dare get on that plane!"

"But—"

"Change your ticket. Or take a bus. Do whatever it takes, but go after him. Don't spend the rest of your life regretting your choices because you're trying to prove you don't need anyone." She peers at Luke as if she can see right through the bricks he's placed between himself and Connor.

She's right. He sits up and fishes for his phone. The woman moves farther away to give him privacy. He stares at the phone. Years ago, he let Connor down because he hadn't understood what love looked like. Now he does, in the big things and the small things. He's not going to let it get away from him again because he's bent on showing everyone he can take care of himself.

His fingers are shaking as he hits Connor's number, and his heart is in his throat waiting while it rings. At last Connor answers.

"Lukey? Is everything all right?"

"No." Luke's crying again. "Baby, I need you. I want to be wherever you are."

Connor doesn't respond right away, but Luke can hear him crying too. "I'm right outside," he finally says. "I never left. I couldn't do it. I was going to watch your plane take off, and you'd never be the wiser. Meet me at the doors."

"I am. I will." Luke stands and grabs his bag. He gives a thumbs-up to the woman and smiles at her through his tears. She grins back. Luke says into the phone, "I love you, and I'm on my way. I'm coming home."

The End

About A.M. Leibowitz

A.M. Leibowitz is a queer spouse, parent, feminist, and book-lover falling somewhere on the Geek-Nerd Spectrum. They keep warm through the long, cold western New York winters by writing about life, relationships, hope, and happy-for-now endings. Their published fiction includes several novels as well as a number of short works, and their stories have been included in anthologies from Supposed Crimes, Witty Bard, and Mischief Corner Books. In between noveling and editing, they blog coffee-fueled, quirky commentary on faith, culture, writing, books, and their family.

Find A.M. Leibowitz online:

Facebook: https://www.facebook.com/amymitchell29

Facebook Author Page: https://www.facebook.com/UnchainedFaith/

Twitter: https://twitter.com/amyunchained

Pinterest: https://pinterest.com/amyunchained

Website: http://amleibowitz.com

Goodreads: https://www.goodreads.com/author/show/8544236.A_M_Leibowitz

By A.M. Leibowitz

Beaten Track Publishing

For more titles from Beaten Track Publishing,
please visit our website:

https://www.beatentrackpublishing.com

Thanks for reading!